Love Me Tender

A MONTANA BORN BRIDES ANTHOLOGY

JANE PORTER
KELLY HUNTER
TRISH MOREY
SARAH MAYBERRY

TULE
PUBLISHING

Contents

Beauty's Kiss

A TAMING OF THE SHEENANS ROMANCE

JANE PORTER

Dedication

For Meghan Farrell.

You are Wonder Girl. Tule couldn't do what it's doing without you.

(And I'd be miserable without a cool Book Girl around!)

Dear Reader

If you've read my books before, you know I love connected stories, and have written numerous series featuring families for Harlequin Presents, Grand Central Publishing and Berkley Books. *The Taming of the Sheenan*s, is my brand new series about five brothers from Marietta, Montana and boy oh boy do these men know how to take over a scene and own the room!

The Sheenans are big, tough, rugged men, and as different as the Montana landscape. I launched the series in December with *Christmas at Copper Mountain,* a story about widower Brock Sheenan, the oldest brother, a taciturn rancher and single father who has been alone too long.

Now the series continues with *Beauty's Kiss*, featuring the 'good' Sheenan twin, venture capitalist Troy, named Marietta's Most Eligible Bachelor by the Copper Mountain Courier several years ago.

But thirty-six year old Troy is more than a pretty face. He's brilliant and ambitious, loyal to his family, and has a secret soft spot for historical buildings, small towns, and brainy book girls.

I hope you'll enjoy Taylor Harris and Troy Sheenan's romance in *Beauty's Kiss*. These two stole my heart as has all of Marietta. Welcome back to Marietta, Montana nestled beneath majestic Copper Mountain!

Jane Porter

Contents

Chapter One

M ontana winters were never mild, and this winter felt even more brutal than normal.

Taylor Harris sucked in a sharp breath at the blast of frigid air as she and Jane Weiss, the new director of the Marietta Chamber of Commerce, stepped from the warm library into the night.

The frigid temperature and biting wind made her eyes water behind her glasses. Taylor fumbled with her key, blinking as she struggled to get Marietta library's front door locked. She had to remove her mitten to punch in the security code on the wall.

Jane stood close by, shoulders hunched, teeth chattering. "You're sure you don't mind driving me to the airport?" she asked, drawing her suitcase closer to her feet.

"Of course not," Taylor answered, shivering as she quickly tugged her mitten back on. Normally she'd be racing home on a night like this for a hot bath, a steaming cup of soup, and a great book in bed. Taylor had been a book lover her entire life and, even at twenty-six, loved nothing more than curling up and getting lost in a great story, reading until the early hours of the morning. So what if it meant she never got enough sleep? Books were her life, her passion. It's why she'd become a librarian.

They set off for the broad, pale stone steps that led to the park and parking lot, Jane's roller bag bumped along next to them.

Taylor glanced across Crawford Park to the tall, domed

courthouse dominating the public park. Even though it was only a few minutes after six, the sky was already dark and the yellow glow of street lamps reflected off the snow heaped onto the sides of the city park's paths. Larger, dirtier piles of snow lined Marietta's streets, thanks to the diligent efforts of the city's snow plows, and now a new storm was predicted to move in tonight, which would mean even bigger piles tomorrow.

Jane glanced anxiously up at the sky. "It's supposed to start snowing later. You're okay driving in a storm?"

Taylor nodded, smiling, amused. "Of course. I'm from northeastern Montana. All we do is drive in snow and ice. It's you I'm worried about. You think your flight will get out okay?"

"I checked with the airline. So far, so good, and I have those alerts on my phone so I'll know right away if there's a change in status." Jane lifted her bag, carrying it down the salted front steps, slightly breathless by the time they reached the sidewalk. "So what are you wearing to the Ball Friday?"

Taylor knew the Valentine Ball would come up, and she dreaded breaking the news to Jane that she'd decided not to attend. "I wanted to talk to you about that," she said carefully. "I've—"

"Don't. Don't say you've changed your mind. You promised me!"

Taylor hated disappointing anyone, much less the best friend she'd made since moving to Marietta six months ago, but Jane enjoyed big events and Taylor did not. "It's just not my thing, Jane, and it's incredibly expensive—"

"You're getting a free ticket for being on the Wedding Giveaway committee."

Taylor adjusted her red and brown striped scarf around her neck, trying in vain to block the wind. "Things have been stressful with Doug and all the changes at the library. I'd honestly rather stay home and unwind. I've got a new book by one of my favorite authors—"

"You can read over the weekend. You don't need to spend your Friday night in bed!"

"Why not?" Taylor exclaimed, as they darted across the

parking lot. "We both know I'm not a Ball kind of girl. I'm a librarian. And boring as mud. Trust me, you'll have more fun without me."

Jane raced next to Taylor, teeth chattering again. "You're only boring because you don't go out and do anything!"

"I like being home. I like reading."

Jane shuddered as the freezing wind whipped past. "You're too young to become a hermit."

Taylor peeled a long strand of hair from her lashes and tugged her knit cap lower on her head. "I'm not a hermit. I'm just an introvert, which means I like people, but I don't find parties exciting. They tire me out—."

"You sound like an old lady!" Jane interrupted, giggling. "But you're young and beautiful and this is a once in a lifetime event. A historic event to commemorate the 100 year anniversary of Marietta's 1914 Great Wedding Giveaway—" she broke off and glanced up at the sky as the first slow, lazy snowflakes drifted down. "It's starting to snow."

"We'll get you to the airport," Taylor said. "You'll make it."

Jane dragged her bag across an icy patch. "So when does it warm up?"

"May? June?"

"*No!*"

"Don't think about it," Taylor said, as they arrived at her car and she clicked the unlock button on her key ring. "It'll just make it worse."

Inside the car, as Taylor turned the engine on, Jane held her hands to one of the vents, waiting for the heat to kick in. "You have to come, Taylor. It's the party of the century. Everyone's going to be there—." she broke off, frowned, hesitated. "Okay, from the sluggish ticket sales, we know not *everyone* will be at the Graff Hotel Friday night, but most of Crawford County's movers and shakers will. It's going to be beautiful. Don't you want to see the ballroom decorated?"

"I do. That's why I've volunteered to help Risa deliver the flowers Friday. But that's enough for me. I love to read about Balls in my Regency romances, but there's nothing in me begging to go to a ball. Besides, even if I went, what would I wear?"

"That's easy. I'll take you shopping, and Taylor, you have to go. We're sitting at the Sheenan table. It'd be rude to not go now."

Taylor backed out from the parking spot, shifted into drive. "Just have catering remove a place setting and chair from the table. No one will even notice if there is eight, nine, or ten at the table."

"Yes, they will."

"No, they won't."

"Yes. They will." Jane exhaled hard before adding in a small voice. "Because you're Troy Sheenan's date."

"*What*?" Taylor slammed on her brakes and stared at Jane.

"He just broke up with his girlfriend and he needed a date and you didn't have a date so I told him—"

"No, you did not."

"I did."

"Why would you do that?"

"He's really nice."

"No he's not. You said he broke your heart."

"Okay, nice is maybe the wrong word. But he is seriously gorgeous and sexy and smart. Very, very smart. And successful. Rich as Midas—"

"Jane, no. He sounds awful. Yuck. *No.*"

"It's just for the Ball. You can go with Mitch and me. We'll drive you home. And I promise that Troy won't make a move—"

"*No.*"

"Although he is by far the best kisser—"

"Don't care. Don't want to know." Taylor's hands tightened on the steering wheel as she moved her foot from the brake to the gas pedal. "And you agreed after that last terrible set up that you wouldn't put me through anymore blind dates." She shot Jane a severe look. "I'm holding you to that promise, Jane."

Jane slunk down in her seat. "I'm not asking you to marry him, just be his date."

Taylor said nothing, her gaze narrowed and focused on the road.

"Normally I wouldn't set him up. I wouldn't want to see him with another woman but you're not... plastic... and you wouldn't be into him for his money..." Jane's voice drifted off. She shifted uncomfortably in her seat. Silence followed.

Taylor clamped her jaw tight.

She was not interested in going to the Ball, and definitely not interested in being set up with gorgeous, rich, sexy Troy Sheenan, Jane's ex-love, whom Taylor had heard *far* too much about over the past few months.

Good Lord. From everything Jane had said, Troy was a handsome, ruthless, self-absorbed playboy. Could anything be worse?

"You'd enjoy talking to him," Jane said faintly, hands knotting in her lap. "He's very smart—brilliant, really—and exceedingly well read. You should see his personal library—"

"*Jane.*"

"He's just got his hands full with his break up, his dad dying, and hosting the Ball for us in his hotel. It's a massive expense that he personally is underwriting."

Taylor flexed her fingers against the steering wheel. "That's not my problem, and it's not yours, either."

"I know, but I offered to help—"

"Wait. You offered to set him up? He didn't ask you?"

"No."

"Oh, Jane." Taylor sighed. "You're still in love with him."

Jane's head bowed. "I know we're not going to be together. And I'm moving on, I am, but that doesn't mean I can't care for Troy, and it doesn't mean I can't want him to be happy."

Taylor just shook her head. She'd been in Jane's shoes once, back when she was in graduate school, and it was a bad place to be. Unrequited love was brutal. All those intense emotions, bottled up inside, making your feelings strong, too strong. "You need to let him go. Completely."

For a long moment Jane said nothing, and then she sighed heavily. "So what do I tell Troy?"

Taylor rolled her eyes. "To be a man and go find his own damn date."

Troy Sheenan was glad to be on the ground, even if he was arriving in the middle of a blizzard. He was a seasoned traveler, accustomed to jetting back and forth between Montana and California to oversee the renovations at the Graff Hotel during the last couple of years, but tonight's flight was rough. Seriously rough. Three endless, unrelenting hours of turbulence that kept him buckled into his leather seat, as the pilots of his private jet searched in vain for some smoother air.

They didn't find it.

But at least he and his crew were safely on the ground and he was free to move, his long strides carrying him swiftly across the snowy tarmac to the Executive terminal.

His rental car, a big black four wheel drive SUV with snow tires, was waiting for him outside the executive terminal, the key already in the ignition, the interior still warm. The paperwork had been handled earlier by Troy's assistant before he left San Francisco which meant he was free to go.

Troy tossed his bags into the back, and slid behind the steering wheel, noting that the snow flurries were coming down thicker and faster. In good weather it was at least a fifty five minute drive to Sheenan Ranch. And it wasn't good weather. He wasn't even sure if Dillon would have been able to get their private drive plowed, which meant he might be four wheeling it. Or stuck.

Any other night he'd just stay at the hotel. He had his own private suite on the fourth floor of the historic hotel, and the suite was always kept ready for him, but if Dad was doing as badly as Dillon said, Troy wanted to get to the ranch tonight and sit with him. Troy hadn't been there when his mom died, and he was damn well not going to be MIA when Dad passed.

The snow was really coming down now.

Taylor sat ramrod straight in the driver's seat, her hands set precisely at ten and two on the steering wheel, her heart pounding harder than she liked.

She wasn't scared.

She'd driven through worse.

And the road seemed fine, not too icy. She just had to keep an eye on her speed and pay attention.

And yes, it was getting harder and harder to see the hood of her car, never mind the road, but she was a Montana girl. She had a good car, a reliable car, and her Subaru could handle the icy roads just fine.

The car would be fine, and she'd be fine, she silently insisted, even as she regretted that she hadn't stopped in Bozeman when she had the chance.

She should have not pushed it. She should have played it safe. But Taylor had thought that maybe the flurries would lighten. She'd thought perhaps once she hit the highway the storm would ease.

She'd thought wrong and now she was driving through a blinding sheet of white, having to pretend her pulse wasn't racing and her hands weren't damp against the steering wheel.

Fifteen more miles, she told herself, checking the windshield wiper speed again. But they were already on their fastest setting and unable to clear her windshield quickly enough.

She couldn't see.

It's okay.

She hated this.

You're halfway home.

Her eyes burned as she fought panic. She wanted to pull over, get off the road but this was a mountain pass and it'd be suicide to pull over here. Another motorist or trucker could lose control and take her out.

No choice but to keep going. No choice but to finish

what she'd started.

And so she sat tall and held her breath and focused very hard on the glow of white where the car headlights shone through the swirling flurries of snow, unable to reach as far as the yellow reflectors on the side of the road. Taylor only knew for sure where she was when she drove over one of the bumps.

Too far right. She was practically on the shoulder. Not good.

She corrected, steering a little more to the left, frowning hard, trying to see the road, knowing it curved somewhere near here, a fairly sharp curve which wasn't a problem during the day but could be treacherous at night. She was concentrating very hard on staying off the reflector bumps and in the middle of her lane when suddenly a row of red lights glowed. It was a big rig truck hitting its brakes.

Taylor hadn't even known a vehicle was in front of her, and she slammed on her brakes to avoid rear ending it, which put her in a skid on the ice.

Braking hard on ice was the absolute wrong thing to do. She was supposed to pump the brakes, supposed to keep the brakes from locking. Too late.

Her tires spun, and her car spun, and she went careening off the shoulder before slamming violently into the metal side guard.

Her airbag deployed, the impact knocking the air from her.

Taylor knew she'd stopped moving when everything grew still and quiet. She sat for a moment, dazed, barely able to see over the airbag.

Cautiously, she opened her door and stepped out into the snow. She shivered as she inspected her car where it had slammed into the guardrail. The guardrail was twisted and bent, but it had stopped her car from going over the edge.

Good guardrail.

"That was close," a deep male voice said from behind her. "You alright?"

"I think so," she answered, swaying a bit as she turned around. A man was walking towards her, his big SUV parked just behind her car, his headlamps on high beams to illuminate the highway shoulder. "Just shaken up more than anything."

The man walked past her, took a look at the guardrail and crushed hood, before returning. "That guardrail saved you."

"I know."

"What happened?"

"The truck in front of me slammed on its brakes, and I had nowhere to go."

"You were following it too closely?"

"I didn't even know it was there."

He nodded. "It's bad. Total white out conditions. None of us should be on the road."

"I just wanted to get home."

"Where were you heading?"

"Marietta."

"That's where I'm going. Let me give you a ride."

Taylor glanced back at his big black SUV with the headlights shining on them. It looked like a new car, and expensive. She gave him the same once-over. He looked expensive, too. Clean cut. Attractive, with black hair, smooth hard jaw, strong, classic features. "Are you safe?" she asked, only half joking.

"Safer than the storm."

"Not sure that's hugely reassuring."

He laughed, the sound deep, warm as well as very confident. "Sorry. Let me introduce myself." He stuck out a hand and smiled down on her, white teeth glinting, and creases fanning at the corners of his eyes. "I'm Troy Sheenan."

Chapter Two

Of course he was, Taylor thought, adjusting the seatbelt across her lap, and then crossing her leg at the knee, trying to make herself comfortable in the big black SUV's passenger seat.

And of course it would be Troy Sheenan who'd plucked her from the side of the road, as if he were a gallant knight, instead of an errant knight.

A playboy.

A *rake*.

It felt satisfying to silently hurl names at him, but it wasn't helping make her more comfortable. She couldn't relax. Couldn't catch her breath.

It was his fault. *Troy Sheenan.*

Taylor's fingers curled into her palms. She stared blindly out the windshield into the night with the thick swirling snow, her chest tight, aching with bottled air.

Of all people to stop...

Of all people to offer to help.

Why did it have to be him?

And worse, why couldn't he be arrogant, and rude, and absolutely despicable? *Dislikable*? Why did he have to be almost... charming?

Nice.

She shuddered inwardly, thinking that he might even be disarmingly nice, if he weren't, well, so...good looking. Jane hadn't lied about that. He was...well, exactly what she'd said he was.

Tall, dark and handsome...black hair, blue eyes, chiseled jaw, dimples.

A man with all those attributes couldn't be nice. Truly handsome men were never nice. They were spoiled, overly confident, *insincere*. They were accustomed to women falling to their feet and throwing themselves at men, bosoms heaving... and so forth.

Taylor's lips compressed and she lifted her chin a fraction.

She couldn't place all the blame on handsome men. Women had to accept some responsibility for their behavior. Just because a man was gorgeous and charming it didn't mean a woman needed to fall for him...

Taylor would *never* fall for someone like Troy Sheenan.

At least, she'd never fall for someone like Troy Sheenan again.

Back in graduate school she'd fallen for a Mr. Charming, and it had broken her heart and damaged her confidence and self-esteem. She'd vowed to never go down that destructive, confusing path again. And she hadn't.

She wouldn't.

She pushed up her glasses higher on the bridge of her nose, suddenly grateful she'd worn them to work today, feeling protected by the big dark frames and the too-thick-to-be-sexy lenses.

She wasn't a plaything, or an intellectual lightweight. Yes, she loved historical romances, and had ever since she'd first read Jane Austen in high school, and then found a Georgette Heyer novel in the local library during her summer vacation. By the time Taylor had graduated with a Masters in Library Science, she'd read everything Heyer wrote (even the mysteries), including a biography just published on the English novelist, and Heyer's work ethic, intelligence, and drive made an indelible impression on Taylor. If Heyer could support her family with her writing in the 1920's and 30's, then Taylor could support her brother with her work.

Taylor didn't need a man or husband to provide. Taylor would provide. And she had. Which reminded her, she'd need to call her insurance agent as soon as she reached the house, and a tow truck, and make arrangements for a rental car. She sighed inwardly, disappointed in herself for losing control on the pass. There were a lot of things going on this week. She didn't need the hassle of being car-less on top of everything else.

Leaning forward, she reached for her oversized leather satchel at her feet. Taylor didn't use purses. She loved her messenger-style book bag and she quickly found the satchel's inner pocket where she kept her phone. Retrieving it, she checked messages but there was no service. They'd get service when they got closer to Marietta and that wouldn't be long now.

"You said you were new in town," Troy said, his deep, low voice breaking the silence.

She nodded as his dark blue gaze briefly slid over her in the dim light of the car before his gaze returned to the road.

She exhaled, hard.

He'd only looked at her for a moment but it was enough to make her insides flip, setting loose a dozen butterflies in her middle. She pressed her phone to her lap, and drew a deep breath to calm the nervous butterflies. "I moved to Marietta at the end of August, right before Labor Day Weekend."

"What do you think of the place?"

"I like it."

"People nice?"

She thought of Judge McCorkle and how he'd handled the sentencing of her brother. She thought also of those who'd been so critical towards Jane and her ideas for the Chamber of Commerce. "Most people."

He shot her another swift glance. "You've met some less than friendly folks?"

There went the butterflies again. She shifted, uneasy. She didn't understand it, didn't understand why he'd make her feel so nervous, but every time he looked at her, every time she met his gaze, her heart raced.

So strange.

Men didn't give her the jitters. And polished, sophisticated men, especially handsome sophisticated men, didn't appeal to her. She wasn't a fan of city men, finding them too smooth, too slick. But even in his dark wool trousers and expensive black cashmere V-neck sweater, Troy exuded strength. Toughness. He had a rugged masculinity that was pure Montana.

Maybe that's what she was reacting to.

If so, she needed to stop. She didn't want to be attracted to Troy Sheenan. And maybe it wasn't really Troy. Maybe it was the accident. Maybe she was still in shock, shaken from the impact, disoriented from spinning on the ice and slamming into the guardrail. Yes, that was it. The accident. She was still shaken up. Relief rushed through her. Everything made sense now. "Most people have been polite to me," she said carefully. "But that's not necessarily true for others. It seems like there are different standards in Marietta. If you are from Marietta, there is one set of rules, and if you're new to Marietta, there's another."

"Can you give me specifics?"

"I don't know that I should. I don't want to criticize your hometown. Suffice it to say, there are some in the community that view newcomers with suspicion, particularly if they're suggesting change. But that is probably true for most small towns. I'm from a small Montana town myself, an hour from Scoby. Hopeville—"

"Hopeville?" he repeated.

She grimaced. "Has to be ironic. There wasn't much *hope* in Hopeville. Our population was less than a thousand and there was no opportunity there, nor much of anything but hard drinking and hard living."

"How did you end up in Marietta?"

"A job," she said.

"What do you do?"

She primly adjusted her glasses. "I'm a librarian."

"You are?"

She heard the note of surprise in his voice, as well as a measure of respect. "I've been hired to take over as head librarian when Margaret Houghton retires in June," she added, feeling a small bubble of warmth. She was proud of her position. She loved her work as a librarian and Marietta's graceful, historic building deserved excellent, modern programs, programs Taylor was determined to implement as soon as she took over.

He shot her a quick, assessing glance. "Impressive."

Taylor's insides felt fluttery all over again. She shouldn't care what he thought. But apparently some part of her—some ridiculous, weak part of her—did.

Annoyed with herself, Taylor stared out her passenger window, noting how the delicate icy flakes stuck to the glass and wondering how she could bring up Jane without making it awkward.

It might not be possible as just sitting next to Troy was making her feel hopelessly awkward.

Even now her pulse raced and her mouth tasted cotton dry, so she gave up trying to figure out how to introduce the subject of Jane Weiss and focused instead on the snow.

It was beautiful, all those thick, whirling, white flakes. Taylor loved the snow and didn't mind the long winters provided she didn't have to do a lot of driving on mountain passes during storms. Thank goodness Troy Sheenan was comfortable behind the wheel. It was obvious he'd grown up driving in snow and ice, too.

"Have family in Marietta?" he asked, a few minutes later.

She pictured her brother, remembering how they'd moved to Marietta together, or how he'd moved with her after she'd gotten hired by the library. Doug was able to get a job, too, as an apprentice to a Marietta electrician but within weeks of arriving in Marietta, he got in trouble and it'd been difficult ever since.

"Not in town, but in Paradise Valley," Taylor said. "My little brother lives—" she broke off, frowning, uncertain how to explain Doug's situation. She was protective of her brother's illness. Not everyone understood depression and mood disorders. Not everyone wanted to understand. Her own parents had thought his diagnosis was a cop-out. More than once Dad had ripped into Doug for being weak and undisciplined. He just couldn't accept that the depression was anything but laziness and selfishness. She gave her head a small shake, shaking away the memory of all the horrible things her parents had said to Doug when he began to struggle in middle school.

She felt rather than saw Troy glance at her.

Taylor swallowed and squared her shoulders. "---out there, in Paradise Valley."

"I was raised in Paradise Valley. That's where our family ranch is," Troy said.

Jane had told her about the big Sheenan spread in Paradise Valley, one of the larger ranches in the area, and it bordered the Carrigan property, the other big ranch. Taylor knew Sage Carrigan as Sage was on the Great Wedding Giveaway committee, and was donating all the chocolates and truffles for Friday's Valentine Ball.

The Ball.

Right.

Taylor prayed Troy had no idea that she was the one Jane had volunteered to be his date. But then, Taylor doubted Troy had a clue. Men listened to women as little as possible. "Beautiful land," she said.

"Your brother's a cowboy?" Troy asked.

"He's... working on a ranch now, yes," Taylor answered, thinking this was exactly what she didn't want to discuss. She was so private about Doug's situation, and so protective of him. He'd been doing better in the year before they moved here, and they'd both been excited about going to Marietta. It had seemed like a great opportunity for both of them, but Doug couldn't find a job right away, and even though he had time on his hands, he wasn't able to make new friends. Within weeks his depression returned. Taylor had been making calls to psychiatrists in Bozeman at the time Doug was arrested. Sentencing him to a halfway house/rehab ranch wasn't the solution. Doug needed counseling, treatment. *Medical* care. But the judge didn't listen. The judge thought he knew best. He was a man, after all. He claimed he knew what a young man needed. Work. Discipline. *An attitude adjustment.*

The very same things Taylor's father had said.

It made her furious. And heartsick. Because both men were wrong. And Doug—as well as thousands of young men and women--continued to struggle and suffer because people were ignorant about mood disorders.

"You sound unsure," Troy said.

Her lips pursed. Troy was perceptive. She had to be careful what she told him, determined to protect Doug as much as possible. "The ranch life is new to him," she said after a slight hesitation. "It's an adjustment."

"Ranching is hard work."

True, and Doug was never supposed to be a ranch hand. He'd gone to school to be an electrician. He was smart and good with his hands, and was very patient with complicated things. He could succeed. He just needed support. He needed someone to give him a chance. But people didn't want to hire young adults with problems. Taylor was discovering that too many people didn't want to be troubled by other people's problems, which made her worry about the future. She worried about Doug being able to have the future he wanted and deserved.

"The physical work isn't the issue," she said after a moment, picking her words carefully, not sure if Troy was friends with the owners of Hogue Ranch. In a small town, you could never be too careful. "It's the... environment. It's not the best place for him."

"What would be better for him?"

"He wanted to be an electrician. He took all the courses and passed all these tests. He just needs to be given a chance, an apprenticeship. And it'll happen. It will."

"So the ranch is just a stepping stone to the next job," Troy said.

"Yes." She smiled, wanting to believe it. Needing to believe it. She loved Doug dearly. It had about killed her going away to college and leaving her younger brother behind with parents who refused to understand not just who Doug was, but what he needed. "That's right."

They lapsed again into silence but this time neither of them tried to fill it.

Troy's powerful four wheel drive made quick work of the mountain pass.

"Almost there," Troy said a little bit later, putting on his turn signal, as they approached the exit for Marietta. It was still snowing, but the flurries were lighter and the snow plows had been working all evening, keeping the city roads clear. "Which part of town do you live?"

"Near downtown, ten blocks north of the library on Bramble Lane."

"Know that street well. I had a girlfriend in high school that lived on Bramble," he said, smiling crookedly, "and one of my best friends, Mason Jones, lived there, too."

"I'm renting a room from the Jones'."

"Then I know right where to go."

Minutes later he was pulling up in front of the one and a half story Victorian home, the pale yellow paint contrasted with lots of creamy white trim, and snow. Mounds of snow. The snow clung to the big evergreen in the corner of the yard and blanketed the shrubs and hedges lining the front walk.

"So his parents rented you a room," Troy said, shifting into park.

"His sister, Kara, did. She bought the house from her parents when they wanted to move to Florida."

"Kara was just a pipsqueak when I knew her."

"She's not a pipsqueak anymore." Taylor leaned forward and reached for her leather satchel. "She's a Crawford County district attorney."

"Is she, really?" Troy grinned. "Good for her. Tell her hello from me. Not sure she'll remember me—"

"She remembers you." Taylor couldn't forget how Kara had positively *gushed* when talking to Jane about the Sheenan brothers during the Chamber's Christmas party. Apparently Jane wasn't the only Troy Sheenan fan in Marietta. "And I'll tell her hello," she added, reaching for the door handle. "Thanks for the ride."

"Glad I could help. And if you need help tomorrow—"

"I'll be fine," she said quickly, opening the door to slide out of the car. She swiftly shouldered her bag and shuddered at the blast of cold air.

"You never did tell me your name," Troy called to her.

Taylor tugged on her scarf, and forced a smile. "Taylor. Taylor Harris."

He laughed softly. "I thought so."

"You did?"

He nodded, his expression amused. "Jane told me all about you."

Taylor suddenly couldn't breathe. "She did?"
"You're my date Friday night."

Troy saw Taylor Harris's eyes widen and her lips part in surprise for a split second before her mouth shut.

She managed a few words, mostly incomprehensible words and then raced up the walkway to the Jones' front door. He stayed put, waiting for her to unlock the door. Once she was safely inside, he shifted into drive and pulled away.

So that was Taylor Harris, the new librarian.

Interesting.

He known Jane had set him up with Marietta's new librarian, but he hadn't expected Taylor Harris to be such a fiery, prickly little thing, nor had he expected her enormous tortoise frame glasses. The glasses practically covered her face.

Troy wondered why Jane would set him up with Taylor for the Ball.

Troy did like smart women, but Taylor Harris wasn't anything like the women he dated. He preferred urban sophisticates, women that were very ambitious and successful… lawyers, doctors, executives, entrepreneurs. Ever since graduating from college, he'd been drawn to women who had big careers and big lives, women who didn't depend on a man and knew how to take care of themselves. Women who preferred to take care of themselves. Independence was sexy. Intelligence and passion was sexy.

But the Ball was just one night, he told himself. And Jane insisted that he needed a date, as it wouldn't be proper to attend a black-tie Ball at his own hotel without someone gorgeous on his arm.

Troy's brow furrowed as he pictured the petite brunette who'd sat in his passenger seat staring out the window.

He'd never in a million years call her gorgeous.

He wouldn't even describe her as pretty. But she wasn't homely, either.

Without her glasses she might be very attractive...

He sighed, wishing he hadn't let Jane talk him into setting him up. He hadn't felt the need to take anyone to the Ball. His brother Dillon would be there, and so far Dillon hadn't asked anyone to be his date. Cormac was supposed to be flying in from California to see Dad and attend the Ball, and Cormac wasn't sure if he'd have a date. The only Sheenan who had a date at this point, was Brock, and he was bringing his fiancée Harley.

But you have a date now, he reminded himself, and it was the perfect date for him since Troy didn't do long distance relationships and he wasn't about to get involved with someone in Marietta.

Much less Marietta's new prickly librarian.

As Troy approached the old, two story ranch house twenty five minutes later, the SUV's snow tires crunching gravel, snow and ice, he noticed that the house was dark except for a light downstairs in the back.

Parking in front, Troy left his bags in the truck, and headed inside. He was eager to see his brother and dad.

The front door was unlocked as always and Troy walked down the hall to the kitchen where the light was shining. Thirty year old Dillon was at the farmhouse style sink, washing dishes.

"How's Dad tonight?" Troy asked, as Dillon caught sight of him and turned the water off.

Dillon grabbed a towel and dried his hands. "Better, now that he's sleeping."

"I saw your text. He had a rough day?"

"He was upset today. He wants to go to the cemetery." Dillon paused, glanced at Troy. "See Mom's grave."

Troy's forehead creased. "Mom's not buried in town."

"I know."

"Her ashes are here."

"I *know*." Dillon tossed the towel onto the counter. "I

told Dad that but he got all fired up, snapped at me that I was being disrespectful and to just do what he asked me to do." He shook his head. "Hard to see him like this. He was always so tough. Now he's like a lost little kid."

"Or a grouchy little kid."

Dillon smiled. "Glad you're back. It's good to see you."

"Why don't you get out of here? Go into town. I'll sit with Dad tonight."

"It's getting late and snowing pretty good."

"It's not even nine and you drive one badass truck. You'll be fine."

"You really want to get rid of me."

"I really want you to have a break. You've been alone with Dad for weeks—"

"Not that long. Harley's been coming over almost every day for a couple hours at a time and then yesterday Brock came with her and the kids and they spent the day here so I could get out, and take care of some banking and shopping. When I came home, she had dinner all made."

"So why hasn't Brock married her?"

"I don't know, but I'm thinking I should nominate them Friday night for that Wedding Giveaway contest. Can't think of anyone around here more deserving."

"True," Troy agreed. "But now, go, get out of here while you can. If you leave now, you could be at Grey's by nine thirty, shooting the shit, playing pool, and flirting with all those girls who have a thing for you."

"All those pretty girls in tight jeans and short skirts are looking for a husband. And I'm happy playing darts and having a beer and making out in my truck, but that's as far as it goes. I'm not looking to settle down, and nowhere near ready to be married."

"That makes two of us," Troy said, before heading upstairs to the master bedroom tucked back under the steep eaves of the eighty year old cabin, the interior walls covered with paneling, to hide the rustic split log walls.

For the next two hours Troy sat by the side of his father's bed in the house that had been home to three generations of Sheenans, and tried not to think.

Or feel.

But that was easier done if he didn't look at his father, who was now just a frail version of himself.

Easier done if Troy had remained in San Francisco, on task in his office on the thirtieth floor in the city's Financial District, or in his sprawling home in exclusive, affluent Pacific Heights with its views of Golden Gate Bridge, Alcatraz and the Bay.

But Troy had come home, and he'd returned for this. To be here. To take some of the pressure from Dillon's shoulders, and ensure that his father was as comfortable as possible in the coming weeks.

Dillon had warned him Dad was fading, but even then it was a shock for Troy to see how much his father had changed since Christmas. His father didn't even look like the same person.

It had always been hard for Troy to return to Marietta. He didn't like coming home, didn't like the memories or emotions, and that was before Dad was sick.

Now...

He shook his head, his jaw tight.

Now he just felt even angrier, but Trey was the angry Sheenan. Trey was the one who drank too much and hit things, broke things. Not Troy.

But whenever Troy did return to Marietta, and the ranch, he felt an awful lot like his infamous twin who was currently spending a five year sentence in jail.

Troy shifted uncomfortably in the antique chair positioned close to the bed, thinking if they were going to continue these bedside vigils for their dad, who was clearly on the downward slope now, then they really needed to get a bigger, sturdier chair in the bedroom.

Footsteps sounded in the hall and floorboards creaked as Dillon entered the dimly lit master bedroom.

"You're back," Troy said.

"Had a couple beers and nearly got into a fight with a punchy little cowboy acting like an asshole around Callan, but Grey threw me out before I could teach that boy some manners."

"You and Callan dating?"

"Callan and me? God, no. I've known her since she was

in diapers but we are pretty tight. We have fun together," Dillon said, running a hand through his thick dark hair, his hair the same shade as Troy's, Trey's and Brock's. Only Cormac was fair, the same dark blonde their dad had been in his early thirties. The rest of the Sheenan boys took after their late mother, Jeanette, who'd been part Indian, part Irish, and one hundred percent beautiful.

One hundred percent beautiful, and two hundred percent crazy.

Troy stretched out his legs, crossing his boots at the ankle. No, that wasn't fair. Mom wasn't crazy. She'd just been terribly lonely and unhappy on the ranch.

It hadn't been the life she wanted, isolated from town and friends, alone except for her husband and her five sons.

Dad should have insisted she learn how to drive.

Dad should have insisted she got into town.

Dad should have taken care of her better.

Troy clamped his jaw, teeth grinding. Or they, her sons, should have, he thought, glancing up at Dillon.

Shouldn't her boys have done more? Because isn't that what sons should do? Take care of their mother?

"How was Dad while I was gone?" Dillon asked.

"He got up once, needing to use the bathroom, and I helped him get there, but the rest of the time, he pretty much slept."

Dillon leaned against one of the columns of the four poster bed. "He does that a lot."

"He thought I was Trey," Troy added.

"Understandable, you're twins and Trey used to live here with him."

"He insisted I was Trey."

Dillon grinned. "So what did you do?"

"Act like I was Trey, and let him lecture me on how I needed to make things right with McKenna and step up and take responsibility for my son."

Dillon's smile faded. "Yeah, well, that's not going to happen."

"Trey loves his son, and McKenna."

"Kind of hard to be a good partner and father in jail."

"He'll get out and he'll get his act together."

"Yeah, but it'll be too late by then, at least, for him and McKenna."

Troy's brows pulled. "You think so?"

Dillon grimaced. "She's getting married again."

"*What?*"

Dillon nodded. "Lawrence proposed last week, after asking Rory and Quinn for permission to marry their sister. Of course, Rory and Quinn, who both hate Trey, said yes."

"If McKenna was our sister we'd hate Trey, too," Troy said quietly, tiredly, aware that Trey would not take the news well. It was a good thing Trey was in jail. Because if Trey *weren't* locked up, there's no way in hell he'd let McKenna, his first and only love, and the mother of his boy, marry another man.

"Who's going to tell Trey?"

"When's the wedding?"

"Not until Fall."

"Then there's no point saying anything now. Something could happen. The engagement could get called off. Why work Trey up when it could be nothing?" Troy nodded at the bed. "I'm going to grab my stuff from the truck and crash. I'll see you in the morning."

Chapter Three

T roy had gone to his truck without his coat and it was cold, seriously cold. His breath clouded in the air as he quickly scooped his bags from the backseat of the big Escalade. He was just about to slam the door shut when he heard a buzzing sound from beneath the passenger seat in front of him.

It sounded an awful lot like a phone.

His heart sank, thinking it was either the little librarian's phone, or the person who'd rented the car before him. Either way it meant that someone, somewhere was without a phone—modern society's lifeline--and probably frustrated as all hell.

Troy opened the passenger door, felt beneath the seat and then the side of the seat by the center console. Found it.

He glanced at the screen with the photo of a young Taylor Harris with a blonde teenage boy wearing a high school graduation cap and gown.

Must be Taylor's brother, even as he noted the five missed calls, and text after text.

Not doing so good.

Need to talk to you.

Call me.

Why won't you answer?

Troy's brow creased, concerned. This didn't sound good at all.

He glanced at the time on the phone's display. It was

quarter past eleven. If he drove the phone back to Marietta, he wouldn't arrive until close to midnight. How could he knock on the Jones' front door at midnight?

But then, reading the desperate texts, how could he not?

Troy returned to the house for his coat and wallet. He told Dillon he'd found a phone in the car and had to return it to town. Dillon suggested Troy just stay in town at the hotel. No reason to drive all the way back so late.

Troy thought it made sense and said goodnight, letting his brother know he'd be back before noon to spend the afternoon with Dad.

Taylor woke up to Kara clicking the light on in Taylor's bedroom. "You've got a visitor," Kara said, covering her yawn.

"What time is it?" Taylor asked,

"Eleven forty-five."

Taylor's mind cleared, and she sat up abruptly, immediately thinking of Doug as she groped for her glasses on the nightstand. "My brother?" she asked, settling her glasses onto the bridge of her nose.

"No." Kara pushed a tangle of dark blonde hair back from her face, tucking it behind her ear. "Your knight in shining armor. Troy Sheenan." She saw Taylor's baffled expression and added. "You didn't even have to track him down in the morning. He found your phone in his car and has brought it back."

Relief flooded Taylor. She'd discovered she'd lost her phone minutes after Troy had left and didn't know how to reach him without calling Jane, and Taylor didn't have Jane's number memorized, just saved on her phone. "It's awfully late to return it, though," she said, pushing back the covers and swinging her legs over the side of the bed.

Kara shrugged. "Apparently he was worried about some of the messages. He thought they might be... urgent."

"From Doug?" Taylor asked, immediately on her feet and reaching for her thick fleece robe from the foot of the bed.

"Sounds like it."

Rattled, Taylor stuffed her arms into the sleeves and tied the belt around her waist. What had happened? Was Doug in trouble? Had he gotten into it with someone? He'd been beaten up once at Hogue Ranch and he'd vowed he wouldn't walk away from a fight the next time. He'd defend himself...even though it'd mean legal complications.

Taylor hated the cold queasy uneasiness filling her. She hated that just hearing her brother's name made her worry. Worry was a terrible feeling, and it seemed like she lived in a perpetual state of anxiety over Doug these past six months. She needed him to get better. She needed him to get the right help and then maybe, just maybe, he'd have confidence again. Hope again. As it was, he struggled to hang in there.

But no matter how dark things seemed, she wouldn't give up on him. There was no reason to give up. Doug was young and still physically maturing and as doctors said, a young male's frontal cortex didn't even finish developing until mid-twenties. Doug just needed to be patient. He just needed to believe in himself, the way she believed in him. He'd already survived six months at Hogue. There were just three months left. Once he completed the program, he could live with her. That was the goal. That was the focus. That was her promise to him.

"Where is Troy?" she asked, combing her fingers through her long hair, trying to smooth and untangle it in one quick motion.

"In the living room. It was the warmest room." Kara gave Taylor a pointed look, her eyebrows arching. "Although maybe that didn't matter, because he's so hot."

"Is he?" Taylor asked, indifferently. She didn't understand all this fuss made over Troy. Yes, he was handsome. But so what? The world was filled with good looking men.

"Seriously hot," Kara drawled.

Taylor rolled her eyes. "Is every woman in this town crazy about him?"

"Every woman with a pulse." Kara winked, and headed back to her bedroom.

Taylor found Troy standing in front of the living room fireplace studying the framed photos on the mantle. She hesitated in the doorway, watching him examine the photos of Kara and her brother growing up.

His dark hair was cropped clean at his nape, showing off his high hard cheekbones and square chin, his strong jaw shadowed with a day old beard. He was wearing a long black wool coat, something you'd probably see in San Francisco's financial district and the tailored wool coat made his shoulders look even bigger, broader, which just emphasized his height.

But then he *was* tall--six two at least--and not the skinny kind of tall, but solid. Muscular. He'd made the huge Escalade feel small and it was probably a very roomy SUV.

"Hi," she said.

He turned to face her. "Sorry to wake everyone up."

As it turned from the mantle, his long black wool coat fell open, exposing his black cashmere sweater, and how it clung to the hard planes of his broad chest.

She'd tried not to stare at his chest in the car.

She had to remind herself not to stare now.

"I'm sorry you had to drive all the way back to Marietta tonight, at this hour." Her voice came out soft, breathless.

She told herself she was breathless because she wasn't accustomed to greeting men in the Jones' living room. She'd had some double dates with Jane, but none of the men had ever picked her up here. She told herself she was breathless because she was worried about Doug. She couldn't admit she was breathless because he was so...so...different...from any man she'd ever met before.

Nervously, she jammed her hands deeper into the robe pockets, thinking she must look as pretty as a roll of toilet paper in her fuzzy gray robe dotted with fat pink pigs, the robe a Christmas gift a from Doug several years ago.

"I didn't want you to panic," he said.

"That was nice of you, because I was, a little bit," she admitted. "I haven't backed up my contacts. Need to." She was babbling. She hated that. But she felt so jumpy. Troy made her self-conscious. And the robe didn't help. She felt silly in the robe. Why hadn't she just put on jeans and a sweatshirt? It would have felt so much safer, and she would have been more confident, than she did greeting him in a pig robe.

Because of course he'd still look urban, and sophisticated.

Dashing.

A prince coming to the villager's house with the glass slipper.

Or in this case, a phone.

"I would have waited until morning," Troy said, walking towards her, "but the messages seemed urgent." He handed her the phone. "Hope everything's okay."

His fingertips brushed her palm as he placed the phone in her hand. Taylor blushed, feeling a sharp tingle where his fingers had touched her palm.

This was so absurd. She had to get a grip. She rubbed at the sensitive, tingling spot even as she glanced at the screen of her phone.

Tons of missed calls. Tons of text messages. All from Doug.

"My brother," she said, heart sinking all over again.

"The one in Paradise Valley?"

She nodded. "Do you mind if I send him a message and make sure things are alright?"

"I think that's a good idea. I can always drive you to him if you need a ride."

She didn't bother to explain there were no visits at Hogue Ranch, and no dropping by. The ranch was a halfway house program approved by the state although Taylor wasn't sure how they maintained their status. They weren't doing much for the men there but making them work.

Taylor quickly shot her brother a brief text. *Everything ok?*

Where have you been? Doug answered almost immediately.

Taylor typed back. *Had a car accident and lost my phone. But I've got the phone now.*

You okay? Doug asked a second later.

Fine. Car's not so good but that can be fixed.

Good. Glad you're safe.

She drew a deep breath and repeated her first question, dreading his reply. *So are you okay?*

For a long moment there was no response, and then, *I hate it here.*

Taylor bit her lip, a fresh wave of dread washing through her, weighting her limbs, making her heart ache.

He wasn't in the right place. He needed a good therapist, as well as a dedicated doctor who could help with fine tuning Doug's medicine. Not all depression medicine worked equally. Every body was different. And bodies changed, and brain chemistry changed, and when that happened, you needed to try a new medicine, or a combination of medicines.

Three months she told herself. Three months and he'd be out and she'd get him the right help. She'd make sure he was seen by the best medical professionals she could find.

He deserved it. Just as he deserved a bright, healthy, happy future.

Before she could think of something to say, Doug texted again. *But I'll survive. I'll make it work. I want to get through this so I can come live with you.*

Her eyes burned and her throat swelled closed. For a moment she couldn't breathe, overwhelmed by love. He was such a good person and it broke her heart knowing how much he struggled. Blinking back tears, Taylor texted him back. *Me, too.*

Will I still see you this weekend?

Wouldn't miss it.

Nite, Tay.

Night, hon.

She slid her phone into the pocket of her robe, conscious that Troy was watching her, and had been watching her the entire time she'd texted back and forth with Doug. "Everything's fine," she said, voice husky.

"No emergency?" Troy asked.

She managed a small smile, eyes still damp. "Emergency averted."

"That's good."

"Yep." She held her smile and yet on the inside she hurt. She hurt for Doug, and from a purely selfish point of view, she missed him. She hated only being able to see him on weekends, for a couple hours on Sunday. It never seemed as if they had enough time to visit, or just relax and hang out together, playing a game, or watching a show in the living room for guests. It was hard for Doug, too, to have so little contact with family. He was still young. He needed family and support. He needed hugs and laughter and the reminder that he was more than his depression, more than the sum of his parts.

"Thank you," she said to Troy, meaning it. "I know it's a long drive, late at night, in terrible conditions."

"Happy to help." Troy reached into his coat pocket for his car keys. "So how are you going to get to work tomorrow?"

"Kara's dropping me off."

"Is she also going to help you get a rental car?"

Taylor nodded. "On my lunch."

"Good. Sounds like you have everything in control."

"Kara's good at that."

"I'd imagine."

Taylor walked him to the front door, chewing on the inside of her bottom lip, screwing up her courage to let Troy know she wouldn't be going to the Valentine Ball. *Just say it. Just say it. Just get it over with.*

"Troy," she said, as he reached for the door knob. "About the Ball Friday night."

He'd started to turn the knob but he released it and faced her. "Yes?"

He was so tall, so big, and movie star handsome that for a moment her mind went blank. For a moment she just stared at him, dazzled.

And then she blinked, and the moment passed, and she remembered why he was in town, and how the big Ball was in just four days.

"I can't go with you," she said quickly, blurting the words before she could change her mind. "And I wanted to let you know now, so you'd have time to find another... date."

Troy didn't immediately speak. His jaw firmed and his

dark blue gaze met hers. "Something came up?"

Taylor thought of all the different excuses she could give him—her brother needed her, she had a library conference to attend out of town, her parents would be in town—but she didn't think it was fair to lie to him, especially not after he'd done her two favors.

He'd been quite the gentleman. She owed him the truth.

"I'm not a black-tie formal event kind of girl," she said. "And I'm happy serving on the Wedding Giveaway committee, and selling tickets, but I never wanted to go to the Ball. Unfortunately, Jane can be stubborn and doesn't really listen." Taylor's voice dropped, deepening. "I'm sorry if I'm leaving you in the lurch, but honestly, there are so many women who'd probably love to go to the Ball with you, and now... one of them can."

Troy drove to the hotel bemused.

The little mouse, his prickly librarian, had just rejected him.

She didn't want to go to the Ball, and she definitely didn't want to go with *him*.

Troy wasn't sure how to react. Wasn't sure if he should laugh, or turn his car around and ask her to explain. Why exactly had she told him no?

Because she wasn't a black-tie kind of girl?

Because she didn't want to go to a Valentine Ball?

His brow furrowed. He slowed as he turned into the Graff Hotel parking lot, windshield wipers moving quickly to bat away the falling snow.

He didn't mind that she didn't want to go. He actually was relieved. They clearly weren't ever meant to be a couple.

And yet...he was so used to women chasing him, pursuing him, wanting him, that it was a bit of a surprise to meet a woman who didn't want him.

At all.

Troy's lips curved as he pulled before the hotel, and

handed his keys to the red-cheeked valet attendant.

He'd been impressed by Taylor's resume over the summer. He'd appreciated her experience and knowledge of modern library science, and now he was intrigued.

Why was she so determined not to attend the Valentine Ball with him? Because he had a sneaking suspicion that she would have gone...if he had been someone else.

T he next morning an exhausted Taylor stood at the kitchen counter, drinking two cups of coffee and a lightly buttered slice of toast.

It had been next to impossible to fall back asleep last night, after Troy left.

She'd tossed and turned, mashing her pillow this way and that.

Sleep had been elusive. She couldn't turn her brain off. And then when she did finally fall back asleep, she'd dreamed she was wearing this fancy pink prom gown with sparkly bits and little puffed sleeves and she was at the Graff Hotel for the Valentine Ball, only it wasn't really the Graff Hotel's 1914 ballroom, but an 1814 ballroom in London. Taylor was there with her brother and Jane and feeling very uncomfortable, very much a wallflower, and Jane kept whispering to Taylor about Lord Sheenan, and how handsome he was. Then suddenly somehow Lord Sheenan was asking Taylor to dance and they were twirling and waltzing around the dance floor...

It had all been so vivid, too.

Too vivid.

The ballroom, the gowns, the self-conscious feeling as she stood against a wall, wishing she were home instead of corseted into the ball gown.

And then the waltz, and the way Troy held her, and the feel of him against her.

She'd liked it.

She'd liked it so much she wasn't even sure who had

initiated the kiss. Him, or her.

That's when she'd woken up. At the kiss.

The minute she'd woken she wanted to be asleep again, dreaming again. The dream was gone.

She told herself she was glad.

But really, she wasn't.

And so baffled, and grouchy from lack of sleep, she finished the last of her cup, rinsed up her breakfast dishes, and then declined Kara's ride to the library, thinking she needed the walk in the frigid morning air to clear her head.

So bundled up in her winter boots and heavy coat, with her striped scarf wrapped around her neck, Taylor walked the ten blocks to the library, down Bramble Lane, the sidewalk mostly shoveled clean and salted.

She had made the right decision about the Ball. She was smart to have told him she didn't want to go. He had plenty of time still to find a date. And this way she could stay home Friday night, and curl up with a book.

She'd be so happy reading. She'd be so very content.

She would, she silently insisted. She loved her books. It was the right decision and she was one hundred percent certain that Troy Sheenan would agree.

On break mid-morning at the library, Taylor made calls, filed reports and begged the Bozeman insurance adjustor to go see her car as soon as it was towed to Marietta's body shop, instead of waiting until the next available opening, which was next week.

Then during her lunch, Kara picked up Taylor from in front of the library and drove her to Marietta's only car dealer to pick up a loaner car for the next week.

The loaner car was an older four-wheel drive Jeep, and sketchy at best, but it was a car and it ran, so it was something.

Taylor had hoped to grab a sandwich on her way back to the library but time ran out and she ended up back at work without eating anything. By the time the Tuesday night book club arrived at five thirty for their meeting, Taylor was dragging.

She needed food, and coffee, or just a big cup of coffee.

But there was no time to get anything before the book

club discussion began and after an hour and a half Taylor's energy and patience was running low.

She loved her job here in Marietta. She loved this library, too.

Although to be quite honest, right now, Taylor wanted to be anywhere but sequestered in the upstairs conference room with the Tuesday Night Book Group. Her stomach was growling, her head starting to throb from hunger, and she still had the Wedding Giveaway meeting to attend. And Taylor couldn't make it to tonight's Wedding committee meeting until she emptied and secured the second floor meeting room for the night.

Emptying the room of this chatty, opinionated group was never easy, but tonight it was starting to appear impossible since three of the founding members of the Tuesday Night Book Club did not like new chamber director, Jane Weiss, and did not approve of the Wedding Giveaway in the first place.

"I'm sorry to interrupt," Taylor said, raising her voice to be heard over the fifteen women, and one man, that made up the group. "But we really do need to wrap up. As I mentioned at the beginning of tonight's discussion, I must get to the committee meeting downstairs—"

Maureen continued talking as if Taylor had not spoken.

Taylor pursed her lips, struggling to keep her temper in check. Maureen was one of the ladies that had made Jane's life miserable last November and December and it was difficult for Taylor to be in the same room with Maureen. Taylor had little patience for people who had nothing better to do than complain, criticize, and make others miserable.

Unfortunately, it was also Taylor's responsibility to sit in on the various book group meetings and help guide the discussion. It was time to guide this discussion to a closure. She cleared her throat and rose from her chair. "It's time to wrap up," she said firmly. "Sadly, we can't go late tonight—"

"Why not?" Maureen demanded, interrupting Taylor with a question she already knew the answer to. "We always go late."

"We've always been allowed to go as long as we want," Virginia chimed in. Virginia was Maureen's best friend and minion. "I can't remember the last time we had to end at seven thirty."

"You know the Wedding Giveaway committee meeting is about to start downstairs," Taylor said, "and I can't join that meeting until one ends, so let's wrap up, and you can continue at the Java Café if you're still wanting to continue your discussion."

"So how are those tickets selling?" Maureen asked, leaning back in her chair and folded her arms across her stout chest.

"I think the committee said they are at two thirds of their goal," Taylor answered, stacking her book and notepad together and then reaching for the novel. "It would have been nice to sell out, but we've almost one hundred and fifty people attending, and that's fantastic."

"Apparently half of those attending have been given tickets to make the event appear successful," Maureen sniffed. "But I'm not surprised you'd have to do that. Who around here can afford to attend a party that costs two hundred dollars?"

Taylor breathed in, and out, her pleasant smile never once faltering. She'd been a shy little girl, and a quiet, polite, and accommodating teenager. She'd never given her parents any difficulty, and it'd been a shock to all when Doug began having issues in middle school. Her parents didn't know how to cope with a troubled son. They must have made a pact not to deal with it...or him. Their failure to take action had made a lasting impression on Taylor.

"I don't believe that's true, Maureen," she said now. "Yes, big donors and underwriters have been given tickets in exchange for sponsoring the Ball, but the committee has sold the majority of the tickets, and it's not two hundred per person, it's two hundred per couple, and that covers dinner, dancing, wine at dinner, and pictures."

Maureen grimaced and stood up, loudly scraping her chair against the hardwood floor. "You'd have to *pay* me to attend a black-tie ball that's being held to launch a wedding contest. Only a Californian would come up with an idea as ridiculous as that."

Taylor opened her mouth to protest, wanting to remind

them that the Wedding Contest was the 100 year anniversary of Marietta's 1914 Great Wedding Giveaway, but the group was rising, and gathering their things, and Taylor realized she'd lost that battle. Better to just let them all go.

As the room cleared, Taylor stashed her notepad and book in her leather satchel before checking her phone. A missed call from Jane. Nothing from Doug. Good.

She then went around the room, pushing in chairs, picking up scraps of paper left behind before turning off the lights, locking the door and heading downstairs to the main floor, taking the stairs quickly.

"Off to the Wedding committee meeting?" Louise, the Children's librarian, asked, passing the foot of the stairs with three children in tow. One of the little girls was Paige Joffee's daughter and the black haired little boy had to be McKenna's son, TJ.

"On my way now," Taylor answered, smiling as TJ chased two little girls around the plant in the lobby corner.

"Apparently Troy Sheenan will be at the meeting, too," Louise said. "Don't know if you've met him, but he's quite something. Marietta's most eligible bachelor and all that."

Taylor arched her eyebrows and pushed her glasses up higher on her nose. Did everyone have a thing for him? "Hadn't heard," she said, trying very hard not to remember her dream last night... and the almost-kiss.

"Jane sent me a text saying she hadn't been able to reach you, but she wanted me to know, which is why I've been hovering a bit in the lobby. I was hoping to give him a hug. I like the Sheenan boys. They've done well for themselves. Very successful young men. Well, all but Trey. Trey's in and out of trouble, but he's not a bad person. He's a sweetheart, he is. He was always my favorite Sheenan." She nodded at the boy who was still chasing the little girls around the potted plant. "See that little guy there? TJ is Trey's boy, and the spitting image of him, too."

Taylor caught a glimpse of TJ's laughing blue eyes and dimples before he chased the little girls in the opposite direction, towards the Children's reading room. "No. TJ is McKenna's son."

"And Trey's son."

Taylor frowned. "Trey and McKenna?"

"You didn't know?"

"No."

"They were quite the item. For years." Louise wiggled her fingers, saying goodbye as she raced after the laughing children.

D illon found Troy in the big Sheenan barn feeding the horses. "You're going to be late," Dillon said, closing the barn door behind him. "Doesn't the meeting start at seven thirty?"

"Yeah."

"It's after seven now."

"I know." Troy brushed feed off his hands, and then wiped his hands on the back of his butt, feeling the stiff denim. "I don't want to do this. Dreading this meeting."

"It was your idea," Dillon said.

"The Ball wasn't."

"But saving the hotel was."

True, Troy thought, adding water to the trough inside one stall.

And what a terrible mistake that had been.

But Troy wouldn't say that out loud, not even to his brother. It'd kill him to admit that restoring the Graff Hotel to its former splendor had the potential to bankrupt him. He should have never invested so much of his own money in one project. A smart investor didn't shell out that much of one's capital. It'd been a mistake to buy the hotel for cash, and even more risky to funnel so much capital into the property. He should have pulled back from the renovation when he realized it was a money pit. But he'd been too proud, too stupid, and too emotionally attached to the project to do the smart thing when he could.

Thank God he was a fighter, and tough. He'd knuckle his way through this battle, because he was nowhere ready to give up on the hotel.

The hotel had only been reopened for six months, after the two and a half year restoration. It'd been a huge job restoring the hotel because it'd been abandoned, boarded up, for over forty years before that. But you wouldn't know it looking at the hotel today. The Graff's grand lobby glowed with rich paneled wood, marble, and gleaming light fixtures, while the grand ballroom and smaller reception rooms sparkled with glittering chandeliers.

And yes, the hotel had virtually zero occupancy since early January, but December had been a good month, with the introduction of festive afternoon tea and company holiday parties on the weekends. But what they needed to do was fill the rooms all the time, because even empty, there were still salaries and bills to pay.

But the hotel was special. She was one of a kind. And while he regretted that restoring her had the power to cost him his company and financial security, he was glad he'd saved her.

Someone had to.

Now he just needed to continue focusing on turning things around, and the hotel staff would. He had a good team here, and everyone in management was committed to making the Graff successful. Troy knew that eventually they could get the hotel into the black. It wasn't impossible.

It was a matter of increasing tourism to Marietta, and getting publicity for the hotel, the kind of publicity that would make the Graff appealing to meeting planners and wedding planners, ensuring that the Graff became the destination of choice for conferences and special events.

"You're in pretty deep, aren't you?" Dillon said, as Troy left the stall and latched the door closed behind him.

"Yeah."

Dillon sat down on a stack of hay bales against the wall, extending his legs. "So just how deep?"

Troy reached for his coat hanging on a peg about Dillon's head. "Deep enough that if things go south, I'd be the one living here, working the ranch, leaving you free to return to Austin."

"That'd be a relief for me, but hell for you." Dillon folded his arms across his chest. "You hate the ranch."

Troy's lips compressed. He wasn't going to even dignify that with a response because yes, he did hate the ranch. He hated everything about it, and always had, which is why whenever he came home he stayed in town at a hotel.

"But then, you don't like Marietta, either," Dillon continued, watching Troy button his heavy sheepskin coat. "Which is why none of us can figure out why you'd hitch yourself, and your future, to that damn hotel. You're the smart, successful Sheenan—"

"You and Cormac haven't done too badly for yourselves."

"Because you invested in us."

"I believe in you."

"And the hotel?"

"Not ready to throw in the towel. I've spent ten years investing in startups. I believe we can still turn things around."

"But why The Graff in the first place? You're never going to make a profit from the hotel. You might not even earn back the investment."

Troy had started walking to the barn door, but he stopped and turned to look back at his brother, and then somehow, just like that, his mother was there. Her ghost. He could feel her at the ranch... in the house, the barn... and her sadness haunted him.

She should have had daughters.

She should have had girls for company. Girls who'd bake with her or sew with her. Girls who'd laugh and giggle and talk to her. Listen to her.

Men weren't good at listening.

He shook his head once, chasing away the past, and the memory of his mother who had loved The Graff. He hadn't restored the hotel for her. That would be idiotic because she was gone. But she had been the one to make him understand that beauty was transformative, and there was value in beautiful things. "Sometimes we do things because we think it's the right thing to do... even when everyone else tells you you're wrong."

Dillon's eyes, narrowed. He studied his older brother a long moment. "Mom would want you to be smart."

"Too late," Troy answered. "Looks like I've inherited her crazy."

Dillon's eyes narrowed another fraction of an inch. "Mom wasn't crazy." He hesitated. "She wasn't happy. That's different from crazy."

Troy said nothing. This was not a subject he liked discussing.

"And yes, Mom and Dad had problems. From what I gather, no marriage is perfect."

"But not all wives take their lives, do they?" Troy retorted.

Dillon flinched. "It's too late to change the past."

"I just wished I'd done something then."

"How could you? You were a kid. We were all kids."

"I wasn't that young. I know something was seriously wrong that night."

"I'm sorry you had to be the one to find her. Dad should have checked on her himself."

Troy shook his head. "Let's not go there."

"But you do. Constantly." Dillon's voice hardened. "It's time you let it go. There's no point in torturing yourself, or ruining your future, over something that's in the past."

"Are you talking about Mom or the hotel?"

"Maybe both."

Chapter Four

Taylor was rattled by Louise's news that Troy would be attending the Wedding Giveaway meeting tonight. She opened the heavy door to the masculine Crawford Room, the private board room off the library's main reading room, wondering why Jane hadn't bothered to tell her that Troy would be coming.

Jane was supposed to be her friend. Her *best* friend in Marietta. And friends did not set friends up, much less with one's gorgeous, popular, ridiculously successful ex.

Most of the committee had already taken a seat at the board room table. Taylor's gaze swept the room, seeing all the usual committee members: Paige Joffee from Main Street Diner, Sage Carrigan from Copper Mountain Chocolates, Risa Grant from SweetPeas florist, Tricia Thorpe from Marietta Travel, Jenny Thorpe, Tricia's new sister-in-law, and McKenna Douglas from Big Sky Photography.

McKenna lifted a hand, gesturing to Taylor.

Taylor moved towards her, seeing McKenna in a new light. Taylor had known that beautiful McKenna Douglas was a single mom, and a talented photographer specializing in wedding photography, but until tonight Taylor had not known that the father of her little boy was Trey Sheenan, Troy's twin. McKenna had never said anything, nor had anyone else. Maybe everyone else just knew.

Or maybe folks here didn't think it was important to

share. Probably the latter, because no one had told Taylor about the tragedy that took place on Douglas Ranch seventeen years ago.

Taylor only found out about the murders by chance, reading through old newspapers and magazines saved in the library's vault.

Taylor, a history buff, had been the one to discover that back in 1914 Marietta had sponsored a big Wedding Giveaway to draw attention to the re-opening of the Graff Hotel following the 1912 fire. She'd shared the news with Jane, who then came up with the idea of a one hundred year anniversary Wedding Giveaway, again highlighting the beautifully restored Graff, and all the merchants in town.

Taylor's interest in history and Marietta's 1914 Wedding Giveaway had been a fun surprise.

The discovery of the Douglas home invasion had been the exact opposite. The horrific crime had sickened Taylor and she'd been afraid to go to Louise and ask her about the news, but she finally did, needing to understand just what had happened.

Louise had found it very difficult to talk about the crime. Apparently the murders had never been solved. For years after the home invasion, locals and the ranching families in the outlying area were jumpy and fearful. Folks wondered if maybe the assault had been orchestrated by one of the Douglas' hired hands. Lots of people felt it had to have been someone who knew the property, the layout of the house, and were familiar to the family, because wouldn't the Douglas' dogs have barked up a storm and alerted the family so they would have had a chance to defend themselves?

Just remembering what she'd read made Taylor queasy all over again, and gave herself a quick, mental shake, needing to chase away the grim details and memories.

"Hello," she said approaching McKenna. "How are you tonight?"

"I'm good." McKenna smiled. "Did you see my wild child with Louise?"

"I did. He's found two little girls to chase which is making him very happy."

"Sounds about right. And Louise? She's managing

okay?"

"She's great. She loves kids."

"She always has. It's going to be awful when she retires. She's been part of the library since I was born."

"She does love her work," Taylor agreed. "I'm going to miss her, too. She's a sweetheart and has been so helpful since I arrived."

"And Margaret? Has she been as helpful?" McKenna asked, even though she had to be aware that Margaret Houghton, the head librarian, did not believe in new-fangled things like computers and the internet and had resisted adding e-books to the library's collection.

Taylor grimaced. "Not as helpful, no."

McKenna laughed. "Didn't think so." She hesitated. "Actually, I was hoping I could ask a favor. I need some help tomorrow night."

"You need a sitter?"

"No. Nothing like that." McKenna pushed a long dark auburn strand of hair back from her cheek, securing it behind her ear. "I need a dress for the Ball, and I hoped you'd go with me to Married in Marietta and give me your opinion. You've seen me. I live in jeans and am useless when it comes to formal attire."

"Of course," Taylor said quickly, pleased and flattered that McKenna wanted to do something with her. "I'd love to."

"You're sure? Dress shopping isn't fun—"

"I would enjoy it. Honestly."

"So you have your dress already?"

"I'm not going to the Ball, but I'd love to help you find a dress for Friday night."

"I thought Jane told me you were going." McKenna frowned, shrugged. "I guess I misunderstood. But if you're up for going with me tomorrow night, that's great. I've lined up a sitter so maybe we can make it a girls night out? Shopping and dinner, or shopping and then drinks after?"

"Perfect. Sounds fun."

And it did, Taylor thought, taking a seat on the opposite side of the table, since there were no spots open near McKenna.

McKenna was something of Marietta's golden girl. People loved her, and were extremely protective of her. McKenna was also influential. Her opinion mattered, and when some folks were critical of Jane back in December, ridiculing her and the Great Wedding Giveaway, McKenna wrote a letter to the editor at the *Copper Mountain Courier*, publicly siding with Jane, stating that the Giveaway would be good for the community, the economy, and particularly the local merchants, and that she not only threw her full support behind the *Wedding Giveaway*, but she'd also volunteered to co-chair the Wedding Giveaway committee with Paige Joffee, owner of Main Street Diner, to ensure the Wedding Giveaway's success.

After that, there'd been a lot less dissension.

A lot less.

Like... *none*. If some folks still weren't happy about the Giveaway, they kept their negativity to themselves.

That was when Taylor learned just how much sway McKenna had in this town. It also made McKenna and Trey Sheenan's relationship that much more intriguing to Taylor.

McKenna was clearly the town's golden girl, but Trey Sheenan was by all accounts, Marietta's bad boy... so what did people make of that?

There was no more time to think about Trey and McKenna as Paige called the meeting to order, welcoming everyone.

Paige went through last meeting's minutes then shared that the Valentine Ball was still shy of its goal with regards to tickets sales, but on the plus side, another twenty had been purchased over the weekend, bringing the expected attendance to 170. Jane still hoped that a few more tickets would sell before Friday, and she'd also given ten pairs to the local radio stations to use as giveaways, in exchange for some last minute publicity.

Paige was answering a question about which radio stations Jane had approached when the board room door opened. A tall man in a sheepskin coat and black felt cowboy hat walked in and all conversation died.

He removed his hat, dipped his head. "Sorry I'm late," he said, his voice deep, husky.

Troy.

Taylor sat up straighter, her stomach flip flopping wildly.

He looked so... different.

"Welcome," Paige said, smiling at him. "Glad you're here."

"Join us," Tricia said brightly.

He nodded again, his narrowed gaze scanning the room, looking for an available seat.

Taylor hated the way her pulse suddenly danced. There was no reason for her pulse to race. It was embarrassing, actually, to feel anything. So ridiculous that she did.

But she wasn't the only one who seemed affected by Troy. Tricia couldn't take her eyes off him, Risa had a touch of pink in her cheeks, and calm, practical, unruffled Paige suddenly looked almost nervous.

It'd been several years since the *Copper Mountain Courier* had named Troy Sheenan Marietta's Most Eligible Bachelor, but apparently he hadn't lost any popularity with the ladies since then.

Only McKenna didn't look thrilled to see Troy. Taylor wondered why.

Troy headed to the table. Last night he'd looked like a city slicker in his cashmere sweater, tailored trousers and black wool coat but tonight he looked imposing in the thick shearling sheepskin coat and scuffed cowboy boots, snowflakes dusting his wide shoulders and long sleeves.

Tonight he wasn't the technology tycoon from California, but a Paradise Valley rancher with Montana running deep in his veins. Tonight he looked like a Sheenan.

Taylor had met two of the other Sheenans in the past month. Louise had introduced Taylor to Brock, the oldest Sheenan, when he and Harley, his fiancé, had brought the twins to the library to do some research. And then just a few days later Taylor met Dillon, the youngest Sheenan, one night at Grey's Saloon. Dillon and Callan Carrigan had been hanging out together, drinking too much, arguing a lot, and apparently enjoying every moment of it.

Brock and Dillon were both big, dark, ruggedly handsome men. And now Troy looked just as tough.

Montana tough.

Taylor couldn't believe that she found this new Troy rather appealing. She didn't want to find him appealing.

He was Jane's ex. Jane's man. Jane's love.

Taylor couldn't forget that, either.

Suddenly Troy's gaze met hers, and held. It was just for a split-second but that split-second was enough to send a rush of blood to Taylor's cheeks.

She dropped her gaze, embarrassed, and flustered. It'd been bad enough telling him she couldn't be his date to the Ball, but now to spend the next hour in the Crawford Room with him?

She prayed he'd take the empty seat next to Tricia.

He didn't.

He took the chair on Taylor's right.

Taylor's heart did a quick staccato as he pulled out the wooden chair and sat down next to her, stretching his legs out beneath the table, boots crossing at the ankle, his denim covered thigh practically touching hers.

"Hello, Taylor," he said under his breath as the meeting resumed.

Her mouth went dry. "Hi," she whispered.

"Get your car situation sorted out?"

She nodded. "Yes. Thank you."

"Good."

The meeting resumed, but Taylor could barely focus on what Paige was saying.

Troy was seriously distracting.

And not just because he was Jane's ex. The man had quite a few attributes.

Like his size. He was a big man... you couldn't ignore him. He filled his chair and all the space around him with shoulders and a big back and hard carved quads.

And a fit man. He had a *body*. And *muscles*. Lots of them. The jaw-dropping, eye-candy sort of body, and now that his heavy coat was off, his snug fitting Henley seemed to stretch over and wrap every sinewy line in his chest and arms, the soft cotton delighting in his dense pecs, flat hard abs, and thick biceps.

Then there was his scent. Which was a lovely, subtle

masculine cologne that hinted at spice and something rich and mellow and smooth... vanilla, maybe?

But these attributes were quickly turning into negatives. His scent and warmth and the sheer physicality of the man was proving most distracting.

Taylor fidgeted unhappily, tugging on her notepad, drawing it more firmly in front of her. She'd been fine until he arrived. Now she couldn't follow the thread of the discussion, the voices around her a whir of sound, the committee members a blur.

Why had he come tonight?

He hadn't been involved in any of the planning for the Ball or the Giveaway, so why come to this last meeting now?

The only other person who seemed troubled by Troy's appearance was McKenna. Taylor caught sight of McKenna's face. McKenna was still pale, her expression now guarded. Shuttered.

McKenna was no longer animated and bubbly, but someone else.

Interesting.

Meanwhile, various committee members continued updating Troy and all, on where things stood for Friday's Ball.

Risa talked about the floral centerpieces, and how there would be flowers everywhere--tulips, roses, lilies, freesias-- the most romantic, lush flower arrangements one could imagine.

Jenny Thorpe, Tricia's new sister-in-law, brought everyone up to date on the band and DJ entertaining the guests. The band would play during the dinner hour and the DJ was to get everyone on their feet after.

Sage Carrigan shared about the chocolates she'd made for the elaborate dessert buffet, and Paige was working on the chocolate fondue fountain with the Graff hotel banquet staff.

Tricia mentioned that the lighting specialist Jane had recommended, would be arriving Thursday from San Francisco to bathe the white and gold ceiling and walls with pink light.

McKenna said nothing, lips curved in a stiff, artificial

smile.

Taylor glanced from McKenna to Troy to the different women on the committee, feeling inexplicably torn, and truthfully, somewhat crestfallen.

It was going to be an incredible Ball. Beyond beautiful.

And Taylor wasn't going.

T roy sat in the library listening to the committee update its members with the Ball details. Everyone was so enthusiastic. The committee had worked very hard. The Ball would be lovely, and successful, he was sure of that. Of course it would have been nice if a few more tickets had been sold, but it was the first time Marietta had thrown such an extravagant party and if ticket sales were the only issue, then he couldn't be critical. Ticket sales were difficult for even professional event organizers.

As he listened to the updates, he tried to avoid looking directly at McKenna, aware that it would just make her more uncomfortable. McKenna was most definitely not good with him here. It hadn't always been the case. They'd once been very close. She was the sister he'd never had. Trey and McKenna had been together off and on since high school, and everyone knew that one day Trey and McKenna would get married. But life kept throwing them curveballs, and it seemed as if McKenna had finally had enough.

He didn't blame her. He couldn't.

How could he blame her for wanting to move on and settle down? She'd been a rock in the face of such chaos and adversity. She deserved a happy-ever-after and she wasn't going to get that with Trey serving time in prison for involuntary manslaughter. True, it was a bar fight he didn't start, and he was fighting to protect a woman. But that punch he threw killed a man and Trey had been in trouble before, so the judge came down hard on him, adding some extra time to the mandatory minimum sentence.

Troy sighed. Dad had taken it so hard when Trey was

sentenced to five years.

It was then that Dad just seemed to give up. Trey was the one who lived at the ranch, managed the ranch. Trey and Dad had been pretty tight, too.

Now, with Dad dying, no one knew what would happen to the one hundred and five year old Sheenan Ranch. Trey might have been the one to run it, but Trey was going to be locked up for another two years at least, and Dillon couldn't remain here in Marietta until then.

Troy was also worried that his bachelor brother Cormac had bitten off more than he could chew by agreeing to raise his goddaughter, two year old Daisy Davis, as his own. It was one thing to be asked to be a baby's guardian. It was another to become the guardian.

Troy shifted restlessly in the library chair, trying not to glance at his watch. He wasn't sure why he'd promised Jane that he'd attend the meeting tonight but he knew why he'd chosen to sit next to Taylor.

Last night he'd been surprised by her refusal to attend the Ball with him.

And then intrigued. And now amused.

He wasn't accustomed to being rejected. In his world, women chased him and he spent tremendous energy dodging his computer and phone, overwhelmed by the number of women texting and calling, instant messaging and sending flirty snap chats. He appreciated a beautiful woman. He admired a smart, beautiful woman. But he wasn't comfortable being chased.

He didn't like feeling hunted.

Back in school he'd been popular. The Sheenan brothers were good looking boys. None of them had ever lacked for girls, or dates. But once he'd made his fortune, women weren't just interested in him, they were interested in his lifestyle.

Maybe that's why he'd chosen to sit next to Taylor in tonight's meeting. She didn't eye him as if he were a tasty steak, or a Thanksgiving feast.

She looked at him with indifference. Maybe even disdain. And that made him curious. Made him want to understand why Taylor Harris disapproved of him. It also made him want to prove her wrong.

Maybe he viewed her rejection as a challenge.

A man liked a challenge. A man liked the chase. Provided he was doing the chasing.

So Troy stopped listening to the committee, he gave up trying to keep track of all the details.... no longer caring to remember what kind of flowers or lighting or chocolate desserts there would be.

Instead he studied Taylor who sat with her legs crossed just above the knee, taking copious notes in her notebook, her pink lips pursed, her brow furrowed in concentration.

She looked so studious and focused with her glasses, cardigan sweater, and long gleaming ponytail. He'd always had such a thing for smart girls. Book girls. His sophomore year of high school he'd spent all his free time in this library, making out with Lani Murphy in any dark corner they could find.

They'd study, kiss, study, kiss.

It had been the best academic year of his life.

Sure, his grades hadn't been so hot but he'd felt like a man, and she'd felt well... amazing.

He tried not to smile as he pictured Taylor back in high school. He was quite sure she'd looked the same. Same ponytail, same glasses, same smart, studious expression.

He wondered if she'd ever spent a high school afternoon making out in the library. Somehow from her starchy expression, he suspected not. She struck him as the kind of girl who believed libraries were about books. Silly girl. He'd love to teach her what dark shadowy corners in libraries were really for.

As if aware of his scrutiny, Taylor turned her head and stared back at him, giving him a significant, no nonsense look that he thought was as sexy as hell.

Until now he'd thought her eyes were brown, a simple chocolate brown, but now he saw they were a hazel green with bits of light blue. Or was it silver?

With her brows arching, dark elegant wings behind the masculine frames, and her hazel eyes snapping fire, he thought she'd never looked quite so bright and beautiful.

If only she understood that she looked very appealing

annoyed.

Quite kissable with her pink lips pursed.

"*What?*" she mouthed at him.

"What, *what?*" he whispered back.

Her nostrils flared as she exhaled hard. "You're staring."

Heads were turning. Everyone seemed to be looking at them now but McKenna, who was looking away.

Troy leaned closer to Taylor. He spoke under his breath. "I like your glasses."

For a moment Taylor just looked at him, her expression incredulous, and then she leaned very close to him, so close he could smell a hint of citrus and orange blossom. Shampoo or fragrance, he didn't know which.

"They're not a fashion statement," she said quietly, tersely. "I need them to see. Now *ssshh*. We're interrupting the meeting."

hy did she say that?

The moment the words left her mouth, Taylor wanted to die of mortification. *Ssssh. We're interrupting the meeting.* She sounded like such a fuddy duddy. Like the crabbiest old woman alive.

Like Margaret Houghton, Marietta's head librarian.

But Taylor wasn't Margaret, nor was she crabby. Taylor was an optimist. And a closet romantic. But even optimists and closet romantics had to know when they were outclassed.

Troy wasn't in her class, or her league, or anything at all that she could be part of.

She and Troy might as well exist on different planets and spheres.

She wasn't a big city girl. She didn't like social functions. She loved disappearing into bed with a wonderful story.

And yes, one day she hoped to find true love... that

wasn't in a romance novel... and she was sure, one day, she'd find Mr. Right, and when she did, he would make sense to her, and suit her, and reflect her morals and values.

He'd be a simple man, too. A homebody. A man who loved books and... and....

Taylor frowned.

What else would he love?

Sports? Hiking? Skiing? Mountain climbing?

Her frown deepened.

She didn't do any of those things. But she did like movies, and she enjoyed some good quality television programs.

She loved B&Bs and scenic drives. She loved visiting historical spots, too, and hoped one day to visit all the national parks in the States.

Surely there was a man out there who'd like her, and want to do those things with her, too.

Surely.

And when she did find him, she'd know he was right. He'd look right. He'd feel right. He'd be right.

T roy had been waiting for the committee meeting to come to an end so he could speak to McKenna. He wanted to come see TJ one night this week while he was home but the moment the meeting did end, McKenna was on her feet and bolting out the door.

Troy tried to follow but Tricia stopped him and asked a question about the suite being donated to the Great Wedding Giveaway for the bridal couple, and by the time he'd answered her question and made it into the hallway, McKenna and TJ were long gone.

He was still standing there, when Paige and Taylor exited the board room, and Taylor locked the Crawford Room door behind her.

"Everything okay?" Taylor asked him, as Louise emerged from the back, turning off lights as she went.

"Yes," he said, but he was frustrated. He loved McKenna. Loved TJ. He didn't want to lose them and he was beginning to worry that maybe he already had.

"Were you hoping to catch McKenna?" Taylor asked.

He nodded.

Paige glanced from Troy to Taylor, and then said goodnight. Paige and Louise left the library together, leaving Troy and Taylor in the hall.

"I'll walk you out," he said. "Make sure you get to your car safely."

"I have a few things to do first," Taylor said. "So don't wait. I'll be fine. Marietta's safe."

"I'm not going to leave until you're safely at your car," he answered firmly.

So he waited while she double-checked that the computers were powered down and the lights were off in the restrooms.

They walked out the front door and Taylor locked the door and set the alarm. Her teeth were chattering as she punched in the alarm code. "It's cold," she said, slipping her glove on.

"It's been a long winter for most of the country," he agreed.

"I take it you all haven't been suffering too much in California?" she asked, shooting him a wry look.

"No. It's been a really mild winter on the West. We could use some good storms in California. Need the rain. We've been in a drought for quite some time."

"Why do you like California?"

"I like startups. Technology. There's a lot of economic opportunity for me there."

They were heading down the stairs for the parking lot and Taylor shot him another quick assessing glance. "You don't miss Montana?"

There was no easy way to answer a question like that, and Troy hesitated, trying to decide how he should answer. "Marietta will always be home, but it's a complicated relationship." He smiled, and shook his head. "That sounds ridiculous, I know. Sorry."

But Taylor seemed fascinated by his response and she

bundled her arms across her chest and faced him. "I have a very complicated relationship with Hopeville, too, so it doesn't sound ridiculous at all. If anything, I find it reassuring."

"You don't go home often?"

"No."

"You don't get along with your folks?"

"I get along fine with them, or at least, I used to until I took my brother under my wing. They didn't appreciate my interference." She shrugged. "But they were neglectful. They didn't treat him the way he deserved."

"That must have been hard for you. You seem very protective of him."

"I am. And it was hard. But it's not Doug's fault. None of it was his fault."

"So you're not just his big sister, but his surrogate mom now."

"You could say that."

Looking down at her small face with the resolute press of pink lips, he felt a funny little pang. She really wasn't like the other women he knew. He was glad. He liked her honesty. He was glad she wasn't trying to impress him. "Would you want to grab a quick bite with me at Main Street Diner? I think they're open for another hour."

She made a face. "It's late."

"I know you haven't eaten. Louise said you had no chance to grab anything before all of tonight's meetings."

"I can eat when I go home."

"Louise said you'd just have soup."

"And I would, it's true."

"She thinks you need some proper meals."

Taylor's lips compressed and yet her eyes were twinkling. "Louise shouldn't be sharing my personal life with you."

"I've known her since I was just a little kid and she has a good heart. I respect her, and appreciate that she's looking out for you."

"I agree. And she's right. I could use some real food. Besides," she added, smiling wider, suddenly sounding mischievous. "It's Tuesday."

"This is good because...?"

"Tuesday means homemade beef barley soup at the diner."

"Soup?" he laughed.

She grinned. "What can I say? I like soup. But don't worry, I'll order a salad, too."

Chapter Five

They cut through Crawford Park, towards the courthouse before crossing Front Street for the Main Street Diner.

Marietta had been so pretty with all the Christmas lights and decorations up. Now it just looked empty and a little dirty with white and gray snow heaped in the gutter and on all the street corners.

Taylor was glad to reach the Diner to get out of the biting wind. Fortunately, at almost nine, the restaurant was virtually empty. The waitress told them they could sit anywhere and Troy left the choice to Taylor.

Taylor selected one of the big leather booths along the brick wall and once seated, she peeled off her coat and scarf and hat, piling them next to her. Suddenly she thought of McKenna, and how McKenna had avoided looking at Troy, and how Troy had gone after McKenna but she'd left without speaking to him.

"I didn't realize until tonight that your brother Trey was the father of McKenna's son," Taylor said.

Troy gave her a wary glance. "You and McKenna aren't close?"

"No, but I like her. I've always wanted to get to know her better, and tomorrow night we're supposed to go look at dresses. Well, she's trying on gowns. McKenna wants me there for moral support and maybe my advice."

"Have you met Lawrence, her fiancé?"

"Briefly, but I do see him around. His office is on Main Street. He and McKenna both work in the same building, down by the Mercantile."

"I don't know him."

"He seems nice, and very devoted to McKenna. He's watched TJ a couple times when McKenna attends the Wedding Giveaway committee meetings. He and TJ will hang out in the children's book section while we meet in the Crawford Room."

"So McKenna is excited about the wedding?"

"I would think so. I imagine I'll learn some details tomorrow night."

"I hope she'll be happy," he said, picking up the menu. He studied it for a minute before setting it aside. "She deserves to be happy. McKenna is amazing, and a great mom to TJ."

Taylor lifted a brow. "But..?"

His big shoulders shifted. "But nothing. Trey had the best girl—the best thing—and he screwed it up."

"Did you love McKenna, too?"

"Of course I love her. Everybody loves McKenna. She's just... that... special, but if you're asking if I was in love with her, that's a no. She was always Trey's girl. Always. I would never, ever go there. Trey's my twin."

"Can't imagine two of you," Taylor answered. "Does Trey really look just like you?"

"We're identical, but we've never dressed alike, or played the twins card. We've always been so different. Trey was quite a bit older than McKenna so they only flirted in high school, and began dating once McKenna had graduated from Marietta High. McKenna's brothers, Rory and Quinn, did not want their sister dating Trey. She was this sweet, good girl and he was the terrible, bad boy but they clicked."

"Opposites attract," Taylor said.

He nodded. "She made him better and he made her laugh, and when it was good between them, it was very good, but when it was bad, it was hell. I don't know how many times they broke off, only to get back together before another bruising break up. They were broken up—apparently for good—when McKenna discovered she was pregnant. It took her a long time to take him back, and then it was magic. Trey proposed, she'd accepted, and they were planning a wedding when Trey got in trouble. Now he's gone for a couple years."

"He got in a bar fight?"

"Some guy was getting rough with his girl over at the Wolf Den and Trey got involved, threw a punch, and the other guy hit his head on a table as he fell. He later died. Trey was arrested, and sentenced to three to five years for involuntary manslaughter."

Taylor didn't know what to say.

Troy shrugged. "It's bad."

"I'm sorry."

"I am, too." Troy lifted a hand, flagged the waitress down. "It's late. We should probably order."

They steered away from personal topics while they ate, discussing the Ball for a bit, and then the Great Wedding Giveaway, before circling back to Taylor's new job at the library.

"I love my job," she said, answering Troy's question. "And I love the building itself. The library has such a great history, built in the 1880's as the third public building constructed during Marietta's short-lived copper boom, and its handsome, with all those tall windows, the high ceilings, the marble foyer and staircase with hardwood floors on the first and second floors—" She took a breath. "But as it is now, it just feels old. I don't know if you've noticed, but the library has a dusty, musty feel. And yet it's clean. The problem is just that it's never been updated. Even the glass display cabinets are filled with displays decades old."

Troy smiled, enjoying how animated she'd become while talking about the library. She was passionate about her work and dedicated, too. The hiring committee had made the right decision, recommending her for the job. "What would you do with the library, if you could?"

"Besides change those ancient displays?" she asked, smiling crookedly. "Well, for one, I'd make the library a true community center. I'd overhaul the electrical—new lights and outlets throughout so people could bring their laptops and study there. I also think that the smaller conference room on the second floor would be perfect for a little café or espresso stand."

"Espresso at the library?"

Taylor nodded. "It's happening at libraries, and can't you just see how good it would be for moms? They could grab a coffee and have a little visit or read a magazine while their kids went to Story Time with Louise. I think Marietta teens and local college students would enjoy a coffee or snack while studying. But of course, Margaret, won't hear of us changing a single thing, library, whether it's one of her faded but 'culturally relevant' display cases, or those hollow antiquated private rooms on the second floor that go unused, unless one of the book groups meet in them."

"This is how it all starts, you know."

"What does?"

"Change. You have an idea, and you get excited and throw your weight behind it and before you know it, you're in really deep and everyone else is wondering what the hell happened."

"Is that what happened with you and your hotel?"

"Pretty much."

"But isn't that good? Look what you've given back to Marietta?"

"Not everyone here is happy about it. Not everyone likes change, even if it's beneficial."

"Why?"

"Because some people are afraid of change. They're afraid it means they might have to grow and change, and that could be hard work."

"Well, I'm not asking anyone to change. I just want to improve the library. I'd like to make the library a thriving community center. Why not let that gorgeous old building become the heart of the community? A library is more than books and quiet spaces. A library should inspire, enrich, and support both individual patrons and the community—" she broke off and bit into her lower lip. "Maybe I am asking for some change."

He smiled, liking her more and more, as well as impressed by her spirit. Who would have thought that the pretty new librarian had such fire? "Good. And don't ever apologize for wanting to do something here, or anywhere.

We need people with passion and vision. I admire your enthusiasm. But can I offer you one piece of advice?"

"Yes."

"Don't fall in love with beautiful historic buildings in small towns."

"No?"

"*No*. It's a maddening love, and very expensive."

She sat back in the boot, expression thoughtful. "I've wondered about that."

"I'm sure everyone has."

"So why did you do it?"

"The hotel is...." his voice drifted off and he stared off, picturing it as it was when he bought it—the boarded up windows, the ratty stained carpet covering the marble lobby, the holes in the walls and then that ballroom, the grand ballroom with its soaring ceiling and gilt trim, and the old reading room with its rich walnut paneling. He could feel the history in the abandoned building, set for demolition. He could picture the dances and the blushing brides and how stately even the old coatroom outside the ballroom must have been.

And he'd bought it on the spot.

For cash.

Because no one would loan him money for that eye sore. No one could see how it'd ever be restored and put back on the market without bleeding the investors dry.

And the hotel was bleeding him dry, but it was also beautiful now. A landmark. A Montana treasure. And he did feel good about that. He had done something right. Maybe not everyone would agree, or understand, but he remembered going to the Graff with his mother and brothers when he was young, just before it had closed, to see the Christmas tree in the big lobby, and have hot chocolate in the restaurant. They'd all dressed up, his mom and her four boys—Dillon wasn't born yet—and Trey had been bored but Troy had been enthralled.

When he grew up, he'd live like this.

When he grew up, he'd give his mother a beautiful palace, just like this.

Troy suddenly became aware that Taylor was looking at

him, and waiting, patiently for him to finish.

He looked into her face, and saw her eyes and her interest and she was interested in hearing what he had to say. Not because he was a Sheenan. Not because he was rich. But interested in what he thought, and felt.

What he knew.

Who he was.

Something inside him shifted. He felt some of the tension he'd been carrying around with him ease. He smiled wryly. "The hotel needed to be saved. It's part of me, and Marietta, and it was supposed to be demolished. The building had been condemned, and I couldn't let it happen. So I didn't."

Her gaze held his, her expression intent. "Do you regret saving it?"

"No."

"Even if it... hurts you... financially?"

"Jane's been talking."

Taylor pursed her lips. She appeared to choose her words carefully. "The whole town's been talking."

"Not surprised. But I have good instincts. I think it's going to be alright."

"You're sure?"

"Yes. Because even if I have to sell it at some point, and even if I take a loss, I've still won. I've given something back to my hometown. I've created something that my children and grandchildren can enjoy. And that makes it all worth it."

Taylor looked down at her plate, and blinked, fighting the most ridiculous urge to cry. Her eyes had burned and turned gritty as he'd talked about creating something for his children and grandchildren. She understood his love for old buildings and the past. She'd always been fascinated by old black and white photographs of Montana's past. If she looked hard enough into one of those photographs she could imagine herself there...

"I wish I could have seen the Graff before you restored it," she said. "But maybe it's good that I didn't. It would have made me sad."

"She was too beautiful to be neglected like that," he agreed.

For a long moment Taylor said nothing, her emotions turbulent, her thoughts whirling. She shouldn't say what she was so tempted to say. She shouldn't even be feeling what she'd been feeling all night.

She should get her purse and coat and go home right now.

Right now without saying a single thing about the Ball. Or maybe, possibly going to the Ball with him.

She couldn't. She'd already told him no. She'd made up her mind. Taylor wasn't flighty. At least, she'd never been flighty before...

Taylor swallowed hard and reached for her leather satchel. She needed to leave before she said something she might regret.

And yet her heart raced. She couldn't remember when she last felt so torn.

"I'm glad we did this," she said. "It was nice. Thank you."

"I enjoyed it, too."

She pulled the satchel onto her lap, and reached for her wallet.

He saw her open the wallet and shook his head. "I've got this."

"It's not a date," she answered.

He smiled. "I know. But I can write it off. It's probably harder for you."

"That's true. There is no budget at the library for meals or entertainment. Not even for technology."

Troy placed several twenties on the table. "Which will change when Margaret's gone in June."

"I hope so." Taylor glanced from the bills to Troy's chest, where the snug Henley hit, just beneath his collarbone, exposing taut tone muscle and golden skin. He was obviously able to get some sun in California. Lucky man.

And then suddenly before she even knew she'd

committed to the idea, she blurted, "Troy, I was thinking about the Ball."

"I'm not surprised. You've been working very hard on the committee."

"I meant. I was thinking about..." Her voice faded. Her courage faded. She couldn't do it. Couldn't put herself back out there. It was too embarrassing. And she shouldn't be going to the Ball. She'd already told both Jane and Troy that. To change her mind now showed lack of stability and judgment. Besides, he might have already found a date.

That stopped her cold.

She studied him, taking in his straight nose, the high cheekbones and his firm mobile mouth quirking in a half-smile. He was so masculine and relaxed... so confident.

She was not.

She'd never had his self-assurance. "Were you able to find a date?" she asked, thinking it was one thing to talk books and technology and historical renovation with him. It was another to discuss... dates. "I was certain you would. Just wanted to be sure. I hate to think I've left you in the lurch."

The corners of his lips curved higher. "Haven't found another date yet, no."

Her heart fell. "I'm sorry."

"It's my fault. I haven't asked anyone else."

"Why not?"

"I wanted to go with you."

Her pulse jumped. "I see."

"You do?"

"Yes."

But she didn't, and Taylor almost kicked herself under the table for saying things she didn't mean, because she didn't see. She didn't understand. She didn't understand why Troy would want to go to the Ball with her. But somehow, between leaving the library and finishing her apple pie ala mode, she wanted to go to the Ball with Troy.

As friends, of course, she added hurriedly.

But she did want to go. She wanted to be part of the historic night and see the ballroom all lit up with pink lights and taste the chocolates and sip champagne...

And it would be fun to go, with him, provided it wasn't romantic. Provided they were... just friends.

Taylor squeezed her satchel, thinking she was most definitely in over her head and yet she was going to press on, and just do this. Of course he could reject her. She fully expected a rejection any moment. "Troy, I was thinking--" her voice quavered, broke, courage once again stalling. She stared across the table at him, no longer certain of anything.

Troy heard Taylor's voice quaver and crack before she went silent. He watched the color storm her cheeks, and then saw her bite down into her lower lip, teeth ruthless and intent.

He was quite interested in what she'd have to say next. "Yes?" he prompted.

"Maybe I could go to the Ball... with you," she rushed and stumbled through the words, before pausing to meet his gaze, her chin lifting fractionally, almost defiantly, "if we went as just... friends."

"Friends," he repeated, looking at her, and trying not to obsess over the fact that her glasses were slipping down the length of her small, straight nose and he itched to lean forward and push them back up. Not because the glasses annoyed him on the tip of her nose—they didn't—he found it quite endearing. She looked like a very young and very pretty librarian. He'd always had a thing for smart girls, book girls and here was the epitome of a smart, book girl before him.

A single, smart book girl. Who also happened to be quite level-headed, and sweet.

Well, her soft pink lips looked quite sweet. He found the bow shape of her lips incredibly appealing. They were the lips of a pin-up, not a prim librarian, and Troy wondered if she'd kiss like a pin-up, or a prim librarian. He was tempted to kiss her now just to find out.

It probably wouldn't do.

It might just scare her off.

As it was, she wanted to be... *friends*.

"I would hope we're friends," he said pleasantly, lazily.

"Yes, but only *friends*," she said, emphasizing the friends part yet again. She sat up taller, shoulders squared. "I was thinking I might enjoy the Ball if it were purely platonic between us."

She *might* enjoy the ball... if it was purely platonic between them.

His lips twitched.

But she wasn't done yet.

"Troy, you seem like a nice man, but here's my quandary—"

"Yes. What is your quandary?" he asked.

She pushed up her glasses, and sighed. "You are Jane's ex and I appreciate that there's nothing between you now, but it makes me uncomfortable, knowing that you were together and that she continues to have... some feelings... for you, so it's best that we be just friends. Nothing romantic. Which is why, if you still need a date for the Ball, I'm happy to be that date, but I just want to be sure we're on the same page, about... romance... and things."

"If Jane were not in the picture, would your feelings be different?" he asked, amused.

Taylor hesitated, frowned, and then tugged uneasily on her ear lobe. "I can't say. I don't know. No... I don't think so. I think I'd still only want to be friends with you. I don't think a romantic relationship would work between us."

She was so earnest that Troy bit down on the inside of his cheek to keep from laughing out loud. Thank goodness he'd grown up in a family of boys and had developed a healthy sense of self-esteem. He might have found her rejection bruising otherwise.

It took him a moment to gather his thoughts.

"What is it about me you don't like?" he asked.

"It's not personal—" Taylor broke off, frowned, dragged her coffee cup and saucer closer to the edge of the table. "Well, maybe it is. And that's not fair of me, but the fact that you and Jane have history, and the fact that Jane continues—" she broke off again, her cheeks turning pink.

Her gaze fell to the table, her long black lashes dropping to hide her eyes. She pushed the saucer again. "She's my friend, my good friend, and I don't want to create problems for you, or her, or me."

"Most admirable," he said, meaning it, finding everything about Taylor interesting and refreshing. "But you do know that Jane and I were friends before we dated, and we dated briefly as an experiment—an experiment that didn't work out—but we managed to preserve and protect our relationship, so that we continue to be good friends today."

"How long were you... together?"

"I don't know that you could say we were ever truly together."

"Jane was in love with you!"

He frowned. "I know she says that—"

"You doubt her feelings?"

Troy stifled a sigh. He shouldn't have ever gone down this path. "No, I don't," he said firmly. "But Jane and I only dated for a couple weeks. Two and a half. Three. For a total of five dates. I knew it wasn't right on date one, but I liked Jane so much. I liked her fire and ambition. She's a great girl, and a marketing genius. It was easy to spend time with her. But at the end of the day, I didn't have... romantic... feelings for her."

Taylor stared at him from across the table, her eyes wide, expression somber. "Then you shouldn't have slept with her."

Troy's jaw dropped. "*What?*"

"You should never sleep with a woman you don't have feelings for." Taylor's soft full lips pressed into a hard, uncompromising line. "Women fall in love through making love. It's a bonding thing for us. Hormones and chemicals and—"

"We never slept together," he interrupted, irritated, not just by the direction their conversation had taken, but by Taylor's low opinion of him. "We never had sex. Jane and I had too much history to just jump into bed together."

For a moment Taylor said nothing, gazing at him intently from behind her big glasses.

For the first time since they'd sat down she seemed to have nothing to say.

Good.

He was fed up with this conversation, as well as having to defend himself. He didn't even know why he felt compelled to defend himself to a little mouse. Except for some ridiculous reason he wanted her to understand how the relationship with Jane had been. Not how Jane had wanted it to be.

"Not everybody clicks," he said crisply, battling his impatience and annoyance. "Not every man and woman belongs together."

He saw a flicker in her wide green-brown eyes and a tiny pulse begin to dance at the base of her throat and he wished to God he could read Taylor's mind right now and know what she was thinking. Feeling.

Did she truly have no feelings for him at all?

Or was she that protective of Jane?

Or was she simply... scared... that they were so different?

"A relationship can't go the distance without friendship and mutual respect," he said, "but there must also be chemistry."

"Chemistry," she repeated, before chewing on the inside of her soft lower lip.

He eyed the lip, seeing how her white teeth bit down into the pink plumpness and he wished it was his mouth on hers.

If only to know if they had chemistry.

It would be such a relief if there wasn't anything between them. It would be the best thing for both of them if he kissed her and he felt nothing... absolutely nothing.

He should kiss her and find out.

Kiss her and be done with this foolishness.

They weren't meant for each other. Troy didn't do long distance relationships. Troy didn't ever intend to live in Montana again.

"You didn't have chemistry with Jane?" Taylor asked quietly.

"No."

She fidgeted with the small ceramic saucer. "How did you know?"

"Because when I kissed her I felt..." He shook his head, not wanting to go there, not wanting to expose Jane but he felt caught, trapped. The villain and blackheart.

"Yes?" Taylor prompted, her voice but a whisper.

"Like her cousin or brother." He hated saying all of this aloud. He wanted to protect Jane then, and now. "She's smart and witty and perfect... for someone else, that isn't me."

He drew a deep breath, feeling awful. He'd disliked breaking the news to Jane eighteen months ago, and didn't enjoy revisiting the topic now. "I ended it quickly with her. Perhaps that was the most hurtful part. We had a great date the Saturday night before, and she was expecting another great date, but instead over dinner I told her that although I cared for her, it wasn't going to work. Would it have been easier by text or email or voice mail? Yes. But it wouldn't have been fair to her. I don't lead women on. It's never been my style."

For a long moment Taylor studied him, her fine arched brows pulled in concentration. "So you could just be friends with me?"

"Absolutely."

He saw relief in her eyes. And then he ruined it all by adding, "As long as I didn't physically desire you."

Her brows shot up. Her shoulders squared. "You *wouldn't* desire me."

"No?"

"*No*. I'm not your type, and you're not my type—"

"What is your type?"

She gestured a hand in his general direction. "None of this."

He should be insulted. Instead he nearly choked on smothered laughter. "Why not?"

"Because we're total opposites. We're oil and water. We're salt and pepper—"

"And yet all those things go so well together."

She glared at him even as her cheeks glowed pink, a dark luscious pink that made her eyes shine and her lips look positively edible. "We won't go together. We won't... click."

"How can you be so sure?"

"I can feel it."

And yet her eyes were very bright and that little pulse at the base of her throat was beating wildly. Erratically. She was very aware of him, and very much engaged in the moment. And Taylor might not admit it, might not even know it, but she was as curious about him as he was about her.

And he was very curious about her right now. About her mouth and her taste and her smell...

"Perhaps you'd feel better putting it to the test?" he drawled, smiling inwardly as her eyes sparked and her teeth came down on the bottom lip again. "That way you can rest," he said, his blood hot in his veins, his body heavy, thick. "Relax," he added, "reassured that you are right, and that there is... *nothing*... here."

Silence followed.

The silence crackled and burned.

She licked the seam of her lips as if her mouth was suddenly too dry.

Just like that, he hardened. At thirty-six Troy Sheenan didn't walk around with erections, or get spontaneous erections. He wasn't aroused by merely pretty faces, either. Not anymore. Because he craved more from a woman than lips and breasts and a firm butt.

He needed more. He needed his mind engaged and his senses engaged. Like they were now.

His pulse drummed harder, faster.

She wondered if there was chemistry.

He'd bet a thousand dollars—no, *five* thousand dollars--there was serious chemistry here, and she was either too innocent, or too inexperienced to recognize it. But this tension, this heat, this frustrating and yet wonderful anticipation *was* chemistry.

"Lean forward," he said.

"*What?*"

"I'm going to kiss you and see if I feel anything. If I don't, then I can safely promise you that if you went to the ball with me, it'd just be as platonic friends."

"But if you do?" she whispered, brows knitting.

"Then I'd probably have a difficult time just viewing you in a platonic light."

"So we couldn't go to the Ball."

"Or we could, and we'd both have a lot of fun, knowing that we're attending a very special event for Marietta, something that might not ever happen again. We'd dine and dance, and sip champagne, and I can promise you that there would be no other woman in the ballroom that I'd rather be with, than you."

Taylor stared at him and swallowed hard.

Tired of talking, fed up with thinking and waiting, Troy leaned across the table, captured her chin in his hand, and covered her mouth with his.

Chapter Six

His mouth felt firm and cool against hers and yet somehow the pressure of his lips against hers, made her skin burn and her lips tingle.

Hot, electric darts of sensation raced through her, making her ache.

Making her want more.

Her lips parted beneath his and she felt the tip of his tongue on the inside of her lip and she nearly whimpered at the pleasure of it.

He ended the kiss, stroked his thumb across her cheek and then sat back and regarded her from beneath lowered lashes.

"Well?" Taylor whispered, amazed that a kiss could feel so good.

"I think we can be friends."

Her heart fell. He felt no chemistry with her, and it's what she wanted. At least, it's what she told herself she wanted. But hadn't she also told him the very same thing?

Taylor pressed her lips together, fighting the sudden urge to cry. "Good," she said huskily. "That's great news."

"So you think you can manage the Ball?"

Her eyes felt hot and gritty and she swallowed hard. "Should I just meet you there?"

"You don't want me to pick you up?"

"Well, if we're just friends, it seems silly to make you leave your own hotel to come get me."

"I don't mind."

"I know you don't. You're quite nice about things like that, and I still appreciate you taking the time to return my phone to me last night."

"Friends do nice things for each other."

She struggled to smile but couldn't. Her eyes burned and her throat ached and she wanted to climb into her bed and pull her covers up over her head and cry.

And she didn't even know why she wanted to cry. It's not as if she liked him. It's not as if she had any feelings for him, either...

"So I'll pick you up," he said after a moment. "How does five forty-five sound?"

"Good," she said.

"Great. It's a date."

Troy walked Taylor back to the library parking lot. He waited until she'd safely left before he started his SUV. He'd eaten dinner but he needed a drink.

He was staying at the Graff tonight, and he could easily get a drink there. It'd be convenient to pull up to the hotel, have valet take the car, and be done with it. He'd get served fast in the bar, too, as the staff at the hotel knew him and jumped to please him, but Troy wasn't comfortable with all the jumping and scraping. The constant display of deference put him on edge. For God's sake, this was Marietta, Montana and he wasn't a Rockfeller but a Sheenan.

One didn't bow and scrape to a Sheenan. Sheenans got into scrapes. Sheenans were tough and practical. Sure, Troy had made some money in the fifteen years since he finished college, good money, money didn't make a man, and money certainly didn't define him.

Troy drove down Main Street to Grey's Saloon.

No one at Grey's bowed and scraped. Grey didn't tolerate airs. The only one at Grey's Saloon with attitude was Grey himself, the surly bastard.

Troy stepped from his SUV, pocketed his keys, entered the corner building, and took a seat at the bar. Tonight it was Reese behind the counter and Reese poured Troy a shot of whiskey, neat, before giving Troy space. Good man.

Troy nursed the whiskey for a bit, welcoming the space and quiet. After a bit, Reese returned and they talked the way men liked to talk, about not much of anything, which was the best sort of conversation because it was never too personal and, therefore, never too uncomfortable. Men didn't need to share their feelings, not like women.

"Another one?" Reese asked, approaching Troy and gesturing to his empty tumbler.

Troy nodded and slid the glass across the counter.

Taylor Harris kissed like a pin up. Her lips were soft and sweet but she kissed with heat.

There'd been serious heat in that kiss. Serious chemistry, too.

Troy hardened again, remembering.

"You're in town for the Ball," Reese said as he placed the fresh whiskey in front of Troy.

"Yeah."

"Who are you taking?"

Troy shifted. "Taylor Harris."

Reese frowned. "Do I know her?"

"She's the new librarian."

"The librarian?" Reese shot him an amused glance. "Not your usual type."

Troy chose not to dignify the remark. He took a long drink from his glass. The whiskey burned going down, a good kind of burn. "So are you going Friday night?" he asked Reese.

"To the Ball?" Reese shook his head. "Not my thing."

"Apparently it's not a lot of folks' thing." Troy grimaced. "Seemed like a good idea back in the Fall, but I've been away from Montana a long time. I'd forgotten that folks here aren't into fancy dress balls."

"Especially in the dead of winter."

"Winter's harsh this year."

"Winter is harsh here every year." Reese leaned against the counter behind him. "I guess it's easy to forget the twenty below zero wind chill when you don't even need a coat in February in San Francisco."

"Oh, you need a coat in San Francisco. But just a thin one," Troy retorted. He raised his glass. "To all the idealistic bastards in the world with more balls than brains."

"The world needs idealistic bastards to balance out the assholes and realists."

"Which one are you?"

Reese smiled darkly. "What do you think?"

"I think there's a tender idealist buried somewhere deep inside you." Troy grinned crookedly. "But I won't tell anyone."

"And I was just about to compliment you for doing a good thing here in this town."

"The Ball?"

"The Graff."

"Huh."

"Marietta didn't need the Graff, but you've done something this town can be proud of. And that's a good thing."

"Maybe you should have been my date Friday night," Troy said.

"You are pretty, but you're not quite my type."

Troy laughed. "I'm crushed."

Taylor couldn't wait for work to end Wednesday. She was looking forward to meeting up with McKenna and going dress shopping at Married in Marietta, because now Taylor needed a dress, too.

It'd been a long time since Taylor did something like this. Even longer since she'd needed to dress up for something. For the last couple of years she'd been focused on work, and getting Doug the help he needed. There hadn't been time for dates or dances... she'd given up being young, and romantic. There was no time for romance, or fun.

But maybe for one night she could just forget about her

responsibilities. Maybe for one night she could just cut loose... have fun.

Maybe.

Taylor must have looked at her watch a dozen times between three and five, and the minute hand never seemed to move. She felt as if she'd gotten a case of Spring Fever, but finally it was five, and Louise, aware that Taylor was going to the Ball with Troy, shooed her out the door, promising Taylor she'd lock up since Margaret had gone home with a toothache earlier in the day.

Taylor headed home to change from her trousers and knit sweater set to jeans and a peach cotton sweater, that was cut boxy and loose in a boyfriend style, before combing her hair and leaving it loose.

Hoping she was dressed appropriately for a girl's night out with McKenna, Taylor drove to Married in Marietta on Front Ave and snagged a parking spot just a block from the store.

Taylor had never been inside the little boutique before, but passing through the front door was like entering another world, an overtly feminine world with a pale plush carpet, soothing neutrals, glittering chandeliers and delicate French inspired furniture.

A sales associate came forward to greet Taylor and offer assistance. "I'm looking for a dress for Friday night," Taylor said.

The sales clerk gestured to the long wall filled with fluffy and shimmering white gowns at the back. "That is our bridal area," she said, before pointing to four rolling racks of gowns in pink, coral and red, "and over there are the formal gowns we've ordered in for the Valentine Ball. We have a little bit of everything here, and I do have more sizes in the back."

Taylor thanked her and headed for the rolling racks of rose and ruby gowns, some filmy and chiffon, others short and fitted, while others sparkled with sequins and embroidery. They seemed to have something for every taste, and hopefully every budget since Taylor didn't have much money.

"Hope you haven't been waiting long," McKenna said,

a little breathless as she appeared at Taylor's side, her cheeks red from the cold. She quickly began peeling off her heavy outer layers. "TJ gave me fits tonight. He decided he didn't want me to go out and made quite a scene."

Taylor turned to McKenna, worried. "Will he be okay?"

"Yes. He just likes throwing his weight around." McKenna grimaced as she placed her coat and scarf and gloves on a fragile white chair. "He's only four but he's already all Sheenan. Not sure why I thought he'd end up with any of my DNA."

"Until last night, I didn't realize his dad was... Trey."

"Troy told you?"

Taylor shook her head. "Louise."

"Not a planned pregnancy. But then, my life doesn't seem to follow any logical plans." McKenna shrugged and turned her focus to the racks of dresses. She rifled through the nearest rack before pausing at a strapless, fitted peach gown covered in sequins that gave way to a silk skirt at the thigh. "How pretty. So romantic."

"I've never worn gowns like these," Taylor said, "at least, not since the Hopeville High prom, and even then, I chose a simple off white dress that seemed classic and elegant. At least, I thought I looked pretty and elegant until I got to the gym and realized the dress looked like a sheet off my parents' bed."

McKenna laughed and pulled out a short, miniscule pink sequin cocktail dress. "I think I wore something like this to my prom."

"Very sexy," Taylor said.

"Mmm. Short, tight, sexy with the highest heels I could find. I wanted to drive Trey crazy."

"Did he love it?"

"No." McKenna hung the shimmering pink number back on the rack. "He was livid." She looked at Taylor, and scrunched her nose. "He wasn't my date. We'd broken up the week before but I refused to sit home crying. So my brother, Quinn, the baseball star, found a date for me, and I went to my prom looking like a million bucks with one of his friends. It made Trey nuts."

"Did you and Trey get back together after the Prom?"

"We did, towards the end of summer. But broke up again by Christmas. Didn't date again for a year since Trey was competing on the circuit." McKenna's smile faded. "We were impossible. Our relationship was impossible. We shouldn't have ever let it go on as long as we did."

McKenna turned back to the rack and quickly flipped through more gowns but Taylor had seen the tears in McKenna's eyes.

"But you're happy now, right?" Taylor asked, worriedly. "You're newly engaged and getting married later this year, so it's okay?"

McKenna held a sleek dark pink gown against her slender frame. The long dress was cut asymmetrical with one shoulder strap and a sequin starburst at the waist. McKenna might not be a dress girl, but she was certainly drawn to gorgeous sexy gowns. "What do you think?"

Taylor noticed McKenna hadn't answered her question. "Very pretty. And that dark coral pink looks great with your hair."

"They always say redheads shouldn't wear pink, but I don't believe in following rules."

"I think it's gorgeous."

"So explain to me why you're not going to the Ball," McKenna asked, handing the dresses to the sales clerk who carried them to a dressing room.

"Well, actually...I am going...now. "

"Good! Great. So you're dress shopping, too. Let's find some things for you to try on. Have you seen anything you like? What's your style?"

"Inexpensive?"

McKenna gave Taylor a pointed look. "No woman wants to look cheap."

"No, I know, but I don't have a big budget."

"I'm sure we can find something pretty that won't break your budget. So what do you like? Long? Short? Fitted? Full? And are you a pink girl, or red, or apricot or purple?"

"I like red better than pink," Taylor said. "And apricot better than purple. And I don't know about the rest. Just pretty. I don't want to look like I'm wearing a sheet from my mother's bed."

"Got it."

For the next half hour they tried on dress after dress, and took turns posing and turning in front of the tall mirror.

In the end McKenna chose the stunning pink asymmetrical gown with the starburst at the waist as it hugged her curves and set off her dark auburn hair, green eyes, and flawless, luminous skin.

"What about you?" McKenna asked. "What are your favorites?"

"I like the red lace cocktail dress," Taylor said, "and the ivory dress with the bronze sequins at the bodice. That was really pretty, too."

"The red lace dress is what old ladies wear to hide their jiggly upper arms," McKenna said, "and the ivory dress is pretty, but it looks like a bargain priced dress. Something for teens to wear to their prom. You're twenty-six and in June you'll be Marietta's new head librarian. You need a dress with wow factor, something that screams stylish, sexy, and sophisticated."

Taylor shook her head. "Not sexy. Definitely not sexy. Stylish and sophisticated is good enough."

"Why not sexy?" McKenna demanded, flipping through more hanging gowns, this time on a search for Taylor.

"Um, I'm not... sexy, and even if I was, I couldn't go to the Ball looking too sexy. My date wouldn't like it."

McKenna turned to face Taylor, hands on her hips. "What? Why not?"

Taylor shifted from one foot to the other. "My date isn't a... date. We're really just friends, and so we're just going as... friends."

"I don't get it. Who are you going with?"

Taylor had wondered when this question might arise. "Troy."

"Troy *Sheenan*?"

Was there any other Troy in Marietta?

Taylor nodded. "Yes." She avoided McKenna's gaze, not wanting to see laughter or mockery in her eyes, because of course Troy wasn't the right man for Taylor. Troy was... well... Marietta's Most Eligible Bachelor. And probably San Francisco's Most Eligible Bachelor, too. "Jane set us up—"

"I knew Jane had said you were going."

"I didn't think it was a good idea to go with Troy, but anyway...we are."

"You and Troy."

"Yes." Taylor's heart thudded, trying not to think about Troy or the kiss, because the kiss had been so good and hot and sweet and sexy all at the same time. "But we're not a couple," she added hurriedly.

"Maybe you should be a couple. He's lovely." McKenna said firmly. "And you are, too."

"But there's no... chemistry," Taylor said, remembering Troy's words. "And he has to have chemistry. You know."

"How do you know there was no chemistry?"

Taylor blushed. "He kissed me."

McKenna's eyes widened. "And...?"

"I thought it was really good."

"Not surprised. He was voted best kisser his senior year of high school. And of course, *I* never kissed him, but Sheenans are good lovers, so. You know."

Taylor glanced around to be sure the sales clerk wasn't listening. "Apparently I'm not a good kisser, though. Troy said... you know."

"Troy told you that you weren't a good kisser?"

"No. He just said... we could be friends."

"Of course you can be friends. You don't want a lover who doesn't care about you."

"He's not my lover. He's not even attracted to me."

"And he said this?"

"*No*. But it was *implied*."

McKenna gave her a strange look. "Not sure your logic is all that sound, which is fine. No one ever said a woman has to be logical all the time. But the one thing that is clear, is that we need to find you the perfect gown for the Ball. Yes?"

In the dressing room, armed with another stack of gowns, all handpicked by McKenna, Taylor tried on one after the other. They were all beautiful dresses, all far more sophisticated than Taylor would have selected for herself. A stunning ruby red ball gown with full skirts and a plunging décolleté; a long, form fitting red sequin gown with small padded shoulders that left her entire back bare; a sweet gown in blush with avant garde roses stitched at the bodice and fluttery folds of fabric falling to her feet.

So many beautiful gowns and yet none of them felt right. She couldn't imagine going to the Ball in any of them. And then, right when Taylor didn't think she could try on another dress, the sales clerk pushed a dress through the curtain and insisted Taylor try it on. "This was in the back," the girl said, "It's a small size, but you're tiny and young enough to pull the look off. "

Taylor warily eyed the gown with the red circle spangles. It was not a quiet little dress, nor a sleek sophisticated gown. It was... eye catching. Maybe even show stopping. It was a dress better suited to a stage or runway...

"It's not me," Taylor said, poking her head out of the dressing room. "It's just too much."

"Put it on," McKenna said.

"Do," the sales girl agreed. "I think you'd look beautiful in it. You have the right coloring with your dark hair and eyes. How can it hurt to give it a try?"

A few minutes later Taylor stepped from the dressing room and turned to let the sales girl zipped up the back of the dress.

She shot McKenna a quick glance as she took a place before the tall mirror. McKenna's eyes were wide, and she was smiling, broadly.

Taylor looked from McKenna to the mirror, and studied her reflection.

And then she did a slow twirl in front of the mirror, unable to believe she was looking at herself.

She looked... incredible.

It was the dress, of course. And the gown's tulle wasn't exactly pink, more blush or nude, and covered with those glossy red spangles and moved and shimmered and reflected the light.

Taylor put a hand to the deep V-neck bodice, and then to the full skirt.

"It's... pretty," she said softly, a bit awed by her own reflection.

"Stunning," the sales clerk agreed.

"That's the dress," McKenna added.

"I think so," Taylor agreed, before reaching for the tag that hung beneath her arm. She blinked, shocked by the price, and read it a second time, making sure she hadn't read it wrong. $3,900.

Three *thousand* and nine hundred dollars.

Good God. Did people really pay this much for a single dress? "It's way too much. Way, way too much."

"But it's perfect," McKenna said. "You look like a princess."

"Anyone would in a dress that costs almost four thousand dollars," Taylor retorted, turning around to be unzipped.

"What?" McKenna cried.

"I know," Taylor answered.

"It is couture," the sales girl said. "One of a kind."

"Not for me. I'm not couture," Taylor said, shaking her head. "I'm an off-the-rack kind of a girl. Eighty to one hundred dollars max on a dress. That's my budget. And the ivory dress with the bronze sequin bodice fit me, and my budget. I'll go with that."

Chapter Seven

With dresses zipped into garment bags and then stowed in their cars, McKenna and Taylor walked down 1st Avenue to Grey's Saloon on Main for drinks and appetizers.

"When does Jane return?" McKenna asked, as they settled into a booth towards the back of the saloon.

"Tomorrow afternoon," Taylor answered, glancing towards the pool tables where Callan Carrigan was playing with a couple of cowboys. Sage had once said that Callan could outride, and out rope virtually any local cowboy, and from the looks of it, she could out play them at pool, too. Callan's sure shots were sending ball after ball into the pockets.

The guys let out a loud collective groan and McKenna turned to watch Callan take a bow. "Looks like Callan kicked butt again," McKenna said.

"She's nothing like Sage, is she?" Taylor said, secretly rather intimidated by Callan, even though they were practically the same age.

"Nope. But none of the Carrigan girls are alike. Just as the Sheenan brothers are all so different." McKenna turned back around, faced Taylor. "Speaking of the Sheenans, explain to me just how it is that you and Troy are going to the Ball together. Jane set you up?"

"Yes," Taylor said, happy to see their drinks arrive. McKenna had ordered a margarita on the rocks and Taylor a glass of red wine. Now all they needed was some food and things would be perfect. "Jane said Troy's dad was dying and he and his girlfriend had just broken up so she was making sure he hat a date for his own Ball."

McKenna touched her finger to the salt rimming her glass. "But didn't Jane used to have a thing for Troy?"

Taylor nodded. "Troy claims it was one-sided."

"I believe it." McKenna licked salt from her fingertip. "Jane's not his type."

"Why not? She's really smart and successful and—"

"A little too abrasive."

"Jane's not abrasive!"

"She's pushy."

"It's her job to get things done."

McKenna shrugged. "I've known Troy as long as I've known Trey, and ever since high school, Troy has liked sweet, smart, successful girls. Nice girls who also happen to be very smart." She lifted her glass, sipped her margarita, green eyes gleaming. "Girls like you."

Taylor nearly choked on her wine. "He doesn't like me."

"He must like you if he's kissed you."

"He kissed me as a test. It was to see if we had chemistry."

"I see. And this is the test you claim you failed?"

"Yes."

McKenna laughed quietly and then sipped her margarita again. "He's playing you."

"He's not."

"Troy Sheenan would never kiss you if there wasn't a little spark. If he felt absolutely no attraction, he wouldn't even bother with a kiss." McKenna shook her glass, letting the ice cubes clink. "Where were you when you kissed?"

"Main Street Diner."

"What?"

"That's what I mean. It wasn't a romantic kiss. He leaned across the table and kissed me to see if there were any... sparks."

"He did this all at Main Street Diner."

"Yes."

McKenna grinned. "Good Lord, girl. He's definitely

interested. He would never kiss you, much less take you to a Ball if he wasn't."

"Remember, Jane arranged the Ball part."

"Troy doesn't do pity dates." McKenna's arched brows rose higher. "Troy Sheenan doesn't have to."

"Maybe not a pity date, but it's not a *date* date. That's why he kissed me. To make sure we could be friends, and so that's what we are."

"But you liked kissing him."

Taylor blushed. "He knows what he's doing."

"You just need confidence."

"I am confident."

"Maybe as a librarian, but not as a woman." McKenna suddenly leaned forward, and reaching out, plucked the glasses from Taylor's nose. "Why do you wear these all the time now? You didn't use to."

"I need them," Taylor answered, sticking her hand out, palm up. "May I have them back?"

"When you first moved here, you hardly ever wore your glasses. Now I never see you in contacts."

"I like my glasses," Taylor said a little stiffly. "And I can't see you right now, so I'd like them back."

McKenna put them in her hand. "Here you go. And don't be mad. I wasn't trying to be hurtful. I'm just curious. And maybe concerned."

"Concerned, why?"

"I don't know. I just kept thinking that maybe something happened." She must have seen Taylor's expression because she quickly added, "I get the feeling that you're hiding, or just hiding behind the glasses. But maybe I'm wrong. Maybe I'm just... projecting."

A whistle from the pool tables drew Taylor's attention and she glanced over at Callan who had her hand out, collecting dollar bills. It seemed she'd just won another game.

"I'm not hiding anything," Taylor said after a moment. "Just trying to... look... older."

"Why?"

Taylor shrugged. "I was told back in early December that I didn't look mature enough. That I was too young. So

I'm trying to dress more age appropriately."

"Age appropriate for what? Too young for what? Take over Margaret's job as head librarian?"

"No." Taylor hesitated, her heart pounding a little too fast, making her suddenly queasy. She really didn't like discussing Doug with others. Family dynamics were difficult enough without other people weighing in. "Take care of my brother."

"You have a younger brother?"

"He's not a child. He's twenty-two. He's... at Hogue Ranch."

McKenna's forehead creased. "That work ranch, halfway house place out in Paradise Valley?"

Taylor nodded again. "He's been there since early September, and he had a chance to be released before Christmas. He was supposed to come live with me, but the judge didn't think I was old enough, and mature enough, to manage my brother—who happens to have some problems--so instead of letting Doug spend the six month probation period with me, he said Doug had to stay at Hogue."

"What did your brother do?"

"He wasn't respectful to an officer."

"I don't understand. Did he hurt someone? Attack someone?"

"No. He was argumentative with a local sheriff who pulled him over for driving too fast. They booked him, and drug tested him and he tested positive for marijuana. He tried to explain that he was argumentative because the sheriff treated him like he was an idiot, and he's not, he was just scared and uncomfortable, and then they labeled him he as some loser, and he's not a loser, either. Doug said in court that he sometimes smokes to manage his depression but the judge said this isn't Colorado or California. If he wants to be a drug addict, go there." Taylor swallowed hard, and again. "Hogue isn't a good place for him. It's hard core. Most men there have been in and out of jail a couple of times, but Doug's not a criminal. He has clinical depression."

"Is that what you told the judge?"

"I told the judge that Doug needed help. Counseling. Better depression medicine. Or a better dose of his medicine. But the judge dismissed everything I said, claiming that I was too young, and too immature, to know what was right for my brother."

McKenna regarded her for a long moment. "You're angry."

"I am." Taylor drew a slow breath and blinked, clearing her vision. "If I were a man, the judge wouldn't have talked to me like I was little girl. If I'd been a local, I can guarantee that my brother wouldn't be at Hogue right now. My brother would be living with me. Kara even said as much after it was all over."

"Kara Jones? The district attorney?"

"She's my roommate. Well, house mate. I rent a room from her, and have been living there since I arrived in Marietta last November."

"And Kara couldn't help you?"

"No. Conflict of interest."

"You'd think the judge would see that as a plus on your side. You live with Marietta's DA!"

"Kara wanted me to ask one of the local ranching families like the MacCreadies or Carrigans or Sheenans to hire Doug. She thought Brock Sheenan would be the perfect person to approach. She said everyone knows Brock, and Brock's solid and no-nonsense, and went to school with the judge's daughter, but I was afraid to approach him. Brock didn't know me from Adam and it made me nervous to get strangers involved. It still does. Doug's had a hard life. My parents treated him different than me. They were not loving towards him--" Taylor broke off, bit down into her lower lip to hold the tears back. "He's spent his life struggling to come to terms with their rejection, and he's allowed to have feelings and be frustrated and figure out who he is, and what he wants, without all of Crawford County judging him."

McKenna waited a moment before speaking. "But you know Brock now," she said quietly. "You've met him, you've met Harley. He has a big spread, too, and is always looking for help, particularly in the Spring. He's got a foreman who has been with him a long time, and his hands are all good people. He'll be hiring a few new guys soon. This would be the time to talk to him."

"But it's too late now. Doug has to remain at Hogue until the end of May."

"Or not." McKenna held her gaze. "I think you should hire a good attorney and let your friends here in Marietta help you."

Taylor said nothing and McKenna reached across the table and tapped her arm.

"Are you listening?" McKenna asked.

Taylor looked up at her. "I am, but McKenna, you grew up here, everybody cares about you here. I'm not Marietta's sweetheart. I'm a nobody here."

"*I* can help you."

"How?"

"I can go to Brock or Cormac or Troy—"

"*No.*"

"Why not?"

"Because I'm not going to beg for favors from the Sheenans. That's wrong. They don't know me—"

"You're going to the Ball with Troy!"

"I explained this already. I'm going with Troy because Jane forced us together."

"Phooey. Open your eyes. Use your brain." McKenna drummed her hand on the table. "Nobody forces Troy to do anything. Not even Trey could get Troy to do something Troy didn't want to do. And Trey was persuasive, and stubborn, but Troy is strong. Troy doesn't take crap from anyone, and he doesn't play games. If he likes you, he likes you, and if he doesn't, he avoids you. And if you're going to the Ball with him, it's because he wanted to take you, and if he's kissed you, it's because he wanted to put his lips on your lips. Nobody made him."

Taylor hung her head, embarrassed. She knew McKenna was looking at her but Taylor didn't know what to say, or how to articulate her feelings. It was hard enough worrying about her brother and struggling to come to terms with how he'd been rejected by her parents and society, without her having to deal with rejection, too.

It was a challenge coming to terms with Doug's depression, and supporting him through his disappointments without her feeling disappointed in herself.

Without her feeling disappointed in her dreams.

Better to not want too much or dream too big.

Better to keep one's expectations small, and manageable.

Better to do everything yourself because you couldn't always rely on others.

"Why are you so afraid to like Troy?" McKenna asked quietly.

Taylor pictured him—tall and so darkly handsome--in his long black wool coat and fitted cashmere sweater stepping from his big black Escalade. The man had a private jet. He lived in some outrageous mansion in the most affluent neighborhood in San Francisco. He lived in a world she didn't know and didn't understand and would never be part of. "He has so much."

"Yes?"

"It's overwhelming to me."

"But you're not a shallow woman. You're not attracted to his things. You're attracted to him. So don't let grumpy old Judge McCorkle turn you into a timid little mouse. Have confidence. Enjoy life. Enjoy your life. You're beautiful—"

"Stop saying that."

"I won't. Because you *are*. Just lose the sweater sets and grandma pearls and men's glasses."

"Even if I dressed like a hipster, Troy would still be out of my league. He's a city slicker—"

"Not true. Yes, he lives in San Francisco but that's because he's brilliant and innovative and it's where technology and opportunity is, but that doesn't mean he's not real. And solid. And smart. And loving. Because he is. He's a wonderful man and he deserves to be treated like a man, and not like a shallow, insincere playboy."

Taylor exhaled hard, feeling naked and exposed. "Is that how you think I view him?"

"Most women think of him that way."

"Well, I don't." Taylor took a long drink from her wine glass, nearly draining it.

She was so private, and she appreciated McKenna's pep talk but it wasn't comfortable. None of this was comfortable and Taylor just wanted the spotlight off of her and this painful conversation to end. "I find this whole conversation uncomfortable."

"Why?"

"Maybe I don't understand why, if you're such a Troy Sheenan fan, you didn't fall for Troy, instead of Trey? Why wasn't Troy the right Sheenan?"

The moment the words left her mouth, Taylor knew she'd said the wrong thing. She didn't even need to see McKenna's face to know it was wrong. She felt it in her heart.

It was spiteful. Mean.

For a moment there was just silence, and the silence made Taylor feel even worse.

"Sorry," Taylor whispered, kicking herself, ashamed she'd said something so unkind to McKenna who had been nothing but kind. "That was terrible. Forgive me."

"It's okay."

"No, it's not."

"It's fine, and actually, it's a very good question," McKenna said, smiling faintly. But the smile didn't reach her eyes. "I'm sure everyone wonders the same thing. Why didn't I fall in love with Troy? My life would have been so different. So much... *easier*." McKenna pushed her glass away from her and glanced at her watch. "Oh dear, it's late. I need to go. My sitter has a big test tomorrow. I promised I wouldn't keep her out too late."

"I should go, too," Taylor said, rising, aware that she'd ruined the mood, and maybe the evening, too. "I really am sorry, McKenna. I shouldn't have been so sensitive, and I shouldn't have said what I did—"

"Stop. It's okay," McKenna said firmly, cutting the apology off. "I'm fine. No harm done. Honestly. And yes, you should speak up. Speak your mind. You can't go through life minimizing yourself, marginalizing yourself, hoping it will please others." She wagged her finger at Taylor, a hint of her good humor returning. "I used to be a big sister, and so I'll tell you what I would have told my sister, Fiona Grace. Don't live to please others. Don't think everyone else knows what's right or true. Listen to yourself, and be true to yourself. That way, no matter what else happens in life, you will always have your self-respect."

McKenna finished buttoning her coat and slipped her gloves on. "And I don't know why I didn't fall for Troy," she added thoughtfully as they started for the door. "Troy is everything Trey isn't. He's good, he's kind, he's responsible. *Successful.* He doesn't drink too much and he doesn't get into bar fights—" She broke off, pursed her lips, and shook her head. "No. He's nothing like Trey, which is why he doesn't make my heart race or my pulse quicken or make me feel special, and beautiful, and new. And Trey made me feel that. From day one. From day one Trey made me feel like I was the most amazing girl in the world." Her shoulders lifted and fell. "How can you not love a man that makes you feel like a goddess... absolutely divine?"

Chapter Eight

T roy was glad that the uncomfortable ninety minute dinner with Judge McCorkle at the Graff was over and he was now free to sit at the bar at Grey's and just relax.

Ninety minutes wasn't long when you were dining with friends or a beautiful woman, but ninety minutes was endless when you were being solicited for a loan.

Judge Joe McCorkle found himself on the wrong side of a business deal and was in financial trouble. Of course he didn't want anyone in the community to know he'd made some mistakes with his investments, and that he'd already taken out a second mortgage on his house to sort things out only to have just dug himself deeper into debt. He'd already approached both local banks and Big Sky Credit Union, and all three had turned him down. Judge McCorkle was a risk. He was also nearing retirement. How could he ever pay the loan back?

For that matter, how could he save his house? His wife had no idea that they could soon lose their home, and everything they'd worked for.

Troy had listened to all this over a dinner of steak and whiskey. He paid for the dinner. The Judge had no money.

The Judge knew Troy had money.

What was a two hundred and fifty thousand dollar loan between friends? Hadn't Troy gone to school with his daughter Susie? (And no, Troy hadn't. Brock had.)

Troy hadn't told the judge yes. But he hadn't told him no. He had to think about it. Had to figure out where the money would come from, and be realistic about McCorkle's ability to pay him back.

The Judge might not ever be able to pay him back.

This wasn't the first time Troy was approached by a Marietta individual needing assistance. It wouldn't be the last.

As Troy entered Grey's, he spotted a half dozen different people he knew. Callan Carrigan was in the far back, shooting pool, with a couple of Brock's young hired hands. Dawson O'Dell and a young off duty sheriff were eating burgers at a table on one side, while McKenna and Taylor were having drinks on the other side.

Interesting, seeing McKenna and Taylor together. He knew from last night that they were going dress shopping together but he hadn't expected to see them.

They were talking, quite seriously, from the looks of things. He hoped they'd had a good evening. McKenna would be a good friend for Taylor. McKenna didn't bullshit and she wasn't superficial, and she was the first to stand up for the underdog.

Even more interesting was seeing McKenna head his way now.

"Hey," McKenna said, coming to the bar counter to greet him.

"Hey, yourself," he said, sliding off thestool. "Hello, Taylor," he added, nodding at the librarian who was hanging back, as if to give them space. Troy turned his attention to McKenna. "You okay?"

She tucked a long dark red strand of hair behind her ear. "Sorry about last night."

"It's fine."

"I wanted to talk to you, but it's... weird."

"I get it."

She shook her head, jaw set, frustration evident. "It's always such a shock... seeing you... even now. I know you can't help looking like him, the rat bastard."

Troy reached out and folded McKenna into a quick hug. "The curse of being an identical twin," he said, dropping a kiss on the top of her head.

"I should hate you," she said, her voice muffled against his chest.

"You should."

She looked up at him, smiling faintly, crookedly. "I don't."

"That's good." He released her, and watched as she stepped back, moving closer to Taylor. McKenna had been a very pretty girl and she'd grown into an absolutely stunning woman with long auburn hair, light green eyes, high cheekbones and a perfect chin, beneath perfect lips. But beneath her beauty was sadness. Her fire and courage didn't completely mask her pain. McKenna had lived through a terrible tragedy and then she'd fallen in love with a man who couldn't get his shit together long enough to protect her properly so that her wounds could heal. Instead Troy just kept hurting her, making the scars and pain worse.

"How's TJ?" Troy asked. Is he doing okay?"

"He's smart as a whip. And a chip off the old block."

"Lucky you."

"Haha."

Troy glanced at Taylor, not wanting to leave her out of the conversation and yet not sure how to include her, before focusing back on McKenna. "I'd love to come see him while I'm in town. If you're alright with that."

McKenna smiled. "That'd be great. He'd love seeing you." She hesitated. "But it is confusing for him. You look, you know, like his—" she broke off, smiled, even as tears glittered in her eyes. "So how is everyone? How's your dad?"

"Dad's not doing well. He's fading fast. I think it'd be a miracle if he makes it another two weeks."

"I'm sorry." She hesitated. "Do you think he'd want... to see... TJ?"

"I'm sure he would. Maybe we can bring TJ by this weekend while I'm still home?"

She nodded and drew a deep breath. "I don't know if you've heard. I'm engaged, to Larry... Lawrence... Joplin."

"Dillon told me."

McKenna glanced at Taylor, who was still hanging back, and then at Troy. "I have to do what's right for me and

TJ."

"I understand."

"TJ needs stability and security. *I* need stability and security."

"We all understand. We do. And we support you. We love you."

McKenna's eyes narrowed and she looked away, focusing very hard on a distant point across the bar. "I haven't told Trey. I'm not going to."

"Okay."

McKenna glanced at Taylor again, and struggled to smile. "I understand you're taking Taylor to the Ball."

Troy saw Taylor's eyes widen behind her big glasses. She looked positively mortified. "Yes," he said, checking his smile. "Taylor has most graciously agreed to accompany me to the Ball."

"That was very nice of her," McKenna said, lips curving. "And that's because she's a *nice* girl, Troy, not like your big city floozies. So please, Troy, be on your best behavior Friday night." She winked and walked out.

McKenna exited Grey's front door so fast, Taylor didn't have a chance to follow. But then, after McKenna's teasing final remarks, Taylor had no desire to follow.

"That was so unbelievably awkward," she murmured, her face hot, certain her cheeks were red.

Troy grinned down at her. "The family history, or the comment about my floozies?"

Heat washed through her all over again. "I don't care about the family history, or if you date floozies. In fact, good for you if do."

She started for the door but Troy, reached out, grabbed the hood on her winter coat and kept her from escaping.

"Where are you going so fast?" he asked.

"Home." She tugged on her coat, trying to free herself.

"And I've just hurt McKenna's feelings so let go, before I hurt yours."

He let her go. "Why did you hurt her feelings?"

Taylor exhaled and shook her head, still upset with herself. "She was being so nice and I'm not that nice. I'm not. And so I said something I shouldn't have, and I think it made her sad."

"What did you say?"

"You don't want to know." She jammed her hands into her coat pockets and hunched her shoulders. "I still feel terrible for saying it."

"Now you have to tell me. What did you say to her?"

Taylor's shoulders rose higher. "She kept talking about you... paying you all these compliments and it was frustrating and so I said... that if she liked you so much, why Trey? Why not you?"

Troy sighed. "Probably wasn't the best thing to say, no, but if its any comfort, I don't think your hurt her feelings as much as touched on a tender spot. People have been saying that to her for years about Troy and me. But she and I are just friends, and what she and Trey had was... special. It's hard to explain but they just... worked. She adored him, and he her."

"So what happened?"

"Trey loves adrenaline. He takes risks and lives recklessly. It was hard on McKenna, never knowing if he was in trouble, or safe. She worried about him on the rodeo circuit, worried about him drinking, worried about him fighting. It just wore her down, and it made Trey defensive." He sat back down on his bar stool and extended his long legs out, arms crossing over his big chest. "So how did the dress shopping go? Did she find something?"

"We both did."

"You both did," he repeated, confused.

She nodded, looking self-conscious. "I hadn't bought a gown yet."

Suddenly he understood. The Ball. They'd gone dress shopping for the Valentine Ball. McKenna hadn't been shopping for her wedding gown. Relief swept through him. "Tell me about your dress."

"No."

"Why not?"

"You'll see it Friday night."

"But you love it?"

Taylor flushed. "I wouldn't say I loved it, but's nice."

"A nice dress for a nice girl. Sounds incredibly sexy."

She rolled her eyes. "As we've just established, I'm not that nice. And the dress *is* nice. It's appropriate for the Ball."

"So it's a ball gown?"

"*No*. At least, it's not how I'd describe a ball gown, but I'm not going to spend a fortune on a dress I can only wear once, so I bought a dress that's pretty. It's long. Formal. And I could still wear it to other things in the future."

"Like what?"

"Are you really this interested in a dress, or are you just giving me a hard time?"

The deep husky laugh seemed to rumble from his chest. "Maybe I'm just interested in you."

"That's ridiculous."

"You are such a prickly little pear, Miss Harris."

Taylor ignored that. Wasn't even going to dignify his comment with a response. "Maybe I couldn't wear my dress to a wedding, since its off white and that's kind of a no-no, but I could wear it to another black-tie event."

"Because you go to so many of those," he teased, his gaze resting on her lips, making her lips feel tingly and hot.

She looked away, had to look away, flooded with emotions and sensation she didn't want. "I might in the future," she said crisply, glancing back at him.

He was *smiling* at her, smiling with his lips and his eyes and his blue gaze was warm and there was this teasing light in the blue depths, a *knowing* light, as if he knew her.

But he didn't. He didn't know the first thing about her.

Correction. He did know a few things. He did know she didn't enjoy Balls and black-tie events because she'd told him that. But other than that limited bit of knowledge, he knew very little else about her, and so he shouldn't smile at her with warm blue eyes and he shouldn't let his lips curve as if they were having a delightful, playful conversation.

Taylor swallowed hard, and pressed her lips together,

trying not to think about how it'd felt when he kissed her at the diner—*so good*—and how he'd smelled—*delicious*—and how hard it had been to fall asleep last night when she kept thinking about going to the Ball with him and dancing with him and having dinner at the Sheenan table with him and his brothers...

Her heart had raced. Just as it was racing now.

Her imagination had gone nearly wild, creating scenarios that could never happen. That would never happen. Swashbuckling heroes didn't fall in love with quiet librarians.

Not unless they'd had a learning disability and needed help with reading. Or filing.

She frowned, watching as he leaned back and dragged a hand through his dark hair, ruffling it. His blue denim shirt, rolled back on his wrist, slid towards his elbow, revealing dense, corded muscle in his forearm and lightly tanned skin.

Shameless. He was.

His gaze met hers, held. His lips curved into a wider, crooked smile. His expression seemed to say that he was enjoying her right now, and maybe even enjoying her a great deal.

Which couldn't be.

It didn't make sense. It didn't work. It wasn't real or plausible.

And did he do this to all women, smile at them and flirt and seduce them with his eyes? Seduce them with the curve of his firm lips?

Taylor wouldn't be surprised if he did. Apparently back in high school, he was quite the expert kisser. He'd probably graduated in college to expert lover.

Annoying. So terribly annoying.

"Why are you frowning at me, Miss Harris?" he drawled, a lock of dark ruffled hair falling forward, giving him a rakish appearance.

"You're such a flirt," she said primly, glancing away, unable to hold his gaze, unnerved by the tension between them.

She felt hot and cold, jittery and nervous, and a little bit dizzy, too. He was projecting some kind of energy, a magnetic energy, and it had heat and intensity and confused the heck out of her.

He laughed softly. "I'm not."

"You are. And apparently you've always been one. Voted Best Kisser your senior year."

"As well as Most Likely to Succeed," he added.

"A truly talented man."

He held up his hands. "To be fair, the vote could have been rigged. My girlfriend was the yearbook editor, and there was some speculation after the results were announced that she stuffed the ballot box."

"You're incorrigible."

"I can't think of anything sexier than a beautiful woman with a great vocabulary."

She laughed because she had to. There was nothing else she could do. "You're also impossible."

"I've heard that. And for your information, I have always liked book girls. Smart girls. Newspaper editor. Yearbook editor. Girl with the highest GPA. Girl with the perfect SAT score. Girl with the biggest brain."

She laughed and pushed her glasses up on the bridge of her nose. "Book girls, huh?"

"Book girls with glasses."

"Stop." But she was smiling and feeling easier, better, than she had all day and she was looking forward to the Ball Friday, more now than she ever had. "And I should go. We have an early morning staff meeting tomorrow—its every Thursday—but tomorrow I'm supposed to present a report on the books I'm recommending we purchase this summer."

"That's exciting."

"Yes, except that Margaret will say we have no money so we can't buy any of them."

"Not as exciting."

"No, but I can try."

"Where are you parked? Can I walk you to your car?"

"No. I'm just down over a block. I'm good."

"I think I should walk you there."

"I don't think its necessary. Marietta has a population of what? Ten thousand?"

"Give or take a few."

"I'm safe."

"You're sure?"

"I'm positive."

"Text me when you reach your car."

"I don't have your number."

"Then we need to correct that immediately," he said, fishing into his pocket for his phone. He scrolled through contacts, typed a message and hit send. "Now you do."

Taylor's phone buzzed in her satchel. She opened her satchel and took out her phone, reading the new text. *Save this number*, it read.

Smiling, she added the number to her contacts. "Saved."

"Don't you feel better now?"

"I'm not sure," she said, and it was a lie, because she felt positively fizzy and warm and wonderful on the inside. "And how did you get my number in the first place?"

"Jane."

"Ah." She blushed. She couldn't help it. "Good night, Troy."

"Good night, Beautiful."

Troy watched Taylor leave, her long dark hair hanging halfway down her back, her brown coat hitting at her hip, giving him an excellent view of her legs. She had great legs. He liked her very much in jeans. He thought he'd probably like her very much out of jeans as well...

Grey set Troy's beer in front of him. "Anything else?" Grey asked.

Troy shook his head. "Nope."

"Alright." Grey moved.

Troy took a sip of his beer. The glass was thick and chilled. The beer was perfectly cold, a hint of ice, but not too frosty. This was exactly what he needed after a depressing dinner with McCorkle and a flirtatious conversation with his favorite librarian.

He'd only just taken a second sip when suddenly Callan Carrigan was at his side, ordering a beer and taking a seat on the bar stool next to his.

"Look whose back in town," Callan said, turning on the bar stool to face him even as she waved off the chilled glass to drink straight from the bottle. "Troy Sheenan, the venture capitalist himself."

Troy gave Callan a long look as she downed nearly one third of the bottle.

He liked Callan. He'd seen a fair amount of her growing up as she and Dillon used to chum around, despite their parents' disapproval. But the Carrigan girls weren't topics of conversation at their house. In fact, the Carrigans were never to be mentioned in their house. The feud between the families had been strong. If Dillon or one of the other boys mentioned Callan or another of the girls, Mom would leave the table in tears, and Dad would start in on his lectures. Or worse.

Troy watched Callan take another long swig from the bottle. Her bottle was nearly empty.

Something was definitely bugging Callan tonight.

"What's up, kid?" Troy asked, taking a sip from his glass, deliberately dropping the nickname he and Trey had given her way back when, a nickname that always fired her up.

Her eyebrows lifted. "Kid, huh? You do know I'm practically running the Circle C these days?"

"Trailing in your dad's shadow, more like." Troy was just teasing but Callan wasn't in the mood.

"You want to piss me off, don't you?"

He gave her another long look over the rim of his glass. She was slender with dark hair that she usually wore in a ponytail—except when she was at the bar on a Friday night looking for trouble. Her slight boyish build made her look far younger than her twenty-five years. But her tight jeans and tank top showed off her curves all the same. "So what's going on? Why are you here? I would have thought you'd be home doing your nails and getting all dolled up for the big Valentine Ball."

"I'm not going to the Ball, and even if I was, I wouldn't be getting my nails or hair done. And it wouldn't take me two days to get ready. Wouldn't even take me two hours. I'd just shower, put on my dress and boots and go."

He shook his head, checked his smile. She was still a sassy, smart-mouth thing, but he liked her sense of humor. He'd always found her refreshing. "So why aren't you going?" He nodded at the young cowboys standing around the pool table looking forlorn now that Callan had left. "Didn't any one of them ask you?"

"I have more fun here. Besides, the Ball's expensive. Two hundred bucks a couple."

"And you're telling me no cowboy was willing to scrounge up two hundred bucks to take you?"

Her cheeks flushed pink. She glanced away, lips compressing. "I was asked. But I said no."

"Wrong guy?"

She shot him a sharp look. "Is there ever a right guy?"

"You don't like men now?"

She gave him another severe look. "Just because I can ride and rope better than any cowboy my age doesn't mean I'm gay."

"Never said you were."

"Good, because I'm not. I just don't feel like dating and doing the whole romance thing right now." She pushed her empty beer bottle across the counter, away from her, and signaled to Grey that she wanted another. "Trying to come to terms with something and its not easy. I'm mad. And confused. But mostly mad."

"Want to tell me about it?"

She laughed once. "You might regret saying that."

He already was. But, he couldn't back out now. "Tell me. If it'd make you feel better."

"I don't know *what* could make me feel better. Except maybe another beer."

Grey arrived, with the needed beer. He popped off the cap and slid the bottle across the counter to her.

Callan snapped it up and took a sip.

Troy frowned. This wasn't normal Callan behavior and he didn't know what to make of it. "What's going on?"

She didn't answer immediately, but then she looked up at him, brows furrowed, expression grim. "I learned some dark Carrigan family secrets."

"How dark?"

"Pretty damn dark."

"Why don't you just tell me? Then I can get back to worrying about my own problems."

"You think this has nothing to do with you?"

Her words were full of challenge—so like Callan. "Maybe you should get to the point."

"Maybe I will. The thing is—our Mom had an affair."

He stared at her. Was this the beer talking? He remembered Bev Carrigan as a very proper sort of woman. Beautiful, with nice manners and a gentle way about her. "You're talking nonsense, Callan. Maybe you should find a nice, gentlemanly cowboy to give you a ride home."

"I don't need a ride home. I plan on crashing on Sage's couch when I'm done here." Callan shredded the label off the bottle. "But first, hear me out. I want you to listen to my story."

"Your Mom's been gone a long time. Why did this come up now?"

Callan's smooth jaw tightened, her expression fierce. "The timing sucks. I couldn't agree more. But with all that's been going on with Mattie and her husband—they split up this fall—Sage decided to come clean. Apparently she's been keeping this secret since she was only twelve years old."

Troy's head throbbed. He had enough drama with Trey in jail and McKenna engaged and Cormac trying to raise April and Darryl's baby as if he was daddy material when Cormac was the least likely of all the Sheenans to settle down.

And now Callan was throwing all her family stuff at him, too.

"Hang on," he said, rubbing at his temple. "Wes and Mattie are separated?"

"On their way to divorced."

"Too bad." He'd seen Wes at a few rodeos. The man knew how to ride a bull. But marriage—that could be harder. "So what does that have to do with Sage keeping a secret?"

"She thought Mattie might be more inclined to work out her troubles with Wes if she knew that our mother had an affair. And that it hadn't ended in divorce for our parents."

Twisted logic, in Troy's mind. But he could sort of see the connection. "How did Sage know her Mom cheated on your dad?"

"She walked in on them."

Wow. That was pretty heavy. And life changing for a kid.

Kind of like him walking in and discovering his mom was dead.

"Sorry," he said gruffly. "That's shitty. For Sage, and for all of you."

Callan took another long drink. "Thing is, Troy, our mother was with your father."

Troy went cold all over.

For a moment he couldn't think, or speak. For a moment there was just silence, and then a buzzing in his head. The sound a radio station makes when you haven't dialed in properly to the right channel.

The buzzing continued unabated.

And he thought of his mom. Not his dad.

Was this why?

Was this the reason for her terrible sadness? For her endless loneliness?

Troy stared blindly down into the pale gold of his beer. He couldn't believe it.

And yet...

He could.

Bev Carrigan and his dad?

"You're sure?" he asked roughly.

"Yep." Her voice was quiet, her expression strained.

Shit.

He wished he'd never stopped in at Grey's. Wished he'd gone straight from dinner to his room. Wished he could have avoided this conversation tonight. Wished he could have avoided this conversation for the rest of his life. "Does everyone know?"

"No one knows. Just you, me, and my sisters."

He drank, and then set the glass down and pushed the half empty glass away. "Lucky you, me, and your sisters," he muttered, reaching for his wallet to drop a five and a couple ones on the counter.

He rapped his knuckles on the counter to let Grey know he was leaving and then glanced down at Callan who suddenly looked very small and young on the bar stool. "My dad's dying," he said bluntly.

She nodded once, her dark braid slipping across her shoulder. "Dillon told me."

"But you didn't tell Dillon about the affair?"

She shook her head. "He's the one who moved home to take care of your dad. Doesn't seem fair to lay this on him, too." She managed a tight, tough-girl smile. "But you're Troy, the V.C. I figured your big shoulders could handle the truth."

Chapter Nine

Thursday afternoon Louise came bounding up the stairs to the second floor landing where Taylor was adding some of the photos and memorabilia of Marietta in 1914 to the second floor display cabinet. Taylor had found them in a box in the library's storage vault and thought it was the perfect time to change displays with the Valentine Ball tomorrow launching the 100 year anniversary of the Great Wedding Giveaway.

"Does Margaret know you're doing this?" Louise asked, stooping to get a look at the faces in one of the photographs.

"Nope."

"She might not like it. She was very partial to the agriculture display. Her dad was a farmer."

"Yes, I know. But the display was almost twenty years old. I think a change is in order." Taylor sat back and dusted her hands on a soft cloth she'd picked up at the Mercantile on Main Street. "And what is she going to do? Fire me? She can't. She didn't hire me."

"You're feisty today."

"I'm just tired of tiptoeing around, afraid of incurring Margaret's displeasure. This library is in the dark ages. It's time it embraced change and technology. Kids read on iPhones and tablets and we should at the very least have New Adult and Young Adult books available for them to downloads." And yes, Taylor silently added, she was still smarting after this morning's meeting where Margaret rejected every single book Taylor had suggested as an interesting read for the local teenagers. Margaret still thought Nancy Drew was the leading series for girls. She couldn't accept that young adults today might enjoy vampires, werewolves, witches or apocalyptic literature stories featuring strong heroines.

"Well, I support you," Louise said. "And you'll have a say in the librarian that's hired to replace me, so be patient and know that change is coming."

"I'm trying," Taylor answered, positioning a new black and white photo of Marietta High with its graduating class of 1914 against a trophy dated 1914 before straightening. "Where is Margaret by the way? Still at the dentist?"

"Yes."

"Good. And I'm finished here, so maybe she won't even notice. She rarely comes upstairs anymore."

"I'm glad you're finished here because you need to come down. Something's arrived for you. It's in the staff room."

"Books?"

"No."

"Magazines?"

"No."

Information on the ALA conference this summer?"

"No."

What then?"

"Just come see," Louise said firmly, but still beaming and clearly quite excited about something.

Taylor dusted her hands off, closed and locked the glass cabinet door before following Louise downstairs, behind the circulation desk, through the small office to the tiny staff room behind.

Inside the staff room, hanging on the antique coat rack, was an enormous silver garment bag with ornate black calligraphy, *Married in Marietta.*

"Lisa Renee dropped it off herself," Louise said. "Just moments ago."

Taylor arched a brow. "It must be a mistake. I'm not getting married, nor do I know anyone getting married."

Louise rolled her eyes. "You know everyone's gone

there for their formal gowns for the Ball. As a matter of fact, you were there with McKenna last night. Miss Renee was not. Apparently one of her sales associates was."

"Yes, and the sales associate rang up my dress and the dress I bought is hanging in my closet at home right now."

"Maybe there was a mistake—"

"There was no mistake. I bought my dress. It's in my closet. This isn't for me."

"But it is. She brought this for you, and there's a card with your name on it," Louise said. "So open it. Read it. The suspense is killing me."

But Taylor didn't want to open the card. She suddenly knew who'd sent the dress and it wasn't McKenna, or Lisa Renee, the elegant stylish manager who did all the ordering for the bridal boutique.

It was Troy. It had to be Troy. McKenna must have said something to him.

Taylor's jaw tightened as she reached for the little envelope tied to the hanger with a silver ribbon. She slid open the envelope's flap and pulled out the creamy white card.

Book girls do it better in red spangles.
Troy

Taylor's heart jumped. Her pulse raced. She knew even without unzipping the garment bag which dress she'd find.

The couture gown.

Taylor peeked into the bag. Glossy red spangles caught the light, glowing and shimmering within.

Her heart fell. She exhaled in a soft, disappointed whoosh.

"Look at that," Louise murmured.

"Mmm," Taylor agreed, blinking back tears. It was such a gorgeous gesture on Troy's part, so exciting, and she loved the thought... she did, but she couldn't keep it. Couldn't wear it. Couldn't ever accept such an expensive gift. "But I have to send it back."

But before Taylor could phone Married in Marietta, Margaret marched into the staff room.

"Troy Sheenan is here, Taylor. He apparently is interested in joining one of the Book Clubs. He asked specifically about the Tuesday Night Book Group. Personally I don't think it's the right place for him, but I'll leave that to you."

Taylor found Troy perusing the New and Notable bulletin board display across from the circulation desk, next to the library's theme table, this month's theme being Valentine's Day, with classic romance novels artfully arranged. *Jane Eyre. Wuthering Heights. Pride and Prejudice. Sense and Sensibility.*

Taylor had fully expected Margaret to reject the theme and choice of books. But she'd left it there, and said nothing.

A victory, in Taylor's mind.

"Thank you for the dress," Taylor said, joining Troy in front of the bulletin board display. "But I can't keep it. I can't even imagine ever accepting something so extravagant—"

"I didn't pay for it," he said, turning to face her. His chiseled jaw was shadowed with a day old beard.

Taylor was surprised how good he looked with a little scruff. She tucked her hands behind her back, fingers threading together. "I'm sure it's not on loan."

"No, it's a gift, from Lily Jewel, the designer. She wants you to wear it and we're to be photographed and Jane is to send the photos to all her big-wig publicist friends who will tweet and share and post the photos on every fashion blog imaginable, ensuring that Lily Jewel's dress is seen by all."

Taylor blanched. "That's a lot of pressure. Maybe it would have been better if you'd bought the dress after all."

"You don't have to wear Lily's gown. You have a very nice new dress from *Married in Marietta* at home."

She smiled at him. "Are you making fun of my nice new dress, that happens to be practical, *and* affordable?"

"Just a little bit."

"I see." But she couldn't stop smiling at him. He made

her feel good on the inside. Bubbly. Happy. It didn't make sense. Opposites shouldn't attract. Big city tycoons shouldn't like small town librarians. Impulsively, she reached up to touch his scruffy jaw. His skin was warm, his jaw was hard, the black bristles sharp against her fingertips. "I kind of like this," she said.

He lifted a brow. "That's good, because I don't always like to shave."

"You... lazy?"

"Can't be clean shaven all the time. Where's the fun in that?"

"You do look rather... wicked."

"And that's appealing?"

She blushed. "Maybe."

"Why is it that nice girls like wicked boys?"

"McKenna says you're the good twin."

"McKenna has never kissed me. How would she know?"

She blushed again. Her heart was beating so fast that her head felt light. "You say the most outrageous things."

"I like to make you smile." He dipped his head, kissed her lips, a swift brief kiss that caught her off guard. "We're going to have fun tomorrow night," he murmured, before stepping back, putting distance between them just as Margaret rounded the corner.

He shot Margaret a quick glance, then looked back at Taylor, his blue gaze gleaming. "Thank you so much, Miss Harris, for the information about the book groups. I look forward to attending my first meeting. I've never been part of a book club before."

Jane arrived at the library just before closing and then stayed to visit with Taylor after Margaret and Louise had left.

The front door was locked and Jane leaned on the circulation desk, watching Taylor swiftly swap out issues of magazines from the plastic protective covers.

"These are all Cormac Sheenan publications," Jane said, tapping the glossy new issues stacked in front of Taylor. "*Montana Living, Wyoming Living, Colorado Living,* and *Big Sky Design*"

"We carry a couple more of his," Taylor said, clicking the plastic binder open, and taking out the January/February issue of *Big Sky Design* for the new March/April issue "I think they are sport oriented magazines. A skiing one, maybe, and a fishing or hunting one."

"He's just bought his third TV station to add to his radio station collection."

"He's quite the media mogul," Taylor said.

"By Montana standards," Jane answered.

"By anybody's standards. TV stations, radio stations, magazines. I think it's incredibly impressive."

"Troy helped him, you know. He gave Cormac a loan so he could buy the first couple of radio stations and then Cormac picked up the Denver-based publishing company for next to nothing a year later, and has turned the publishing company around."

Taylor clicked the binder closed and reached for *Wyoming Living.* "It'll be interesting to meet Cormac tomorrow night. I've been curious about him. I hear he's the only blonde Sheenan."

"He's pretty hot... channels Channing Tatum. Some girls like that." Jane paused, flipping through the magazine. "I always liked brunettes. With blue eyes."

Like Troy.

Taylor's chest squeezed and she held her breath a moment. Did Jane still love Troy?

Taylor reached out, put a hand on the magazine Jane was flipping through, stopping her from turning any more pages. "We need to talk," she said quietly.

"I thought we were talking."

"About something important."

"What?"

"Are you madly in love with him?"

"Mitch? No. We've only had a couple of dates."

"Not Mitch. Troy." Taylor leaned on the counter and

stared intently into Jane's face, trying to read her expression. "You're here for Troy. I've done the research. The whole wedding giveaway in 1914 was the clever brainchild of a Graff employee back in 1913, trying to figure out how to generate publicity to the reopening of the hotel after the 1912 fire." Taylor gave Jane a pointed look. "Just as you are now the clever person creating a publicity event for the new owner of the Graff Hotel."

"That's what I was hired to do, yes, but I didn't take this job for Troy. I took this job because it was an exciting opportunity and there was a big fat salary which paired nicely with Marietta's cost of living—substantially lower than San Francisco's--meaning, I could bank some money, starting saving up to buy my own house."

"So you're not here to make points with Troy?"

"It doesn't hurt to make points with Troy. He knows everyone, everywhere. The man is connected."

"You love him."

"No."

"You want him back."

Jane grimaced. "No. It'd just be a waste of both our time and, to be fair to him, I knew he was never into me, but it was fun being out with Troy. Heads turned. Everyone paid attention. I felt sexy and beautiful when we were together, but I knew something was missing.... not from my side of things, but from his. He didn't feel anything. There were no sparks. I pretended not to know, or notice, but when we kissed, I could tell he didn't want to kiss me. And to be honest, it was a turn off."

"So you don't love him."

"I've been telling you that for weeks."

Taylor felt as if a massive weight tumbled from her shoulders. She breathed in, and then out, and in again, feeling lighter than she had in ages.

"I wanted him to love me," Jane added. "But apparently he felt more brotherly towards me." She slumped onto the counter. "Do you know how often I hear that? Why do men just want to be my friend?"

"You're smart. Ambitious. That's scary for men."

"Why?"

Taylor grimaced. "I don't know. Men are stupid."

Jane burst out laughing. "Did you really just say that?"

"Of course I don't mean all men, but I think men are far more insecure than they like to let on. I just don't think they've evolved as much as we woman would like to think they have."

"Are you a feminist, Taylor Harris?"

"I don't know if I'm a feminist or a realist. But I can't help thinking that men might be hampered by all their testosterone, while estrogen allows women to be flexible. Because we have to be flexible. Our lives are all about growth and contraction."

"I had no idea you were such a deep thinker."

Taylor shrugged and smiled. "Book girls rule."

Jane shook her head, smiling. "You're a nut, and for your information, I wouldn't have ever set him up with you, if I didn't think you could be the right one for him." She hesitated a moment. "Troy's liked you from the beginning."

"He didn't even know me until he scooped me up on the side of the highway."

"He knew about you long before that. Troy was a big part of you getting this job, Taylor."

"*What?*"

"Come on, you knew that. He's a board member for Marietta's Friends of the Library—"

"I did not know that. I thought Cormac was."

"Troy replaced Cormac over the summer. There was no way Cormac could care for Daisy and continue with working and holding volunteer positions on all the various non-profits, so he let most the volunteer work go."

"Wait. I'm getting confused. Daisy isn't Cormac's daughter?"

"Daisy was the daughter of Cormac's best friends, Daryl and April Wilde. Daryl and April died in that big accident on the Las Vegas strip last June. I'm sure you heard about it. The accident was all over the news. Now Cormac is raising their baby."

"Wow. I didn't know all that. And I definitely wasn't aware that Troy had been part of the hiring committee."

"He was one of the ones that recommended you."

"There were some who didn't want me?"

"There were some who thought the library should replace Margaret with someone older, and more mature."

"Like Judge McCorkle, maybe?" Taylor muttered.

Jane's eyebrows shot up. "How did you know?"

Taylor's jaw dropped. "He wasn't part of the hiring committee!"

"He was. Along with Annabeth Collier, Chelsea's mom, Sharla Dickinson, the principal at Marietta High, and Samuel Emerson of Emerson Ranch."

"Ella's Dad."

Jane nodded.

"How do you know all this?" Taylor asked.

"Committee meeting notes are always saved in a city Dropbox folder I have access to as Director for the Chamber of Commerce."

"So you know Marietta's dirt."

Jane grinned. "I do."

"People should be nicer to you."

Jane laughed as she reached for her coat and purse. "Yes. Yes, they should." She slipped her coat on. "What time is Troy picking you up tomorrow night?"

"Five forty-five, so we can be there at six, since that's the start of the cocktail hour."

"I'm planning on being at the hotel by five thirty. Just to be on the safe side. Mitch is going to meet me there since I'm going so early."

"That's no fun."

"It's okay. I don't think Mitch and I have all that much in common anyway. He's a sports nut and I like the arts."

"He is a high school football coach."

"Exactly. Good looking, hunky as heck, but once again, not the right guy for me."

That evening at home, instead of curling up with a book, Taylor gave herself a manicure and pedicure as she sat in the living room with Kara. The TV was on but Kara was reading through a huge stack of legal briefs and Taylor wasn't really paying attention to the television program.

"What color did you decide for your nails?" Kara asked, without looking up from her paperwork.

"Red."

"Good choice. So you've decided to wear the Lily Jewel gown?"

"No. Can't wear it." Taylor frowned at the smudge in her little toenail and debated redoing the nail, and then figured it was fine. No one would be looking that closely at her feet. "It's too... everything... for me. And I'd be terrified I'd tear it or spill something on it."

"She's giving it to you."

"Well, I'm giving it back. She should have someone rich and famous wear that dress. Not a boring librarian like me." Taylor screwed the cap on the nail polish, and stretched, relaxed, and happy. "I can't believe I'm saying this, but I'm really looking forward to tomorrow night."

"*Finally.* I've been worried about you. You have Marietta's hottest bachelor taking you to the Ball. You should be counting your blessings, girl."

"I know." Taylor glanced down at her glossy red toes and fingertips and then up at Kara, and then did a little excited wiggle, unable to contain her excitement. "I am."

Friday afternoon Taylor had planned to leave work an hour early to go get her hair done. She'd wanted a blow out so her hair would be sleek and shiny and she could wear it down, but just before she left the library she spotted a tall lanky body perched on the edge of the wooden bench seat in the drafty library foyer.

His coat was open. His dark blonde hair mussed. She knew who he was immediately.

Doug.

Her heart fell. It was bad. Terrible. He'd broken one of the rules of his probation, leaving Hogue Ranch without permission.

Taylor hadn't even been able to speak. She just looked at him sitting on the bench, his head bent, his thin body angled forward, hands braced against his knees.

She sat down next to him. "Doug," she whispered, unable to think of anything to say. All those months at Hogue...all that time....

He didn't say a word. He just reached out and took her hand. Held it tightly.

His hand was icy cold and his fingers wrapped around hers, holding her hand snugly, desperately. She felt his pain. Felt his anger and pain and desperation.

He was in trouble. Not just trouble with Hogue, or the law, but trouble emotionally, psychologically.

"It's okay," she said.

He shook his head. His shoulders heaved. He made a rough sound deep in his chest. He was crying. Or trying not to cry. Either way, it broke her heart.

She wrapped an arm around his waist, hugged him, feeling the crisp frost on his coat. He was chilled through.

"What happened?" she asked.

He wouldn't look at her. He turned his head so she couldn't see his face. "Can't live like this. Can't continue like this."

For a second she couldn't breathe. "The depression's back?"

"It never goes."

"Then we don't have you on the right medicine."

"I've been telling everyone that, but no one listens."

"I'm listening."

"It's too late. They'll arrest me now for leaving the ranch."

"But if you needed help, medical help—"

"It doesn't matter." He ran his hand beneath his eyes. "Doesn't change me. Doesn't change my future. Can't live like this, Taylor. I'd be better off dead."

"Well, I wouldn't. I couldn't imagine life without you."

She squeezed him again, pressing as close as she could, needing to send love into him, through him, healing love, and hope. She needed hope, too. She loved her brother more than anything. Her parents might have abandoned him, but she couldn't. She wouldn't. Ever. "We just need the right doctor and the right medicine and we just have to take it one step at a time."

"I'm so sorry, Taylor. I'm so sorry for everything."

"It's not your fault. Your brain is wired differently, but it's still a beautiful brain, and you are a beautiful man and we're going to get this sorted out. I promise."

He lifted his head and looked at her. "You think?"

She inhaled as she saw his black eye and swollen nose. "What happened?"

His head dropped again. "Nothing."

Something had happened. His face was black and blue. "Who did it?"

"Doesn't matter."

"Of course, it does."

"I tried to avoid the fight. I did."

"How did it happen, and with who?"

"Doesn't matter. I left Hogue. I broke my contract. I'll be going to jail."

"Maybe. And maybe not," Taylor said, remembering what McKenna had said about hiring a good attorney. Maybe it was time to ask for favors from her friends here. McKenna knew the right people. Maybe it was time to reach out and ask for help. Brock Sheenan might be a good person to approach. The worst thing he could do was say no. "We'll go to Kara's," she added. "Make some calls, come up with a plan. Alright?"

"Who will we call tonight? Isn't that Valentine Ball taking place this evening over at the Graff?"

The Ball.

Troy.

For a moment she'd forgotten all about tonight's Ball. Remembering, made her breath catch, and her heart tumble to her feet.

She wasn't going to be able to go.

She was going to miss tonight after all.

She blinked back tears, hating herself for even feeling sorry for herself. Doug was in trouble. Doug needed her. She couldn't desert him now.

"Yes," she said. "The Ball is tonight. So let's go home. Work on that plan, okay?"

Chapter Ten

T roy was in the shower in his suite at the Graff when the text arrived. He didn't notice the text until he'd finished shaving and dressing. It was while he was adjusting his tie in front of the bathroom mirror that his phone, left on the gleaming white marble counter, caught his eye.

He had a message.

He picked up the phone, checked it. It was from Taylor. *Doug showed up at the library this afternoon. He's gotten himself into some trouble. Can't go tonight. So very sorry. Apologies!!*

He read the message a second time, disappointment washing through him.

She was bailing on him at the last minute, and yes, her brother was more important than the Ball, but he'd be lying if he didn't have some mixed emotions. He told himself she wasn't rejecting him, but in light of all the ups and downs of the past week, perhaps he should have expected this.

Perhaps Taylor Harris was not the most reliable woman. Perhaps she was so wrapped up in her brother that there wasn't time for anyone, or anything else. Or perhaps her brother was in crisis as she'd said... which meant that of course she needed to be with him.

Troy had a twin brother that was always in some sort of trouble. He knew better than any that there were some situations beyond one's control. And this was one.

His disappointment over not attending with Taylor shifted to concern for her. She probably wasn't happy at all right now. And God knows what trouble Doug had gotten himself into.

Troy frowned at his phone, wondering if he should call her. Did she need help? Was there something he could do?

Troy dragged a hand through his still damp hair before shooting her a brief response.

Family comes first. Do what you have to do and don't worry about me. But are you okay? Do you need anything?

He hit send on the text and slipped his phone into the pocket of his black tuxedo trousers and went to work styling his hair and giving his tie one last little tweak.

He still needed to slip on his jacket, but he looked alright. Shouldn't embarrass himself or anyone else tonight.

He was perfectly fine going to the Ball solo. And it's not as if Taylor was the only one to cancel on the Valentine Ball at the last minute. Dillon had decided to stay home with Dad. And out in California Daisy had a violent stomach bug so Cormac chose to stay with her instead of getting on a plane for Marietta.

He respected both Dillon and Cormac for making good choices. And if Taylor's brother, Doug, was in trouble, then she was doing the right thing, staying home with him.

Fortunately, Brock and Harley were still joining him at the Sheenan table, and Jane and Mitch would be there, too. So what if it was now a table of five instead of ten? Sheenans liked having some elbow room.

Taylor read the text from Troy and it was a very nice text from him. He'd said exactly the right thing, behaved as a gentleman should, but it didn't make her feel better.

She didn't want to miss the Ball.

She didn't want to sit and watch TV with Doug, or order a pizza as Kara had suggested. But that's what she was going to do, because it was the right thing to do.

Kara disagreed. She thought Taylor should still go, and she reminded Taylor that she was at the house tonight, wrapping up some work stuff so she could take off next week to go skiing with friends from law school without worrying about anything. "I'm here," Kara said. "I'll keep him company. We'll have pizza—"

"I've already told Troy I'm not going."

Until that moment, Doug hadn't any idea that Taylor had been invited to the big Ball and he was upset that Taylor was missing the event because of him.

"Why don't you go?" he asked Taylor, joining his sister and Kara in the kitchen where they'd been trying to decide on what pizza to order. "It's still early. You can make it."

"It's fine—"

"It's not," he interrupted. "It's bad enough I screwed up my probation but I don't need to screw up your life, too."

"You're not screwing it up."

"All I've ever done is screw it up." He leaned against the counter and dug his hands into his jean pockets. "Taylor, I'm not going to go anywhere tonight. I'm not going to do anything bad. I'm going to eat pizza and watch TV and crash early. I'm tired. But I'm not dangerous. I'm not psycho. Not a flight risk. I'm not going to do anything stupid tonight. I've done enough, walking out of Hogue. I know I'm in trouble."

"I don't think you're in as much trouble as you think," Kara said. "We'll take some pictures tonight of your black eye and bruises, and tomorrow if need be, Taylor can take you to a doctor and get a medical exam. The photos and exam will serve as evidence that Hogue isn't protecting you, and that you're in danger there. I'm not able to represent you, but Doug, in my opinion, if you're getting beat up at Hogue, you need to leave, and you have grounds to leave. We just need the right attorney and we're going to work this out."

Doug glanced at Taylor and back to Kara. "You really think so?"

"Hogue was never the right place for you," Kara said. "And it's time we sorted this out, once and for all." She gave Taylor a look. "And you... you really should go to the Ball. If you stay home tonight, Doug's just going to worry and feel guilty, and responsible, and there's no reason for that. There's no reason for you *not* to go. Get dressed, do your hair and drive over. Surprise Troy."

"Surprise Troy," Taylor repeated.

Kara nodded. "Live a little."

"Or live a lot," Doug added with a lopsided smile.

Taylor looked at her brother, saw his hopeful expression and felt the warmth steal back into her heart. Maybe they were right. Maybe it was time she lived.

A lot.

A half hour later Taylor stared at her reflection in the bathroom mirror.

Her breath caught in her throat as she gently touched the skirt of her pale pink tulle gown, the tulle dotted with glossy red spangles. She watched herself in the mirror as she lightly ran her hand up the gown's fitted, boned bodice to the plunging neckline.

The ball gown pushed her breasts up, squeezed her waist smaller, and shaped her hips, revealing far more of her slender frame than Taylor was normally comfortable with, because good librarians didn't show off their breasts, or flaunt their hips, or draw attention to any other part of their bodies.

But tonight Taylor didn't want to be a good librarian.

Tonight she didn't want to be a librarian at all. She didn't want to be the smart one, or the good one, or the responsible one who was always rescuing, protecting and defending her brother.

No, tonight, for one night, she'd be someone else. She'd be someone different, someone beautiful and glamorous and fun, and she'd go to the Valentine Ball at the Graff Hotel and have fun.

She wasn't even sure what fun felt like, but she knew that whenever she was with Troy she felt good.

She felt happy.

That's the feeling she wanted tonight. Good and happy.

A knock sounded on the bathroom door. Taylor opened the door and faced Kara. "What do you think?" she asked shyly.

Kara's eyes opened wide. "You're wearing the Lily Jewel gown."

"You said I should live a little." Taylor lightly stroked her fingers across the full skirt with the circle spangles. "I feel like a walking carnival or circus."

"You look gorgeous."

"It's the dress."

"It's *you*, in the *dress*." Kara walked around Taylor to inspect her properly. "I love that you're also wearing your hair up. Very chic."

"There was no time to get a blow out."

"Looks good." Kara tilted her head to the side. "What about earrings?"

"I have my diamond studs."

"Those will work. And your make up looks good. I love the eyeliner and mascara, too."

"Thought I'd better wear more make up since I've got my contacts in."

"You're a knock out."

"No—"

"Yes," Kara insisted. "Poor Troy. He isn't going to know what hit him."

I t was almost seven by the time Taylor reached the hotel, and snowing. Taylor parked her car as close to the hotel entrance as she could manage, and held her full skirts up to keep them from dragging in the snow and ice.

Entering the hotel's grand lobby with the marble floor and tall columns and rich dark paneling, Taylor felt her heart skip a beat.

She felt like a princess attending her first Ball. It was

exciting. Thrilling. And she did feel pretty tonight, truly pretty, and that never happened. Normally she felt smart, practical, helpful, *useful*. Not lovely or delicate, and certainly not ridiculously feminine.

But her gown was ridiculously feminine with the dotting of red spangles that reflected light, making her feel like a Valentine that had come to life.

She couldn't wait to check her coat and enter the ballroom. She wanted everyone to see her gorgeous dress and most of all, she wanted Troy to see her in this dress.

He said Lily Jewel had 'given' her the dress, but Taylor knew that gifts like that didn't just happen. Troy orchestrated the gift. Taylor wasn't sure what he said or did and right now it didn't matter. All that mattered was that she would soon be attending her first Ball with the most handsome man she'd ever met.

Even though it was almost seven, lots of people were still arriving and the entry hall outside the hotel's grand ballroom echoed with laughter and chatter as couples arrived for the Valentine Ball, and checked their coats and greeted each other.

Taylor handed over her winter coat and then shivered as she stepped away from the coat room, feeling almost naked in the strapless gown.

But she wasn't naked, she was a walking Valentine... light, lovely, delicious.

She wasn't going to allow herself to feel one negative emotion, either. She wasn't going to let herself feel doubt or fear.

No, tonight was a celebration, of not just one thing, but many things--the restoration of the historic Graff Hotel, the launch of the 100 year anniversary of The Great Wedding Giveaway, and the intrepid individual who dared to take risks, and dream.

T roy saw her enter the ballroom, passing through the tall double doors alone, and then hesitate in the doorway, her ball gown gleaming in the pink lighting, a clutch pressed to her chest, her dark hair pulled up in an elegant chignon, reminding him of a young Audrey Hepburn.

Striking features, and wide bright eyes. No glasses tonight. She'd left them home.

She scanned the ballroom.

He pretended he didn't know her and imagined the man she was looking for—her boyfriend or lover. Not her husband.

It wasn't that she was too young to be married—many women in Montana married young, choosing their high school or college sweethearts—but she didn't have a married look. She didn't appear settled, although he wasn't entirely sure what settled would look like, but married women carried themselves differently. They had a different confidence about them—perhaps it was complacency—that young, unmarried women didn't have.

Either way, in the doorway, she was truly lovely, and in that moment he realized she wasn't merely pretty, but beautiful, and delicate, in her romantic ball gown with the sweetheart bodice.

Troy walked towards her, wondering how she'd managed to sneak away from the house to be here, hoping she didn't regret doing so, either. He was so happy to see her. So glad she'd come after all.

There was no other woman he'd rather be with tonight.

But then, from the heavy staccato within his chest, and the silver heat in his veins, he suspected that there was no other woman he'd rather be with, any night.

"Taylor," he said, reaching her side.

Her head turned sharply and she looked at him, smiling. "Hello, Troy," she said, her voice soft, light. Even her dark eyes were so full of light they sparkled. "You look very dashing tonight."

"And you look stunning, my lady. You are the belle of the Ball."

"I hope you still need a date. Please tell me you haven't

replaced me."

"I could never replace you."

"So full of flattery."

"I am speaking the absolute truth. There is only one Taylor Harris and I very much want her."

She blushed. "Why?"

"I have a secret soft spot for book girls. I happen to think you book girls are very cool."

Her eyes lit up and her lips curved. "I've always said the same thing."

"As you should." He offered her his arm. "Shall we find a glass of champagne and then locate our table? Dinner is about to be served."

"Sounds wonderful."

At seven thirty Jane went to the microphone and welcomed everyone to the Valentine Ball and the launch of The Great Wedding Giveaway. She pointed out the handsome wooden box in the back near the chocolate fountain. The box had been made by the French wood carver and furniture designer, Laurent, for the occasion. All nominations and submissions of couples for the Wedding Giveaway would go there. Jane added that she'd taken a peek inside the box just a few minutes ago, and there were at least a half dozen entries inside.

Jane thanked Troy and the staff at the Graff Hotel for hosting the Valentine's Ball, and then asked all the committee members on the Great Wedding Giveaway to stand. Taylor shyly stood, noting that nearly every table had a committee member at it. The Great Wedding Giveaway had been a lot of work but Taylor was glad she'd volunteered. She'd gotten to know some wonderful people in Marietta, including McKenna Douglas who waved to Taylor from across the ballroom.

Taylor sat down again and Troy refilled her champagne flute. "Have I told you how beautiful you look?" he asked, leaning towards her, his blue gaze resting intently on her face.

"Yes." Taylor settled her pink napkin across her lap and looked up at him. "It's because I'm not wearing my glasses tonight."

"I like your glasses."

"I'm getting lots of advice from friends that I should ditch them again."

"Again? You don't always wear glasses?"

"I hadn't since jr. high, but since taking the job here in Marietta, I started wearing them exclusively, thinking that people would take me more seriously if I looked more academic."

"You shouldn't have to dress to impress others."

"I shouldn't, no, but it seems as if I do." She shrugged, smiled. "And let's not talk about that tonight. I'm sick of me. I want to know all about you."

"I think between Jane and McKenna, you've heard plenty."

Taylor laughed. "Kara's told me a few juicy tidbits as well."

"See? You know everything already."

"I don't know anything about your life in San Francisco, or the girlfriend you just broke up with," Taylor said, leaning back as the servers placed the salad course before them. The salad of woodland greens, dried cranberries, toasted walnuts and feta cheese made her mouth water, but she was far more interested in hearing Troy's answer than eating.

"I like San Francisco. It's a great city. I hope to always have a home there."

"How long have you lived there?"

"I've been in California since I left for college at eighteen. I went to Stanford University in Palo Alto."

"You studied?"

"Electrical engineering and computer science."

"So computer science was your minor?"

"I was a double major, and then a graduate degree in the same."

She eyed him with new respect. "You are smart."

He grinned. "I am more than just a pretty face."

She laughed. "I can't believe you just said that."

"It was a calculated move on my part. I wanted to make you laugh, and I succeeded." He reached for a candied walnut and popped it in his mouth. "So what do you like better? My brains or my beauty?"

Taylor loved the glint in his eye and the hint of mischief in his smile. "Your sense of humor." She sipped her champagne, enjoying the cold tart fizz in her mouth and the way the bubbles warmed her going down. "Tell me about the girlfriend."

"Which one? There have been many."

"The last. And why have there been so many?"

"So many questions."

"I'm curious about you. And the women you love." She took another quick sip of champagne. "And leave."

One of his black brows lifted. "I'm not out to break hearts. I'm just not going to settle."

"So what was wrong with the last one?"

"There's not much to say. She was a lovely woman. We dated for a number of months, but it wasn't a forever relationship. It couldn't go the distance."

"Why not?"

"We had different values and goals, as well as a different vision for the future." He saw her expression and shrugged. "She couldn't understand my love affair with The Graff. She came from money. Her family is old money in San Francisco, and big philanthropists, but she doesn't believe in rescuing decrepit buildings in the middle of nowhere. She believed my money would have been better spent funding a museum or donating to the San Francisco arts."

"That's why you broke up?"

"There were other issues, fundamental issues about identity, integrity, and loyalty, and I appreciate that her family is a well-known family, and I appreciate that she is an heiress in her own right, but I'm not jumping through hoops for anybody. I am who I am, and that's a Sheenan, from Marietta, Montana. I don't come from big money, and I don't care what others think of me. I don't want a woman that cares more about society's opinion than mine. I want a woman who is herself and has a strong sense of self, because our relationship has to be based on mutual respect, not status or public adulation."

"Was she beautiful?"

Troy suddenly closed the distance between them, kissing her lightly on the lips. "You are more beautiful." He kissed her again. "And smarter." His fingers brushed her cheek, his thumb stroking over the sweep of her cheekbone before kissing her a third time. "And one hundred times more intriguing. Any more questions?"

She stared into his deep blue eyes, lost. In the back of her mind she was sure there were more questions, dozens of them, but her head was spinning and her heart was racing and she just wanted to go somewhere private and kiss some more. "No," she murmured. "At least, no more right now."

The night just got better from there.

Dinner was wonderful and Taylor talked to Harley and Brock, Jane and Mitch, aware of Troy's arm resting lightly along the back of her chair. Now and then his hand would move to her back, and he'd touch her, a soft caress to the middle of her back, a light touch at her nape and she'd tingle and burn.

It didn't feel like a first date or a Valentine Ball. Being with him was exciting and yet somehow familiar. She was strangely comfortable with him. Had they known each other perhaps in a different life?

Taylor darted a glance at him as Jane and Mitch headed off to the dance floor.

Troy smiled at her. "Yes?"

"Just wondering if you were doing okay."

The corner of his mouth tugged. "I'm alright. And you?"

"I'm alright, too."

He lifted her hand, carried it to his mouth and kissed her palm. "Do you want to dance?"

"Not if you don't."

"I'm happy being with you. Don't care if its here, or on

the dance floor--" he broke off as Taylor stiffened. "What's wrong?"

"Judge McCorkle," she whispered, nodding at the couple approaching. "I don't like him."

Troy looked from the judge and his wife to Taylor. "Why not?"

"It's... personal."

"Did he say something to you?"

"I'll tell you later."

There was no time to say anything else as Judge McCorkle and his wife were upon them. Troy rose, and Taylor more reluctantly. The judge ignored her but greeted Troy effusively.

It was Troy who introduced Taylor to Mrs. McCorkle. "Sarah, I don't know if you've met Taylor Harris."

"No, I haven't," Sarah McCorkle answered. "It's a pleasure to meet you."

"She's the new librarian," the judge boomed.

"Yes, I know," his wife answered.

"How is your brother?" the judge asked, fixing his narrowed gaze on Taylor. "Staying out of trouble?"

Taylor squared her shoulders and lifted her chin. "How thoughtful of you to remember him." She smiled at the judge, a wide dazzling smile, thinking she'd kill him with kindness. "I will be sure to let Doug know you asked about him."

And then Troy saved her, wrapping his arm around her and squeezing her close. "If you'll excuse us, this is our song. We have to dance."

"Now?" The Judge said frowning.

"Yeah, now." Troy kissed the top of Taylor's head. "You remember how it was when you fell in love. You'd do anything for your girl." And then Troy took her hand and, with their fingers laced, drew her after him onto the crowded dance floor.

It was a slow song and when Troy found a spot for them he pulled her into his arms. "You don't like Judge McCorkle," he said, settling a hand low on her back.

She shivered at the touch, thinking it was delicious to be held so securely. "No," she said, tipping her head back to better see Troy's face. "And I appreciate you standing up for me, but you didn't have to tell him we were in love—"

"I was just speaking for myself."

Taylor blushed. "We're not in love."

"Again, speak for yourself."

Taylor didn't know where to look. "You're not in love with me."

"No?" He gazed down at her. "What else do you want to tell me?"

"I mean, I appreciate you going to bat for me..." Her voice faded as she got lost in Troy's blue eyes. "But there's no way..." She frowned. "Is there?"

His head bent and his lips covered hers. "No," he murmured against her lips. "No way am I going to let you go..."

Chapter Eleven

A half hour later Troy and Taylor wound their way through the crowded dance floor back to their table. Taylor was breathless as she sat back down in her seat. Troy had loosened his black tie. His cheekbones had a lovely dusky color. He was so incredible. Handsome, witty, kind, sexy...

He should be out of her league.

He was out of her league.

But she'd stopped caring or trying to prove anything. She just wanted to feel, and feel good, and right now she felt amazing. This entire night was amazing. And maybe Troy was exactly her type. "That was so fun," she said fanning herself and reaching for her ice water. Her heart was beating fast. "I loved it. What a great DJ. He's got everyone dancing."

"I don't think I've ever seen my brother Brock dance before," Troy said, signaling the server that they wanted another drink. "It's great to see him so happy."

"Harley is wonderful."

"She is," he agreed.

"Thank you for making this possible," Taylor said.

"The Ball?"

"No, this," she said, gesturing from him to her. "I tried so hard to get out of this date but it's the most fun I've had..." Her shoulder lifted, fell. "... ever? Thank you."

The waiter materialized with a tray and their cocktails, his drink and another champagne for her. She took her flute but frowned at the raspberry bobbing among the tiny bubbles.

"What's wrong?" he asked.

She looked up at him. "I never drink more than two of anything, but I think I've already had at least... three."

"This would be your fourth," he agreed. "But you've had dinner and you've been dancing. And if you're worried about driving—"

"Not worried about driving. Not planning on driving anywhere." She looked at him. "You do have your own suite here at the hotel, don't you?"

She saw the gleam in his eyes before his lashes dropped. "I do," he said.

"So no, drinking and driving isn't my concern."

"What is your concern then?"

"Losing my head. Which could easily happen after two. And God only knows what happens after three."

The corner of his mouth quirked. "All hell breaks loose?"

"Maybe."

"Maybe we should find out."

"You think?"

He smoothed a loose tendril back from her cheek, and studied her face, his gaze lingering on her lips. "Could be interesting to see what happens when Miss Harris loses control."

She reached up, to lightly drag her nails down his cheek. He felt good. So good. And so real. She wanted to kiss him. And more. "I'm not good at this stuff," she whispered.

"It's just you and me, baby."

Her heart did a painful double beat. "I'm afraid I'll get this part wrong. I'm not a big city girl—"

"Don't want a big city girl. I like my small town girl just fine."

She smiled. "You know all the right things to say."

"I know what I feel and I know what I want. And I want you, Taylor."

"Why?"

"You just seem like you were made for me."

Taylor had no answer for this. Silence stretched. She

gulped her champagne.

And he just waited, lifting a black brow, his expression quizzical, and maybe even gently mocking, but she didn't mind.

He was looking at her, waiting on her.

It was all about her. And she liked it. She loved it. She loved the way he focused on her. Loved the piercing blue of his eyes. Loved the intensity in his gaze. When he looked at her like this, she felt strong. Real. Powerful.

She was a woman who could do anything. And love big.

"Can we take our drinks to your suite?" she asked.

"I think we absolutely can." He stood, held out his hand to her. "Come with me."

They didn't make love that night. In Troy's suite they kissed for hours and did everything one could do without going all the way before finally falling asleep in his bed.

Taylor woke up sometime in the night and turned on her side to watch Troy sleep.

It had been years since she'd slept next to a man. It was hard to sleep when so many different emotions raced through her, making her insides feel raw and tender.

A week ago she would have never thought this was possible. Even two days ago she wouldn't have thought this was possible...

Now look at her... in bed with Troy, falling for him, hard. So hard.

And yet somehow it felt right. Him, her, together...

Everything worked. *They* worked. She didn't know how, didn't know why, but maybe she didn't have to have all the answers. Maybe it was enough to just feel wonderful.

T roy woke up Taylor with a kiss. "Hey Sleeping Beauty," he murmured, "It's almost six. We better get you home. Don't want to worry Kara or Doug."

"Can't go yet," she said, wrapping her arms around his neck to prolong the kiss then sighing with pleasure as he shifted his weight over her. He was warm and strong and hard and felt so good against her. "We have time."

"You're sure you want to do this?" he asked, settling his hips between her thighs.

"Not going home until we do."

And so they made love, just before dawn, as the first snowflakes of the new storm began tumbling down.

Later, snuggled up against Troy, Taylor sighed, relaxed and perfectly content. "Mmm, that was lovely."

He wrapped his arm around her, holding her to him. "Who would have ever thought that Marietta's new librarian was such a wild thing in bed?" he teased.

She gurgled a laugh. "I don't know how wild I was. You were the one with all the moves... and oh, you have some moves."

"I dig your body. But then, I'm pretty crazy about you."

Taylor wrapped her arm over his, and squeezed. "I will miss you when you return to San Francisco."

"I've been thinking about that, too."

"When do you leave?"

"Tomorrow, early afternoon."

She was silent, aware that Marietta would feel so different without him. She pressed her fingers to his hand, fitting her fingers between his. "When do you come back again?"

"I'm going to try to return next weekend. Dad doesn't have much time left." He dropped a kiss on the top of her head. "And I don't think I could handle going more than five days without seeing you."

Taylor smiled slowly. "So I'll see you next weekend?"

"If you want to see me."

"Oh, I want to see you." She pushed him onto his back and leaned over his chest, smiling down at him. "And kiss you and make love to you—"

He reached up, cupped the back of her head and drew

her face down to his. "I don't think I can wait that long," he murmured.

"Then let's not. Because this long distance thing might be hell."

Epilogue

April 18th

Actually, the long distance thing wasn't as bad as they'd imagined. At least, for Troy, the distance hadn't been a problem so far.

He was commuting weekly between San Francisco and Marietta, leaving San Francisco every Friday night, to spend the weekend in Marietta. Sometimes he'd spend the week in Marietta, too, trying to be with his father as much as he could in his father's final days. Thankfully he'd been home, at the Sheenan Ranch, when his father died the first week of March, and as hard as it was to say goodbye, it was time.

Troy was in Marietta, too, when Doug Harris received a letter from Judge McCorkle, letting Doug know he could finish his probation at home, provided he continued to attend weekly counseling sessions.

Taylor showed Troy the letter. "You were behind this," she said to him.

Troy shook his head. "I know nothing about it." And it was true. Troy hadn't needed to address Doug's situation. Judge McCorkle wanted his loan. He wasn't about to risk upsetting any of the Sheenans.

And now Troy was back again, this time to escort Taylor to the Wedding Giveaway's Spring Gala at Emerson's big barn tomorrow night.

Taylor was looking forward to the barn dance. Troy was just happy to have time alone with Taylor. An entire weekend alone if they chose to skip the barn dance and hide out in his suite. She wouldn't have been able to do it before, but now that Doug had gotten a job on Brock's ranch, a real joy, a paying job, Doug was happy out at Copper Mountain. He liked Brock's cowboys and the easy camaraderie in the bunkhouse and said he'd already made a couple of friends.

"Things are working out," Taylor had said when they'd tumbled into bed earlier this evening.

"Yes, they are," he agreed.

Now, close to midnight, they'd just made love again, and were warm and relaxed. Taylor was curled up against him, smiling and practically purring with pleasure.

His little librarian was not a shy thing in bed.

"Come with me to San Francisco for a week," he said. "We can fly out together, spend the week in California, and then have you back the following Sunday in time for work Monday."

She opened her eyes, looked at him. "I wish I could—"

"Why can't you?"

"Doug."

He kissed her, his hand tangling in her hair. It was meant to be a quick reassuring kiss, but the moment her lips touched his, he just wanted more. That was the thing about her. It didn't matter how much he had of her, it was never enough.

When the kiss finally ended, he stroked her flushed cheek then watched her sit up. "What about Doug?" he asked.

"I worry about him."

"I know you do, but Taylor, he's a young man—" Troy saw her lips part in protest and he added firmly, "—on his way to becoming a mature man and he can handle you being gone for a week. It's good for both of you to have some independence, and you can rest easy knowing he's at Brock's and nothing's going to happen to him there. Everybody in the bunkhouse will keep an eye out for him, and there's no one more maternal than Harley. She's one of five kids herself. She'll take good care of Doug. You know that."

Taylor lay back down next to him, nestling close. He wrapped his arm around her, holding her, feeling her tension. She was still so worried.

"What else?" he asked.

"My job."

"Will be waiting. No one's going to fire you over taking a few days off, and good grief, wouldn't it be nice to miss one week of that horrible Tuesday Night Book Group?"

Taylor giggled and then her giggle turned to a heavy sigh. "But Maureen will talk. The *gossip*."

"And if it's not Maureen, then it will be Carol Bingley, who used to gossip about all us Sheenan boys. But what I've learned is that even if you don't go, or do anything bad, those same folks will talk anyway. It's not personal. It's just what they do."

She stifled another sigh "True."

He smoothed her long dark hair back from her face, kissed her bare shoulder. He'd loved it when she'd giggled a moment ago. She sounded so young and carefree and it made his heart lift, happy. He'd never met anyone he'd wanted to make laugh the way he wanted to make Taylor laugh. He'd never met anyone he'd wanted to love the way he wanted to love her.

Taylor Harris deserved the sun and the moon.

And Troy Sheenan was damned determined to give her the sun and the moon and all the stars in the sky, too.

"I love you, Taylor." He kissed her again. "And if you're not ready to leave Marietta yet, that's okay. San Francisco will always be there. You come see my world there when you're ready."

She was silent a long moment. "Is that where you'd want to raise your kids... in the city?"

An interesting question, one he hadn't asked himself before but now that she'd put it to him... no. He didn't want to raise his kids in a big city. He'd want to raise them here, in Marietta. "I think my kids would have to be raised in Montana. With you here, it once again feels like home."

She sat up, pulling the sheet with her. "You'd live on the Sheenan ranch?"

"No. We'd find our own place." He saw her eyes widen at the use of *we*. "Preferably a big house on Bramble Lane," he added, tugging on a long strand of her dark silky hair.

"That way during the summer our kids could walk to the library to see their mom."

Taylor blinked hard, her eyes turning liquid. "Are you saying what I think you're saying?"

"I want to marry you, Taylor." He hesitated a moment, and smiled crookedly. "I couldn't imagine any woman more perfect for me."

She knocked away the tears. "And you wouldn't mind if I wanted to work after we got married and had kids?"

"Of course not. You're my book girl. How could I take you away from what you love most?"

"But maybe I love you most," she said softly.

"That's a good answer." Smiling, he reached out to catch the next tears before they could fall. "But there is no reason you can't have a family and do the work you love. I believe in you, Taylor. I believe you should be who you want to be. If you want to continue at the library, I'm one hundred percent behind you. If you want to work part-time, then that's what you should do. And if you want to stay home, I'm good with that, too. But I love you too much, and respect you too much, to make life decisions for you."

"You are one evolved man, Troy Sheenan," she whispered, leaning over to kiss him.

He pulled her down on top of him, kissing her back, tasting the salt of her tears. "My mother taught me well."

"I wish I could have met her, Troy."

"I wish you could have, too. She would have loved you. You would have been the daughter she never had."

"I hope we have a little girl. We could name her after your mom."

"I hope we have a little girl, and I hope she looks just like you."

"But without the big glasses."

"I'd love it if she wore big glasses. It'll help keep all the boys away."

Taylor punched him lightly in the shoulder. "I thought you said you loved me in glasses."

"I do. But as you know, I'm highly evolved."

Taylor didn't know whether she should laugh, cry or punch him again. "So most boys don't like girls who wear glasses."

"Well, we both know that most boys are fools. Let's just say *I* personally think book girls should rule the world."

She laughed and kissed him. "You are so good with words."

"I mean every word I say." He clasped her face in his hands, and kissed her slowly, thoroughly, completely. "I love you, Taylor, and I want to have a life with you, and read books with you—"

"Read books?"

"Sssh. I'm not finished. And take walks with you, and travel to interesting places with you, and make beautiful babies with you, and grow old with you. How does that sound?"

"Quite nice, actually," she said, smiling and snuggling closer. "I approve the plan. And I suggest we move forward. Immediately."

What A Bride Wants

A MONTANA BORN BRIDES NOVEL

KELLY HUNTER

Dedication

To Jane Porter and the wonderful gang at Tule Publishing. Thanks for your laughter, the endless encouragement, and for the opportunity to come play in Marietta.

Dear Reader

Writing into a pre-built fictional world is always a challenge and a pleasure. The small town of Marietta, Montana has been crafted with such love and care, and the people that inhabit it are so real to me now that I want to sit down to drinks and a meal with them at Grey's Saloon. I want to eat Sage Carrigan's salted toffee on a regular basis and stroll through Bramble Park in the summertime and in the snow. I just want to live there.

The Great Wedding Giveaway is a Marietta Chamber of Commerce initiative, aimed at bringing tourists to the town and encouraging a thriving destination wedding trade. In *What A Bride Wants,* we see the launch of the Great Wedding Giveaway during a Valentine's Day Ball (see our Pinterest boards for more). My heroine enters my couple in the wedding giveaway as an act of support for her hero, and united they stand in the face of great turmoil and danger. Will they win the competition?

I don't think they can wait that long.

I hope you enjoy Ella and Sawyer's story, and then look forward to the rest of our Montana Born Brides.

Happy Reading,

Kelly Hunter

Contents

Chapter One

"Yes, I know he's perfectly presentable and possibly a very nice person. Second-born son from a good ranching family. All good things. It's just that when he looks at me he sees Emerson Holdings and award-winning bloodlines – money on the hoof. He doesn't see *me*."

Ella Grace Emerson leaned against the walnut desk and watched with fond exasperation as her father paced the length of his study. He stopped and stooped to add another block of wood to the fire that sat snug within the stonework of the study's western wall. A huge picture window took up most of another wall and in the distance loomed the soaring, snow-clad Crazy Mountains of Montana.

The charity dinner they'd just returned from had dragged on late into the evening. They'd been seated at a table of eight that had included Joe Carter and his middle son Max, and the blatant matchmaking efforts of both fathers had been enough to set Ella's teeth on edge.

Max's half-baked interest in her good-self had done the rest.

"It was worth a try," her father argued. "You and Max have similar social status, similar interests. It *could* have worked well."

"That's what you always say. And it never does. Daddy, I am *not* a cow to be bred. You need to let me find my own man."

"But you *don't*." Samuel T. Emerson threw up his hands. They were good hands, big and scarred and strong. They'd picked her up over the years and held her tight when she'd come off a horse. When her mother had died. When her high school crush hadn't invited her to the prom. "Where are you going to find this man, Ella Grace? Out here with the cattle? Roaming around Marietta? Livingston, maybe? At least Livingston has more variety than Marietta, but wait... you never go there. You're buried here. You could travel anywhere. Canada. Australia. Europe. But you don't. You haven't had a holiday in three years."

"Has it really been that long?"

"Ella Grace, you're twenty-five—"

"Hardly on the shelf."

"—And opinionated as all get out, for which I take complete responsibility."

"Surely I should take *some*—

"And I would see you happily settled before I die."

"I am happy. And I don't feel at all unsett—" She broke off as his words filtered through, and stood up hastily so that she could keep him in view as he headed for the sideboard and the crystal decanters of liquor that lived there. She eyed him worriedly, tried to look closer, but was hampered by flickering firelight and a face full of shadows. "Wait. Dad, are you sick? Is that what all this is about? You're *dying*?"

"No! No faster than the next man. Lord, Ella, but you'd test the patience of a saint." Her father poured himself a hefty two fingers worth of bourbon and downed the liquid in one long swallow.

"Where's mine?"

"You're not the one second guessing everything you're about to say." He put down the cut-crystal glass and turned to face her, his blue eyes not nearly as bright as they'd once been. He seemed to stoop a little, his suit sat his shoulders more loosely than it once had, and it dawned on Ella that, sick or not, her father was getting old. "Ella Grace, I've spoiled you rotten. You're used to giving orders and having them obeyed. You'd cut a man down as quick as look at him, especially if you know that he has ranching interests of his own. Why do you do that? I've taught you everything I know about cattle production and ranching, and I know you love this life and this land. Max would have been a good fit for you and the business both, but you made no effort with him tonight at all. None."

"You're wrong. Max and I both made an effort to get to know each other at the start of the evening, but there was no spark." Did she really have to spell it out for him? "Isn't this my prettiest dress?" The gown was several years old, but still stylish enough to make her feel good about wearing it. It made the most of her breasts and showcased her toned and slender arms. It cut in at the waist and out again to fall softly over her hips. It was neither too sexy nor too old-fashioned. The color was a deep and luscious scarlet and suited her creamy skin and dark brown hair to perfection. Ella *had* made an effort to dress well tonight. She'd even worn jewelry and that practically *never* happened. "Don't I look presentable?"

"You look beautiful," her father offered gruffly.

"And," Ella smelled her wrist and wafted it gently in her father's direction, "I smell like gardenias. And Max smelled good too and looked very presentable, but there was no attraction between us. And if there's no chemistry now, what with both of us looking our best and being on our best behavior, what hope is there for chemistry later on? Daddy, I want the spark. The lightning bolt." *The lust.* "And then once that's in place I'll see what I can do when it comes to cultivating the love."

"I so wish your mother was here."

"Daddy, please—" Her mother had been gone for fifteen years now and sometimes Ella wished for her too, but not nearly as often as she once had. "You're doing okay." She crossed the room to stand in front of him, touched him gently on the forearm – a little reminder that she was still here, living and breathing. They both were. "We're both doing okay. Aren't we?"

"Yes." He cleared his throat and covered her hand with the warmth of his own, patting it once, twice, and then that was enough when it came to Samuel T. and rampant displays of affection. "I should send you to Dallas. *Make* you go and live amongst people your own age."

"But I *have* lived in Dallas. For a year. In a little concrete box of a dorm room." Ella shuddered. "Dallas got old fast."

"Or I could put a personal ad in the paper for you," he grumbled. "Lapdog wanted for headstrong cattlewoman of marriageable age."

"I do like lapdogs." Ella nodded encouragingly. "Not that I've ever had one. And let's face it, Max wouldn't have made a very good lapdog at all. He'd have been opinionated and commanding, and eventually he'd have wanted to run this place." And then all the other places they owned, given that Emerson Holdings consisted of not one ranch but three, along with a sizeable livestock transport business. "That's *my* destiny."

Her father groaned. "I miss her so, *so* much."

"I know you do." Ella reached up and put her arm around her father's shoulder. He was a good, strong man and a fair boss, and she loved him to bits. He just had a thing about wanting to see her married.

Ella had nothing against the notion, but she knew what she wanted in a partner and it was a hard combination to find. A man as strong and as capable as her father. A man who was driven. A man who had pride. *A man who had no interest whatsoever in running Emerson Holdings...* and therein lay the crux of the problem. If Ella was the one running the ranch, what else was there here for such a capable man to do? "I know you want me to find someone, and I want to, I do. And he'll fit me and Emerson Holdings to perfection, you'll see. Just let me do it my way."

"Your way's not working."

Stubborn old goat, but she hugged him again anyway. "Neither's yours."

E lla hadn't taken her father's words to heart but she didn't dismiss them either. It wouldn't hurt her to be a bit more sociable, catch up with friends. Marietta had a population of ten thousand fine souls and saw its fair share of tourists. It wasn't exactly a thriving metropolis, nestled as it was beneath soaring mountains and surrounded by valleys and rich grazing land, but it wasn't a two-bit town either. There were places to go if someone wanted to kick back and relax. Grey's Saloon gave good food and music and whatever beverage a heart desired. Or there was the newly refurbished Graff Hotel with its fancy restaurant and bar. She'd mentioned both options to her father when she'd told him she was heading out for the evening with her old school friend Joanna Talbot. Her father had liked the idea of Ella strolling around the Graff Hotel – preferably in a ball gown.

Which was undoubtedly why, come Friday night, Ella and Jo ended up dressed in jeans and thick winter coats as they headed for Grey's Saloon instead.

"Grey's is good." Jo was a bubbly brunette who'd left Marietta to study pre-med in California, and returned two years later with remedial massage and acupuncture diplomas in hand. Word of mouth and Jo's capable touch had turned those qualifications into a thriving business. "There's a new bartender filling in for Josh. He's Australian – you should hear him speak."

"Accents are good."

"It's not just the accent, it's the voice as well. All smooth and low, with a big fat rumble of just-try-me running straight through it."

"You *are* smitten."

"Me and every other woman in Marietta, regardless of age, creed, or marital status."

"No one's that hot."

"No, but he's a really good start."

"Is he married?"

"No."

"I want to walk in and be wildly attracted to him," said Ella. "I want to be a believer."

"That's the spirit. Is Samuel T. still throwing second-born sons of wealthy ranchers at you?"

"Yep."

"Anyone interesting?"

"Nope."

"You know, you could direct some of them my way. I could find a real soft spot for the second-born son of a wealthy rancher. Even a third-born son. You should organize a party out at your place. A midsummer night's ball."

"*Me?* Organize a ball?"

"Why not? You organize everything else. Your father would be ecstatic and so would I. Remember me? Your poor single friend?"

"No balls. The Graff Hotel is having a ball. Go to that."

"I *am* going to that. And so are you."

"We're having a barn dance in April, if that helps any? My father offered the ranch as the venue the other day and the chamber of commerce took him up on it. It's promo for a big wedding giveaway competition. Apparently Marietta's going into the destination wedding trade."

"But that's wonderful! Entertainment on our doorstep. *Brides* on our doorstep, brightening our day. I may need to invent a bridal relaxation massage package."

"You should."

"Tell me you're inviting me for a sleepover on the night of the dance."

"You're invited for a sleepover the night of the dance."

"I *knew* we were friends for a reason."

They'd reached the doors of the saloon. Jo moved forward and pushed her way inside. Soft wafts of warm air met them first. Then the mellow twang of well-played acoustic guitar drifted over them. Ella looked toward the scarred wooden bar to the bartender behind it, but it was only Reese Kendrick, the saloon manager. Reese was gorgeous, no question, but he was a hard man to know, and an intimidating man, period. The only woman to ever undo Reese had been Loreli Grey... and Loreli was long gone.

A waitress headed their way. Ella knew her too. Mardie Griffin had been two years ahead of her in school and effortlessly popular, but all that had fallen away when she'd met a man who'd led with pretty words and followed up with his fists. Mardie had divorced him eighteen months into the marriage, and these days worked her butt off at Grey's to keep herself and her one-year-old daughter fed.

Mardie greeted them with a cheerful smile. "Ladies. Table for two?"

"Booth, if you can swing it," said Jo.

"I can swing it."

"Sawyer working tonight?" Jo asked next.

"Not you too." Mardie's voice was dry, very dry.

"Ella Grace wants a look. She's hoping he'll spark a little something deep down inside. I'm hoping to say I told you so."

Mardie laughed. "He's not exactly docile. And I don't think marriage is on his agenda."

"It's not on mine either," offered Ella.

Mardie slid her a puzzled glance. "So what was with the ad? Not that it wasn't awesome, because it was."

Ella blinked in confusion, and then shrugged it off. Maybe Mardie was talking about some television commercial. Given that Ella rarely watched television at all, it stood to reason that she had no idea what the other woman was talking about.

They were halfway to the booth when Ella realized that something other was going on. Lots of eyes in this here saloon for it was Friday night and a snowy, wintery one at that. Lots of eyes fixed on her. A pair of women laughed suddenly, over by the bulletin board. Reese Kendrick looked her way and there was a warning for her in his dark, dangerous gaze... and what the hell was that for? Ella had done nothing to fan his ire of late. That she knew of. "Am I missing something?" she asked warily.

"The ad," Mardie answered, equally wary now. "*Your* ad. In the classifieds."

Ella shook her head. "I never put any ad in the classifieds."

"Go Ella!" A wolf howl followed, and Ella had no idea what that meant either.

"Mardie, I'm lost."

"How about you settle in that booth right there and I'll bring you the paper."

"Yes, but what's that got to do with anythi—"

Mardie slipped away fast and Ella walked to the booth

on suddenly wooden legs. She eased into the bench seat and frowned when Jo took the seat opposite. "Do *you* know what she's talking about?"

Jo shook her head.

"I have a really bad feeling about this." It was that sinking sensation, the one she only got when she'd screwed up but good.

And then Mardie was back, drinks tray in hand and the local newspaper tucked under one arm. "Here you go, ladies. Two grapefruit daiquiris on me. Ella, yours is a double 'cause you're going to need it." Mardie set the pretty yellowy-orange colored cocktails down in front of them. The paper got slapped down on the table next. It was open at the personal classifieds.

Someone had drawn a fat red circle around one of the ads. Within the fat circle was a photograph of Ella.

"But I didn't *put* any ad in the classifieds," Ella protested, and then memory kicked in...

Lapdogs.

Her increasingly frustrated father, when it came to Ella settling down and giving him grandchildren.

Oh, *no*.

Ella whimpered, there was no other word for it. She'd become a whimpering woman.

"Would someone please tell me what's going on?" demanded Jo.

"I may have annoyed my father the other night," Ella offered jaggedly. "More than I thought. A lot. He's been threatening to send me to Dallas. I refused to go, and then there was talk about putting an ad in the paper. I didn't think he'd *do* it."

"An ad for what?" asked Jo.

Ella couldn't bear to look.

Mardie sent her a sympathetic glance. "Apparently Ella's after a docile house-husband."

Jo snatched for the Copper Mountain Courier at the same time Ella did. Ella got there first and wore Jo's slender body slamming up against her side a heartbeat later.

"Oh, look," Jo said helpfully. "A picture of you. And it's a good one."

"Color too," Mardie pointed out. "Only colored ad on the page. Makes it *pop*."

"Make it *stop*," muttered Ella as Mardie hastened away, trying to disguise her smile.

The heading on the ad was arresting.

DOCILE HOUSE HUSBAND WANTED

They read in silence. Moments later, Jo's hand crept up to cover her mouth.

"If you laugh—" Ella threatened darkly. At which point her sweet and ever loving childhood companion did a mighty fine impression of someone about to cough up a cow.

It was a full one minute and thirty-seven seconds before Jo could even speak. "I'm not laughing. I was choking."

"Have you read down further?"

Jo nodded vigorously. "I particularly like the bit about him needing to be able to cook, clean, iron, keep a tidy house, and raise well-mannered, obedient children."

"And the rest?"

"Well, who wouldn't want a man who's committed to due diligence, the greater good, and sparkling silverware?"

Ella drained her drink in one long swallow and signaled for another. "I'm going to kill him."

"Shush. If you tell everyone about it beforehand, you're not going to be able to claim temporary insanity. What do you think *excellent remuneration package* means?"

"It means I'm going to kill him."

Another grapefruit daiquiri got plonked down on the table in front of her. They must have had it waiting. "It's still on the house," drawled Mardie. "Reese says don't do anything stupid. Me, I figured you might want to know that some bright spark pinned the ad to the bulletin board too. You want me to take it down?"

"I want a piece of paper," Ella grated.

"Better than a gun," Jo said and Mardie nodded her agreement.

By the time Mardie returned with a writing pad with the saloon's logo scrawled across the top, Ella's temper had settled to a slow seethe and she had her chin up and her mortification almost under control.

"You ready to order?" Mardie asked. "Not that I'm rushing you."

"Give us another few minutes." The title would need to be eye-catching. Large print.

PERFECT LOVER WANTED

"Oh, yay," said Mardie and was gone again before Ella could gift her with a glare.

Instead, Ella underlined her heading and started in on the specific skill set required.

"Experienced, attentive, innovative—

"Male," Jo added. "You'd better put down male."

"Experienced attentive innovative *male* bedmate required for hardworking cattle dynasty heiress with no time to meet a man and no desire for a husband of any kind, docile or otherwise. Should I ask for references?"

"Yes."

"References required. Ability to alienate meddlesome father essential."

"You need to ask for a photo and a phone number as well. I know how this works."

Ella dutifully wrote "Attach photo and contact details below."

"Please," said Jo. "*Please* attach photo and contact details below. You don't want to come across as demanding."

Ella dutifully added please to the front of the sentence. "It still sounds demanding."

Jo's lips twitched. "How odd."

Ella ignored her and signed her name with a flourish. "There. All done."

"Good. Now burn it."

"No."

"Ella Grace, I know what you're thinking, and as your dear childhood friend it is my *duty* to— Ella!" Jo's voice was rising, the further away Ella got from the table. Ella was halfway to the bulletin board, her shoulders back and her gaze firmly fixed on her destination when Jo spoke again. "Ella, this is a really bad idea."

"No, I'm really liking it."

"You won't in the morning."

"My future won't look so hot in the morning anyway, what with me murdering my father and being a wanted fugitive and all. I've decided to live in the now." Ella reached the saloon's bulletin board, glared at the offending personal ad, and briskly cleared a space next to it. She stole two pins from the school band's flyer and another pin from a postcard advertising the local library, and stuck her own ad up on the board. If Samuel T. Emerson wanted to make her private life public then, dammit, she'd make it public.

She studied the ad, tilted her head to one side. Something was missing. Ella uncapped the pen and wrote MUST HAVE SPARK across the bottom in big bold capitals. Might as well live in hope.

"Jo, have you ordered yet?" Ella wasn't quite yelling. Jo wasn't quite doubled down on the bench seat trying to stifle her giggles. Reese wasn't quite ready to throw them out. Yet.

"Not, but I'm having the beef and the potato bake."

Ella smiled brightly. "Hey Mardie, we're ready to order. I'll have the trout."

Sawyer pushed through the swinging doors that fed from the storeroom out to the run of Grey's long bar. One of the beer taps had been spluttering like a fuel-starved engine and he'd had to go and tap a new keg. The saloon had been quiet enough when he'd left, but it was buzzing now and for no discernable reason that he could fathom.

"What's up?" he asked Mardie as she swung by with a round of empties for him.

"Remember that personal ad in this morning's paper? The one for the docile house husband?"

"Hard to forget."

"Ella Grace didn't put that ad in the paper after all. Her daddy put it in on her behalf."

Sawyer didn't know much about father-daughter relationships, but he sure as hell recognized public embarrassment when he saw it. "Father of the year."

"Ella's just written her own ad and stuck it up on the board next to the other one. She's after a lover. One who can annoy the living bejeezus out of her father."

Sawyer smiled. He liked the defiance inherent in Ella's actions. It tugged at heartstrings buried deep in his past. He knew how it felt to pull up short of parental expectations. Sawyer glanced over the customers again. "Which one's Ella?"

"Booth eight. The smaller brunette."

Sawyer looked over toward the booth. Aha. *That* brunette. He'd seen her come in, along with her friend. She wasn't all that big and she wasn't all that curvy now that she'd shed her winter coat, but there was something about her that drew the eye and held it. Her confidence, maybe. Or perhaps it was just the liveliness in her eyes. He always had been a sucker for bright eyed women, no matter the actual eye color.

Hers, he noted, were the vivid blue of cornflowers on a sunny summer's day.

"You should go read Ella's *other* ad." Mardie fished in her apron pocket and came up with a phone that she held up at eye level and pointed his way. "Let me take a photo of you first, 'cause you might want to answer it. C'mon Sawyer, *use* those dimples, look naughty—not *that* naughty, and... wow. You're really photogenic, aren't you?" Mardie's smile came at him sunny side up and full of mischief. "Hold the fort for me, lover boy. I'm just going to run this through the printer."

"Yeah, no, Mardie, I don't much like having my photo up on any walls. Got a thing about avoiding the limelight. And the wrath of *Reese*." And the press.

Then again, maybe it wouldn't hurt.

Sawyer thought back to the ridiculous personal in the paper that morning and couldn't help but laugh.

"There. Behind the bar. Look," said Jo, and Ella looked and then forgot what she was talking about in favor of looking some more, because he was hot, smoking hot, and he was heading out from behind the bar and striding toward the bulletin board with a sheet of white paper in hand.

His shoulders were broad and his face was a collection of strong planes and angles, no softness anywhere, and then he stopped at the board and read the ad and his eyes crinkled as he smiled, and there – right then and there – Ella felt the world around her slip a little sideways.

"Any spark yet?" Jo wanted to know. "Because *that* is Sawyer."

"Could be the two daiquiris," Ella muttered as she dragged her gaze away from him and reached for the water jug on the table. "Phew. Is it hot in here? It's hot in here."

"I knew you wouldn't be immune."

"Let's not be hasty." Ella took a quick sip of water but she couldn't quite keep her gaze away from the masterpiece that was Sawyer. "Good grief, look at those shoulders. They're almost as wide as your average door. Must make life difficult – always having to sidle in sideways."

"I thought you said you wanted to be a believer."

"I do. I do want to be a believer. How do I make him speak?"

"I hear the usual approach is to say hello." Ella and Jo watched in silence as Sawyer pinned a bit of paper below her ad. Looked like a photo. And a phone number.

"Could be he's pinning up someone else's reply," Ella said. "No need to be all... hopeful."

Except that Sawyer turned and looked straight at her and his eyes were green, honest-to-God, no-other-color-involved, deep forest green. He quirked his lips and showed off a dimple in his cheek, and then he turned and sauntered back to the bar, easy as you please.

"I think I'm in lust," Ella wheezed. "After all these years, it's finally happened. I feel like I've just been hit by an eighteen-wheeler. What do I do?"

"Are you going to listen to my advice this time?" Jo looked skeptical.

Ella nodded frantically.

"Breathe."

Chapter Two

"You can buy her a glass of water," Reese told the customer at the bar flatly. "With ice and lime."

Reese Kendrick wasn't big on words but he *was* big on maintaining order in the bar. Sawyer liked that about him; liked that Reese's fearsome reputation was usually enough to shut down trouble before it began.

Trouble was, those warring ads on the bulletin board had taken on a life of their own. Sawyer might have been the first to pin up his picture but he hadn't been the last. The ad for the perfect lover now had three more responses beneath his own, and the ad for a docile house-husband had two.

One of the house-husband contenders had sent dessert over to Ella's table instead of a drink. And she'd eaten it. Well, strictly speaking, Ella's friend had eaten most of it, but Sawyer still figured it for a nice play.

Bets were going down all across the saloon as to what the delectable Ella Grace was going to do next. Meanwhile, the number of beverages being sent her way was hitting double digits, hence Reese's decision to cut her off.

Reese sent the man away with a glass of sparkling water.

Reese was currently eyeing *him* with the flat bleak gaze of a man lining up a sniper shot.

"What?" Some kind of defense was clearly needed. "I was *helping* when I answered that ad. What if she'd had no takers? That would have been really embarrassing."

"You're such a sweetheart," said Mardie from the other side of the bar, and then went and spoiled her defense of him with a snicker.

"Ouch. Who babysat your daughter the other day when you had to go to Livingstone?" He pointed to his chest. "Me. The sweetheart."

"I already thanked you for that, even though Mrs. Burrows saw you out walking Claire and now thinks I'm a twice fallen woman with a weakness for truck-stop trash."

"Your baby was screaming because she was bored. I defend my right to walk her around the block. We picked up fallen tree branches and Claire tried to eat them. Happiness ensued."

"You let my baby eat trees?"

"No, I let her *try*."

"Trees aside, you *do* know that the father you've pledged to help annoy is Samuel T. Emerson, of Emerson Holdings?" Reese told him dryly. "Ring any bells? Because you're living in one of his bunkhouses."

Sawyer probably should have made that connection himself; what with the Emerson name being plastered all over the transport trucks, not to mention the trucking company signage itself. "Gotta hand it to old Samuel T. He does provide good sleepover accommodation for his drivers. Clean room, good shower pressure. Really good mattress."

"You don't care who he is, do you?" said Reese.

Sawyer smiled. So did Reese.

"All this rebel bonding," Mardie grumbled. "Sawyer, how *did* you manage to rent that room at Emerson's Transport?"

"I asked. Man called Ray gave me the option of rooming by the week, cash in hand."

"You're not even on the books," Mardie told him bluntly.

Sawyer slid the last of Mardie's drinks order onto the tray. "Don't have to be if I can be out of there in ten minutes."

"Did you come by that drifter mentality the hard way, or were you just born to it?" she sniped, and Sawyer thought that maybe, just maybe, he didn't deserve that and that her comment was mostly meant for someone else. From all accounts, Mardie's ex had been a drifter too, and that probably wasn't the half of it. Sawyer had come up behind Mardie on his first day working the bar – she'd been trying to reach for a fresh bottle of top shelf whisky, and he'd watched her flinch hard then go utterly rigid when she'd realized he'd hemmed her in. He'd stepped back slowly, giving her space, lots of space, and almost let her reaction pass.

Almost.

"Okay, so next time we do that, how about you stand over there and tell me what you want down from the shelf and I'll get it for you?" he'd offered carefully, and watched some of the stiffness ease from her thin shoulders.

"Deal," she'd said in a low, ragged voice, not even turning to look him in the eye.

He hadn't asked questions. Hadn't really needed to.

They'd come to an understanding since then, and these days she trusted him enough that she could ask him to babysit her kid for a couple of hours while she went and had some x-rays taken. These days he understood her well enough that he could brush off some of her more cutting comments about his drifter lifestyle.

Most of the time.

He moved down the bar. Mardie stopped him with quiet words. "I'm sorry, Sawyer. That comment was uncalled for. It wasn't meant for you."

"We're good," he told her gruffly, for the echoes of a battered woman were all around her. "I do drift. I'm not a stable influence." And this conversation was cutting way too close to the bone and it was time he found a way out of it. "Mind you, I like to think I have a *few* useful qualities. Skills, even."

"Yeah, running your mouth," muttered Reese.

"Your customers love my mouth."

"And his eyes." Mardie was already turning away with the loaded tray of drinks, her smile firmly back in place. "His dimples. His muscles. His ass. His utter lack of humility..."

"Find out what the odds of me landing the perfect lover position are," he called after her. "See if you can raise them. I'm just warming up."

"I'm glad to hear it," said a new voice, a feminine voice, mellow and assured. "Because for a former frontrunner, you're slipping behind. You haven't even bought me a drink."

"That's because you're cut off." Sawyer turned and there she was, all creamy skinned and restless, and even prettier up close than she had been from afar. He met her gaze and felt the force of it, the singular focus of it, and he was glad he hadn't still been talking when he turned her way because he might not have been able to finish his sentence. Some people kept their energy contained. This woman didn't seem to live by that particular philosophy at all. Instead, she exuded a vibrant energy and the air around her seemed to shimmer beneath its impact.

That, or he was getting dizzy.

He took a moment, remembered to breathe, and then smiled his best lazy smile. "I was thinking flowers for you instead of a drink."

"At this time of night? Where would you get them?"

"There's some out back in a vase. I'm not sure who they belong to but I doubt they'll be missed."

"*Stolen* flowers," she murmured. "Tell me, do they smell sweeter?"

"They do." He let some rumble enter his voice. He'd wooed women before; he knew what worked for them. And for him.

"My father's going to love you," she murmured.

"Trust me, he won't. Although seeing as that's the point, I'd say we're good to go."

"I'm going to need some references."

Damn but she had a pretty mouth. Generously proportioned. Soft and supple looking. "I never kiss and tell."

"Convenient."

"Discreet."

"I'm really not after discreet," she told him politely. "I'm looking for a noisy, attention-getting affair with a man my father will find thoroughly unsuitable."

"For you I could be indiscreet." She leaned forward. It seemed only polite that Sawyer lean forward too.

"May I make a confession?"

"I'm all ears." Her eyes really were the most amazing shade of blue.

"It doesn't even have to be a real affair. It could be a pretend one."

From somewhere beside him, Reese snorted. Ella Grace Emerson swayed back and eyed Reese reproachfully. "You cut me off."

"I know."

"I've had two. Right at the start of the evening."

"Considering the first one was a double, that makes three. And you're still cut off. Ella Grace, I don't care who started this debacle, you or Samuel T. I do know that you're asking for the kind of trouble that isn't welcome here. So unless you want to wake up tomorrow morning naked in some joker's bed, with a splitting headache and no notion of how you got there, I suggest you take control of what you've started and change the way some people are thinking. Two choices, Ella Grace. Either you shut this down..." Reese's voice had hardened. "Or I will."

"Do you really think that's where those ads are sending us?" she asked skeptically.

"You never can tell."

"Give me your pen," she said, and Reese handed her a fat black marker with an air of quiet warning.

Sawyer watched as she stalked over to the bulletin board and crossed out the docile house husband ad completely. A groan went up from two of the tables, but it was friendly still, there was laughter still. Reese might have a sixth sense for trouble, but it wasn't upon them just yet.

Ella Grace turned and held up her hand for attention.

As if she didn't command the room already.

"Sorry," she said. "Really not after a husband. It was a joke. Carey and Ry, I'm flattered and truly grateful that you decided to play along. I've every confidence that you'll make fine husbands one day. *Really* fine if you plan on using that ad as your guide."

Ladies cheered. Carey blushed. Ry stood and raised both arms in victory. And then Ella's hand was back in the air again.

"As for the lover wanted ad, it's been pointed out to me that I may need to put a little more thought into that as well before, uh, taking action. So that notice is coming down too." Groans this time, and more laughter, all still on the bright side of sociable. "I do apologize for the misdirection, people, but I hope there's no harm done. And, um, for everyone involved, this round's on me."

"I like her," Sawyer murmured.

Reese gave him a flat stare.

"What? She did exactly what you asked her to do and she did it with style. Tell me you didn't admire that."

"She'd have impressed me more if she'd never started it."

'Well, yeah, but where's the fun in that?"

"I'm surrounded by children," Reece said, but he gave Ella a nod when she returned to the barstool. Ella's girlfriend joined her moments later, grinning hard.

"There we go," Ella said briskly, with the air of someone dusting her hands. "No one wants to marry me, no one wants to take me home and showcase their sexual prowess, and Sawyer here thinks I'm a lunatic. My work here is done."

"I love your life," said her friend. "It's big. It's got balls. What are we doing for an encore?"

"I don't know about you but I'm spent. Possibly broke. And for some strange reason I'm also cut off from the alcoholic beverages. Want to go to your place, watch bad action movies and eat s'mores? I can put the round I just offered people on my account." Ella shot Reese an enquiring glance. "Do I have an account here?"

"You do now."

"My father will be so pleased."

She was such an autocrat, decided Sawyer. It helped that she also had a fine sense of the ridiculous. And, y'know, bright blue eyes.

She looked at him curiously, as if she couldn't quite figure out what to make of him. He quirked a brow and she seemed to come to some sort of decision. "Would you like to have lunch with me tomorrow?"

"Are you still on about the pretend lover thing?"

"Yes." Ella ran a hand though her tousled dark tresses.

"No."

"Which is it?"

"Okay, maybe I *do* want my father to realize that he can't control my love life the way he controls the breeding habits of our cows, but I don't necessarily plan to use you to make him see the light. That would be unfair of me. I just figured, okay, maybe he's right and I do need to get out more and expand my social circle. It wouldn't hurt to do *that*. Besides, it's only lunch. It's no big deal. A little company. And forget what I just said about cows – you don't need to know their breeding habits, or mine. I'm just..."

"Babbling?" he offered helpfully.

"I know." She sighed. "I never babble."

He'd been here three weeks and two days, he'd been hit on half-a-dozen times a night and never once had he taken anyone up on their offer. He didn't share his bed with strangers. Didn't start things he wouldn't be around to finish. But this woman... Ella... he could stand to know a little more. "What time for lunch?"

"Noon."

Ella's girlfriend nudged Ella hard. "Ella, play nice and preserve his ego. Try and make it sound like a question."

"Oh. Right." Ella nodded and tried again. "Noon?"

It was no less a command than the first time she'd said it.

Reese coughed – probably to hide his amusement.

Sawyer smiled, sweet and slow, not bothering to hide his. He liked this woman. His body thought she was hotter than the sun and his brain wanted to know just how long she could keep a man on his toes. "All right, princess. I'll see you tomorrow at noon. Look for me by the frozen fountain in Bramble Park."

Chapter Three

S awyer woke to the knowledge that he had a lunch date
with a woman with cornflower blue eyes and a way
about her that had engaged every bone in his body.
How long had it been since a woman had caught and held
his attention like that? Not since Zoey, and he'd been barely
twenty-four back then. Too young to know the trouble he
was bringing down on her in the shape of his family, and too
powerless to stop it from happening.

Zoey had been the only child of a wealthy father too. A
Spanish princess rather than a Montana born one.

Apparently he had a type.

Loud thumping on the door interrupted his not-so-
pleasant reverie. That. That was the sound that had woken
him.

He could sleep through the sound of trucks coming and
going, and the shouts that went with linking up the rigs,
because those noises didn't concern him. This noise, on the
other hand, did. He muttered a response that might have
sounded like "Coming", or it might have had a suggestion as
to where the noisy thumping person could go. He hauled up,
wrenched open the door and stood there blinking into the
sun, belatedly grateful that his low-slung PJ bottoms were
on his body rather than on the floor.

Ray the truck yard foreman stood there, fidgeting. Ray
knew the hours he kept, knew he'd be asleep. Ray wouldn't
have woken him for nothing.

"Ray."

"Boss wants to see you."

"Whose boss?"

"Mine. His daughter didn't come home last night. Seems Samuel T. heard you might have something to do with that."

"She's not here."

"Good."

"Good gossip grapevine though. Speedy. I think she went to her girlfriend's place for cookies and pillow fights."

"He'll see you in five minutes."

Ray backed away, message delivered. Sawyer didn't bother shutting the door, he just rifled through his carryall for jeans and a clean T-shirt, dressed fast, splashed his face with water, and ran wet hands through his hair. He brushed his teeth. He had a couple of day's growth on his face but he didn't have time to shave. He reached for his coat and an apple on the way out the door.

He did have time to eat.

Samuel T. Emerson was a good looking man, with eyes almost as blue as his daughter's. He wore the same sort of well-worn work clothes as his employees, something that lifted him a notch in Sawyer's estimation. Sawyer's own father wouldn't be caught dead wearing anything but a hand-tailored suit.

"So you're Sawyer," the older man said, and Sawyer nodded and examined the skin on his apple. It had been a long time since he'd offered up a yessir. "And you met my daughter last night."

Another nod as Sawyer bit into the apple and chewed thoughtfully, and then swallowed before answering. Manners and all that. "I'm meeting her again for lunch today."

"Are you buying or is she?"

Sawyer smiled, slick and fast. "How 'bout I get back to you on that?"

The older man eyed him coldly but Sawyer remained unperturbed. He'd grown up with colder stares than this one. Meaner ones. He took another bite of his apple. And chewed.

"I know about the ad my daughter put up on the saloon bulletin board. I know how contrary she can be."

Again, Sawyer took his time chewing and swallowing before answering. "Something you might have considered when writing *your* ad."

"Perhaps." Samuel T. smiled mirthlessly. "What brings you to Marietta, son?"

"The road, mostly. Work I like. Real pretty little town."

"Are you looking for more work, Mr. Sawyer?"

He could have told the older man that he only had three more weeks left at the bar before Reese's regular bartender returned from his break, but in Sawyer's experience handing over that kind of ammunition never ended well. "Why? You got any?"

"What can you do?"

"Jack of all trades."

"Do you have an education?"

"Ivy League, can't you tell?"

Ray snorted. Sawyer smiled and continued to eat his breakfast. Happens he did have a Harvard education, courtesy of his mother's American connections and his family's abundance of money. His father had wanted him to have a business degree so that's what he'd enrolled for. His father had once been of a mind to position Sawyer somewhere within the family's extensive brewery holdings. Right up until his older brother had stopped that line of thinking dead. "I may know a little something about the liquor business," he offered. "Running a bar and the like."

"Grey's already has a manager. A good one."

"Noticed that."

Samuel T. looked him over again, with eyes that missed nothing. "Do you know cattle?"

"I know what they look like." Sawyer sighed. "Samuel, can we cut to the part where you tell me the bunk room is no longer available and you try to run me out of town?"

"What makes you think I'm going to do that?"

"You're here."

Samuel snorted. "Son, I know my daughter. Last thing I'm going to do is run you out of town, even if I could. She can get real ornery if you take her toys away."

"That a warning that your daughter's a spoiled princess?"

"Well it should be. She has a good heart though, and there's nothing I'd like more than to see her in love and happily settled."

"Hey, woah! I answered the *other* ad."

"So you did." Samuel reached for his hat. "Pay for lunch, Sawyer. Get to know my daughter, if that's what you both want. Court her if you've a mind to. I'll give any man a chance to earn my respect and hers – even a casual worker living out of one of my bunkhouses." He put his hat on and fixed Sawyer with a steady gaze. "Just don't play my daughter for her money, because that won't end well for anyone."

"I'm not that money driven."

"Maybe you're after permanent residency."

"Australian father, American mother." Sawyer studied his apple core, decided he'd had enough and tossed it in the freshly emptied office bin. "I'm already a citizen."

Samuel stared at him long and hard. Sawyer stared back.

"Are we done?" Sawyer asked with the quiet menace he usually reserved for unruly bar patrons.

Finally the older man nodded, as if he'd made some kind of decision. "There's a new brewery opened up on the outskirts of town. It's owned by a Texas oil man, name of Jasper Flint. Maybe you should talk to him about a job if you've a mind to stick around this real pretty little town."

Samuel left Sawyer and Ray standing in the little container-built office as he headed down the steps and off toward a huge livestock transport rig already loaded with cattle. Seemed like the old man was going to deliver some cattle himself. Moments later the engine rumbled to life and Samuel T. turned the truck toward the exit gates.

"He give every man a chance to prove his worth?" he asked, and Ray nodded.

"What happens if you fail him?"

"It's your loss."

Ella didn't usually spend Saturday mornings at the park on the outskirts of Marietta's town center. There was winter feeding to attend to, along with the unloading of stock and getting them drenched and immunized while they were still in the yards. Extra hands were always welcome. That was where Ella should be, where she wanted to be, because it was safe and familiar and she could be herself.

Ella wasn't entirely sure what she was doing here, or what had come over her last night when she'd asked Sawyer out to lunch. In the light of a cold winter morning it really didn't seem like such a good idea.

But an Emerson didn't go back on her word or renege on her invitations, and Bramble Park did look lovely draped in winter white. The baby snowplows had been through the grounds already, clearing the paths and running a wide circle around the frozen water fountain. A bunch of kids pelted snowballs at one another over in the direction of the courthouse, using tree trunks for cover.

Sawyer wasn't anywhere to be seen. Ella was only a couple of minutes early, but still...

Maybe he wouldn't show.

She stamped her feet to ward off the cold and then figured that she should probably stop with the stomping in case Sawyer took it as a sign of impatience. She wondered what time his bartending shift had finished. Maybe 1:30 am? Although if he stayed on through clean up... 2:00 am? Would he shower when he got home? What time would he have woken up this morning?

Maybe he wouldn't show.

Ella shoved her mittened hands beneath her armpits and figured she'd give him another five minutes before leaving. Probably better if he didn't show. That way he could remain a fantasy for years.

And then Ella turned around and there he was, all rugged up against the cold and heading toward her along one of the snow-bitten pathways and lord but he was big – it was the shoulders that made him seem so, had to be, because his legs – currently encased in faded denim – were just normal. Okay, maybe the legs were somewhat lengthier than normal. Okay, nothing about him was normal and everything was superb – may as well admit that now and be done with it.

Ella had wondered if she'd been imagining the deep kick of lust in her belly she'd felt when she first set eyes on Sawyer last night.

She'd wondered if the lust had been a fleeting thing.

Nope.

"How much do you know about cattle, Sawyer?" she asked when he reached her. He was dressed for winter – as she was. Thick coat and gloves, waterproof boots with thick grip rubber soles. Winter gear tended to swamp Ella. It didn't swamp him.

"You're the second person to ask me that today. Why do you ask?"

"I wondered if you were one of those rugged Australian Snowy Mountain men."

He grinned at her. "No."

Shame. "So how did you get your, um—" she waved her hand in his general direction. "—physique?"

"Hard labor and genetics. Hey, I bought us lunch. Well... it's either our lunch or my dinner, depending on whether you have any suggestions as to where we can eat it. I like the outdoors. Having said that, finding a picnic spot in Montana in the middle of winter with the ground under four foot of snow is a little more challenging than finding a picnic spot in Australia. I brought a picnic blanket though. Waterproof."

"You're really not from around here, are you?"

"No. Are you trying to tell me that you've never picnicked in the snow?"

"Sawyer, I have never picnicked in the snow."

"Would you like to?"

Ella studied the cloudless blue sky. It *was* a very fine winter's day.

And Sawyer had such very tempting dimples. And when

he reached into the pocket of his coat and pulled out a big bag full of Sage's chocolates, Ella was sold.

"You've discovered one of Marietta's best kept secrets," she said as Sawyer tugged on the ribbon around the cellophane. "Sage Carrigan is a world-class chocolatier. Which ones did you get?"

"The salted toffee with dark chocolate swirled into it." The cellophane opened to reveal a generous supply of it.

"I'm liking this picnic a lot already," she told him, as she plucked a chocolate from his hand and popped it in her mouth.

Which finished the conversation for quite some time given that the toffee was chewy, the chocolate dribbly, and the salt crystals just made the mix perfect.

Sawyer didn't seem to mind. He just took her hand in his and stomped his way through squeaky, part-packed snow – leaving yeti tracks behind him – until he found a spot that spoke to him.

Hard to know what it said.

He withdrew a blanket from the pack on his back and spread it out. He took off his gloves, held his hand out and helped her be seated and then sat opposite, set the chocolates in front of her and started pulling more food from his pack. A loaf of crusty bread. Crumbly cheese from the deli. Two locally made beers. Spicy avocado dip and crackers, two containers of rare-roast-beef pasta salad from Ginny's Café. Two containers of apple crumble, also from Ginny's Café – and there was another Marietta culinary experience to savor.

Ella loosened her scarf but decided against taking her woolly hat off, no matter that she'd spent an inordinate amount of time straightening her hair this morning in anticipation of having to do just that and not wanting to look a complete mess when it happened. If Sawyer wanted to picnic outside he would just have to deal with her staying bundled up.

"I'm glad I'm hungry. Are you hungry?" she asked, kneeling up and then sitting back down again, this time with her padded coat between the snow, the thin blanket and her butt.

"Yes. Do I get to eat the apple pie first?"

"I ate the chocolate first." She reached for another one of Sage's confections. "And second. Is Sawyer your first name or your last one?"

"Last."

He sounded as if he was going to leave it at that, but she gestured for him to keep going and then nudged his leg with her foot when he missed that cue.

He nudged her back but he did offer up more. "My first name's Cameron. Got a few people who call me that. My mother. A couple of aunts. A few more people call me Cam. Here in Marietta, it's just Sawyer."

"What does your father call you?"

Sawyer tensed, then deliberately reached for a takeout container full of pie and the plastic spoon that went with it. "Nothing. We haven't spoken for a while. Family rift."

"Is it mendable?"

"No."

"Do you talk to your mother?"

"On rare occasion."

"Brothers and sisters?"

"I have one brother. We don't get along. Told you I had experience when it came to alienating family." He eyed her steadily, and those eyes were even more amazingly green in the daylight than they had been at the bar. "What about you, Ella of the twenty questions? What's your background?"

"I was born here. Raised here, and sometimes raised in Texas because we have a couple of ranches there as well. I like horses, I breed arguably the best stud Angus cows in three states, and I raise fat cattle. I lost my mother to cancer when I was a kid. My father never quite got over it, or found another love. I did get over it eventually, but some of the side-effects took hold and they're a part of me now. I stick close to home because I like living in a familiar world where the people don't come and go every five minutes. I like waking up and looking out the window and knowing the mountains are always going to be there. Could be I'm slightly set in my ways. But I'm aiming to shake that up. I may even go traveling for a while."

"Where to?"

"Don't rush me."

Sawyer grinned around his spoonful of pie. Ella stripped off her gloves and reached for the beef salad and added a hefty sprinkle of Sawyer's crumbly cheese. The bread really couldn't be ignored either. Maybe she could make a roast beef salad sandwich without making too much mess.

Turns out she could.

Sawyer eyed it hungrily, so she rolled her eyes, handed it over and started making another one. "*This* one's mine."

"Never said a word."

"No, but you *looked*."

"You're ornery."

"So I've been told. How do you do it? Travel around all the time?"

"I like seeing new faces," he told her. "New places."

"Don't you miss home?"

"No."

She studied him thoughtfully. Hard to say if he really did mean that. She didn't know him well enough to tell. "Where *is* home for you?"

He was silent a long time. "Sydney, probably. It's where I spent a lot of my childhood. But my mother's American and I have dual citizenship, so... big place, North America. Takes a while to get around it."

"Have you ever thought about settling down anywhere?"

"Once or twice."

"What stopped you?"

"Guess it wasn't what I was looking for."

Conversation lapsed as they ate haphazardly. Good sandwiches. Sweet and cold beer.

"Your father came to see me this morning," he murmured.

"How'd he know where you live? I don't even know where you live."

"I'm staying in one of the bunkrooms at Emerson's Transport."

Ella grimaced. Yep, that'd do it. "What did he want?"

"Meet and greet."

"What did he *say*?"

"Not a lot."

"C'mon Sawyer, spill. I need to know whether to berate him or not. I'm thinking yes, just on principle."

"He warned me against chasing you for your money."

"*Are* you planning to chase me for my money?"

"No."

"That's a relief. Are you planning on chasing me at all?"

"I'm not sure yet."

"You're not exactly crazy about me, are you?"

There were those dimples again. He should register them as a lethal weapon. "Don't rush me."

She laughed because he was playful and smart and those dimples encouraged laughter. "Where'd you go to college?"

"What makes you think I did?"

"Gut instinct."

"See, if I told you, you'd put me in a different box. And I like the box I'm in."

"The international man of mystery box does have a lot going for it," she said agreeably. "Apart from making me feel downright home grown."

"They do grow many fine products around these parts."

"You said products. The minute you start talking supply and demand, I'm going to call you a marketing major."

"Did you get a tertiary education, Ella?"

"I went to University of Texas for a year. I tried business. Pulled some good grades, probably because I'd already learned a lot about business from my father. Maybe I'll go back one day and try a few more subjects but right now I've no plans in that direction."

"Because your father knows it all?"

"Because I have a really good life here and I don't want to leave it."

"So you have everything you want right here?"

"Well, my father would say I need a husband, and while I'm not wholly opposed to the idea I'm not entirely convinced that I *need* one. I could do want *and* need, I guess. Best of both worlds. And I really want to do lust, husband or not."

His eyes smiled down at her, as if he found her highly amusing. "Have you ever *been* in lust?"

"No, but I'm ever hopeful. You've no idea how long I've waited to feel the lust."

He was sitting on the picnic blanket, leaning back on his hands, pure sun-spelled, lounging male. "There's a chance I could teach you something about that." His voice had roughened. Best bedroom voice ever.

"Now is good." That wasn't too pushy, was it? She was just being accommodating.

Sawyer's gaze was very intent. "Trouble is, lust can strip your control. Make you vulnerable. Make you want to do naughty things in a public park with half a dozen people looking on. You ready for that, Ella?"

Chances were he'd just hit a kink she never knew she had, what with the tight knot of heat forming in her belly and all. "So if I were to slide on over and straddle your legs and sit in your lap and just nibble on something..."

"We might both learn something."

Ella was already moving, skirting the food, straddling his legs so that she was kneeling above him at first before sitting herself tentatively just above his knees.

"Closer," he ordered gruffly.

And...*oh!* Well.

"Better?"

"You're really, um, hard-bodied. And warm. Phew."

"We've been sitting in the sun."

Yeah, winter sun. In the snow. Minus double-digit degrees.

"Would you like to take the lead?" he murmured, his lips brushing her ear while her body went soft and pliant. "Or do you want me to do it?"

"You." Chances were she could learn something. "You lead."

With his lips he drew a lingering path from her ear to her lips, stopping at the edge of them so she could draw breath and prepare. He still leant back on his hands, leaving her a way out should she want to take it. She liked that about him. And then he lifted his knees and slid her more snugly into his lap, the smile in his eyes as cheeky as the maneuver.

"You've done this before," she accused.

"You wanted experience."

True. "What else you got?"

"This." His next move was pure, slow-motion beauty as he leaned in and brushed his lips against hers. Nothing but a tease and a torment, not even all that warm. And then his lips were on her again, opening, coaxing, and *now* they were warm, and Ella responded with a gasp and a great big need for more.

He was good at kissing, better than good, and his lips tasted like salted toffee, and his big hand was gentle as he cupped her jaw and took from her whatever the hell he had a mind to take.

A lazy taste. A hint of teeth against the curve of her lip and it was effective. So, *so* effective, and she shifted against him and gave in to the temptation to wrap her arms around his neck and slide a little deeper into the moment.

There was no park. No people who might be watching.

She'd wanted lust, wanted to know the strength of it and what it could do. She never imagined that it could make the world around her disappear.

And then his arm came around her waist and he shifted beneath her until he had her pressed hard against him, positioned just right for—

She was whimpering again. She was an undulating, whimpering woman and her body knew exactly what it wanted to do with him, even if some small fragment of her mind was trying to tell her something else.

"Not here." His voice was gruff and halfway to pleading. "Ella, pull back. Public park. Children."

"What about them? Pregnancy is very unlikely; you're not even naked yet."

"Children *in the park*." His hand slid to her neck, his thumb tracing circles behind one ear, just beneath her woolly hat. He slid it down her back in what was probably meant to be soothing fashion. Instead, she rode the rough pressure of it all the way down to her hip.

And then he tipped her sideways, tipped her onto her back and she was staring up at the sky and then at Sawyer, who'd opted to sit up and reach for the pie she hadn't yet eaten. He held it out toward her.

As if pie could compete with the taste of *him*.

She sat up and took it grudgingly.

He smiled at that. "There are a dozen people watching us. If you were wanting your father to hear about our wild display of public affection, consider it done."

"Oh." She glanced around. They had indeed attracted plenty of attention. "I'm sorry about your reputation. It's probably just been trashed."

"How so?"

"See, I've never been quite so..." Ella searched for the right word. Crazy? Reckless? *Forward?* Yeah, she didn't feel like mentioning any of those. "I've never been quite so *enthusiastic* in my approval of someone before. And you're not from around here. Chances are you'll be seen as a troublemaker, just dying to lead me astray. *Are* you dying to lead me astray?"

"I don't know about the *dying*. That's something I'd rather avoid. Are you going to eat that pie?"

"No." Sawyer's stomach was a bottomless pit, but she didn't hand him her pie. Instead, she held it firmly out of arm's reach, an action which served only to amuse him more. "Are you going to lead me astray?"

"Yes." He smiled sweet and lazy. "I do believe I'm inclined that way."

"Oh, good." Ella smiled back, bright as a daisy, and handed him the pie.

Chapter Four

There was a downside to taking up with Marietta's Ella Grace Emerson, Sawyer discovered, when he arrived for his shift at the saloon three days later. Sawyer had known they were making their date public when they'd had it in the park in full view of anyone with eyes to see. They'd met for coffee the day after that, and this morning Ella had been in Marietta getting parts for something or other so he'd met her at Ginny's Café for an early lunch. Which seemed to suggest to some people that Ella had spent the night with him.

He'd thought he'd be able to handle it, handle her.

He'd been wrong.

He tried to ignore the renewed interest in his good self and his background, but halfway into his shift Mardie was slanting him worried glances and Sawyer was damn glad that Reese wasn't around to watch him grow clipped with the customers and free with his scowl.

The fine folk of Marietta were nosy, he understood that.

They were protective, he understood that too. They wanted to know if he was good enough for their Ella Grace.

And that wasn't a question he wanted to answer.

The picnic had gone well. Sawyer liked Ella Grace Emerson, really liked her. They'd strolled through the park after lunch. He'd kissed her again, standing up this time, in the hope of better control.

Yesterday after lunch he'd ended up pinning her

against a tree, the rough bark digging into his fingers as he slaked his hunger, and hers, because he hadn't been alone in his passion, oh no. Ella Grace had matched him gasp for soaring gasp.

He wanted to know what she was like first thing in the morning. He wanted to see her astride a horse. Tending her cows. He just plain *wanted.*

And then he wondered what it might be like to have Ella at his side on a more permanent basis and that scared him, that thought, because sooner or later his family would find out and his family was seriously dysfunctional, and exposing a woman to that wasn't something he ever wanted to do.

"Hey, Aussie." Mardie didn't corner him until the end of the night when she was counting cash and Sawyer was tallying up the beverages that had gone over the bar. "Want to tell me what's wrong?"

"Nothing's wrong."

"Sawyer, sweetie, you're a little more transparent than you think. You've been brooding half the night. Is it Ella? I heard about lunch."

"Everyone heard about lunch."

"So? Ella got what she wanted. You got what you wanted. Sounds like a fine time was had by all."

Sawyer shrugged. He started measuring the spill in the beer trays into a stainless steel bucket. They'd had a good night when it came to beer sales but there was more spill than usual. "How many new kegs did the boss tap tonight?"

"Three. And he swapped out the new Jimmy's Creek Blonde before it was due, because a couple of our regulars thought it tasted off."

"He tip those drinks down the sink or did they go into the spill?"

"Didn't notice."

Sawyer figured they *had* probably gone into the spill and that the trouble with the Blonde keg would account for the extra.

"Spill volumes make more sense now?" asked Mardie.

"Yeah, we're square."

"I swear, under all that lazy charm you're as thorough as Reese."

"Good to know."

Sawyer hadn't changed his name. No matter where he went, he never did that. If Reese or the bar's owner, Jason Grey, wanted to search for Cameron Sawyer on the Internet and start putting two and two together, the information would be there. Youngest son of international brewery magnate Laurence Sawyer. Youngest son of Catherine Allbright-Sawyer. Brother of Richard Sawyer, the golden child who was brewery heir and rampant psychopath...

Though maybe that last bit wasn't on the Web. Yet.

Yeah, Cameron Sawyer had a heritage and a history all right.

But it wasn't one he wanted to share.

Mardie was still frowning at him and this time he called her on it. "What? I'm good, Mardie. I'm fine."

"You really don't like talking about yourself much, do you? You don't like people getting up in your business."

"Does anyone?"

"Is that what got you so terse with people tonight?"

"Probably." Sawyer met Mardie's gaze square on. "Yes."

Mardie sighed. "You're a nice guy, Sawyer. Mind you, I'm the worst judge of men in the world."

Sawyer felt his lips hitch toward a smile. "Thanks."

"My point *being* that if you have something to hide I'm not going to pry. People are entitled to their secrets. But."

"There's always a *but*."

"*But*, if you ever did happen to fall into a sharing mood, I can personally vouch for Ella as someone who knows how to listen. Someone who can keep her mouth shut and just be there for a person. She did that for me, and we weren't best friends to begin with, if that's what you're thinking. I used to have other friends. Fair-weather friends who didn't even try to stick around when my going got ugly."

"You're not helping. I need to like Ella *less*, not more."

"Oh... well, why didn't you say so? I'm sure I can help you there. Ella's opinionated, she doesn't tolerate fools, she can buy and sell you and chances are she's smarter than you. If she is, she'll let you know."

Sawyer grinned.

Mardie laughed. "It's not working, is it?"

"What do you mean it's not working? I'm daunted. Dismayed."

"Try saying that *without* the goofy grin on your face." Mardie shook her head. "Sawyer, my friend, when it comes to Ella Grace, you are well on your way to gone."

Maybe Mardie's words were meant to be playful, but after they'd finished for the night and left lock-up to the taciturn Jason Grey... after he'd seen Mardie to her car and watched her pull out onto the road... Sawyer headed walked the few blocks to the park again, rather than to his pickup.

So far he'd had three dates with Ella, though you could hardly call a stroll down Bramble Lane and a mug of hot chocolate afterwards a date. A man *couldn't* be thinking of forever after only three dates. It was too soon, way too fast. Not even on the menu. That kind of thinking was crazy in more ways than one.

His breath huffed white and his throat stung with the sub-zero air, and Sawyer hunched down into his jacket and found a bench to sit on, before pulling out his phone and looking up what time it was in Spain. Lunchtime. A good time to call. He took his time thinking about what he might say, and whether it was wise to ring at all, then he found a number and dialed it and waited. He needed to talk to someone who understood the consequences of him introducing a woman to his family. Someone who wasn't family. Preferably a woman who'd been there, done that.

He needed to talk to Zoey.

'Cameron!" She always sounded glad to hear from him, and he adored her for that. He always remembered why he'd fallen for her in the first place when she did that.

"Zoo. How's things?"

"Cameron, how many times do I have to tell you not to call me Zoo?" It was an old tease, and a hauntingly familiar reply, and he felt himself unwind just a bit because of it.

"Maya's six now. And Amalie four. How did that happen? And Manuel has just bought us a summer house in Andalusia. I'm well, Cameron. We're all well. And you?"

Zoey had got married eventually, to a man who adored her. She had two little girls, dark eyed and happy. She had a good life.

He shouldn't have called.

'I'm well, Zoey." He was, wasn't he? "I'm fine."

"Cameron." Zoey had the gentlest scolding voice in the world. Effective though. "I can hear that you're not."

"I met a girl."

Zoey's silence weighed heavily on him. Sawyer stared at the snow clad trees, at the shadows cast in their wake and then at the stars in the sky, and waited while Zoey found her voice.

"You can't lock your heart away forever, my friend," she offered quietly. "You have too much to give. What's she like?"

"She's fearless, Zoey. And I never want to see that taken from her."

More silence.

"He's still there. Doing what he does." His brother. Richard Sawyer, family golden boy. Protected by family money and their father's clout. Above the law. Barely constrained by it. And driven by passion after passion, one of which was to destroy anything and everything his younger brother held dear. Zoey had been in Richard's sights once. Because Cameron had claimed her. Because Richard had wanted her.

And Zoey had paid a hefty price.

"I don't know what to do."

"Have you spoken to your mother about her?"

"No."

"She might be able to gauge things. She might be able to help."

"Did she help you?"

Zoey's silence was telling. "Your mother was blindsided," said Zoey eventually. "As were we all. Don't discount her as an ally though, Cameron. She was very kind to me. And very fond of you."

"Yet she supported Richard's behavior."

"I don't believe she did. Your mother was silenced, like the rest of us. There's a difference."

"I've had a couple of dates with her. Three." Four, if he counted the night they'd first met – which couldn't be counted as a date at all given that he'd been working. "Already I'm trying to figure out how I can make this work."

"I like her already."

"She breeds cows."

"So does Manuel. Bring her to Spain, I want to meet her. She'll be safe here with us, you know that. Richard's reach does not extend here."

"You don't know that for sure." One of the main reasons Zoey was safe now was because Sawyer was no longer in her life. A phone call once a year was one thing. Going to visit her and Manuel was a different level of involvement altogether and one he would never attempt.

"Are you still restructuring the soft drink industry up in Alaska?"

"No, I finished with that six months ago. I'm a bartender in Montana now."

"Cameron," she scolded again. "Bartending? But why?"

"Why not? I like the people. It seemed like a good idea at the time. Did I mention that I bought a house on the Washington coast just south of Seattle? The aim is to live in it more than three weeks a year."

"I like that aim. Maybe you should fill your house with a woman to love and a family to raise. Does she know? Does this woman know who you are?"

"No."

"My friend, that is not a good start."

"I know."

"Your family will always be your family, Cameron, whether you choose to acknowledge them or not."

"I'd rather not."

"I know that. And yet..."

How do I do it, Zoey? How do I keep her off his radar?"

"You don't. You stand your ground and you be prepared for whatever comes your way – both of you. You can't do that if she remains unaware. Tell her who you are. Tell her what you fear. It's her best protection."

But Sawyer didn't want to tell Ella who he was, didn't want to lay that filth before her. His silence said it for him.

"You said she was fearless. Let her be that for you." Zoey's voice had thickened, her accent had become more pronounced. "I wish I could have been that for you. *Te deseo amor*, Cameron. I wish you love. Always."

He closed his eyes. Wished her all the love in the world right back. Just not his. "You too, Zoey. You too."

Chapter Five

Sawyer called Ella from the chocolate shop the following lunch time. He'd been driving himself crazy with indecision all morning. A little more of her wouldn't hurt anyone, he'd think with one breath. Don't be a player, he'd scold himself with the next. And with his third breath he tossed around the notion of telling Ella who he was and the challenges he faced and letting her make her own decision.

She seemed like a woman who might appreciate not having decisions made for her.

"I need a chocolate recommendation," he began. "I ate them out of salted toffee and dark chocolate swirls."

"You want the dark-chocolate-coated ginger strips." It was noisy at her end. Windy. "Trust me, your life will never be the same again."

"What are you doing?"

"Shifting early-calving cows to a more weather-protected part of the ranch. There's more snow forecast."

"Talking to you can be very daunting."

"Does that mean you don't want to come out and see for yourself what goes on around here? Because that was my next move. I was giving you one more day to make *your* next move."

"Good of you."

"I *know*. Have I mentioned that cows with frosted eyelashes are the cutest things ever?"

"You really are a cowgirl, aren't you?"

"Born and bred. Am I tempting you?"

"Are you dusty, dirty and wearing cowboy boots and a plaid shirt?"

"I am neither dusty nor dirty. You're thinking of summer clothes or possibly Australia. Right now my hands are half frozen inside my gloves, my jeans and boots are cold and damp and my waterproof jacket isn't quite living up to its name."

"Are you at least wearing a cowboy hat and sitting astride a horse?"

"I'm sitting astride a snowmobile, greenhorn. But I do have the hat."

Sawyer took a moment to picture her as described. Then he pictured her coming apart in his arms. No telling how many times he'd pictured *that* in the past twenty-four hours. "How'd your father go with our public display of affection in the park?"

"He hasn't mentioned it. But everyone else thinks you're a dreadfully bad influence, so I'm calling it a win. If you head out here mid-afternoon we should be done with the cows, I can make an effort to be more presentable than I am now, and I can take you up into the ranges and we can get stranded in the mountain lodge overnight. Bring the ginger strips."

"And here I was going to suggest dinner and a movie."

"It's a very nice lodge. Open fireplace. Hearth rug. Food in the pantry."

"Here's the thing." He stood in the chocolate shop. Looked up and saw just how many people were listening in and decided to take this conversation outside. "The kind of privacy you're talking about isn't going to make resistance easy. We get up there and get cozy, and you *know* what's likely to happen between us. Yesterday should have made that very clear."

"It did. Am I being too forward?" She didn't wait for his reply. "I am, aren't I? I blame the lust. Come on out to the ranch, Sawyer, and take a look around. I'll take the lodge off the menu. You can put dinner on the menu. I would love to have dinner with you. Very respectable pastime."

"Do you always backtrack quite this rapidly?"

"I'm impulsive, in case you hadn't noticed. Backtracking is part of the deal. It happens every time common sense takes hold." Ella sighed heavily. "I've been sitting here waiting for a cow to get up but I don't think she can. I may have to shift the others and come back to her. What time did I say I was getting in this afternoon?"

"Mid afternoon."

"Better make it later."

"You want a hand?"

"You can tell a lot about people by the way they handle cattle," she mused. "It'll show you the man. Or the woman, as the case may be. I really hope I don't disappoint you. How soon can you get here?"

"Depends where you are."

"I keep forgetting you're not from around here. That was a compliment, by the way." She gave him directions. "Takes about fifteen – twenty minutes to get here from Marietta. Dress warm and bring a change of clothes."

Twenty minutes later, Sawyer was driving his pickup through one of the prettiest valleys he'd ever seen. Bad weather was indeed closing in on them, the sky confirmed it, but it hadn't yet arrived and the landscape sat bathed in that weirdly intense glow that photographers loved.

Ella and her father ran a beautiful operation. One where the fences glowed white, the barns were full of hay, and the ranch house itself sprawled low and loose in the foothills of a vast mountain range. Grazing cows shone glossy black and strongly muscled against the snow and every vehicle on the place was at most only a couple of years old.

Plenty of fat in Emerson's bottom line, from what Sawyer could see.

Plenty of time to figure Ella for a chip off the old block when she came into view around the side of the main barn, for she was dressed for work and her pace was brisk as she pointed to a place to park, up beside a snowmobile that had an accompanying sled loaded with hay.

He got out and reached back across the seat for his gloves and a woolly hat. "Hey."

"Just this minute loaded," she told him with a cheerful grin. "I'm aiming to get out to the cow and back before this weather hits. She's calving, which is much better news for us than her being down for reasons unknown. She's also one of our maiden heifers and she's about three weeks early... that, or she got put in the wrong group... which is why we need to take another look." Ella handed him some goggles and reached for the pair slung over the seat of the snowmobile. "You ever driven one of these things?"

"Yeah. We used them all the time in Alaska."

"What were you doing up there?"

"Restructuring a soft drink company."

Ella turned to look at him. "Who *are* you?"

"Ginger strip?" He was going to tell her. He would. He just needed to find the right time.

He pulled one out of the bag in his pocket and dangled it in front of her, and she took it and thanked him and bit into it with one hand while she straddled the snowmobile and motioned him to get on behind her. She slipped her goggles on and moments later set the machine to moving.

Ella drove with a confidence that came of long experience and a preference for speed that Sawyer enjoyed. She sped them across flat snowy grazing land and then began to climb the foothills. Not once did she let up on the gas.

Sawyer tucked his hat more firmly over his ears. Cold wind peeled across the bare sections of his face. Ella was bearing the brunt of the biting wind and she didn't complain. They crested a ridge and she slowed to a halt and pushed her goggles up but she didn't get off the snowmobile so neither did he. He pushed his goggles up too and stared out over the valley below them.

"The creek forms part of our border," she said and pointed to the thin, snaky line cutting through the valley floor. We're also bordered by the road and the ranges." More pointing ensued. And then she pointed uphill, toward a rough track that climbed steeply. "They run a big snowmobile race across the range every year. It starts here. Occasionally I win it. People say it's because I have the home advantage across some of the course. I prefer to think that I really am just that good."

"I guess that's why you don't seem to mind when the front end of this thing lifts four feet in the air."

"That's just because we're back-heavy at the moment."

It wasn't *just* because of that. "What are you like in powder, and without the sled on the back."

"Sawyer, I am goddamn poetry in motion."

Sawyer grinned at her total lack of modesty. "Please tell me you wear a helmet."

Ella turned and flashed him a killer smile. "I do. We just haven't put them on this time because we're going so *slow.*"

Yeah, not that slow.

"What does your father think about your relationship with speed?"

"He prefers to call it my reckless disregard for safety. That answer your question?"

"Yup."

"My father had me take lessons from a national race champ a few years back – in the interests of improved safety. The extra speed was just one of those happy coincidences. The champ even offered me a place on his race team. Alas, that wasn't all he wanted and unfortunately there was no spark. I'm a little particular about that. Ask anyone."

"How 'bout I take your word for it?"

"Or you could do that." She shifted her goggles back over her eyes and got them moving again, and then turned back toward him. Sawyer immediately wanted her to turn back and watch where she was going. He pointed dead ahead, his arm bracketing hers. "What's that? Halfway up the mountain?"

"That's the lodge. You're really rather big and all-encompassing when you set your mind to it, aren't you?"

"You need more room?"

"No. Warmest I've been all day." She leaned back against him and he tucked his arm beneath hers and wrapped it around her waist. Even with all her layers of winter clothing he could still gather her close with ease.

Long time since he'd offered a woman that kind of closeness and protection.

Long time since he'd done anything but pull away. "I

like your ranch," he rumbled over the whistle of the wind and the noise of the snowmobile. "It's big. It's wildly beautiful. It's well maintained."

"My father's pride and joy," she yelled back.

"Thought that was you?"

"No, I'm third in line – behind the bulls. I just get shown off a little more often than the other two because I can talk."

But Ella didn't do much talking the rest of the trip, and Sawyer was content to save his breath, enjoy the ride and the feel of Ella in his arms, and the sense of purpose that came of heading out to tend an animal that was in Ella's care.

Responsibility and ownership. How long since he'd felt the weight of that particular combination? Oh, he'd go in and take responsibility for a broken business and nine times out of ten he could turn it around, but he never took ownership. Not in the way Ella and her father had taken ownership of this place. Not in the way his own father had agonized over decisions regarding the brewery and probably still did.

They reached Ella's stranded cow a good fifteen minutes later. The cow was lying on her side, all stretched out, and Ella stifled a curse and was off the snowmobile, sinking into the snow and cursing before stomping her way to the sled and cutting the string on the bale of hay moments later.

"She won't want to eat but if you put some by her head, I'll do the back end and see if I can figure out where she's at with delivering." Ella gathered up an armful of hay, so Sawyer did the same. The cow mooed at him and tried to sit up as he tromped toward her. He tromped a little more gently so as not to frighten her more.

"Hey, girl," he murmured as she craned her neck to see what Ella was doing.

Ella, who was spreading hay out over the snow and moving in close to examine the cow's rear end and then cursing up a storm – to be specific.

"We have feet," she said when he joined her. "Hind feet instead of front feet. The calf is breech. Which does explain why mama cow is taking her time."

"What do we do?"

"Pull."

Ella stripped off her gloves and started taking off her coat. Then she took off the plaid shirt he'd teased her about on the phone, leaving just a short sleeved T-shirt and hopefully some kind of thermal wear under that. The shirt went over the seat of the snowmobile, the coat went on the ground on top of the hay and then Ella knelt on the coat and, without further comment, slid her hand over the feet of the calf and into the cow.

Her whole hand.

Then up to her elbow.

Then more until she was almost in up to her armpit.

"I hope you're not squeamish," she offered with a grimace, as she blew a strand of wayward dark hair out of her face. She followed her words with a quick gasp of pain as the cow's stomach rippled and the cow out-and-out groaned. "It's mighty squeezy in here when they start contracting."

"Uh huh." That was pretty much all he had by way of comment. Long time since he'd been lost for words.

Then again, he'd never before seen anyone use a cow as a hand puppet.

"The good news is that the calf's not that big and the front legs and head are where they need to be. Heart's still beating. You just need a bit of help, don't you, baby?"

Ella withdrew her arm slowly, to the accompaniment of more contractions. She rubbed at her wrist and took a deep breath, let it out, and reached for the two little sticking-out feet. And then she braced *her* feet against the rump of the cow, waited for the next ripple of the animal's belly and pulled, using her entire body as leverage. She gained an inch or so of back legs.

And the minute the contractions stopped, they slipped back to where they'd been before.

"Okay, then." Ella slid him an assessing glance. "So. We have a couple of options. Want to get your gloves off and join me? I'll direct, you pull, and come the next set of contractions I think we might be in business."

He took his gloves off. Took his coat off too and draped it around Ella's shoulders. "I know you said you wanted to get down and dirty with me, but this wasn't quite what I had in mind."

"It's not exactly my first preference either, but at least I get to see those muscles of yours at work. There's a bonus right there." She made room for him and he settled down beside her on the coat atop the hay and then the snow. She put her hands on his, and they were cold and sure and ever so slightly sticky as she guided them toward the legs of the calf. "You want to get a good grip just above the hock, and instead of pulling up toward the tail, we want to pull out and down a little as the pelvis appears. Don't pull until she's pushing. Try and work with the cow."

"Got it." He had two warm and slimy little hocks in his hand and a woman at his side that he wanted more than ever. He was hopelessly out of his depth. "Work with the cow. I've never worked with a cow in my life. What does that even mean?"

Ella grinned and snugged in alongside him, sharing her warmth and part of the coat. She'd bracketed his waist with her thighs, her legs tucked up under her as she leaned in against his shoulder and set the palm of her hand between his shoulder blades. "Just have a little tug. Test the resistance. Get a feel for it."

"Have a little tug, she says. It's like my favorite fantasy ever. Minus the cow." And the hay. And the cold and the storm front coming in. And the life or death situation.

Ella ran her other hand down his forearm and rested her fingers around his. "I love this stuff. Makes me feel useful. Okay, here we go. You need to pull hard and smooth, and don't stop until I say so. 'Cause she's getting ready to push."

Push the cow did, and Sawyer took a deep breath, took a firm grip and pulled.

And then pulled that little bit harder.

"Steady," Ella murmured. "Nice and even, just a little bit more. Out and down. Yes, just like that." And then the cow kicked and shifted, and then the calf's back legs were out and then the pelvis and then the rest. One slimy, limp little calf, and Ella was moving forward, putting the palm of her hand to the baby's chest, just behind its front leg, and then that hand was moving again, pulling mucous away from the mouth and stripping it from its nose and then the calf was moving, and coughing and Ella was calling it a good girl and moving away, cleaning her hands and arm with snow, and then the hay, and then finally wiping her hands on her jeans before reaching for her shirt. "I *will* shower before dinner. I promise."

Sawyer laughed as he got to his feet in order to avoid being trampled by one very eager mama cow who was up and turning toward her calf. Moments later she was nosing and nudging and licking its little face. "What now?"

Now we wait for the calf to get to its feet and have a drink. Ella glanced at the sky, her eyes narrowing. "And then I think we might help dry the calf off and put it on the sled, and get them to shelter with the others. The cow will follow."

Ella picked up her coat and shook it out, put it on and shoved her hands into the pockets. "Brrr. Bit chilly out."

"And you do this how often?" he asked politely.

"Not that often." She looked bright eyed, rosy cheeked and utterly content. "You did well, bartender."

"What would you have done if I hadn't been here?"

"Used the calf pullers strapped to the sled. But a hand-pull has more finesse, and besides, I wanted to see what you could do. You've a strong and steady way about you, Sawyer, underneath all that charm. You made it look easy and I know for a fact that it's not. Gonna make a cowboy out of you yet."

"Let's not get carried away."

"You don't want to be a cowboy?"

"Put it this way... did you ever dress up as a kid?"

Ella nodded. "Annie Oakley, sharpshooter."

"I was the fireman."

Chapter Six

It had turned five by the time they'd got cow and calf settled with the others, all of them protected from the worst of the incoming storm by a stand of trees and a horseshoe shaped hill. It was the most protected corner of the ranch when the weather was coming in from the south east and was a godsend when it came to winter calving.

Sawyer had followed her lead, easy as you please, when it had come to getting the calf onto the sled. He'd held the calf in place, with Ella driving and the anxious mother cow bringing up the rear. Not too fast and not too slow, with one eye on the encroaching weather and the other eye on all concerned. They unloaded the calf and the rest of the hay once they reached their destination, and Ella waited until cow and calf had settled before bumping shoulders with Sawyer to get his attention. "Now we can go."

He nodded, and she took him the fast way back to the barn, stopping only for Sawyer to open and close gates along the way. Driver drove, passenger got the gates. It was a time honored tradition – ask anyone on the land. And still...

"Am I bossy?" she asked once they were back at the barn and she'd parked the snowmobile and sled up against the western wall, just shy of the big double doors that now stood closed. Fat flakes of snow drifted down on them, not a blizzard yet, but not far off. Sawyer's pickup would get them the house with this amount of snow on the ground, no problem. Hard to say whether it'd get them to Marietta tonight though. "Did you find me bossy out there?"

Sawyer glanced her way, his gaze disconcertingly direct. "If you're talking about telling me how to pull a calf, I needed direction and you gave it. Doesn't make you bossy. It makes you strategically resourceful and me grateful."

"Strategically resourceful," she grumbled, even as his words filled her with pleasure.

"It's a compliment. Confident, capable, strategically resourceful women are incredibly hot."

"Even ones who've just had their hand up a cow?"

"It was more like your entire arm."

"Yeah." Ella sighed. "Really not the image I was hoping to present."

"Ella."

They'd reached the passenger side door of his truck. Next second he'd opened it for her, reached for her hat and tossed it inside. He smiled down at her with those crinkly eyes and the dimples and Ella couldn't help but smile back. It was a tentative smile though, maybe even anxious. She knew who she was, good traits and bad, and sometimes she wished for more subtlety and finesse, and sometimes she wished that her mother had lived long enough to teach her how to be less of a cowhand and more of a lady.

She *had* wanted Sawyer to see who she was and the world that she loved.

She'd also been hoping to break him in a little more gently.

"That memory of you with the cow is going into the memory bank alongside the one of you presiding over Grey's Saloon." He tugged his gloves off and tossed them in the truck too. "And the one of you sitting in the snow making sandwiches, and the one of you getting altogether lost in a kiss. And now I have one of you with snowflakes in your hair. It's a collage, this picture I'm building of you." He kissed her, sweet and fleeting, and then he set his lips to the spot on her cheek where a snowflake had just landed and Ella felt like melting right along with it. "And it's amazing."

"I bet you say that to all the girls." How could a few muttered words and a whisper of a kiss make her feel this gooey inside?

"No." He pulled away, his smile crooked and his eyes troubled. "I don't."

They reached the house and Ella took him through the side entrance, straight into the mudroom where they shed their coats and boots and hats and anything else that was wet. Sure, he was a visitor, but he'd also been a cowhand for the afternoon and hopefully they were past standing on ceremony with each other. From there she took him through the huge galley kitchen, with its bank of east facing windows and from there she showed him through to the adjacent wash room; the one with the super pressure and the oversized shower head. She gave him towels and fresh soap. She may even have sighed wistfully as she'd watched him close the bathroom door behind him.

"I'm going up to another shower," she said, loud enough so that he could hear. "Help yourself to tea, coffee or whatever else you want when you come out."

"Okay."

Ella went to her room and set her own shower to scalding and then she got in and scrubbed everywhere, twice, before declaring herself squeaky clean and starting in on her after shower care. Lotion. Comb. Teeth. Towel wrapped around her while she stood in her walk-in-closet and wondered what to wear for a night out at a restaurant or a night snowed in here, the latter seeming more likely by the minute given the way the snow was coming down outside.

She stood there for a full five minutes, undecided, before stalking back out to her dresser and picking up her phone. Hopefully Sawyer had his phone on him too.

He picked up on the second ring. Guess that was a yes.

"I'm still in the bedroom, trying to decide what to wear," she told him without preamble. "And I usually don't much care what I wear. It's very odd, this desire to please you. Do you think it has something to do with the lust?"

"Everything to do with the lust," he told her dryly. "You

want to hope that the level of lust fades as you get to know me better, otherwise you're going to want to please me *all the time*."

"I can see how that would get tedious, but back to the now. What shall I wear?"

"You're really task oriented, aren't you?"

"I think it's a family trait. I'm also standing here in a towel and it's getting chilly. At this point, clothes would be good."

Silence.

"Sawyer?"

"I'm trying to decide if you're torturing me deliberately."

"Rest assured, that is my intention."

"Wear whatever's comfortable, Ella." There was a smile in his voice. "Rest assured you're going to torture me anyway."

Ella grinned as she went back to her wardrobe. She narrowed her eyes and gnawed on her lower lip before finally reaching for her favorite pair of jeans. They were low slung, soft to the touch and perfectly comfortable.

Bonus points for being blue.

She had a yellow top in there somewhere, with three-quarter sleeves and a pretty sweetheart neckline. Team it with a burgundy, hot-pink and grey plaid shirt and she still looked country but not staggeringly so. Add a ring for her forefinger – a wide white-gold one – and a yellow band for her hair and she figured she looked ready for just about anything, which she was, and relaxed, which she most definitely was not.

How many times had she shown visitors around the house? Too many to count.

How many times had she fretted about what to wear while doing so?

Never ever before.

Cameron Sawyer was a bad influence. And that was before she factored in all the naughty things she wanted to do with him.

Ella found him in the kitchen, looking freshly washed and smelling of pine and lime soap. A tall glass of water sat beside an almost empty bag of Sage's ginger strips. He'd made himself at home, but not overly so and she liked his restraint, his awareness of borders.

"I made the mistake of opening them before I left Marietta, and then eating them all the way here," he said, pushing the chocolates toward her in silent invitation.

"We've all made that mistake." She took *one*, and vowed to resist the rest. "You want a tour of the house? People usually do. The architect was a Norwegian who settled here as a young man. He had a thing about honoring the landscape and the materials it provided. Revolutionary back then."

"A tour would be fine."

"And then we should probably decide what we're going to do this evening." Not that she was being directive. Or bossy. Or anything.

Much.

Ella swung into tour guide mode, leading Sawyer through the house to the front door. The tour started on the wide entry porch that had been built to look imposing and to complement the landscape and the stunning mountain views that the house commanded. She showed him the reception room with its rough-hewn wooden furniture and exposed wooden beams. She drew him through into the lounge for more exposed beams and a bank of floor-to-ceiling windows. She took him into her father's study where her mother's portrait hung, for no other reason than that she wanted her mother to get a good look at this man with his wide shoulders and dimpled smile, this man who Ella was in lust with.

Sawyer studied the portrait openly before looking back at her with a question in his eyes.

"Cameron Sawyer meet Caroline Grace Emerson. My mother."

He didn't comment that her mother was very beautiful, which she was, or that Ella favored her in looks, which she did. He didn't talk about the diamonds and sapphires at her mother's throat and in her ears.

"She looks happy," he murmured.

"I think she was. She and my father were so very much

in love. At least, that's how I remember them. What about your parents, Sawyer? Are they still in love?"

"I don't know." Sawyer smiled faintly. "They seem well suited. Compatible."

"Is your mother happy?"

Again he hesitated. "My mother's very reserved. Hard to know what she's thinking or feeling."

"How long since you've seen her?"

"Three years, maybe four."

"You should try and see her more often."

"Now you're being bossy."

"Guess I am. Still, she is your mother. Maybe you should think of her as an underutilized strategic resource."

"Yeah, no. Pretty sure that's not going to work either. How about I say that I hope she's happy and leave it at that?"

"We're really quite different when it comes to family, aren't we?"

"You noticed."

Hard not to, thought Sawyer grimly, and hot on *that* thought came the notion that now would be a good time to tell Ella what he needed to tell her about his family. He looked to the window, at the snow now falling thick and fast. Ella followed his gaze and frowned.

"What are your thoughts on eating in and staying overnight?" she asked. "Because I have a sneaking suspicion that unless we leave now we're probably not going to get out. And even if we do get out, I'll probably not get back in tonight. Or you could go and I could stay," she added belatedly.

"Where's your father?"

"He went to Livingstone with a load of hay. He'll either be back soon or he'll stay put for the night."

Sawyer frowned. He'd been perfectly willing to annoy Ella's father, what with his continued interest in Ella and the kissing in the park, but this was a whole new level of inappropriate behavior.

"We won't be completely alone," she offered next. "Carl and Jem live in the bunkhouse by the barn and there's a rope line between them and the barn and the house. It's under snow, but it'll pull up if anyone needs to get about in a whiteout."

Better, but only slightly.

"I'm really sorry to put you in such an awkward position."

"You keep worrying about my reputation. Do you ever worry about yours?"

"Er... mine's pretty sound," she offered lamely.

"You barely know me." That was the crux of it. "You don't know who you're getting mixed up with, Ella."

"Reese employed you."

"*He* barely knows me."

"Mardie trusts you."

"Are you really going to trust Mardie's instincts when it comes to men?"

"Ray gave you a room."

"In a truck stop bunkhouse." He glanced outside again. "Will that calf be okay out there in that?"

"Ha!" she said. "You can't imply that you're bad news with one breath and ask about the welfare of the calf in the next. That's not how it works."

"Could be a ruse."

"Could be, but I trust my instincts. The cow and calf will be fine. They're in a well sheltered pocket – that's why it was so important to get them there this afternoon. As for us staying here tonight—" Ella shrugged. "Whether my father returns or not, I figure we'll be fine too."

"Where do you get your certainty from, Ella?"

"No one ever showed me how to be any different." She glanced up at her mother's portrait and then quickly looked away. "It's a turn-off, isn't it?"

"No."

This time her glance was for him and it was a startled one. For all her bravado and strength, Ella Grace Emerson had some vulnerabilities too.

"No, it's not a turn-off. Don't ever change."

"Oh. So."

"Couple of things I need to tell you about, Ella. About me. About my family. Before we settle in for the night."

"Good things?"

"No."

"Yeah, didn't think so. Do we need wine? I think we need wine. And a fire in the living room and a casserole in the oven." And then the phone on her father's desk phone began to ring. Ella reached out and picked up.

Her father, unless Sawyer had missed his guess.

He listened as Ella told her father that she'd shifted the pregnant cows to the shelter of the foothills and that there was a calf on the ground already. She told him that, yes, Carl and Jem had shifted the rest of the stock to more sheltered locations. She told him she'd see him in the morning.

"You didn't tell him I was here," Sawyer said when she hung up.

"Wouldn't want to worry him unnecessarily."

"Ella." There was a warning in there somewhere.

"You need to let people make their own mistakes," she told him firmly. "Living room fire, do you think?"

Maybe he did need to let people make their own mistakes.

Ella shot him a quick smile and headed for the kitchen. Sawyer headed for the living room and lit the fire. Five minutes later he found her standing in front of the wine rack in the kitchen, looking thoroughly undecided.

"This is getting ridiculous," she said. "There's more wine in the cellar, but if I go down there I could take hours. First I'm wardrobe challenged and now the wine."

"Maybe you're simply tired and in need of a little rest and relaxation." Maybe he should leave his confessions for another time.

Yeah, no.

He reached around her, pulled a Shiraz cabernet from the rack and tucked it in her hand. "This one. Not too old, not too new, good body and smooth as silk going down."

"Thank you, bartender. I appreciate it."

He opened the bottle and poured into the two large wine glasses sitting on the bench beside a still frozen loaf of crusty bread.

"Beef casserole's in the oven."

"Great. It'll go with the wine."

They returned to the living room. Ella lit the candelabra - one set on either side of that enormous window, another set on a side table beside the doorway through to the hall.

"In case of a power outage?" he asked as he sat on the bank of lounge chairs that ran the length of the room. Enough room for eight people to sit comfortably. As for seating two...

"Not really in case of power outage." Ella settled in beside him, wine glass I hand. "We've a generator and plenty of flashlights. A lot of the time we light the candles because people like the atmosphere."

"Of yesteryear?"

"Yeah."

"Feels like church."

Another quick grin split her firelit face. "Cozy confessional. You wanted to tell me something but we were interrupted and waylaid."

Sawyer hesitated.

"Or we could just talk about regular things. Like how long you plan to stay in Marietta?"

An easy question.

Until he factored in her.

"I have another three week's work at the saloon before Reese's regular bartender returns."

"You're better at bartending than Josh is."

"I don't want his job."

She gave him a measured look. "Where will you go after that?"

"Washington State." And at her enquiring look, "I have a house there."

"You have a house?"

"Bought and paid for. I've lived there exactly three weeks out of the past fifty-two. It's not really working out."

"Why not?"

"I thought I wanted it. But." There was always a *but.* "It's a little out of the way. It sits on a cliff overlooking the Pacific, just outside a sleepy little seaside town."

"I guess *parts* of that equation might fit with what I know of you," she offered dubiously. "I'm liking the view I've got going in my imagination."

"It does have good views. Nothing quite as spectacular as your views, but the ocean has its own charm."

"Do you surf and swim?"

"Yes."

"It's starting to make a little more sense."

"There's a really good wood-fired-oven pizza place in the town," he offered. "Little hole in the wall operation. In the mornings they do six different types of bagels."

"Now you're talking."

They lapsed into silence.

Now, he thought. Tell her now.

But he sipped at his wine and stared into the fire instead.

"What kind of work will you do there?" she finally said.

"The lower floor is set up as a business hub, with a formal meeting room, high-speed communications, records room, and plenty of workspace. The idea was – is – to use it as a base and get more strategic when it comes to the company restructuring jobs I take. Get in, get out, finish up the work from home. Although that has its drawbacks too."

"Sawyer, you mystify me. You're comfortably situated with a home and well-paid work that you seem to be able to take or leave at whim. Forgive me for being wildly impolite, but are you rich?"

"It's all relative, don't you think?"

"Yeah, no."

"I come from an extremely wealthy background but I started again from scratch. I'm not even in the same league as the rest of my family, but I'm certainly not destitute by any means."

"So you *are* rich."

"Yes."

"So why on earth are you working at Grey's and living in a bunkhouse?"

"Nobody gets that, do they?"

Ella shook her head.

"I like working at the saloon. Coming into a new place and figuring out what makes everyone tick and how they fit together. I like finding out what's important to people and what's not. It helps me do my other job – the one where I look at revenues and deals and then start ripping up management plans. Spread a business out on paper and it's all too easy to forget that we're playing with people's lives."

Now it was Ella's turn to look at the fire.

"What do you do when people fall for you, Sawyer? Either as a bartender or in your corporate magician incarnation? You're rich. You're smart. You're absolutely gorgeous and of marriageable age. Why aren't you hooked up?"

There. Right there was the opening he needed. And he knew damn well that Ella had given it to him deliberately. "Confession time, huh?"

"Your call."

It was time. Past time. "There was a girl. My girl."

Ella sipped at her wine and listened.

"Zoey was twenty-one, I was twenty-four and we were living together. I'd asked her to marry me."

"And she said no and broke your heart?"

"She said yes and made me very happy."

"Hnh," said Ella. "So much for that theory."

"Problem was, my brother wanted her too, and at the engagement party he stood up and told everyone that she was carrying his child and that she needed to marry him and not me. It was a complete lie. I knew it. Zoey knew it. My mother suspected it. But."

"But?"

"You don't know my brother. He had a lot of power, even back then. A lot of people positioned inside his web. He was very convincing."

"I hate him already."

Sawyer smiled wryly. "Zoey and I went ahead with our engagement, regardless. Richard didn't get what he wanted that night, but the damage it did to Zoey's reputation was irreversible. The gossip mongers attacked her."

"Tell me she stuck it out."

"Would you have?"

"Yes."

"For a month, she did. Zoey's no weakling. But it was a month during which my brother pursued her relentlessly; never mind that she wanted nothing to do with him; never mind that Zoey lived with me. He'd corner her on her way to work and on the way home, and when I started taking her to work and picking her up he'd get to her *at* work. He was at every social function we went to and he was obnoxious. And then..." Sawyer cleared his throat. "Then he tried to rape her. To make the statement he'd made at our engagement party true."

"Oh."

There was a world of sick horror in Ella's quiet exclamation. And Sawyer let it sit there.

"Anyway, that was the end of it for Zoey. She'd had enough. She was living in fear. I wanted her to press charges, but she broke the engagement and took off back to her family in Spain instead. In the end she did it with my blessing. Zoey's fine now. She's safe. She's married and very much in love with her husband, who adores her."

"Didn't your brother follow her?"

"No. As soon as Zoey broke our engagement Richard lost interest in her. But he hadn't quite finished with me. We were working in the family business, him in management, me in marketing – mainly because we were better off working apart. I'd had some success marketing one particular product we'd developed. A mixer – alcohol lite. It did good things for our bottom line. My father liked that and praised me for it. Richard and I had grown up with him getting all the praise and me getting none, so it was a big thing. A big change."

"Why did your father never praise you?"

"I think maybe he wanted to at times, but there was always Richard and the fear of what might set him off. Even as a kid he was uncontrollable." Especially as a kid.

He took a breath, let it out. "My brother framed me for embezzlement and presented the evidence to my father. My father didn't want to believe him, but he couldn't get his head around the notion that Richard had framed me either. He couldn't believe that anyone could carry that much hate. Easier to believe that I got stupid and greedy."

"Your father is a very foolish man."

"You *are* black and white, aren't you?"

"He should have dug to the bottom of it. The lies, the attempted rape... all of it. And *you*... maybe you should have stayed and fought for your rights and for your place within family."

But Sawyer just shook his head. "It was tearing my family apart."

"So you just up and left?"

You don't sound impressed.

"Jesus, Sawyer." She reached for a fat cushion and smacked him with it. It wasn't particularly soft. "You let him *win.*"

"I have a good life."

"Without *family.* Though by the sound of it they weren't worth much anyway. How could they stand by and watch that happen, Sawyer? How?"

"There's big business involved. Someone had to take the fall for the embezzlement."

"How about *nailing the person who did it*?"

"My father made his choice."

"Your father's a moron."

Yep. Definitely black and white. Not that he didn't enjoy Ella's indignation and her fire on his behalf, because, well...

Maybe he had an ever-so-mild craving for fierce, blind trust.

"Is that it?" she wanted to know. "Any more skeletons?"

"No, I think we're done."

"Oh, we are anything but done." Ella set down her wineglass on the little side table. She took Sawyer's and set it there too, and then she was sliding into his lap, all warm and fragrant woman. "We've barely begun, and you don't scare me, Cameron Sawyer. You and your screwed up family."

"You're something else, you know that, don't you?"

"Do you like it? Do you like what I am?"

"Yes."

"Then let's get back to where we were at the park, shall we? You were showing me a few things about lust."

She'd just shown him a few things about loyalty and acceptance and there was every chance that she'd break him, regardless of relative size, but he summoned a smile and tried to get with the plan. But not before one last word of warning.

"He's still out there, Ella. My brother and his world of hate."

"I hear you. And now I want to touch you." She followed her words with the brush of her fingers across his shoulders. "Fill up on you." A kiss for the edge of his lips and then another, more centered and a moist lick of tongue. "Learn what makes you tremble and what makes you blush. We good?"

"Yeah." It was just lust, this trembling in his hands as he reached for her. Base need, not reverence, as he buried his hands in her silky dark hair and returned her kiss. "We're good."

"What would you take from me, Sawyer, if your brother wasn't hovering in the shadows? Would you want love as well as the lust? Would you be freer with your own heart?"

"Probably." She stole a kiss and then another. "Yes."

"Would you claim a home for yourself? Would you settle?"

"I might." She scraped her teeth along his jaw and reached for the buttons on his shirt. "Yes."

"You do know that I'm taking everything you say with a grain of salt, given that I'm seducing you while you're saying it?"

"Good idea," he managed hoarsely, for the pad of her thumb had just stroked over one of his nipples.

"Last question, I promise," she whispered, and he groaned, because her hands had found his belt buckle and both body and brain heartily approved. "Have you ever thought of starting your own family? Have you ever dreamed of babies to love and a woman who'd fight for you and love you and stand by your side, no matter what?"

"No." While the candles flickered with revelation and his heart broke wide open. "Yes."

Chapter Seven

Ella knew where she wanted him. Stretched out naked on the rug in front of the fire, with cushions and blankets all around him and his body a study of shadow and light. It had been a good look for him in her imagination. Enough to make her all flustered and needy.

The reality was even better.

"Let me," she murmured, as she put her hand to his chest and encouraged him to ease back against the pile of cushions. "Can I?" she pleaded, as she drew his arms above his head and circled his wrists with his fingers and then dragged her nails back down his arms, skirting the outside of his armpits and then on to the muscles along the outer edges of his torso. Lines that ran in to his waist and then down over the cut of his hips and the silky skin of his inner thighs, and, oh, the noises he made. The ragged, jagged breath. "You're so beautiful," she whispered.

"That's my line."

Ella leaned over him, hands to either side of him now, and ghosted her breath across one of his nipples and watched it pebble tight. "I want another line." She used the tip of her tongue to wet it, tease it, and finally to suck it into her mouth before releasing it with a pop. "A better line."

"Take your clothes off."

Sawyer had undressed women before, if his expertise in that area was anything to go by. And then he rolled her on her stomach, brushed her hair to one side of her neck and put his lips there and lit her up completely.

"Lust," he said in a voice that promised heaven. "Needs to be built."

And then he trailed his lips down her back, finding all the best places. Spots that made her gasp and squirm and heat up and grow moist. He lifted her up as her knees shifted into place beneath her and his big hands kneaded her buttocks, exposing her, playing her to perfection as he slid one hand lower until his thumb found the exact right spot and circled it.

She pressed into the touch, eager for more. She'd become a wanton whimpering woman and she loved it. "Sawyer?" He added a blunt knuckle to the mix, giving her something to grind down on and, oh, sweet mercy, she needed it, needed more.

So this was lust. Blind, mind-altering desire because why else would she be moistening her lips and spiraling beneath his touch, no intercourse required.

"Not yet, not yet, not yet," she whimpered.

"You can go again," he murmured, and then he was shifting around, his lips trailing over her buttocks before joining his fingers, gliding a path straight to her clitoris and taking over from his thumb. She screamed out, no inhibitions left, as hands and tongue brought her to soaring, trembling completion.

He let her topple sideways after that, onto blankets and pillows as he settled down on his back beside her, farthest from the fire, smug as a well fed wolf.

Ella felt her own lips tug into a smile at his obvious state of readiness. She'd get to that soon, just as soon as her sated body started moving again and her lungs had enough air. "Be right with you."

"Relax." He eased back onto one elbow and curled around her, his knees tucked in under her buttocks. "I'm not going anywhere."

Not tonight, at any rate. She took his hand and threaded his fingers through her own. She let her eyes grow slumberous as she memorized every curve and plane of his body. And then slowly, deliberately, she slid her hand over the outside of his, raised it to her lips and licked a long stripe across the center of his palm. "Show me," she said, and wrapped his hand and hers around his erection.

The effect on Sawyer was instantaneous. His eyes closed, he bit his lip and a ripple ran straight through him. She'd never seen a more responsive man. "Kink?"

"Big one." As he set up a slow stroking rhythm, his grip firm and his body pushing into it. Ella looked, debated, and then set about adding the swipe of her thumb to the head on the upstroke. And then, well, maybe she had to leave him to it while she brought her hand back to her lips and tasted.

The sounds he made were another feast for her senses. "I think we might need condoms now," she murmured. "Please tell me you have some."

He rolled back and reached for his jeans, and she let him coat up before sliding into place on top of him, wriggling until she felt the press of him against her and then dipping inside. She shifted slightly at the insistent pressure, for he was proportional everywhere and no one could ever accuse him of being a slight man.

"Easy," he murmured, stilling beneath her and running a gentle hand down her side, but Ella didn't want easy, she wanted *him*. Now. And inch by all-encompassing inch she made it so.

Ella had never felt so full, every sense engaged, drilling into her, he was all around her. She'd never had her senses be so completely engaged. And then she put her hands to his hips and lifted all the way up and then slid back down, reveling in the friction and the drag, a drag Sawyer facilitated by splaying one hand low over her stomach and pressing down on her clitoris with his thumb.

"You're right." She closed her eyes and bit down on her lip to stop the helpless noises from escaping. "I *can* go again."

And then Sawyer began to move and Ella surrendered herself to him completely.

Lust.

Lost.

Love.

By the time they were done, Ella had felt them all.

"Middle name?" Ella asked as they ate dinner in front of the fire some time later. She was dressed, sort of, in that she had her underwear on. Sawyer had opted for jeans, no shirt, and she wasn't complaining.

"Franklin."

"Seriously?"

"Ask my mother. I have no idea why."

"Favorite movie?"

"It's got hobbits in it."

"Best friend?"

Sawyer hesitated. "Zoey Alvarez."

Spanish surname. *My* woman, he'd called her. *The* woman. The one who'd been driven away. Ella didn't like the twinge of jealousy that went through her but it was there. "Are you still in love with her?"

"No."

"Sure?"

"Very sure." He held her gaze with a steady one of his own.

Okay, then. Maybe she really did need to let go of that jealousy. Sawyer and Zoey had shared good times and bad times. The worst times. The bond between them might not be love anymore but it was always going to be strong. "Okay, I can work with that. Favorite type of music?"

"New Orleans Jazz. Sometimes Bluegrass. Yours?"

"Country," she told him. "And then Western."

He grinned at her. "We're going to have to fix that."

"Greenhorn, you can try."

Ella didn't quite know how this led to them ending up in bed again, her bed this time.

But it did.

Chapter Eight

Morning-afters were problematic, decided Sawyer, as Samuel T. Emerson stepped through into the kitchen from the side door and stopped dead.

It was half ten and the roads were supposedly still under a foot and a half of snow, although perhaps not anymore, given that Ella's father was definitely, undeniably here. Sawyer was here too, smelling of sex and this man's daughter, and he was pretty sure he had a bite mark on his stomach, just above the cut of his hip.

And another one on his shoulder.

Ella was in the shower.

Ella had woken him at dawn to listen to the weather report, because apparently cowgirls did that, and then she'd burrowed back down into the bed clothes hooked an arm over his chest and slid straight back to sleep. Sawyer had gathered her closer, buried his face in her hair and done the same.

They'd woken again not ten minutes ago. Sawyer had come down for coffee and a shower of his own, and, yep, Samuel T. Emerson was still standing there.

Eyes narrowed.

"I see you got the position," Samuel said.

"Kind of not thinking about it in quite those terms, Samuel," he offered quietly.

"What kind of terms *are* you considering?"

Good question. Sawyer ran a hand though his hair, not

entirely sure it would do in lieu of a comb. Samuel's gaze fixed on a spot of skin just under his arm, a place Ella had really liked, Sawyer looked down and hastily lowered his arm because... more marks.

Awkward.

"You want to go and put a shirt on, son?"

And then Ella barreled in, dressed, thank God, took in the scene and smile brightly.

"I *thought* I heard someone pull up," Ella said casually. "Did you get a look at the group two steers on the way?"

"They're fine," her father replied dryly. "Aren't you going to introduce me to your friend?"

"Haven't you already met?"

"Ella," her father said, and the one word warning was enough to set her back some. Not so confident now as she backed up and began the introduction.

"Cameron Sawyer, this is my father, Samuel T. Emerson. Daddy, this is Cameron. Cameron kept me company last night."

Her father's eyebrows rose. Ella held his gaze with a steady one of her own. "Is now a good time to tell you that if I have my way he'll be doing it again?"

Sawyer would have probably chosen a different time, but that was just him.

"How about you get an old man a coffee, Ella, while I think on it?" her father said gruffly, before turning a carefully neutral gaze on Sawyer. "What do you think of the place?"

"It's beautiful."

"Impressive?"

"That too."

"Best valley on God's green earth. Where are you from, Cameron?"

"Sydney. Noosa. Copper Creek. Brisbane."

"And Washington state," said Ella, moving in and reaching around him for the jar of coffee grounds.

"Not exactly a stable existence."

"No."

"Glad to see we're all getting along," said Ella. "But I think I might have left something in the living room, so..."

She glanced up at Sawyer. "I just have to go and do a couple of things. In the living room."

Most of their clothes were still scattered across the living room. The wine was heaven knew where. Good idea for someone to get to them before her father did. And Ella was the only one who knew where all the rugs and cushions went.

Well, except for her father. Sawyer gave her an almost imperceptible nod.

"Grab his shirt while you're there," said her father.

Guess no one had ever accused Samuel T. of being slow.

"Go," Sawyer nudged her with his shoulder as Ella's cheeks went bright red. "Your father and I can stay here and bond."

"Is that likely?" she murmured.

"Notice that I'm willing to try."

Ella shot her father a quick glance, and then stood on tiptoe and kissed Sawyer's cheek. "Thank you." Her smile could have gotten him to do just about anything.

He was so screwed.

Ella left. Her father stayed and took a seat at the kitchen bench. Still awkward. "How do you take your coffee, Samuel?"

Strong and black, with one."

Sawyer made the coffee in silence and sat it down in front of the other man. He was used to serving others. He saw no slight in it. If he were in Samuel T's shoes he'd want a coffee too.

The older man left the coffee on the bench and ran his hand across his mouth instead. "Wish my wife was here," he offered at last. "Twenty years she's been gone and I still miss her every damn day."

Sawyer hadn't tended bar on and off for years without learning a thing or two about encouraging another person to share. "Ella showed me her portrait."

"That wasn't her. It's too serene. Caroline could walk into a room and set my world on fire."

That'd be right, thought Sawyer. It was hereditary. "Mr. Emerson, I'm not about to tell you that this isn't what it looks like. It's exactly what it looks like. As for where it's going I can't say, because I don't know. But I won't hurt your daughter. I'll put myself on the line before I do that."

Samuel T. reached for his coffee. "Maybe that's all a father can ask."

Sawyer never meant for him and Ella to become inseparable, but one week passed and then another, and not a day had gone by without talking to her on the phone or seeing her at the saloon or in the mornings before he started work. By mid-morning Ella had usually already put in half a day's work at the ranch and had no hesitation when it came to sauntering into the truck yard and hammering on his door. Her father didn't think it was a good look for her.

Sawyer agreed.

Not that Ella had taken the slightest notice of either of them. Short of buying or renting a house in Marietta, there was nothing to do but start getting up and into town earlier and texting Ella his whereabouts before mid-morning, or if she was short a hand, heading on out to the ranch. She was still trying to make a cowboy out of him. He was still telling her it was never going to happen, but the truth was he enjoyed the physicality of it and he *loved* seeing Ella in her element.

He had a midday start at the saloon today but he was meeting Ella for an early lunch at the deli. He'd been expecting to see her in her usual work wear, but today she'd gone all dynasty princess on him and was wearing good jeans and boots, a pretty shirt, and jewelry.

"What's the occasion?"

"Ball gown shopping at the local bridal wear shop," she offered glumly. "And trust me that never ends well. By the way, I have a spare ticket for the Valentine's Ball at the Graff Hotel next weekend. It's a big affair. Huge. Think ballrooms and chandeliers, fairy lights, pink champagne and feathers."

"Feathers?"

"Okay, I'm not sure about the feathers, but it's to launch a big competition. They're giving away a wedding. Do you have a formal suit?"

"Er..."

"For the ball, not the wedding," she offered somewhat dryly. "Although I'm pretty sure that Mr. Armani or someone of his ilk is going to tailor-make you a wedding suit, should you win the competition."

"How do I win the competition?" he asked warily. "I don't just have to walk through a doorway or something, do I?"

"You and your significant other would have to write a persuasive five-hundred word essay on why you want to get married. And then agree to a whole flood of publicity."

"I'd rather elope."

"I'm sure you're not alone. Meanwhile, I need a gown. Maybe even a pink gown. Possibly with feathers. Or sparkles. Or something."

"Good luck."

"And *you*, should you choose to accompany me, will need a suit."

"With feathers?"

"I think not. Will you come? Will you even be here?"

There was an underlying thread of anxiety to her words that Sawyer didn't like. "I finish up at the saloon Tuesday week. Nothing stopping me from heading to my place on the Wednesday, picking up a suit, airing the place out, and being back here on Friday. You can come too, if you want?"

"I do want." Ella's wistful expression confirmed it. "But we've a new bull buyer coming to the ranch on Thursday and my father's away. May I take a rain check?"

"You may."

She leaned forward, over the table, and kissed him square on the lips in front of half of Marietta, Montana, and Sawyer grinned and slid his hand in her hair and made it count.

"It's not working, this attempt of yours to cultivate a bad girl image," he said when she pulled back. "Too many people around here have known you since birth. I live in a truck stop bunkhouse and work behind a bar. I'm a lean, mean flirting machine and I'm becoming respectable by association."

"You don't flirt anymore, according to Mardie."

"She lies."

"Will you come to the ball?"

"Yes."

"Can I come to your bunkroom tonight?"

"*Hell*, no."

"You're as bad as my father." She sat back, her gaze speculative and her smile playful. "Did I mention that my father's away?"

T uesday afternoon and the end of Sawyer's stint behind the bar at Grey's Saloon rolled around all too soon.

Reese offered him on-call work and guaranteed him Friday and Saturday nights if he wanted them. Mardie thumped him on the arm hard and got alarmingly teary-eyed when he told Reese, no.

"She'll be fine," Reese said as she stalked from the kitchen. "She just doesn't want you to go. Figure you might have a few people in that position." Reese's gaze sharpened. "Come on through to the office. I want to show you something Jason found on the Web this morning. Breaking news."

The news was... significant.

Richard Sawyer – businessman and CEO of JB Brewing Industries—was going down. Embezzlement, forgery, three counts of assault occasioning actual bodily harm, one count of sexual assault, and an apprehended personal violence order taken out against him that cited intimidation, harassment, stalking, and more assault. And they'd still granted him bail. Laurence Sawyer, former CEO and major shareholder of JB Brewing, had been given conditional board approval to step in and mop up. The predominantly family-owned brewery was on the brink of collapse, blah blah, blah blah. The scavengers and speculators were having a field day.

Sawyer sat back in the office chair and blew out his breath. He felt sick just looking at it. "Does Jason know that he's my brother?"

Reese nodded. "He dug a little deeper after reading that."

"Tell him you can't pick your relatives."

"He knows." Reese smiled thinly. "Does Ella know your family background?"

"She knows some of it." Sawyer shoved a hand through his hair. "My brother's been heading in this direction since—" God, even as a kid, the things Richard had done to get his own way had been extreme. "Long as I can remember."

"Where do you stand in all of this?" Reese nodded toward the monitor.

"Out of it." And yet... "Doesn't matter how far you run, does it? When it comes to family you're never really gone."

It took Sawyer ten minutes to throw his gear in the pickup, and eleven and a half hours to get to his Washington home. From there he phoned his mother, and there was no *hello* or *how are you?* forthcoming, just a quietly defeated, "You've heard."

"Yeah."

"I did a very foolish thing when you left. I never told you. I was so *angry* with your father for brushing Richard's actions aside. As for Richard, then and now..." Her voice broke. "How did I create such a person, Cameron? What did I *do*?"

Sawyer closed his eyes on the view from his bedroom window. A sweeping ocean view. "He just was."

"When you left, I sold half our shares in the brewery and put the proceeds in trust for you. They were mine to sell, so I did it. Your father and Richard have been struggling to control the business ever since. I think that's what pushed Richard over the edge."

"What he did to Zoey was already over the edge."

"They granted him bail."

He couldn't keep his bitterness down any longer. "Did it ever occur to you that maybe you should have left him behind bars?"

"Yes." He could barely hear her. "I wasn't the one who paid Richard's bail. Nor did your father. He got the money from somewhere. Nowhere good."

"Buy back into the business, Mother. You'll probably *make* money if you buy in now. Give Dad the control he needs to run things his way."

"No. That money is for you."

"It's what I'd do."

"Then come home and do it."

"Mum—"

"Cameron, I'm at the end of my rope. Your father's barely sleeping, Richard's God knows where and I don't know how much longer I can hold this together. You've always been the strongest of us all. The best of us. Come back to us, please, if you could just consider it."

"I have a life here. A woman I don't want to leave behind." There, he'd admitted it. "You're asking me to walk her into that?"

"No. I—no." His mother sounded defeated. "I didn't realize."

Sawyer paced. He'd been pacing ever since he picked up the phone.

"I'll let you go," she murmured.

"I'll come alone. I'll give you one month and I can be there by mid next week, but I can't help you if you don't co-operate. Buy back the stock. Get me a seat on the board. I'll send you my CV. Tell my father to give that to the board as well. Tell him I'll not be his yes man but I will support good management decisions. Tell him I know damn well that he's always been good at those. Unless it involved Richard."

"Richard—"

"Deserves what he gets."

"Cameron, we do this and he'll come after you. I'm not guessing. I'm sure."

"I know. Where does he think I am now?"

"I don't think he knows."

"Tell him I'm on my way. And I will be, just give me a few days. Tell him I want my life back. And I want my family back, and I want to be able to offer the woman I love safety and security rather than a life full of fear. I'm not coming home to hold Richard's hand, Mother. I am done with staying out of his way. I'm coming home to finish him."

Chapter Nine

S awyer had left. Ella heard the news third-hand when she went to Emerson's Transport on Wednesday morning to find him. She wasn't impressed. Gutted, more like. Upset enough to call in on Mardie at the saloon. Mardie, who'd taken one look at her and told Reese she was taking her lunch break now and had then proceeded to sit Ella down in front of a plate of fried food.

Sawyer phoned her while she was still at the bar contemplating the delights of fried onion rings dipped in mayonnaise. He was at his beach house in Washington. Ella didn't even know the name of the town, and it seemed a little late to ask.

"I didn't think you were leaving quite so soon. Couldn't you have said goodbye?"

Mardie nodded vigorous agreement. Damn right he could have said goodbye.

"I'll be back on Friday – with a suit for the ball. I wasn't exactly thinking in terms of goodbye."

"You weren't?" Now she sounded tentative as well as needy.

"I just have to sort out a couple of things while I'm here. I will be back, Ella. Don't give my ticket away."

"I won't."

"See you soon."

"Yeah."

And then he was gone.

Ella met Mardie's troubled gaze with one of her own. "He said he'd be back in time to take me to the ball."

"Yeah?" Mardie's face brightened.

"Do you think he will be?"

Mardie nodded. "Sawyer says he's going to do something, he does it. That's my experience of him. What's yours?"

"Same."

"See? We can't *both* be wrong."

Ella smiled wryly. "Pretty sure we can."

Mardie rolled her eyes. "Hey, Reese. Is Sawyer going to get back here in time for Friday's ball?"

"Ask him," said Reese.

"See?" Mardie picked up a fried onion ring, dragged it through the mayonnaise and offered it to Ella, dripping and all. "Reese says he'll be here, and Reese is male and *never* wrong."

"I heard that," muttered Reese. "Don't you have work to do?"

"See?" Mardie murmured sagely. "Never. Wrong."

Ella worked herself to exhaustion for two days solid, until on Friday lunchtime, her father ordered her to get on up to the house and stay there and get ready for the ball.

"I haven't heard from him these past two days," she muttered, and her father stopped stacking hay and regarded her narrowly. "At all."

"Phone him."

"You think I should? He said he'd be here. I don't want him to think that I don't trust him to keep his word."

Ella's father just looked at her.

"You know he's not in Marietta anymore?"

"Ray said." Her father took his cap off and wiped at his brow with the sleeve of his shirt. "Still. I presume he owns a phone?"

Ella nodded.

"Text him. Ask him what time he'll be here."

"Oh, that's clever."

"Yeah," her father drawled dryly. "I'm Einstein."

"Could be I'm feeling just a *little* insecure." Ella held up her forefinger and thumb about an inch apart and watched her father smile. "But I will. I'll text him. I'm not sure I ever gave him a time we had to be there."

The doors opened at 7 pm. Before that, there were drinks in the bar. Dancing commenced at eight. At some point during the evening someone would launch Marrietta's Great Wedding Giveaway competition. As far as Ella was concerned, as long as they turned up before pumpkin hour she could still say she'd been to the ball.

Although turning up a few hours *before* midnight would be better. "I'll call."

"That's my girl."

But when she called, Sawyer's phone was either turned off or out of range.

Ella picked her way through a late lunch and then decided she needed to make bean soup with ham hocks. She took a shower once it was simmering gently, but there was no sense putting on her ball gown yet. She had soup to stir and biscuits to make first.

Her father came in just at six, took one look at her and the soup and the kitchen counter covered in biscuits, and wisely headed for the emergency kitchen whisky instead. "Did you get hold of him?"

"Not yet. But he'll be here. He will. And then I'll get dressed." Ella pulled a fresh batch of biscuits from the oven and dumped them on the cooling rack on the counter. "Biscuit?"

Her father took a biscuit and wisely opted not to say another word.

Sawyer turned up just at dusk, wearing a suit tailor made for those magnificent shoulders and bearing an armful of mixed colored roses. He stood on the front porch, with the mountains in the background and Ella thought she'd never seen anything more magnificent.

"These are for you," he said and held them out to her. "There would have been chocolates too, only Sage sold them because I didn't get there before closing time. And I don't know if you still want to go to that Valentine's ball with me or not, but we could." He took in her jeans and plaid shirt. "If you wanted to."

She took the flowers from him. "I've been waiting for

your call."

"I did call."

"On *Wednesday*."

"Yeah, but I said I'd be back for the ball."

"It never occurred to you to phone again today and confirm it?"

"It did occur to me. There should be a message on your mobile. Or four."

"Oh." Still. "Mardie thinks I should skewer you for leaving without notice."

"Mardie's mean."

"My father hid all the shotguns."

"Smart man."

"It's a good thing I don't have an impulsive streak."

"Yeah. Hey, Ella." All of a sudden he looked uncertain. "Got a couple of things to mention. Updates, of a sort. The kind could impact on whether you want to go to the ball at all. With me."

Ella reached out and dragged him in and shut the door. "What do you mean?"

"Is your father in? Because maybe he needs to hear this too."

"My father's in his study." And that was where she headed.

Her father took one look at them both and headed for the whisky.

"Where's mine?" Ella said as she set the flowers on the sideboard.

Silently her father poured two more.

"Here's the deal." The playful note in Sawyer's voice had disappeared and about three ton of steel had taken its place. "My older brother is going down for rape, corporate embezzlement, assault, and half a dozen other assorted felonies. This isn't a surprise because he's done it all before." He pinned Ella with a troubled green gaze. "Still want me to take you to the ball?"

"Of course."

"I'm heading home next week to help save the family brewing business. It's called JB Brewing and it holds a significant global market share. It's not a small corporation and I don't rightly know how long it will take to fix. I'd ask you to come with me, but until Richard is behind bars its best if you don't. It's not safe for you there."

It was a lot to take in. Ella ran a nervous hand around the back of her neck and slid her father a glance. Her father stared back, stony eyed. "Sawyer's brother isn't all that nice," she offered.

"So I gather."

"So, uh." There was a distinct possibility that she probably should have mentioned Sawyer's brother to her father earlier.

She turned her gaze back on Sawyer. "Who was she this time?"

"One of our corporate execs. The good news is that she pressed charges and has the will to see a nasty court case through. And then she'll probably sue JB Brewing."

"I'm inclined to say good for her."

Sawyer's lips hitched a little higher around the edges. "Let's just say she won't lack for support. The bad news is that Richard made bail. He's had to surrender his passport but I don't like it. He has a tendency to think that rules and regulations don't apply to him. If Richard finds out about you there's a chance he might come here looking for you, as a way to get to me. I've left him precious little else by way of leverage."

"I can handle it."

"Ella—"

"I can."

"Here's a recent picture of him."

Ella took the paper Sawyer held out and studied his brother's handsome face before passing it to her father. Sawyer's brother didn't look like a power-tripping egomaniac, and that was probably part of the problem. "No one comes onto this place without our notice. We can show the photo to Jem and Carl, Ray, and the boys. If your brother comes poking around here we'll know it. And then we'll handle it. Right, Dad?"

Her father nodded, his eyes flat and hard.

Sawyer looked torn.

"Sawyer." She waited until his gaze had shifted from

her father back to her. "You need to trust us on this – no going back to Australia and obsessing over what if. I'll be careful. We will *all* be on guard."

"Never meant to bring this kind of trouble down on you, Ella. Never wanted you to have to live in fear."

"This isn't fear."

"I'll fix it," he said raggedly. "I *will* neutralize him. Help put him behind bars, and then maybe *he* can get help, I don't know. And then I aim to come back and court you properly this time. Dinner and the movies. Weekends away somewhere special. Cows. Line dancing. Rodeos. The works."

Ella liked the sound of that. "You can line dance?"

"You can teach me."

"Where would you live?"

"I haven't really thought about it yet, but it's not a problem. I could keep the house on the coast, buy well in Marietta and still have change." This time Sawyer's words were for her father. "Sir, I'm not a pauper, whatever my former employment and living arrangements might have suggested. I can provide for your daughter."

Her father cleared his throat. "Ella could build here, on the northern side of the ranch, tucked into the shelter of the foothills. We could build a new road out; that way there'd be more privacy for everyone involved."

"I'm right here," Ella said, before they decided to build her a castle. Although...

"We were just considering options," said her father.

Sawyer nodded. "Options."

First real smile she'd seen on his face all night. "Your dimples aren't always going to save you, Sawyer. If I go and get changed into my gown, I don't want to come back down here to find my future lodgings all organized for me, got it?"

Ella wanted *input* into those future house plans, dammit.

"Drink?" her father asked Sawyer pleasantly, pushing a glass toward him.

"I'm driving. Maybe something soft."

"Good thinking," she murmured. "Save your thirst for all that pink champagne."

"Maybe just the one whisky," she heard Sawyer say as she swept from the room before her smile split her face in two. Sawyer was back. Back with intent, and whether his brother aimed to make trouble or not, Ella wanted *this* Sawyer. The one who stood taller than before, and who looked at her with a world of quiet determination in his eyes. She wanted him just as much, if not more, than she'd wanted the old Sawyer.

And that was saying something.

Ella practically floated to her room and into her closet. She looked at the gown hanging against the wall and hit the ground with a thud. Lisa Renee from the bridal store had assured Ella that pale pink did wonderful things for her complexion and that the cut of this particular gown did amazing things for her figure. The sequins and the feathers, well, they were just for fun. They, too, were pale pink and there weren't that many of them. They were very discreet – sequins on the bodice, feathers at the hem. Elegant even.

What on earth had possessed her?

By the time Ella had put her makeup on, tried to do something with her hair and shimmied into her gown, she looked like a carnival kewpie doll. Oh, this was bad. Lisa Renee had good taste. Excellent taste. People *relied* on her to have good taste.

Clearly, when Lisa Renee had bought this she'd been having a meltdown.

Ella reached for her phone. Perhaps meltdowns were contagious.

"I'm looking at my gown and wondering whether *you're* going to want to go the ball with *me*," she offered when Sawyer picked up. "Too many feathers. And did I mention the sparkles?"

"I like sparkles. Did I mention that I've booked us a suite at Graff's Hotel?" he answered. "Two nights. The Valentine's package."

"And what might the Valentine's package include?"

"Turndown and chocolates, champagne breakfast in bed, a massage at some stage tomorrow, dinner at the hotel tomorrow night and a pink teddy bear."

Oh. Well. So. "I'll think about it," she muttered. "Don't

go anywhere." And hung up.

Still, she hesitated. Fiddled some more with her hair and chose a perfume to dab at her wrists and behind her ears. Lisa Renee had persuaded her to buy pale pink stilettoes to go with the gown. Pale pink stilettoes for a woman who lived on a ranch. Ella let loose a nervous giggle. She was never shopping at Lisa Renee's again without at least two girlfriends in tow for backup.

At the last minute, she reached for a black velvet cape that tied at the neck with a black satin ribbon. It suited the gown. Gave it a fairytale air.

It was her mother's.

Ella stared at her reflection in the full length mirror and suddenly all she could see was her mother, a mother who she missed more than ever.

"You'd like him, Mama. I know you would. I think I love him."

Yeah, so there was that.

The sound of someone clearing his throat at her door made her whirl around, hand to her hair in nervous anticipation of it being Sawyer and that he'd just overheard her, but it was only her father.

"Oh, thank God."

"I left him nursing a whisky in the study," her father offered dryly. "I thought you might like to wear these." He held out a black velvet case and she knew before she even opened it that she would find her mother's diamond and ruby earrings nestled within. "You look beautiful, Ella Grace."

"Really?" She was starting to get a little teary.

"Really."

"He's a good man, Daddy. This other business with his brother and his family? He needs to go back and fix it. He'll be stronger for it."

"I'm not going to judge the man by the actions of his brother, Ella Grace. I'll judge him by his actions toward you."

"How's he doing so far?"

"It could've started better." He gestured toward the jewelry, and his eyes suddenly looked as watery as hers felt. "Take them. Don't be too long. Your man's down there climbing the walls waiting for you. I remember that feeling and not with a whole lot of fondness."

"I'll be there."

Her father left. Ella put her mother's jewelry on, repaired her eye makeup and took a deep breath as she stared at her reflection in the mirror. "You with me, Mama? You going to lend me your grace tonight?" Ella nodded. "Good, because I need it."

She smoothed her lipstick with her finger, wiped her fingers on a tissue and picked up her little black clutch. "Let's go get my man."

S awyer didn't seem to have much to say when he saw her. He looked and looked, but he just didn't seem to have any words. Then his face lit up with a smile that looked as if it came from within, and Ella felt a corresponding lightness sweep across her body. He liked it.

He liked her.

He cleared his throat, but there were still no words.

"He likes it," Samuel T. told her dryly.

"I really do." Sawyer had found his voice and it was rough and warm with a flattering thread of awe shot through it.

"Are you ready to go?" she asked.

"When you are."

Ella kissed her father on the cheek and then moved toward Sawyer. It felt right, moving toward this man with his broad shoulders and his troubled soul. "You look very respectable." She preferred him naked in front of the fire, but a black dinner suit and tie was an exceptionally fine alternative. "Tailor made?"

"The rack stuff doesn't fit. It's the shoulders."

"So I see." Ella ran an admiring gaze over him, delighted when he colored up just a little. "Are you worried about being recognized at the ball? In relation to your brother, I mean."

"Reese knows. And Jason Grey. Jasper Flint might have an inkling by now – he came by the bar the weekend before I left and asked some fairly pointed questions."

"Do you *want* people to know who you are?" Ella thought in an important enough question to ask it before they got to the ball. "Who *else* you are?"

"I've never hidden my identity, Ella. I just haven't always advertised it, because people used to judge me in relation to Richard and I didn't like it. I daresay I won't like it any better this time around but it's still going to happen."

"Not around me."

Sawyer showed her his second genuine set of dimples for the night. "I can deal. I don't need protecting."

"So you think."

They left her father to his whisky and headed for Sawyer's ride. He'd swapped his battered pickup for a late model Audi fitted with snow tires. It was a beautiful vehicle, but it was going to take some skill getting it off the ranch without getting it stuck. Mind you, he'd somehow driven it in, so maybe there was hope for them yet.

Sawyer drove with a confidence born of great skill. He didn't have quite the relationship with speed that Ella had, but given the conditions maybe that was a good thing.

They had valet parking at the Graff Hotel this evening, that was new, and they also had a doorman and an attendant taking coats. "Promise you won't laugh," she murmured, tugging on the ribbon at her neck, the one that held her cape in place. And then the cape was gone and she stood there, revealed, and she hoped to heaven that the ballroom was as extravagantly decorated as she felt.

"Beautiful," said the coat attendant, and Sawyer nodded and offered his arm. Ella took it, uncertain of what the evening might bring but determined to not waste one more thought on feathers and the wearing of them. Ella liked feathers. End of story.

How they had managed to fill the Graff Hotel ballroom full to overflowing with people was anyone's guess, but they'd done it. The grand old room had kept its sculpted ceiling features and decadent chandeliers, but the down lights had been replaced by thousands of dangling fairy lights and pink and red themed decorations were everywhere. They had a band up on the stage and a podium for the making of announcements. Smack in the middle of the room stood a confectionery table, loaded with Valentine's Day candies.

"Does Marietta usually go all out for Valentine's Day?" Sawyer murmured, as a passing waiter offered them champagne, wine, sparkling water, or juice. Ella took the champagne, Sawyer took the juice.

"It's the launch. The one hundredth anniversary Great Wedding Giveaway. Here, read the poster." There was one pasted to the wall below a side chandelier. "The dress – very important."

"What type of dress would you choose?"

Maybe it was idle conversation but Ella gave it the consideration it deserved. "Something strapless and romantic. And, look, they even give you a selection of bridal nightwear."

"You really think a bride's going to need nightwear?"

"Your Neanderthal is showing."

"Guess I could work around the nightwear," he murmured. "Why the sudden interest in weddings?"

"Hey, I'm just reading the poster. The suit, flowers, hair and makeup, wedding cars, the wedding and reception venues, drinks and food, entertainment, the cake. What more does a happy couple need?"

"Lust?"

"You're so right. And love." Mustn't forget the essentials. "I still can't believe how many people are here and how glamorous everyone looks. I expect you've been to events like this before."

"A few."

"I'm trying very hard not to be too daunted by your other life and the people who populate it. And I'm not talking about your brother." Ella spotted another poster, this one situated behind the bar. A beer ad. And a JB beer brand. "Just how embroiled in the family business do you aim to get?"

Sawyer looked conflicted.

"You're going to be in it up to your armpits, aren't you?"

She'd wanted a man who had other things going on in his life – business interests that didn't involve ranching. Could be she'd gotten a little more than she'd bargained for. "You're going to need that ground floor office space in your Washington house. That's if you get back to the states at all."

"I said I'd be back." He leaned in close and his lips brushed her hair. "Have I ever given you cause not to trust me?"

"You mean apart from the masquerading as a rudderless drifter bartender?"

"I *was* a rudderless drifter bartender. And then I found something I wanted to keep and things changed." He looked down at her, his green eyes intent. "I'm not returning home because I want back in to the family business – I aim to help fix it and then get gone."

"But you could do more with it if you had a mind to. If you wanted to. Business is so global these days. You could probably work from anywhere. You could commute."

"From Marietta to Australia?"

"I hear people do it all the time."

He looked suitably amused. "You've heard no such thing."

"You could start a trend." Ella sighed and decided that subtlety was getting her nowhere. "All I'm saying is that if you get back to Australia and find that you need to spend a little longer there than you originally intended, you'd have my support. I know what home means and I know that sometimes people need to be there. I could visit you. I'm all about the travel."

Sawyer snorted. "You lie."

"For you I'd try."

"Ella." His voice had softened. "Australia isn't home for me – even if I call it that sometimes. Washington isn't home for me either – even though I have a house there. I'm going back to sort out family stuff because of what I want to be able to come back and offer you *here*."

"And, um." She wasn't waiting breathlessly for a wedding proposal. She *wasn't*. This sudden overwhelming desire to get married was simply the result of the wedding vibe all around them. "What might that be?"

He leaned closer, lips to her ear. "A life without fear. With me."

"Well, well. Isn't this cozy?"

The voice had enough oily venom in it to send a shudder straight through her. Sawyer went rigid and his gaze shot to hers in silent warning, but his movements were smooth as he straightened and turned toward the newcomer's voice.

"Richard," Sawyer said evenly.

"Hello, brother."

"I really didn't think you'd be stupid enough to come here." There were similarities in their big bodies and in their facial features, decided Ella, although Sawyer was bigger and more vibrant in every way. "You're wanted at home."

Richard's face contorted into an ugly sneer and he no longer resembled Sawyer at all. Not even a little bit. "You need to leave the folks at home to me."

"I don't think so."

'You know, I wondered, when I heard you were coming back – after all these years – I wondered why? What would make my little brother return?"

"It appears I've been asked to clean up your mess."

"You think you're going to get a seat on the board and return the big hero – you're not," his brother warned. "You think that bitch is going to put me behind bars. She'll be lucky if she can testify. As for our beloved *parents—*" Richard almost spat the word. "They're mine. They've always been mine."

Sawyer had taken a step forward, getting all up into his brother's space, or maybe just trying to put Ella behind him, out of sight and away from his brother's notice.

Yeah, no.

Ella tilted her chin and stepped up beside Sawyer, elbow to elbow, presenting a united front. "Funny how times change," she said. "You must be Cameron's embezzling rapist brother."

"Oh, aren't you sweet." Richard's eyes glittered with a frenzy, that might have been chemical and might have been madness.

"You need to leave," Sawyer told him.

"What, and miss all this? Oh, I don't know. Maybe the

little lady here can introduce me around. Love the feathers, by the way. So very showgirl. Do *you* pole dance?"

"I never did get the hang of it," she murmured sweetly, putting one hand firmly on Sawyer's suit-clad forearm to hold him back. "I was always too busy out on the range – learning how to shoot. But if it's introductions you want, I'm sure I can help you. The sheriff's just over there, along with two of his deputies. And I know he's wearing a suit, but it looks a little bulky around the chest and chances are he's carrying concealed. Law men. They're just never off duty, are they?"

"Cameron, where did you find her? She's divine."

"And is that Reese over there next to Jason Grey? You'll love Reese. Ex-special forces. He's a bar manager now. Safest bar in Montana. You'd think he'd get sick of taking out scum, but it must just never get old."

Cameron had stepped back and taken her with him, slanting her a half-amused, half-warning glance. "Where'd you learn to trash talk, Ella?" he asked, pulling a phone from somewhere inside his jacket.

"You've never shown stud bulls, have you?"

"The mind boggles."

"Who are you calling?"

"My father's lawyer. He gave me this number to call. Something about Richard having had to surrender his passport as a condition of bail. Because if he leaves Australia, then it just gets messy, what with warrants and international borders and extradition orders and all that. And of course the breaking of bail conditions."

"All that just to deliver a threat?"

"I never said he was smart."

Ella looked up to find Richard melting away into the crowd. "He's leaving."

Sawyer handed her the phone. "Wait here."

And then he was striding toward the exit, after his brother.

Ella headed for the sheriff and handed him the phone. "It's some lawyer in Australia," she told him. "Tell him Richard Sawyer's here in Marietta making threats against his brother, the woman he allegedly raped and his parents. I don't really know what happens next." She flashed the sheriff a bright smile, handed the man standing next to him her pink champagne and went after Sawyer.

Her father's pickup stood beneath the hotel portico, possibly awaiting the attention of valet parking, but she couldn't see her father anywhere.

Sawyer and his brother stood off to one side of the entrance, away from bright entrance lights and prying eyes. It probably wasn't wise to join them, given the cold and the wobbliness of high heeled shoes on icy ground, but she could stand witness, given Richard's liking for violence and aggression. Better to do this with eyes on them than not. And then Sawyer's brother saw her and smiled, and a chill went through her veins as he began to draw a handgun from behind his back.

"Sawyer!"

Before she could think, before she could run, Ella heard the familiar sound of a gun being cocked just behind her, and then her father's gruff voice telling her to step aside.

But Sawyer had this. With impressive swiftness and a few well-placed punches, Sawyer had his brother pinned to the wall with the gun at Richard's throat. Everyone stood frozen for what felt like forever and then finally Sawyer stepped back and let his brother go.

Not until Richard was at least thirty feet away from him did Sawyer lower the gun.

Her father lowered his too. "Why aren't you wearing your cloak?"

"Why are you even here?"

"Ray phoned. Said someone had been sniffing around the bunkhouse after Sawyer. He didn't like the look of him."

"Neither did I."

"Are you sure this is the one you want, Ella? You could just walk away. No one would fault you."

"You didn't teach me to walk away."

They watched in silence as Sawyer's brother walked unsteadily back toward the hotel, toward her father's pickup.

Her father began to raise his gun again and Ella stayed him with her hand. "If Cameron wants to stop him from leaving, he will."

"Did he threaten you?"

"He liked my feathers."

They watched some more as Sawyer's brother got in the pickup and drove away. Ella's father sighed.

"That was way too easy," Ella said. "Did you leave the keys in it?"

"Habit."

The sheriff came through the hotel doors and headed toward them, handing Ella back the phone without comment. Moments later, Sawyer walked up, shedding his jacket and draping it around Ella's shoulders. His brother's gun was no longer on show. Probably a good thing. Sawyer eyed her narrowly. "Didn't I tell you to stay inside?"

"Like that was ever going to work. Notice that I didn't interfere."

"I'm still a little unclear as to whether this guy's even within my jurisdiction, but I'll do my best," said the sheriff. "Lawyers and their double speak. Where is he?"

"I want to report a stolen vehicle," said Samuel T. Emerson.

And the good sheriff smiled.

Sawyer's encounter with his brother had left him with a faraway expression and a frown between his eyes. He didn't seem to be riding the adrenaline high of having a gun pulled on him or of disabusing his brother of that notion with a force that was all his own. Maybe he'd done this kind of thing before. Maybe he hid his disquiet well. Ella took his hand in hers and turned it over, looking for damage.

"I'm fine, Ella."

Maybe on the outside. "Do you want to go after him?"

"No, I—no. But I should."

"Or you could let the authorities do what they do best and leave it to them. Do you waltz?"

He looked at her, his gaze faintly incredulous.

"He came here looking to ruin your evening." Maybe

he'd come here with even grimmer intentions, but Ella didn't want to dwell on that. She squeezed his hand lightly and bumped shoulders with him instead. "Do we really want to give him the satisfaction of having done so? I don't think so."

Sawyer laughed. It was only a little laugh, but it was there.

"Ella Grace Emerson, would you care to dance?"

"Why, thank you, kind sir, I'd love to."

He was light on his feet and he made her look graceful as they whirled around the dance floor beneath a ceiling of fairy light stars. He'd done this before. Not until he'd slowed and pulled her in close for movement sweet and slow did Ella tear her gaze from his to see what others thought. Her friend Joanne stood watching them with the biggest smile in her eyes. Reese Kendrick had a half hitch to his lips that for him equated to a broad smile. Jasper Flint was eyeing them with an air of quiet calculation and so was Jane from the chamber of commerce. Ella lifted her chin: let them calculate all they liked. Ella was exactly where she wanted to be and no-one, well-meaning or otherwise, was going to take that away from her.

She turned her gaze back to Sawyer, to those brilliant green eyes and the smile in them, and the dimples in his cheeks, and felt blessed.

"I don't know how it happened," she murmured. "But all he's done is to make me want you more."

"That's 'cause you're ornery."

And then a smiling young woman thrust a piece of paper in between them. Several pieces of paper, stapled together. An entry form, no less. For The Great Wedding Giveaway. "We're a little low on entries so we're giving them out to likely-looking couples," she said. "And you two look gorgeous together. Love the dimples. And the dress." And then the smiling cupid was gone.

"We should enter," said Ella impulsively. "No, wait. Does that mean I just proposed to you?"

"Pretty much."

"Then I take it back."

"You don't want to propose to me?"

"Absolutely not. I want *you* to propose to *me*."

"We should enter," Sawyer said, dimples and all. "And support Marietta's fine endeavor." Sawyer's delicious rumble held the teasing edge she'd come to love. "Help me fill it out."

Ella found her little clutch purse which had a pen in it, and then they found a shadowed corner of the ballroom's bar and dispensed with names and addresses, nationalities and dates of birth – the easy parts. When Ella stared at the blank lines where those five hundred loving words were supposed to go, she took a deep breath. To hell with supporting the town, it had all started with lust.

I saw him and my body said I want that, she wrote and then handed the pen to Sawyer.

I saw her and smiled.

"That's it? That's all you've got?" she asked and Sawyer rolled his eyes and added some more.

I saw her and smiled. She smiled right back and I trembled.

He handed her back the pen.

I spent time with him and my heart soared.

I got to know her and I couldn't stay away.

I saw the hunger in him, and the strength, and wanted more.

I shared my deepest fears with her and she kissed them away.

He remade his world for me and carved a place for me in it.

She shared her world with me and I gave her my heart.

I love you, and I don't want to win The Great Wedding Giveaway. It's a wonderful prize, but I can't wait that long when all I've ever dreamed of in a man is standing right in front of me. It's you, Cameron Franklin Sawyer. All that you are. All that we can be.

Elope with me.

No.

Marry me.

Yes.

She dropped the pen as he spun her into his arms and lifted her, kissed her, and, as always, the world around them faded away until there was only him. And lust. And a love so big it filled her heart to overflowing.

"I love you, Ella. With all that I am and all that I can be. I'm yours. Will you marry me?"

"Yes." Ella kissed him again, promptly lost herself once more in the warmth of him and the taste of forever. "Yes."

Chapter Ten

Six weeks later Ella waited impatiently, two horses saddled and at the ready, as Sawyer drove up to the ranch and stepped from his pickup. He'd been in Australia for a little over a month helping his father refinance the family business, and he'd be going back again before he was through, but he'd kept his promise to return and Ella could barely wait for his smile and his touch.

This was what happened when wild longing turned into bone-deep love. You wanted a person to go and do what they had to do, you gave them your blessing and one-hundred-and-fifty percent of your support, and you vowed that when they came back you'd give them time to settle and room to breathe.

She'd been doing so *well* with all of that.

And then Sawyer set both feet on the ground and turned, and Ella launched herself into his arms, glorying in the way they closed tightly around her as he swept her off her feet. Video calls were wonderful things but they couldn't compete to having a living, breathing Sawyer in her arms, swinging her around, his deep laughter wrapping around her heart.

"You've no idea how much I've missed you," he muttered. "I couldn't wait to get back."

"I'm coming with you next time." Ella proceeded to lay kisses from his neck all the way to his temple. "You've no idea the number of people who are putting in for the ticket.

Apparently I'm not all that good at patiently waiting for you to return."

"Who'd have guessed?" His voice slid through her, a deep delicious rumble shot through with laughter. "How would you feel about one month in Australia—one month here for a while?"

"I'd feel good." Better than good. And then his lips were on hers, strong and sure and the greeting turned into a homecoming as one kiss slid into the next, each one notching the heat up that little bit hotter until finally, for the sake of breathing room, Ella broke away.

"You keep kissing me like that and I'm likely to agree to anything."

His dimples put in an appearance as he smiled, which was just plain *mean* when it came to Ella retaining her decorum. "I know you've had a long trip, but how do *you* feel about heading up to the lodge tonight?" she asked him as he turned his head to eyeball the horses. "It's private and warm, I stocked it full of food yesterday afternoon and we can get as naked as we want there. Nakedness being a priority to my way of thinking. I want you stretched out in front of the log fire there. I've been dreaming up all sorts of variations on that particular theme. Long live the imagination, I say."

"How do the horses fit in?"

"They're for getting there. We can drive up the mountain as far as we can, and then take the horses from there. It shouldn't take too long. Okay, it might take a while. Especially if I have to teach you how to ride on the way. We can go slow. I'll probably die of anticipation on the way. You haven't changed your mind about wanting me, have you?" That last question came out so needy that she immediately wanted to take it back.

"Ella, are you babbling?"

"I don't babble." Much.

Could be she was a little nervous as to how Sawyer's time in Australia might have changed him. But he didn't look all that changed. His hair was a fraction tidier and his face looked a little bit more tanned, but the light in his eyes when he looked at her was just the same and his kisses felt as magical to her as ever. "Do you still want to marry me?"

He stepped back, set her at arms-length and eyed her sternly. "Ella Grace soon-to-be Sawyer, what kind of question is that?"

"A needy one," she admitted. "I just—"

"Yes," he interrupted gruffly. "Yes, I want to marry you. I even have a ring for you this time. There was a distinct lack of a ring last time we discussed this, as I recall. Maybe you're feeling that lack."

"You are so right. Let's put my neediness down to that. It's nothing at all to do with feeling achingly vulnerably head over heels in love with you."

He shared a smile made for soothing the skittish. "Would it help if I told you that I feel exactly the same way about you?"

"You should probably say that a lot."

"I will. Would you like your ring now or would you rather wait until there's a crackling fire in the background rather than two horses and several farm vehicles in the background?"

"Now. Definitely now," and then as an afterthought, "please."

Sawyer dug in his pocket and pulled out what looked like a scrap of black velvet. The material fell aside to reveal two rings, one a plain white band and the other ring considerably more ornate. It had three blindingly white diamonds set in a row across the band, all of them enormous. And that was before she took into account the scattering of smaller pink stones winding their way around the base of the others.

"Whoa!"

"So, was that a good *whoa*?"

It had definitely been an unladylike *whoa*. A lady would have aimed for a quietly pleased gasp. "Sawyer, it's gorgeous!"

"They're Kimberley diamonds." Sawyer slid the engagement ring on her finger and then brought her hand up and kissed the inside of her wrist. "Don't lose them in a cow."

"I would *never*. I'd go in after them."

His dimples put on a show. "Good to know."

"Shall we show my father?" Ella tilted her fingers this way and that, making the diamonds catch the light as Sawyer wrapped the wedding ring back in velvet and slid it in his pocket. "I think we should. And then he'll want to know what you've been doing this past month, and then he'll try and show you his new bull, to which you will say 'tomorrow' because if you go admiring bulls today we are never going to get away in time to make it to the lodge before nightfall."

"And that would be bad."

"Especially seeing as I want to take a couple of quick detours along the way to look at possible building sites for a safe and private little mountain cabin."

"Don't you already have one of those?"

He definitely had her measure. She favored him with her most angelic smile. "Or a sprawling family home. I've been talking with the grandson of the architect who built the ranch. He's a big fan of his grandfather's work and he has lots of ideas of his own. Fusion architecture. It sounds very appealing."

"I really shouldn't have left you alone for a month, should I?"

"So. Much. Time on my hands." She took his hand and tugged him towards the house. "Not that I'm impatient but the sooner you say hello to my father the sooner we can get away. He'll be happy to see you and he'll *really* like the ring. He can say I'm engaged if I have the ring."

"He really doesn't mind you marrying me, does he?"

"He knows what I want and he knows what I need, and you're it."

"My brother—"

"Is not you."

"—is likely to be in prison for quite some time, but he will get out one day."

"And if he comes for me and mine ever again he'll regret it. I protect what's mine."

"That's my line."

"I want a different line. A better one."

"I'll try and deliver it naked."

And off she went on yet another naked Sawyer-induced fantasy. "We probably only need five minutes or so with my father. Remember the lodge and the open fireplace? You naked amongst all the rugs? I would really like to remember it well and that won't happen if we don't actually get there. We're on a tight schedule, especially if we have to walk the horses through the snow to the lodge... and since you don't know how to ride."

He grinned wide and boyish as he glanced at the horses. "I know I don't know anything about cattle. I never said I couldn't ride."

"Have you been holding out on me, cowboy?"

"Not anymore and never again." He swung her into his arms again and Ella was only too willing to stay there. "I love you. I'm always going to love you, need you, care for you and want to be with you." He ducked his head, brushed his lips against the tender lobe of her ear and Ella whimpered with want and with need as heat unfurled low in her belly. "We are going to have the most amazing life together," he promised.

And she believed him.

Epilogue

From the bulletin board of Grey's Saloon, the pen of Mardie Griffin, and accompanied by a snapshot of the blissful bride being swept off her feet by the groom...

Last Saturday, former bartender Cam Sawyer married Marietta's own Ella Grace Emerson beneath a blue summer sky and with the soaring Crazy Mountains of Montana right behind them.

Ella was attended by Joanna Talbot and Mardie Griffin, who loved their beautiful muted caramel-colored gowns of silk and taffeta almost as much as they loved their bridesmaid necklaces. General consensus has it that both Jo and Mardie looked very fine indeed (both Mardie and Joanna are currently seeking the perfect lover and/or a domestic God of a husband).

One of the groom's attendants was a beautiful and mysterious young Spanish woman, whose husband also attended as a guest. The other groomsman was a childhood friend of Sawyer's named Joe.

The groom's brother was not in attendance because he's doing a nickel and dime, but the groom's parents were there, dressed to impress and looking rather pleased with the show. They have Ella for a daughter-in-law now — damn right they should be pleased.

The reception took place in the Emersons' ever-so-atmospheric and freshly painted and re-floored big barn.

Rumor has it that Ella stole all the Graff Hotel's fairy lights for the occasion, but the Graff fairy lights are pink and Ella's were white and I have it on good authority that Ella purchased them herself, so... She probably purchased them in anticipation of all the future Emerson barn dances she's going to host for her dear single friends.

The quality of the beverages provided by the groom's parents had to be tasted to be believed. Maybe the drinks spectacular was because JB Brewing is back on its feet now, with no small thanks to Sawyer, but I figure the elder Sawyers would have spent up big on their son's wedding anyway. His mother thinks Sawyer makes the sun rise. His father only thinks he hung the stars.

This isn't quite the case.

I know for a fact that Ella and her bridesmaids hung most of those shiny little stars while Sawyer was out somewhere delivering a calf with Samuel T.

The country and western band sounded absolutely brilliant, even if they did sometimes play the blues, and the dancing lasted until dawn. Coincidentally, this was around the time the bride and groom slipped away.

As the sky grew lighter, our very own bartender Josh took up one of the band member's guitars and showed us all how bluegrass should be played. He's so good, in fact, that our altogether taciturn Jason Grey waxed lyrical (his exact words were 'You're not bad') and then proceeded to offer Josh a Sunday afternoon solo gig at the saloon – for double pay.

I'm still trying to convince Reese that we need a Happy Hour then too, but that's an announcement for another day. Back to the wedding.

The big breakfast cook-up the next morning was a treat, and the gift boxes guests received on their way out the barn door contained complimentary coffee vouchers for several of Marietta's wonderful cafés and a selection of Sage's chocolates to devour on the drive back to town.

Congratulations, Ella and Sawyer, from your friends at Grey's Saloon. We love you both and wish you every magical, love-soaked moment this world possesses.

Second Chance Bride

A MONTANA BORN BRIDES NOVEL

TRISH MOREY

Dedication

*To Jane Porter
and all at Montana Born Books,
who offered this writer a ray of sunshine
during one of the toughest years of her life.
Thank you for helping me rediscover
the sheer joy of writing.
xxx*

Dear Reader

Who doesn't love a wedding? The gowns, the flowers, the color and the sheer glamor of it all—what's not to love? And that's all besides the romance and hopes and wishes for the happy couple, who've found their perfect partner and their happy ever after.

I was totally chuffed to be invited be part of the Spring Brides series, to write a story that links with novellas by some of my favorite writing colleagues and friends. It was pure romance, pure escapism, all dressed up in a gorgeous frothy wedding gown.

That's not to say I didn't give my heroine, Scarlett, plenty of grief along the way. Scarlett is a twin and she's the flaky sister. Her older sister by five minutes, Tara, is the sensible one (and yes, their mother is a dyed in the wool *Gone with the Wind* fan). With Scarlett's own wedding plans gone askew, she gets to help out hero Mitch at another wedding, that turns out to be the kind of nightmare we all hope won't be our own. Oh, I had so much fun writing this story!

It was so lovely to be able to bring Scarlett and Mitch together at the end. These characters so deserved one other. I really hope you enjoy reading their journey into married life together as much as I enjoyed writing it.

And then watch out, because Tara's story, *Almost a Bride* by the incomparable Sarah Mayberry, is up next!

Much love and romance to you!

Trish Morey

Contents

Chapter One

Mitch Bannister needed a cold beer and a hot woman, preferably in that order. The cold beer would go down fast, he knew, but the hot woman—well, it had been a while, and so he'd rather linger over that particular pleasure.

He strode down Hannan Street, feeling the beat of the summer sunshine through the shirt on his back, knowing he'd made the right decision to spend the first of his seven days R&R here in the outback town of Kalgoorlie.

He could have headed straight to Broome, where his best mate, Robbo, was to be married later in the week, and where the pre-wedding party was already underway. But then, as much as he liked his mate, this was one wedding he wasn't particularly looking forward to.

Alternatively, he could have headed to the city, to Perth. Plenty of his workmates went back to the big smoke when they'd finished their rostered fourteen days straight at the mine. But Mitch wasn't a fan of the big smoke. He preferred his country wide open, with a sky that went forever and then some.

Besides, it wasn't like he had anyone waiting for him back in the city.

He almost snorted aloud at that thought. Kristelle had made damn sure she wouldn't be waiting for him barely ten minutes after his suggestion that they needed a break. Ten whole minutes before she was warming someone else's bed.

Ten minutes more and she was marrying the dumb arse.

And that was fine. Really it was.

Right now he was still so relieved at having escaped her clutches that he wasn't interested in diving back into that particular shark pool again.

Right now he preferred his life without complications, even if this meant turning up at the wedding alone. Not that he was about to arrive looking like he'd gone without, mind. Because it had been a while.

Which was why a temporary woman for the next hour or so suited him just fine.

He checked the street sign at the next corner. Perfect. Just a mere block or so back from here he'd find Hay Street and the place someone had told him about that promised exactly what he needed.

A cold beer, a hot woman and no complications.

The concept had a hell of a lot going for it.

Desperate times call for desperate measures.

Aunt Margot had used those exact words when, as a ninth grader, Scarlett had dumped an entire box of platinum hair color on her head and turned her honey blonde hair green, sending her mom into hysterics. Aunt Margot had calmly uttered the phrase as she'd reached for a bottle of ketchup and shoved Scarlett's head over the kitchen sink.

She'd remembered that saying while she'd been in Perth. "Go to Kalgoorlie," a girl she'd worked tables with in a cafe there had told her when Scarlett had looked at her pay slip, despairing that it would take forever to save the fare home. "That's the place you can make the fare home in a couple of weeks and it's legal."

She'd balked at the suggestion then.

Legal or not, she wasn't *that* desperate to go home.

Until her twin sister had emailed with the news of their mom's diagnosis and a plea to get back to Marietta as quickly as possible.

She'd added up the numbers that night and worked out it would take more than half a year of saving at her current rate in the cafe. Aunt Margot's words had played over and over in her mind as she'd tossed and turned in her backpacker hostel single bed. And she'd figured it might be a desperate measure, but these were desperate times indeed.

She could bury her pride for a couple of weeks, surely? And then she'd go home to Marietta and forget this whole sorry saga ever happened.

And the best thing? Nobody else need ever know.

Which was why she was right at this moment sitting nervously in an office in Kalgoorlie being interviewed by an unexpectedly bookish-looking fifty-something woman named Bella. And right now, desperate times were the only thing keeping her from bolting for the door.

"So, have you ever done this kind of work before?" the woman asked, and Scarlett was tempted to answer, *well, I've had sex, how different can it be?*

"Sure," she said instead, feigning a confidence she didn't feel as she brushed a flake of nothingness from her arm. Because she was twenty-six and of course she'd had sex, though probably not half as much as what her up-tight sister no doubt imagined. And then she added, "Back home, in the States," just in case the school librarian posing as a madam asked for references or something.

"Okay, that all sounds fine," said Bella, "and now I need you to fill out this form. But I will need your real name, sweetie, for the records."

"Um, Scarlett Buck is my real name."

The woman blinked and looked doubtful. "Scarlett Buck *is* your real name?"

"Seriously."

Bella's eyes glittered like she'd hit pay dirt. "So welcome to Bella's Belles, Scarlett Buck. I can see we're going to get along just famously. Now you finish off the paperwork and I'll grab you something to wear. I've got just the perfect outfit in mind."

Bella didn't believe in wasting time. Barely an hour later Scarlett was dressed as a cowgirl, and that was kind of funny, because she kind of was, but still this cowgirl felt out of place here in the Australian outback town of Kalgoorlie.

In fact, wearing a pink cowgirl hat teamed with her own pink spangly boots and nothing more than a black corset with pink bows and tiny panties in between, she could almost imagine she was back circa eighteen-seventy, preparing to strut her wares along the balustraded balcony of Marietta's Grey's Saloon. Which is exactly where she wished she was right now—in Marietta, at least.

But it wasn't eighteen-seventy and Marietta was more than fifteen hundred dollars and an entire half world away from the down-under escort agency she'd just signed on with.

Except it wasn't exactly an escort agency either...

It was a house of ill repute.

A bordello.

A brothel.

And maybe it was a legal brothel courtesy of the mining town's rich historic past and a bending of the State laws.

But it was still a brothel.

She swallowed, despairing of both desperate times and desperate measures and of being forced to make such a choice.

Not your proudest moment, Scarlett Buck.

Maybe not, but she'd done some crazy stuff in her time and she could do this if she had to.

After all, she rationalized, it was just sex.

All she had to do, she figured, was to take her mind off it. Think about something else. Something boring. Something dull to take her mind off what was happening.

She could do that.

After all, she'd jumped out of an airplane once. Climbed out onto the wing of a tiny plane in spite of a lifelong fear of heights, and calmly waited for the instruction to jump, all thanks to her six times tables. She'd got all the way to *eleven-times-six-is-sixty-six* before her chute had cracked open above her head and she'd realized her arithmetic had given her fear of heights a run for its money.

And if she could do that?

She could do anything!

Empowered, she swept aside the bead curtain to the Ruby Room. The glow from fringed lampshades bounced red light between richly textured wallpaper and red velvet sofas, soft music playing in a place that hummed with the promise of sin.

This was where the clients would be introduced to the girls.

This was where they would make their choice.

And if they chose her?

Her palms grew damp, her stomach wobbled, her boldness wavering. It was what she wanted—needed—and yet...

She perched down on the edge of the nearest sofa, crossed her legs and fiddled with the bows on her corset before uncrossing her legs again. Because if they chose her, then she'd soon have the money to get home to her mom. To her sister.

Oh hell.

Of course she could do this.

"I heard there was a new girl."

Scarlett jumped. She'd thought she was alone, but now her eyes were beginning to adjust to the low light, she could see the woman sitting on a sofa across the room, a magazine in her lap, her skin fair, her lips red and her long black hair gleaming under the lights like a silken curtain.

"Is it that obvious?" Scarlett said, trying to sound light but painfully aware of the nerves in her voice. Any minute someone was going to figure her for the impostor she was and throw her out.

But then the woman smiled. "First day in a new place is always the hardest. I'm Jasmine," she said, her name as exotic as her looks.

"Scarlett."

"You're American?"

"Yeah. From Montana. You?"

"Thailand," she said, shifting the magazine to smooth down the fluffy hem of the red baby doll that floated just above her slim thighs. "Bella's is a good place to work. You'll like it."

Scarlett very much doubted it but she smiled and

nodded her thanks anyway. There was no point explaining she'd only be here until she made enough money for her fare home.

And then Bella walked in with her grey bob and pearls and looking so much more like a school librarian than any madam she could possibly have imagined.

She clapped her hands, "Look lively girls, Rule number one, let's not keep the customer waiting."

Uh-oh.

Scarlett was so not ready for this. Oh, she might be Scarlett Buck, the flaky twin, the girl with the anti-Midas touch who could turn golden opportunities into dust and managed to do so with infuriating regularity. She might have driven her sister to despair and her mother to drink on too many occasions to count, but to be forced to this?

Jasmine rose from the sofa and flicked back her hair, no trace of hesitation. Whereas she—

Barely-contained nerves got the better of her.

Time.

She needed more time—just a few more minutes to get used to the idea. 'I'll sit this one out,' she offered. "Jasmine was here first, after all."

"Nonsense!" boomed Bella as she took her hand and hauled her off the sofa in a very un-school librarian kind of way. Before Scarlett knew it she was lined up alongside the other girl and Bella was reminding them to smile. "Nothing like being thrown in at the deep end, I always say."

Great. So much for getting used to the idea. Any moment now a middle aged man with grey hair and a paunch would come sauntering through that door and size her up to be his sexual plaything for the next however long and still she would have to smile and make him feel like she wanted nothing more than to hop into the sack with him.

Just sex?

Oh, Scarlett Buck, you have really have done it this time.

She raised her eyes to the ceiling and sent one last silent prayer to the heavens and her family and anyone else who might possibly be listening up there and could help: *I'm sorry. I'm really sorry. But it won't be for long, I promise, and after this I'll never, ever, disappoint you, ever again.*

And then she heard Jasmine's, "Welcome to Bella's, I'm Jasmine," and a cold shiver of apprehension snaked down her spine as she summoned up a smile. She opened her eyes, her hundred watt smile fully charged and ready to dazzle the client despite the nerves clawing at her insides. "Welcome to B—"

She stopped and blinked, and tried again. "Welcome to..."

But there was no finishing. Because it didn't make sense. Because *he* didn't make sense. She'd been expecting middle aged and desperate whereas the man in front of her was anything but. He was nowhere near middle aged for a start, his short cropped hair dark blonde and thick, and—she flicked her eyes down his denim clad legs and up again—there wasn't so much as a hint of a paunch in sight.

Far from it.

Instead, he was *built*. Six foot two of hard-packed built, if she wasn't mistaken, with a face that looked in the glow from the red light like it had been chiseled from outback rock itself, full of rugged angles and red planes and secret, shadowed depths.

Since when did someone who looked like him have to visit a place like this?

"You must forgive Scarlett," Bella said from what sounded like a long way away. "She's new."

"Excuse me," she said, snapping to, her smile getting tangled in the confusion on her lips. "Welcome to Bella's."

And with that he was gone, disappeared with Bella back into the office to make his choice.

Like he needed time for that.

She dropped back into the sofa, her face in her hands. Oh god, was there nothing she could do right? Nothing she couldn't screw up?

Apparently not.

She might as well pack her things right now.

"Scarlett!"

She looked up, resigned for the dressing down if not the sacking from Bella she knew was coming, that she knew she deserved. "Yes?"

"Congratulations." Bella looked as surprised as Scarlett felt. "You just got your first client.

Chapter Two

"M e?" Scarlett looked over at Jasmine. "But...?"

"Don't worry about me," said Jasmine, flopping back down on the sofa, "I've got a regular coming in at two, it would be nice not to have to rush."

"But..."

"Well, get going," said Bella, shooing her with her hands. "Rule number one, remember?" Scarlett remembered all right. Don't keep the customer waiting.

And she also remembered what she was doing here and why. Cold hard cash. Soon she'd have the price of a one way ticket home. The first client—the first day—would be the hardest. It would get easier after that.

Keep telling yourself that!

So she put on a brave face, collected her client and calmly led him to the room that would be theirs for the next however long, while her insides buzzed and frayed. And not just because she was nervous about what was coming.

But because of him.

Her first impressions hadn't told her the half of it. He had the rugged good looks and the broad shoulders of a Montana cowboy, not to mention long legs and strong thighs that were born to be wrapped in denim, and probably then around a horse or a bull. Even the way he moved said he knew his place in the world.

Somehow she knew he'd be no slouch in the sex department.

And didn't that just make her insides buzz all the more?

"Shower first," she said with a tight smile, handing him a bundle of towels and whipping her hand away at the zap as their fingers brushed.

And he took them and turned and she reminded herself to breathe as he headed for the private bathroom.

The breathing helped.

Right up until the moment he stopped short of the bathroom and sat down on a chair instead, pulling off one of his boots. The second one followed, landing with a thunk on the carpeted floor. His socks were off before she could blink. He was already standing, putting his hands to his belt when she found her voice.

"Um, what are you doing?"

He paused, considering her a while. "Is that a trick question?"

Her eyes narrowed. After three weeks in Australia, she was becoming aware that Australians didn't always say exactly what they meant. It was kind of funny when she could keep up. But how did you respond when you weren't sure? "I don't—think so."

"So what's it look like I'm doing?"

"You're taking off your clothes?"

He smiled, and she damn well wished he didn't look so happy with it. "Bull's eye."

"But..."

"But... *what*?"

She blinked as he stood and undid the belt at his jeans and then unzipped his fly. She felt every one of those zipper teeth scorching a heated trail down her backbone. "Nothing."

"You're not shy, are you?"

"No! I'd just hate for you to catch cold."

He hesitated with that, the start of a smile tweaking his lips. "I didn't expect Bella's Belle's to take care of *all* my physical needs."

"All part of the service," she said breezily, willing the floor to open up and swallow her whole and spit her out the other side of the world. Anywhere would do. Anywhere at all would be preferable to being here. "Which reminds me," she said, latching onto an alternate means of escape, albeit temporary, "how about I get you a beer or something?"

"Had one," he said, a slight frown creasing his brow while the fingers of one hand casually flicked open the buttons of his shirt. In spite of herself and her needing to flee, her feet stayed exactly where they were as her eyes were drawn to his chest, tan-skinned and dusted with hair. Firm skin. A dusting of hair rather than a forest. Just the way she liked it. Her fingers curled into fists, nails biting into her palms to stop them aching to reach out and run her fingers through it. "And the last thing I want right now is brewer's droop."

She blinked, and had to drag her eyes away to meet his. "Excuse me?"

"Too Aussie for you, sweetheart? I do want to be able to perform."

"Oh." Heat scorched her cheeks and she looked away, although she wasn't really sure it was because she was embarrassed at his words, or because he'd peeled off his shirt and dispensed with his jeans in quick succession, leaving nothing to cover him but a band of black, that hugged the nether regions of his body and left nothing to the imagination.

Absolutely nothing.

Suddenly her lungs felt as if they were flapping around like freshly landed trout on a lake shore. She put a hand over her chest to try to calm their flailing tails before they flapped right out of her. "Right," she managed at length. "That would a shame."

He looked at her then, his eyes going from the cowgirl hat on her head all the way down to her boots and back again until her skin tingled inside and out, and he smiled a broad hungry smile that this time set every organ inside her flapping. "Cowgirl, that would be all kinds of tragedy."

And he turned and swiped off his underwear, picked up his towels and padded naked to the private bathroom.

Breathe she reminded herself, as the sight of the most perfect male buns she'd seen in a long time disappeared from view. Buns with dimples nestled just above, either side of the spine that bisected the two perfect halves of his back.

Buns that sent a rush of heat to her blood and a tingling anticipation between her thighs.

Because soon he and his buns and his dimpled spine and his hungry eyes would be back and they'd climb onto that big wide bed together and make love and...

Whoa, right there!

What the hell was she thinking, constructing some kind of fantasy version of what was happening here? There was no *making love*. No matter what his hungry eyes might say, this was sex, pure and simple. A business transaction pure and simple, nothing more.

Business, she reminded herself, as she busied herself checking that everything was in order even though she already knew it was—the sheets freshly changed, the box of Kleenex at the ready, the condoms that were waiting on the bedside table.

Three condoms, she couldn't help but notice.

Gulp.

Mitch wasn't sure what he'd been expecting, but it sure hadn't been the green-eyed cowgirl waiting for him in the bedroom. Sure, she looked hot enough with scarlet hair that matched her name and dressed in that cute little black and pink number and those perky little boots, Oh man, if those provocative little boots on the end of those pins were enough to make him hot under the collar, it had definitely been too long. Yes sirree, he'd been looking for hot. He just hadn't expected the skittishness.

But then, Bella or whatever her name was had said this girl was new. Maybe that was why.

Or was that just part of the act?

Maybe some guys went for that?

He shrugged as he put his face into the stream of water to rinse his hair. He had no idea what other guys went for. But he'd handed over his credit card and he was paying the money and he was already half primed in anticipation.

Something about that nutty combination of black satin and pink bows and red hair and green eyes and a name like Scarlett—because what else could she be called in a place like this? Whatever, he could do a hell of a lot worse than an hour or two with someone who looked as good as this temporary cowgirl.

And if it meant he'd be in a better mood by the time he got to Broome for Robbo's wedding, so much the better. He didn't want to go anywhere near Kristelle with anything like a hungry look in his eye or she'd take it a sign of victory. And he was so not giving her one of those.

He felt himself wilting and cursed, snapping off the flow of water. Why the hell would he be thinking about Kristelle when he had princess in boots waiting in bed for him, and when he was paying for her time?

Why waste a minute of it?

S carlett was sitting on the bed, her legs crossed, trying to look casual when the guy emerged from the bathroom. It was his fault entirely that she wasn't able to carry it off, emerging as he did with his hair beading moisture at the ends and with a towel slung low on his hips.

Dangerously low.

Dangerously... *delicious.*

Just business, she reminded herself, when in truth it was all she could do not to drool at that glorious expanse of chest and abs, and that beguiling line of hair that separated the two sides of his abs and circled his belly button before heading south and disappearing under a knot of fluffy white towel.

She looked up and found him smiling at her, and she knew she'd been sprung. But he looked so good when he smiled that it was all but impossible to stop herself from smiling back. And somewhere in the back of her mind she knew one shouldn't drool at a client, or smile without having to make some kind of effort. Shouldn't actually be tingling at the thought of having sex with this man. But the way he looked at her made it so damned hard to remember this was business.

He took her hands and hauled her to her feet. "I thought we were going to bed."

And the jolt she felt on contact, a hundred times more powerful than when their fingers had brushed, warned her that the six times tables or even the sevens weren't going to cut it. It was time to bring out the big guns.

One times eight is eight.

Two times eight is sixteen.

"Sure," she said, with her head back in a Marietta Elementary School classroom with a wall filled with numbers and tables and charts and old Mrs. Henson with her stick pointing out the next line in the chant and she felt better already.

Three times eight is twenty-four.

"In that case," he said, as he swiped the hat from her head and spun it away into a corner, "it appears one of us is over-dressed."

Four time eight is...

He touched his hands to her shoulders—long-fingered hands that brought with them that jolt of electricity and the wall of charts and tables blurred and faded in the knowledge that these hands—these electric long-fingered hands—would soon be all over her, and that thought damn near sucked the air from her lungs along with her recital.

Four times eight, she persisted, finding her place. Four times eight is thirty-two.

Good. She just needed to stay in control. Who was the client here after all? She made a move to twist out of his arms, to sit down on the big wide bed. "I'll just get my boots off—" But he stopped her descent, her shoulders held fast in his big hands, fingers squeezing into her flesh, and she knew that if her knees buckled under her right now, she would not fall.

And given the way the muscles in his arms and chest had contracted as he'd supported her, it was a wonder her knees hadn't buckled.

Forget muscles!

Think boring.

Five times eight is forty.

Six times eight—

"How about we leave the boots on, cowgirl, at least for now." His voice was husky low and so sexy that there was only one way for her pulse to go and that was into overdrive. And that was before he dipped his mouth to her throat, drawing her closer as his lips set fire to her skin, sending her senses damn near into meltdown.

She heard a sigh, and realized it had come from her, as he collected her close against his chest, his hands molding her to him, from shoulder to waist to butt, his mouth doing wicked things to her skin, the drumbeat of her blood blocking out rational thought, so that she wondered the point of an eight times table, anyhow?

It made no sense at all.

Nothing made sense beyond the desperate need to lace her arms around his neck and drink in the feel of him, hot and hard against her.

God, but he smelt good, of clean skin and lemon soap and all overlaid with the scent of masculine desire.

She shuddered against him. He was like Christmas and New Year all rolled into one; the surprise package under the Christmas tree and the fireworks on New Year's Eve. He was the birthday present she'd always wished for and never gotten, and the blessing she would have given eternal thanks for at Thanksgiving.

He was the lover she'd imagined meeting when she'd knocked on that ordinary door on an ordinary house in a middle-class suburb in Perth.

And didn't that sluice a bucket of cold water over her right there? How cruel life was that it would send her a man who could make her feel like this now. Here. In this place.

A place where she had no wish to feel anything, least of all this heavy, pooling heat between her thighs.

Vaguely was she aware of the towel at his hips tugging loose between them and falling away at the same time as his hand curled over her breast, his thumb tracing the line where skin disappeared under fabric.

His mouth moved lower and he kissed her there, his

tongue flicking fire across the skin of her breast and she gasped, knowing she'd lost any semblance of control—times tables long forgotten, her senses in disarray.

A day or two more—a few more clients—and she'd be used to this.

And part of her rebelled.

She didn't ever want to get used to this.

She didn't ever want to be numb to something that felt so good.

Didn't want something that felt so good as to be ultimately meaningless.

She felt his hands at her back, felt a tug and a loosening and his hands easing the corset down and her nerves turned to panic with the knowledge that she couldn't do this—could no more turn off from what was happening than pretend that up was down or that night was day.

Couldn't bring herself to do this, whatever the reason, and knew that her mother would never in a million years expect her to.

"Actually, you know, maybe not," she said, wriggling away on an bubble of panic that came out half way to laughter, while her fingers held on tight to the front of her loosening corset.

He growled approvingly against her ear, his warm breath threatening to break her resolve as his hands skimmed her body and honed in on her panties instead. "You want to keep it on with the boots? Kinky."

"No! *Yes!*" She shook her head and tried to wriggle away. "But no, that wasn't *actually* what I meant."

"So what—" he said, not letting her go and nuzzling the skin below her ear so that she almost purred with it, "—did you mean?"

She pulled herself away from his hot-as-sin mouth. "I meant, you seem like a nice guy 'n' all... " She searched for the words. "But I'd rather not have sex right now, if it's all the same to you."

Finally she had his full attention. The hands at her hips stilled as he pulled his head back to look at her. "You'd rather —*what did you say*?"

The hungry growl in his voice was gone, she noticed,

replaced by a tone a lot less friendly. And it was a shame to make him mad when he seemed like a nice guy, but she guessed he had a right to be just a little cranky. She shrugged and smiled apologetically. "I don't know about you, but it's just not working for me."

His hands fell away from her, his blue eyes disbelieving, his lip tugged up into a what-the-hell without the words. "You're kidding me, right?"

She shrugged. "I'm real sorry, truly I am, but under the circumstances, I can't see the point of going on with this. So—uh—if you don't mind, you might put your clothes back on and—" her fingers did a little walk in the air between them—"go?"

His face screwed up. "Is this some kind of game? Because I didn't pay for the innocent virgin package or the comedy bedroom capers. Straight-up sex, that's all I'm here for. That's what I chose you for."

She swallowed and held her ground, which he wasn't making any easier for her. He looked gorgeous even when he was angry. Angry, naked and utterly gorgeous. There should be a law against it.

"Well, there's the problem in a nutshell right there," she said, clutching her loose corset to her breasts like a shield. "Because I didn't choose you."

"What?"

"Nobody asked me what I wanted."

"What?"

"I'm real sorry."

"You already said that," he growled, as he plucked up his underwear and his jeans and thrust his legs through the holes like he was punching fence post holes in the ground. "Okay. I'm going."

She swallowed. She felt bad, she really did, just not bad enough to change her mind again. "I'm sure Bella will give you a refund. Or maybe Jasmine—"

"Forget it." No way was Mitch staying in this nuthouse a moment longer. He swiped on his shirt, stuffed his feet into socks and shoes. "What is your problem anyway?"

She blinked up at him and for a moment he feared those big green eyes were going to spill with tears, reminding him of another time and another's tears. Being spun back to that time was just what he needed to get the hell out of here before things got a whole lot uglier.

"Forget I asked," he growled, as he pulled open the door. "I don't want to know."

Chapter Three

"I 'm hoping to find work."

Mitch was nursing what was left of his second beer at a table in the front bar of the York Hotel when he heard it: the unmistakable twang of an American accent. A strikingly familiar American accent. His head snapped up and sure enough, she might be baring less skin than the last time he'd seen her, and have tied her hair back into a long rope of a braid for sure, but it was her. With hair that color, it couldn't possibly be anyone else.

And for the space of a second, until the shock of seeing her again dissipated and her words actually registered in his brain, he was half thinking she must have followed him here. Except he'd left Bella's more than an hour ago and there was no reason after what had happened—or more to the point, what hadn't happened—that she'd want to follow him anywhere. He was in no rush to renew their acquaintance. He pushed back in his chair, shrinking back into the shadows, wishing he had a hat to pull down over his face like they always did in the western movies he used to watch as a kid.

She let the big backpack drop from her shoulder onto the floor where it landed with a heavy thud. A backpacker then, he thought, as his eyes took in the view of her from the back in a little white shirt and faded jeans. That made sense. The west was full of backpackers, come to make their fortune, or at least enough money before moving on, while it seemed the rest of the Western Australian population was busy working at the mines.

"Are you hiring at the moment?" he heard her ask the young barman, who, given his accent and his blonde northern European looks, was no doubt a backpacker himself.

The young barman shrugged. "You'll have to ask the boss," he said, gesturing towards the fifty-something woman returning from the lounge bar behind. "Maude does all the hiring."

"What's that, lovey?" the woman said, hearing her name.

"This girl wants to know if there are any jobs."

"I'm new in town," Mitch heard her say, "And someone at the bakery told me she'd heard you had a vacancy."

The woman frowned and tossed a dish towel over her ample shoulder before placing her hands wide apart on the bar and all but resting her bust on the counter. "Yeah we did. But I'm sorry lovey, not any more. We just hired a new girl yesterday."

"Oh." He saw her shoulders drop even though she managed a tight smile. "Okay," she said, wearily, "thanks anyway."

She was lugging her pack from the floor and already turning to leave when he heard Maude say, "Have you tried Bella's? They're always looking for new girls."

He saw her eyelids droop, witnessed the intake of breath, before the girl turned back with a weak smile and said, "Thanks. I'll keep that in mind."

And then she was gone.

Mitch sat there for a while after she'd left, contemplating the foamy residue sliding slowly down the sides of his glass. So the cowgirl had lost her job. Or given it up. Either way, he shouldn't feel bad, it was clear she wasn't cut out for it. It wasn't like he'd done anything wrong.

Damn it, he hadn't done anything at all.

Other than leave Bella's a few hundred bucks poorer and a whole heap less satisfied.

So much for no complications.

The wooden bench outside the York Hotel had been soaking up the summer sun and was way too hot to sit on for long, but Scarlett had only realized that once she'd sat down and felt the sun's bite through her jeans. But right now a too-hot slab of wood beneath her butt and the sting of the sun on her shoulders were the least of her worries. Because she had walked the length and breadth of the main street looking for work and all she had to show for it were pairs of aching feet and shoulders. And the soul-destroying realization that Scarlett Buck had failed in spectacular style yet again.

It really shouldn't come as a surprise, she figured, given her life history, and yet this failure stung more than most. Maybe because there was no getting out of this one: no older-by-five-minutes sister close by to help her out of a sticky situation, no Aunt Margot to run to when her sister had despaired of her and there was no one else to turn to.

So she was stuck here, half a world away and at least fifteen hundred dollars from home and it was nobody's stupid fault but her own that she was even here. Nobody else to blame for spending her entire bank balance on a one-way ticket to Australia when everyone had warned her against it and she'd gone ahead and done it regardless. And nobody to blame but herself that she'd taken a second to email Tara, all excited when she'd got the gig at Bella's to tell her she'd be home in no more than a week or two.

So premature.

So typical.

So stupid!

And now Tara was wanting to know her flight details and when she'd be home and when Scarlett could be the one chasing her mother's appointments rather than her sister having to fit them all in to her shifts.

Which would all be perfectly fine and reasonable given Tara had shouldered the load and ferried their mom back and forth for her medical tests and shopped and cleaned for her while Scarlett had been traipsing half way around the world in the—okay, what had turned out to be futile—pursuit of true love. Except she wasn't going to be coming home any time soon after all.

What was she going to tell her sister now? That she'd been so turned on by her first client in her new job, that she'd freaked like some tensed-out virgin and been told to pack her things and go? What would her police officer twin sister make of that?

She could hear her entirely calm and sympathetic response right now.

"You took a job in a brothel?"

"It's not that bad, it's legal here, just like in Reno."

"It's still a brothel!"

"But it's okay, because I left before anything actually happened—"

"But you took a job—in a brothel!!!"

By that stage, her strait-laced police officer sister would be practically foaming at the mouth, and things would most likely go downhill from there.

No, it was better Tara didn't know.

Ever.

Because then there was no chance she might tell their mom. God knew, their Mom had way too much to deal with right now as it was.

Early Onset Parkinson's.

When her sister had told her the news, she hadn't believed it. Only old people got Parkinson's, didn't they? And Mom was what? Forty-five? Surely she was way too young. But no, the doctors were certain that the sometime falls she'd been having, the shakes and unsteadiness that she and Tara had put down to a couple of bourbons at night, had a far more sinister cause.

Who could blame their mom for getting depressed about it? Who wouldn't be depressed when there was no cure and when you knew that bit by bit, you would lose control of your movement and functionality and everything in life you took for granted. And now her mom needed her and she needed to be with her mom and instead here she was, stuck in some tiny podunk Australian town with no quick way of getting home. God, she was all kindsof fool. But she would make it up to her mom and her long-suffering sister one day. Come hell or high water, she'd make it up to them.

Tears squeezed unbidden from her eyes and she cursed and pressed the heels of her hands into her face. Dammit, she would not cry! She might be bone tired and in a tight spot, but she was twenty-six years old for heaven's sake. She would not damned well sit here and feel sorry for herself! She'd never get home to help her mom that way. No, she'd pick herself up and dust herself off and find a job and somewhere to bunk down for as long as it took to save up enough money for the fare and then she'd go home. End of story.

She swiped the tears from her cheeks and blinked to clear her vision as she stood, swinging the pack over her shoulder in the process.

She didn't see the man coming.

She didn't see anyone coming for that matter.

But she sure as hell felt him.

I t took a few moments for Mitch's eyes to adjust to the sunlight when he left the relative darkness of the pub, and by the time he saw her, sitting on the bench at the edge of the veranda, he was already half way to her. His footsteps slowed. God, what were the odds?

Then again, who needed odds? It was small town coincidence, he decided, and pure dumb luck.

He almost turned around and walked the other way but why should he? She was the one with the problem, after all. Besides, just like she hadn't noticed him in the bar when she'd turned up half an hour ago, she hadn't noticed him now, hadn't so much as turned her head towards him—or anyone else walking by for that matter. Just kept staring blindly out across the wide Kalgoorlie street, seemingly oblivious to the moving streetscape and everything and everyone around her. She looked younger than she had at Bella's, looked lost and lonely and at the end of her tether, and for a moment he was reminded of another girl, lost and lonely and desperate.

No!

Not your problem, he told himself. She's not Callie. It's just the guilt talking. *Move along, nothing to see here.*

Someone lurched into him from behind and belted out a curse, before staggering off along the veranda, more than a couple too many beers under his belt.

She noticed none of it. Just muttered something before dropping her face into her hands.

Perfect. She was so focused on whatever was on her mind, she wouldn't even notice when Mitch walked right on by. Which he was seconds from doing when the drunk in front of him lurched suddenly to the right at the same moment that the girl sprang up and around, the pack on her back connecting with the guy and sending him sprawling. The drunk stumbled, wrong-footed, across the veranda, before crashing into the pub wall with a loud, 'Oof!' and all hell broke loose.

"I'm sorry!" she cried, reaching for his arm to steady him, her eyes big and too late noticing the world around her, once again. "Are you okay?"

"You bloody bitch!" the drunk bit out, peeling himself off the wall slowly before wheeling around with a speed that should have been impossible given his intoxicated state.

"Ah hell," Mitch muttered, knowing dumb luck wasn't done with him yet.

The drunk flung out his arm as he spun, the back of his elbow heading straight for the girl's jaw.

Mitch wrenched her clear with one hand, blocking the man's arm with the other. "Calm down, sunshine. We don't hit women here."

The man either didn't hear or didn't care, just kept on coming, his face twisted and malevolent as he swung his other fist wildly around. Mitch caught that one too. "Little bitch knocked me over," the drunk snarled, as he tried to twist his limbs free. There was spit coming from the side of his mouth and he stank of stale beer and sour body.

"I didn't see him," she pleaded, all big green eyes in a face bleached of color, and if she was relieved to see it was Mitch coming to her rescue, it didn't show.

"You weren't bloody looking, bitch!"

"Calm down!" Mitch gave the drunk a shove, not letting go of his arms just yet. "You're drunk and you can't walk straight. Go home and sleep it off."

"I don't have to take orders from you." He pushed hard against Mitch, a lumbering mass of drunk whose blood alcohol level was higher than his IQ, and Mitch had no trouble slamming him up hard against the wall. "Didn't you hear the lady? She said she was sorry. How about you accept her apology and go home? Before the police want a bit more than just an apology from you." The drunk blinked bloodshot eyes at that, the logic of Mitch's words filtering through the fog of alcohol clouding his brain. "I'm goin'," he said Not that it stopped him letting let fly a few more curses after Mitch set him free with a shove, and he staggered off down the street.

The few pedestrians who'd stopped to watch a free show filtered off until just the two of them and an uncomfortable silence remained. He should go too, he thought, before things got even more awkward between them. It wasn't like he needed to be reminded of what they might have been doing earlier today if she hadn't decided it hadn't been working for her. It wasn't like he needed another lesson in humiliation.

"I didn't choose you."

The words had stuck in his craw ever since she'd uttered them. Well, fine. He'd done his good deed for the day. He could choose not to hang around here any longer.

Move along.

And he was moving along. Heading back to his blessedly uncomplicated life even if that did come with its own frustrations.

"Wait."

He stopped and glanced at the veranda. "Now you and I both know you don't really want me to."

"At least let me thank you."

He didn't bother glancing, this time. "You don't have to

do that."

"I do. Let me at least buy you a coffee or something."

He turned, all set to say no again, but he saw her looking up at him, her face still pale, and he felt the shadow of his little sister in the hurt and despair in her eyes and his gut twisted so tight he couldn't breathe.

What if someone had been able to help Callie but they'd chosen to walk away instead?

What if this girl needed help and he walked away now? Before at least making sure she was okay? Would it kill him if he stopped long enough to find out?

The girl made like she was going to say something, her lips poised half way to a word, but then she closed her mouth and gave her head a shake, as if she'd decided against it. Instead she hauled her backpack over her shoulder. "Sorry," she simply said, before she turned to go. "I'm the last person you'd want to have coffee with."

She was right and she was wrong. He'd been happy to leave her at Bella's. Would have quite happily lived his entire life without their paths ever crossing again. But they had crossed, and she'd needed help, and if he wasn't mistaken, she still did.

And maybe she didn't particularly want his, but hell, it seemed to him like she could hardly afford to pick and choose.

"Coffee would be fine," he said. And just in case she needed to have it spelled out, in case she might imagine he was still trying to collect on the money he'd dropped at Bella's, he added, "Just coffee."

Her lids shuttered down, long lashes lingering a while on her cheeks. Not a blink, but a measured pause for a measured response, before she opened her eyes on a nod, "Just coffee then," she said, "I owe you."

He didn't argue the point. Just nodded and felt himself smile.

Her face relaxed enough to smile back, just tentatively, but it was a start. She looked summer fresh, dressed as she was in a lacy white cotton vest with faded jeans tucked into tan boots and her scarlet hair braided into a thick rope down her back. Girl-next-door pretty, with clear skin and a wide mouth and eyes almost too big for her face—until she smiled and the curve of her lips somehow balanced it all out.

He looked away before he could dwell too much on how good she looked, because that wasn't why he was having coffee with her, and pointed out a cafe across the street that had stools along a bench overlooking the street and where he knew they'd both be more comfortable than sitting face to face. She wouldn't let him carry her pack, even though it had to weigh twice as much as she did. Independent, mistrustful, or just plain stubborn, he didn't know what she was, but he couldn't help but find a measure of respect for her, right there.

"What can I get you?" she asked, checking out the drinks menu. The cafe was busy with the afternoon tea crowd, but they found a couple of stools like he'd hoped at the front.

"Long black," he said.

Americano, she translated in her head approvingly. But then, he hadn't struck her as a cappuccino or a soy latte sort of guy. Her stomach rumbled and she thought longingly of food—how long had it been since breakfast? But cafe prices were too extravagant for her limited budget. Every dollar would have to count now, more now than ever—and so when the waitress came for their order, two long blacks was the extent of it.

She pulled a few coins from her coin purse and stacked them in a pile, and when that was done, stared out at the passing traffic, grateful that the man beside her seemed content to just sit and watch too. And it was easier looking at the traffic than looking at him sitting beside her and being reminded of how he looked dripping wet and naked but for a fluffy white towel lashed around his hips.

Don't go there, she told herself, just say what you need to say.

And she was about to, but his leg brushed against hers, denim against denim, and she jumped. Hoo-ee, if the guy wasn't electric or something. "I really could do with that coffee," she said, looking over her shoulder as she poked a few strands of hair back behind her ears.

"It'll come," he said. "You're bound to be a bit shook

up."

She smiled. If only he knew what was shaking her up. Well, there were a couple of things shaking her up, and only one of them was him, and if she didn't say something soon about the other, she'd burst.

"About before," she started, her eyes still fixed on the moving streetscape. "I'm real sorry about what happened."

"Not your fault. He was drunk."

She squeezed her eyes shut. "Not that before. The other before. At Bella's."

A pause.

"You don't need to explain."

His voice had a gruff edge to it. He was still sore about it, she could tell, and that was fair, but she still needed to explain. "No, listen." She dragged in air that tasted of summer dust and small town, and it struck her that it wasn't that different from how summer air smelt back home in Marietta. Except it was winter at home now and the air blowing down off Copper Mountain and whistling along Main Street would be cold and clear, and her mom would no doubt be doing battle with the central heating and losing again. She shouldn't have to struggle with that on top of trying to cope with everything else. Scarlett turned away from the traffic and thoughts of home. What was the point? It would be months before she'd get home now. "Bella told you I was new. I was brand new, as it happens. You would have been my first."

His eyes opened wide. Really wide. "First? What, first time ever, you mean?" He sounded appalled.

"Oh hell no," she said, laughing. "Not *that* kind of first. Just first in my new ex-job. But I do feel bad about it and I just wanted you to know, it wasn't you or anything you did, it was me."

Their coffees arrived and she was grateful for the interruption before she'd gone and told him how it had been damned near impossible to stop and wouldn't that have been embarrassing? She breathed in the bewitching aroma of her coffee instead. It smelt strong and rich and exactly what she needed right now.

'It wasn't you—it was me.'

Funny, Mitch thought, that was almost the same thing Kristelle had told him, only the other way around. It was kind of refreshing not to be blamed for something for once.

"How about we forget about what happened before and start again." He held out his hand. "The name's Mitch. What's yours?"

She frowned a little as she regarded his hand. "Scarlett," she said, raising her eyes as she slipped her hand warily into his. "But you already know that."

It took a moment for the name to register, maybe because her hand was smooth in his and came with a burst of feel good that reminded him just how good she'd felt in his arms. And because his body didn't need a reminder of what he'd been so close to having and missed out on, he let her hand go and focused on her words instead. "Like Scarlett O'Hara in *Gone with the Wind*?"

She rolled her eyes. "Yeah, the very same. Mom's the original *Gone with the Wind* Windie. Would you believe, I have a twin sister called Tara."

"Seriously?"

"Oh yeah. Mom even has a poster of Rhett Butler hanging above her bed."

Her voice went quiet at the end and she lost her smile, her eyes a million miles away, her hands fiddling with the ends of the thick red braid dangling heavily over her shoulder.

"You miss them?"

She sighed. "Hell, yeah." And then she looked up, a forced smile that couldn't mask the tension around her eyes, and he figured there was something majorly unsaid right there. "But that's normal when you're so far from home, right?"

"Sure it is. So where is home, Scarlett?"

"Montana. A little town called Marietta, not far from Bozeman. Ever heard of it?"

"Can't say that I have. Haven't spent a lot of time in the States, though I did get to New York once." He sipped his coffee. He remembered it well. Kristelle had wanted a treat for their two month anniversary. A week 'somewhere special', she'd said.

Looking back, he could see it had been a test. *'How much do you love me?'* she'd been asking even then. *'How much am I worth to you?'*

But back then it had suited him. He'd always wanted to go to New York City and why not indulge her? There were only seven days out of every twenty-one when they could even see each other, which was hardly conducive to getting to know someone.

At that stage, he'd still thought she might be worth getting to know.

The taste of the coffee turned bitter in his mouth.

More fool him.

"Kalgoorlie reminds me a lot of Marietta, actually." The girl alongside him looked thoughtful as she swirled her coffee cup in her hands, before she took a sip and turned her attention out the window. "All these gorgeous old buildings with balconies and verandas." She turned to him, "Marietta started as a mining town too, you know, but not with gold like here. They found copper up on Copper Mountain and for a while the town did really well, but then the copper ran out and Marietta almost became a ghost town for a while."

She screwed up her nose. "Anyhow, that's probably way too much information. The point I was getting to is that Marietta's about as different from New York City as this place here is."

She was wrong about the too much information. Mining was in his blood, it was part of who he was and what he did fourteen days straight of twelve-hour shifts. He could listen to her talk about her town's copper history all day. Then again, he could listen to her talking about anything. Her accent matched her boots for pure country and the way her face lit up when she was talking about her home town, he could almost see it projected from the depths of her green eyes.

"I believe it," he said. "Like chalk and cheese." Like the world of difference between Scarlett and Kristelle, it occurred to him. And then he wondered how he could be so certain when he'd known Scarlett for all of ten minutes and they'd hardly got off to an auspicious start.

But now that he'd put the two women side by side in the

same thought, his mind began to play with the germ of an idea.

A mad idea, sure, but it had possibilities.

And if it helped his lonesome cowgirl out into the bargain, everyone was a winner.

The more he mulled it over, the more perfect it became until even his coffee started tasting better.

Because he wasn't interested in commitment, and if he wasn't mistaken, she had a hankering to get home. What could be better? She could still be his temporary cowgirl—only for a few days instead of the few hours he'd imagined.

It could work.

Hell, it would be worth turning up with Scarlett on his arm just to see the look on Kristelle's face.

"Anyhow," Scarlett said, swallowing down the last of her coffee before she stood and reached for her pack. "I better get moving. Thanks for, you know, helping out and—um—well, for the conversation." She pointed to her small pile of coins. "I've left the money for the coffee."

And Mitch knew the moment was now. He'd wanted to help her and he wasn't sure how, but he wasn't naive enough to think that a conversation over a cup of coffee was going to magically solve all her problems. But something else might...

"Where are you headed?"

"Oh, you know," she looked out the window longingly, and he could tell she didn't have a clue, "I thought I'd just check out the town a bit."

"And where are you staying?"

"Excuse me, but I don't think that's any of your business."

"Okay, let me put it like this. Seems to me that you need money to get home but you haven't got a job, and I'm guessing, the way you're lugging that pack around, that you haven't got anywhere to stay either."

Her green eyes opened wide with shock and indignation. "What? What's it to you anyhow?"

"Simple," he said, knowing he'd hit the mother lode. "Because I've got a proposition for you."

Chapter Four

carlett laughed if only to cover up her disappointment. She'd had plenty of propositions before and she was pretty certain of what this one might entail. And there she'd been thinking he was one of the good guys. There she'd been thinking she'd almost miss him once she walked out of here. "Thanks but no thanks."

"You haven't even heard what I'm offering yet."

"You think I need to? A proposition, you said. Sounds to me like you're still looking to collect. Though I really don't understand why you'd want to throw good money after bad."

"After what happened before, do you really think I'd be insane enough to offer you money for sex?"

Heads at nearby tables swiveled at the S word. Conversations and clatter stopped and all ears angled closer. She scanned the faces looking at her, held out her hands in a shrug and smiled. "Can you believe it? He's still sore because I turned him down. What's a girl to do?"

"Good for you," said one nodding grey-haired matron at a table nearby.

"Make him work for it, I say," added her friend.

"Hear, hear," said someone from another table, "make him sweat!"

Scarlett laughed and bowed a little. "Why, thank you all for the advice. I'll be sure to do that. I'd just hate for him to think I was easy."

"Hell, Scarlett," he said, "I *know* you're not easy." He

took her by the hand and hauled her pack over his shoulder and said, "Let's blow this joint."

"Have fun, you two," called the first woman after them. "Don't do anything we wouldn't."

"Well, that leaves plenty of scope!"

The cafe dissolved into shrieks of post-menopausal laughter that followed them out onto the street.

"Why did we have to leave?" Scarlett asked, still smiling as she waved back to her new friends through the big open window. "That was just getting to be fun."

"How was I going to negotiate anything with the entire cast of the *Golden Girls* listening in? I'd be toast."

She laughed and it felt so good. He was still holding her hand, his fingers warm and sure around hers and she liked it. Liked it? She damn well near sizzled with it. It was the best she'd felt since she'd landed in Perth and called the number she'd rehearsed so many times she knew it by heart.

And look how that ended.

A sliver of fear wound its way around her stomach and pulled tight. "Hey, are you married?"

He looked down at her, his expression guarded. "No-o-o."

The knot slipped undone and she found she could breathe again. "Good."

"And just for the record, I'm not looking for a wife."

"Even better. Nothing personal, but I'm not looking for a husband either."

"Excellent," he said, "so we understand each other."

She wasn't so sure about that. There was plenty she didn't know about him, but she did know he had nothing to worry about on her part. After making a complete ass of herself over Travis, she was so not going down that road again in a hurry. In fact, it was high time she stopped doing everything in a hurry. Maybe if she took her time and seriously considered the pros and cons of things a little more before she dived—headlong—in, she wouldn't get herself into these messes. Maybe it was time to act a bit more responsibly like her sister, with her good sense and her good job and her oh-so-sensible fiancé.

Then she thought about Tara's history teacher fiancé,

Simon, for a moment. Hmmm, well, maybe she didn't especially want one of those, exactly, but she could do responsible if she really set her mind to it, she was sure.

Meanwhile this man's hand was warm around hers, his fingers long. Was it sensible to be holding hands with a man you barely knew? Maybe not, but she could hardly expect to get this sensible thing down pat in one shot.

"This should do." He pulled her down next to him onto a bench outside the information center, where there was not a golden girl in sight and no risk of their conversation being overheard except in meaningless snatches in passing. He released her hand to let her pack down onto the ground.

"Jesus, that thing's enormous, I thought backpackers traveled light. What the hell have you got in there?"

She shrugged as he settled back down alongside her and cursed the lack of interest on eBay. "You really don't want to know. So tell me, Mr. Mitch *deal-or-no-deal*, what exactly is this proposition of yours?"

He looked at her, at her startlingly red hair and her green eyes and a mouth that made words sound too cute to be real and wondered if he was making the biggest mistake of his life. Then again, life had been pretty dull lately and it was a hell of a way to go. "I was right about you needing money to get home, wasn't I?"

She stretched her long legs out and stuck her hands in her jeans pockets and looked out at the traffic. "Maybe."

"That's okay, I don't need the details. That's your business. All I need is a favor." *And something to distract me from those legs.*

Clad in denim with cute little rips in all the right places and ending in those fancy cut leather boots, they were long and lean and the best thing he'd seen since he'd eyeballed them unwrapped back at Bella's. And while he told himself her legs weren't the reason he was asking her to do him a favor, he sure wouldn't object to seeing them unwrapped again sometime soon.

Maybe he would.

And that was a worry when he was supposed to be doing this to help her out.

So much for being altruistic.

"So what's the favor...? Earth calling Mitch?"

He looked back up, wondering just how long he'd been missing in action thinking about little tears in jeans that opened when she moved and revealed a tiny glimpse of tan skin beneath. "Yeah, here's the plan. I need a temporary girlfriend, or someone to act as my girlfriend. Just for a few days. For a wedding I have to attend this weekend."

"So why do you need a pretend girlfriend?"

"Because it's my ex getting married."

"Well, that's a no brainer. Just don't go."

"Not possible. She's marrying my best mate."

"Ah." This time she nodded. "But I'm sure he'd understand if you choked, given he's marrying your ex and all. He'd probably rather you weren't there anyhow."

'Yeah, you'd think so, wouldn't you? Trouble is, he's asked me to be best man."

She sat up. "What the hell? And you said yes?"

"Only because he didn't tell me who he was marrying before I agreed to do it."

She stretched back out again. "Wow. So does this guy have it in for you or something?"

"No, like I said, he's a mate." And Robbo was. They'd met at university and done two years of engineering together before Robbo had decided that he preferred counting things to building them and switched to accounting instead. He still worked for a mining company, but his place was firmly behind a desk in the big city head office.

"Yeah, I can see that. A good mate, clearly, because in case you hadn't noticed, he's marrying your ex."

"I had actually noticed that." And he couldn't really blame Robbo for jumping at the chance, because Kristelle was really something to look at and Robbo had never had much luck in the female department. He must have thought all his Christmases had come at once when she'd knocked on his door bemoaning Mitch's failings.

"Okay, so let me see if I've got this straight. You're stuck with going to this wedding, because you're the best man, only he's marrying your ex and you don't want to go alone because you don't want to look like some kind of loser?"

Good grief. So maybe this wasn't his best ever idea.

"Thank you for your succinct and incisive assessment, but can we drop the loser angle? Maybe I just don't want her to think I'm available."

"Why? You think she's still got the hots for you or something? Then why would she marry someone else?"

Who knew? "Look, Kristelle and I were together a couple of months all up—most of the time with me on shift so we didn't get to see that much of each other. And it was it good at first but it clearly wasn't going anywhere, so I suggested a break."

"And let me guess. She didn't take it well."

He thought back to the tears, the melodrama, the breast beating and the incessant 'whys.' "Yeah, you could say that."

She nodded. "So you think she's marrying your friend to get back at you."

He shrugged. "I know it sounds crazy."

"Maybe they really love each other. How long have they been together now?"

"Three months."

"Wow. She is a fast worker."

"Oh yeah."

"So basically you don't trust her or her motives."

He thought back to her final words. *You'll be sorry. I'll make you sorry.'* At the time he'd thought nothing of it. She was angry. She'd get over it. Hell, it wasn't like they'd ever professed undying love for each other.

It was Robbo who'd explained that as soon as Mitch had left Perth and gone back to the mines, Kristelle had turned up on his doorstep in tears needing comfort. And finding it, apparently, though Mitch had stopped Robbo short before he could tell him all the gory details. And it was Kristelle who'd apparently begged him not to tell Mitch they were together so as not to upset him. Like hell. More likely so she'd have Robbo wrapped around her little finger before Mitch could warn him to run like hell.

No. He didn't trust her one little bit. "Not entirely."

"But what can she do? She's marrying someone else."

"That's just it. I don't know if she'd try anything, but I sure wouldn't put it past her. The simple fact is she'll have less opportunity than if I turn up alone." He looked at her.

"Think of your role as insurance."

She screwed up her nose. "I'm not sure I can do insurance. It sounds awfully dull."

"Then think of it as being a guard dog."

She smiled. "Now *that* I can do."

He looked at her with new admiration. "I always wanted a red headed Rottweiler. So—will you do it then?"

"What's in it for me?" she asked, but she was smiling and he had a good feeling about this.

"You're doing me the favor. You name your price."

Was he for real? "Okay." She stuck up her chin. If he wanted a pretend girlfriend for a few days, it was going to cost him. "If I'm going to even think about this—just think about it, mind—I'm going to want fifteen hundred dollars on the table. Cash. Paid in full the day after the wedding."

He didn't even blink. "Done. Plus expenses of course. So you'll do it?"

"Um." Had he really said 'done'? Could she really have the funds to go home in just a few days' time and all she had to do was pretend to be someone's girlfriend? It was that simple? Hope, that fragile bubble of hope, that had been dashed and bruised and battered by today's disappointments, peeled itself off the floor and sucked in air.

"Oh, and you'll need something to wear for the wedding of course. Unless you've got something suitable in your backpack."

Suitable for a wedding? Now, that *was* funny.

"Nope. Nothing suitable for a wedding," she said, with a straight face. "Absolutely nothing."

"Okay." He looked at his watch. "We'll go shopping tomorrow. So, what else do you need to know? Will you do it?"

It was all happening so fast. She liked fast. She thrived on fast. But it was her downfall too, she'd learned. Things looked so good on the surface, she didn't bother with the details. She had to learn to bother with the details. And there was one detail that was unsaid, and sizzlingly unsettling, and it couldn't stay that way.

"What about sex?" she asked. 'Will that be expected as part of the pretend girlfriend deal too?"

"We'll have to look like a couple. You'll have to share the villa they've booked for me."

"So that's a yes?" Damn, did she sound too hopeful?

"Sex is actually outside this arrangement."

"So, that's a no?"

He smiled and that killer combination of blue eyes and smiling mouth almost did her head in. "That's not what I said."

Oh hell. What was that supposed to mean?

"So what's it to be Scarlett?"

"Hang on a minute, I have to think about this." She squeezed her mouth and her eyes tight shut, the cogs in her mind spinning around, putting the brakes on the *Hell yes!* response that she was renowned for. If she was going to be more responsible she was going to have to stop doing that. She was going to have to seriously think about this. Think about the pros and cons and what could possibly go wrong, because sure as God made little green apples—if she didn't, something would.

Pro, she thought: it was quick easy money, quicker than even Bella's had promised to be. And it was all expenses paid. *Bonus.*

Pro: she wouldn't even have to confess to Tara that she'd been sacked from a brothel. *Yes!*

Pro: she'd get to spend the next few days with a guy who came with an electric touch that made her toes curl. All that rampant electricity. All that masculine heat. Just remembering how he'd felt naked and next to her sent her pulse tripping all over again.

Oh hell. She turned her mind to the cons before she'd talked herself into it on the pros alone.

Con: she'd jumped before at the chance for quick easy money, and look how that had turned out.

Con: she didn't really know this guy. He could be an axe murderer for all she knew. Why should she believe his story about a jilted lover and her need for revenge when he could be packing an axe?

Con: if she ended up dead, Tara would never forgive her. Oh, maybe that should be a pro?

Con: she'd get to spend the next few days with a guy

who came with an electric touch that made her toes curl. All that masculine heat. Ooh, but that was a pro too. Then again...

"Excuse me?"

She was still tossing up whether spending more time with this guy was a pro or a con. She didn't appreciate the interruption. She didn't bother opening her eyes. "What?"

"What are you doing?"

She cracked open her eyes and peeked up at him. "What do you think I'm doing? I'm thinking."

"So why's it taking you so long?"

"Because I'm weighing up the pros and cons. Making a sensible decision. I always jump into things and it always goes wrong. This time I'm determined to do the right thing."

"Fine," he said, "just keep in mind that the wedding is Saturday."

"That's three whole days away." She closed her eyes again.

"But our plane leaves in two."

She cracked them open again and looked at him. "What plane? Where's the wedding?"

"Broome, on the north west coast. Pearl capital of Australia. Sandy beaches, camel rides at night and the best sunset in the world. And if the weather gods are favorable, the not-to-be-missed Staircase to the Moon. Are you coming?"

She blinked, his words adding six more *pros* to the mix right there. "Well, why didn't you say so?" She'd heard about Broome while she'd been waiting tables in a cafe in Perth. Heard the buzz about the Staircase to the Moon effect across the mud flats at full moon and how it wasn't to be missed if she could get there. She'd given up all hope of getting there this visit. Assumed it was just another addition to the bucket list of things in Australia that she'd have to go home without seeing this time.

"So?" he said, staring at her like she was crazy, "Will you do it?"

"Hell, yes!" she said, punching his arm and with a smile that felt a mile wide. "Besides, it wouldn't be fair to let you turn up alone and look like some kind of loser."

"What's your name?"

Scarlett was sitting on an arm chair in his rented apartment doing a Sudoku while Mitch was on the phone to his travel agent or airline or something. He'd found her a single apartment in the same complex and she'd stashed her pack away and hung up her dress—*the wedding dress—new, with tags—that continued to go irritatingly bid-less on eBay*—in the little closet. And now she was waiting for him to finish whatever he was doing so they could go out for Chinese food.

"Hey!" He was frowning when she looked up. "What's your name?"

"Scarlett," she said back, wondering why he was having such trouble remembering her name. She'd told him, what, twice already?

"No. Your second name."

"Oh. Buck."

"What?"

"Buck. Scarlett Buck. Have you got a problem with that?"

"Buck? No, no," he said shaking his head to whomever was on the phone, though they would miss the head shaking completely. "I said Buck. B-U-C-K. B. For brandy. Not—" he laughed. "Yeah, not that." He raised his eyebrows at her and she laughed and went back to her Sudoku as he pulled out his credit card and finished the reservation.

"All done," he said, repocketing his cell, "Ms. Scarlett Buck."

Something about the way he said her name alerted her. She looked up from her puzzle. "Yes?"

He was smiling. "Cute name."

"Yeah. Bella thought so too."

His smile widened. "I bet. Probably thought she was going to make a killing. Guess you must have had a bit of a rough time growing up though."

She screwed up her nose. "You better believe it. Tara

and I spent an entire childhood being pooped on from a great height because of our name." She shrugged. "'We got so used to it after a while that someone would say something and we'd just laugh and say it was water off a Buck's back." She grinned up at him. "They breed us tough in Montana."

He liked it. "Beer?" he asked, as he pulled a Corona from the fridge and held it up. He pulled out another and flipped both lids when she nodded. "What's she like, this sister of yours?" he asked, as he handed her the longneck and sat down in the other arm chair, his elbows resting on wide-apart knees. He had his shirt sleeves rolled up and his forearms were strong and lean, and she didn't know what it was about him but just looking at him was intoxicating and one beer would likely put her over the limit. Lucky she wasn't driving. "Same as you?"

She laughed at that, happy to be distracted. "Hardly."

"But you're twins, right?"

"We're twins, but not identical. We're pretty different, when all's said and done."

"How so?"

She shrugged. "Tara's real pretty—"

"Not so different then," he said, and she felt a bloom of heat burst open inside her right there.

She bowed her head and raised her beer at him. "Thank you, kind sir. What I was going to say, is Tara's real pretty only she doesn't like to show it too much. I mean, she's got the most gorgeous long blonde hair, but she pulls it back real tight and wouldn't be caught dead getting a color—well," she lifted up her hair, "anything like this. And she's real sensible and does everything right." She took a sip of her beer. "Whereas, and you may have noticed this, I tend to be the one who jumps in feet first and, more often than not, *bucks up*."

He laughed into the neck of his beer before he took a draught. "Sounds like you're pretty hard on yourself. She can't be that perfect."

"Ha, then listen to this. She doesn't just have a good job, she's a cop—a patrol officer over at Bozeman and she's marrying sensible Simon the history teacher later this year. No doubt about it, Tara is the perfect daughter."

"Definitely hard on yourself."

She shook her head and threw her legs over the arm of the chair and looked up at the ceiling, the bottom of her beer resting on her belly. "You know, I think I'm just starting to realize how much grief I've put everyone through these past twenty-six years. Tara's the sensible twin and I'm the flaky one, the one who dropped out of school, the one who spent more time under the bleachers researching anatomy with boys than cheering my sister on her ribbon-winning way from up top. And sometimes I've thought Tara's just being a party pooper when she gives me advice or tells me not to do something, but I'm starting to see that sometimes she's even a little bit right. Well, a lot right, actually, come to think of it. Sometimes I think I should be more like her."

He sipped his beer. "Interesting."

He was being polite, she was sure. She'd seen Amtrak timetables that were more engaging than the details of her family's dynamics. "What about you? Have you got family somewhere around?"

"Mum's still going well in Melbourne. Dad died a few years back. Heart attack."

"Nasty. Our Dad left when we were thirteen. I think Mom would have been a lot happier if he'd had a heart attack." She looked over. "Oh, damn, I probably shouldn't have said that."

"No, it's okay."

She smiled her thanks. "So, any other family?"

His lips pulled tight. "I had a sister. Once."

Crap. She'd done it again. She really had to learn to quit while she was ahead. She put her beer down. "I need the bathroom."

She was half way to her feet when he said, "Thank you," from whatever dark place he was inhabiting.

"What for?"

His eyes, when he looked up, were more gray than blue, a clear sky scudded with clouds. "For not saying you were sorry like it was somehow your fault, like most people do."

That was a hard one to respond to. "I am sorry though, but for your losses. Especially for your sister. Because as much as my own sister drives me crazy trying to protect me,

I can't imagine life without her."

He took a deep breath and smiled uncertainly as he raised his beer. "To sisters, then," and she picked up her beer and they clinked bottles.

"I'll drink to that."

T hey had Chinese food in a restaurant nearby, honey shrimp—except they were called prawns here—and crispy duck with fried rice washed down with an almost local Margaret River white wine. The food was small-town Chinese restaurant good, and Mitch talked about his fly-in fly-out job at the mines, about the fourteen day shifts filled with twelve hour work days and big meals in the mess and maybe a swim before bed and then getting up the next day to do it all over again. Scarlett listened and crunched shrimp tails between her teeth and sucked honey off her fingers and thought that maybe it wasn't such a crazy idea that she'd come to Australia after all, or she would never have known about any of this kind of lifestyle.

Or more importantly, that otherwise she would never have met Mitch. Maybe she should send Travis a thank-you postcard from Broome? She was halfway tempted.

And Mitch watched a woman who could follow his every word and ask questions while eating with gusto and relish and who wasn't afraid to get her fingers dirty in the process. And he liked it. A lot.

When she licked her fingers clean, he wished she'd offered them to him first.

And then he smacked his lustful thoughts down hard. He was trying to help her out. Offer her a solution to her problems, so that whatever was bothering her would disappear.

At least, that had been his intention.

Now that she was coming with him to Broome he wasn't so sure of his motives. She was fun. A breath of fresh air into his highly regulated existence. A temporary cowgirl for a short-term problem.

And while sex wasn't part of their deal, that didn't mean he wouldn't welcome it if it happened. He wasn't looking for commitment but where was the risk? She was going home in a few days. And they were going to be sharing a villa after all. Sure, it was a big villa. Loads of space for two.

Loads and loads of space.

And one really big bed.

Chapter Five

T hey went shopping the next day, to a boutique in a building that would have been right at home in Marietta: an old three level Victorian with arched windows and a veranda that had been prettified up outside in pinks and whites. Inside was a confection of dainty bow-legged furniture topped with flower arrangements and there were crystal chandeliers hanging from the ceiling and wall-length mirrors reflecting the rows and rows of tulle, satin, and silk dresses.

Scarlett had to pause for a second, remembering a trip not long ago to the local bridal store, *Married in Marietta*, where she thought she'd found the bargain of the century. A two thousand dollar Vera Wang designer last-season gown marked down to three hundred and fifty bucks, all because some poor woman had been stood up at the church and wanted to return it. It had been crazy because she'd only gone in to the store for a look around because the town was full of the talk of the Graff Hotel's one hundredth anniversary Great Wedding Giveaway. She knew she'd never be part of that, because she was so full of thinking about Travis and all his talk of soul mates and forever that she was dreaming what-ifs. But when she found the dress, it was like a sign. An omen.

Even if it came with more yards of frothy tulle than she'd had frosty winter mornings.

Even if it teetered so very dangerously on her own

personal borderline between classy and meringue. What the hell did that matter?

It was a Vera Wang two thousand dollar dress on sale for three hundred and fifty bucks.

And she'd had to have it.

Travis would love it, she'd told herself. He'd get the surprise of his life when she turned up on his doorstep, and then she'd be wearing it in mere weeks! She'd beat her sensible sister down the aisle and wouldn't she be the good daughter for once?

Idiot!

"You okay?"

She looked into Mitch's sky-blue eyes and blinked away the past. "Yeah. Let's do this."

He made her try on a dozen gorgeous cocktail dresses, any of which she would have been perfectly happy to wear, but he only let her stop when he found *it*: emerald green and the perfect foil to her hair, in a strapless design that hugged her breasts and fitted slim over her waist and hips in layers of ribbon-wide satin.

"You look amazing," he said, and it wasn't his words that warmed her through and through, it was the husky quality to his Aussie drawl and the raw heat in his eyes. If she'd had any qualms that he was dressing her to make his ex feel bad, they were banished before they could take root. He was dressing her for him.

She'd never thought blue was a warm color, not until now, not until she'd felt this slow, warm glide of his eyes over her form leaving a smoking trail of heat.

So sex wasn't part of this deal?

Didn't mean it wasn't going to happen.

Shoes and accessories were next. He took his time, not rushing and not checking out the sale items like she was, but going for top shelf every time.

She wondered whether he was as attentive a lover as he was a shopper.

And then she remembered that first encounter in Bella's, and the hot stroke of his tongue against her breast.

Oh yeah!

"We should work out some kind of story," he said, when the shopping was done and they stopped for a bite of lunch, "for when we're in Broome. Someone's bound to ask how we met." Like Kristelle for example.

"Sure. So who are we expecting to meet up there? Apart from your ex and her lover."

He shot her a dark look. "We're staying at the same resort as Robbo and Kristelle and their parents."

She raised her eyebrows. "What, with the bride and groom and *both* sets of parents?"

"Yeah, and the bridesmaid. Sharon, I think her name is."

The reality of the task ahead suddenly loomed. Maybe this wouldn't be quite the cake walk she'd imagined. Pretending to partner Mitch for an ex who might or might not be out for revenge was one thing. But questions would invariably be asked and the lie would grow and grow, and barefaced lying to decent people whom she had no wish to deceive and who'd never and were never likely to do her or her nearest and dearest any harm was another thing entirely. "That sounds like fun," she fibbed. "Will there be alcohol?"

"Lots, I'm hoping. The villas have full butler service with all the trimmings."

"Excellent." Those butlers would no doubt be busy. "So what's our story then?"

"I'm thinking we keep it simple. We met in Kalgoorlie. You were backpacking around Australia and we bumped into each other."

"Now there's a bit of creative genius."

"So what would you say?"

"No, I like it, let's keep it simple. We met in Kalgoorlie. No lie there. Me the hapless tourist and you who just happened to be in town for a few days. Almost the truth. How long have we been seeing each other?"

"Long enough to cover a couple of my leave periods. Let's make it a bit over a month."

"Okay. I was barely in Australia back that far, but nobody's going to check my travel arrangements surely?"

"Exactly how long have you been here?"

"Not long. Not relevant. I'm sure it won't come up. So we met in Kalgoorlie and clicked and the rest, as they say, is history."

"Yeah," he said uncertainly, "That ought to do it. What do you think?"

"Perfect," she said. She just loved a man who spent time on the important things. Like shopping.

"I'll get this one," she said, going to pick up the tab as they left.

"Hey." His hand came down on hers. "All expenses paid, remember?"

"Yeah, and you just paid for some absolute doozies. So allow me a little pride."

He took his hand away. "Your wish is my command."

"Atta boy," she said with a smile. "That's definitely more like it."

The girl at the cash register punched in the order and brought up the total. "That'll be twenty-five dollars and seventy cents, thanks."

"There you go," she said, handing over the notes and change she had ready in her hand. The girl counted it and flicked her eyes up suspiciously.

Scarlett had already turned away. "So where to next?"

"What about your change?"

"I gave her the right money." She turned and the woman waved all okay.

"So how did you know how much it would be before she'd put it in?"

She shrugged. "I added it up."

"But there were no prices on the tab."

"But there were on the menu."

"You remembered?"

"It's not rocket science, Mitch, it's just a lunch tab. Now, what do we do next?"

They spent the rest of the day sightseeing. They walked the length of the main street, most of which Scarlett had already seen in passing, but this was stopping to check out the history of the buildings. And then Mitch took her to the town's biggest attraction. Scarlett gazed over the massive Super Pit, the gold mine that was more than a mile long, half that wide and a quarter mile deep and that never slept, the sides stepped and dusty from the endless parade of giant trucks up and down the tiered terrain twenty-four hours a day.

It was late afternoon by the time they got there, and Scarlett's feet were aching in her boots, but the view was breathtaking, the slanting sun casting a golden glow over the walls of the massive mine. Copper Mountain back home in Marietta had always seemed the biggest thing in the world to her, a huge backdrop to the town she'd grown up in, but this thing—this mine—was mammoth.

"Is this like what you do up north?"

"Kind of, but it's iron ore country up there, rich and red like you wouldn't believe."

"What do you actually do there?"

"Lots of things. As a mining engineer it can be anything from feasibility studies to mine planning and open cut design to budgets and reports. It can be physical one day and then you're stuck in meetings the next. But it's good. What do you do back home?"

She crossed her arms along the wire fence barrier and looked out over the vast hole in the ground. "Well, that's a hard one. Drop out of things mostly. I worked in the local diner for a while. Tried a bit of work at the salon where Mom works as a nail technician but it didn't appeal. I'm not really qualified to do anything. Apart from screwing up. If I could make a living from that I'd be doing great."

He was about to tell her she was being hard on herself again, but she was leaning her head on her arms looking at him and her green eyes were smiling and the sun was turning her scarlet hair as red as the Pilbara country where he worked. The breeze was turning the loose tendrils of hair around her face into snakes and he thought, *beautiful* and couldn't help but lean closer.

"You'll find something," he said, snagging a flying tendril and curling it behind her ear, knowing there just had to be something amazing in store that deserved this woman.

"Yeah, that's what Aunt Margot says. She says sometimes the way isn't clear straight up but you're on the right track all along even if it winds around a bit. She's got this Joseph Campbell quote she reels out at me whenever I'm feeling like I should be doing something serious with my life. It goes like this. She took a breath and looked skywards, as if she was concentrating on the words. '*If you follow your bliss, you put yourself on a kind of track, which has been there all the while waiting for you, and the life that you ought to be living is the one you are living*'." She smiled and looked around. "How cool is that? It makes me feel better anyhow."

"I like the sound of your Aunt Margot."

"Yeah, she's cool too. Always knows the right thing to say at the right time."

"It won't be long now until you see her."

"Yeah." And she did that measured blink of her eyes thing again and turned her head back out over the pit before she'd opened them. "Not long."

"Uh-oh, that's not good." Scarlett turned off her phone, peeved to find there were still no bids, to check out whatever Mitch had found. "What's not good?"

Mitch gestured up to the TV in the corner of the bar by the ceiling as he put down their drinks. "The weather in Broome. They reckon there's a system sitting off the coast and they're worried it could make landfall late tomorrow or the day after."

She looked up at the screen, at the chart that bore no resemblance to the weather charts she was used to at home and meant nothing to her now. "What would that mean exactly?"

"Anything from a bit of a blow to a full-on cyclone."

The weather map disappeared and the news went back to a recap of the headlines. She pulled her wine glass closer. "Oh, that's definitely not good news for a wedding. Will they have to cancel?"

"I suspect not. They're already all up there, having a pre-honeymoon honeymoon before the real honeymoon in Bali."

"Two honeymoons?"

"You can never have too many honeymoons, apparently."

"And we'll be okay to get up there?"

"Looks like it at this stage." He shrugged. "Be awful to miss it."

"Yeah, I'd be without a job."

He twirled a spare beer coaster in his fingers. "I'm sure I could find something else you could help me out with."

A waitress arrived with their food, hamburger and hand-cut chips—aka fries—for him, salt and pepper squid for her. "Yum," she said, because it was easier thinking about the food than about his last comment. Did he really mean what that had sounded like? More fool him if he didn't realize he didn't have to pay her for sex. She'd do that for free.

The squid was excellent, melt-in-the-mouth tender with just the right amount of spice. Her thoughts were even spicier. She put her knife and fork down knowing she'd burst if she didn't speak. "Can I ask you something?"

"Sure." Mitch was feeling mellow. He had a cold beer, a damn fine hamburger and the prettiest woman in the pub sitting opposite him. Right now he would have agreed to the sun not coming up in the morning.

"Why did you choose me?"

"What?"

"Back in Bella's—why me? I messed up my lines and stood there staring at you with my mouth open looking like a goldfish. I thought for sure you'd choose Jasmine."

He frowned. "You mean the Asian girl?"

"Yeah. Why didn't you choose her?"

He considered his hamburger for a while. "Because she was tiny."

"I know. She was exquisite."

"Yes. No. Tiny. I felt like a giant next to her."

"Oh."

Mitch looked up at her. He'd knew that kind of 'oh'. It was loaded. Clearly he'd said something wrong.

"And you looked cute."

"Thanks, but you don't have to do that."

"Do what?"

"Try to make me feel better by pretending you were interested in me all along."

Bam, there it was. "Who says I was pretending?"

"Me. You're just saying that to make me feel better. You wouldn't choose Jasmine because she was tiny. And so you chose me because I wasn't."

He put his hamburger down. It was his favorite, one with the lot, which in this part of the world meant onion, salad, bacon, cheese, beetroot, pineapple *and* pickles, so putting it down was a tough ask, but still he did it, because he'd just made a discovery, and he wanted to ruminate on that for a while. Because it seemed to him that even when a hamburger was complicated, it was still simple. There was a lot to be said for a hamburger. A hamburger might come with pickles, or sesame seeds on top, but it never came with a *Catch 22.* "I swear I will never understand how a woman's mind works."

"Then you're not really trying," she said.

He sighed. "So how about I just have a thing for redheads?"

"Uh-uh. I'm not falling for that one. You know it's not really red and now you're just trying to make stuff up."

"So maybe I have a thing for women in corsets and pink boots."

That was probably closer to the mark. "You mean, wearing nothing else but?"

"Hell, yeah. I loved those spangly pink boots. And

maybe I have a thing too, for teensy tiny pink bows that look like sugar and like they might melt in your mouth."

"You remember the pink bows?"

Did she really think he'd forget? "You're kidding me. I do believe those pink bows were the ruination of my sleep for these last two nights."

The slow burners inside her kicked on. Who needed alcohol when you were sitting opposite the man who kept you awake and wanting into the early hours, who'd just admitted she'd done the same to him. "Tell me, why do we need two rooms here in Kalgoorlie when we'll be sharing only one in Broome?"

"You know why. Because sex was never part of this deal." He paused. "And because up in Broome we won't have a choice if we want to look convincing." She liked that he didn't sound too thrilled about it.

She angled her head. "You know, I've been thinking about that convincing thing," and across the table from her, Mitch didn't move a muscle. "We'd be far more convincing in front of your friends if we were an *actual* couple."

He jacked up one eyebrow. "You think?" And it warmed the cockles of her heart that he didn't need her to explain.

She smiled, their eyes locked, green with blue, flickering at the edges with heat. "I know. New lovers are just so convincing, don't you think? They can never keep their hands off each other."

She liked the way the fingers of his hands curled on the table. Liked it that he probably didn't even realize he was doing it. "It's your choice, Scarlett," he said, his blue eyes as heated as a gas flame. "This time you get to choose." And his voice was husky and low and thick with wanting and she had a burning desire to hear it from the pillow next to hers.

"Mitch Bannister," she said, taking his hand, "I choose you."

And for the first time in his life, Mitch Bannister failed to finish a hamburger with the lot and chips. But only because he had more important things to do.

They'd barely got outdoors before he'd backed her up hard against a veranda post

"What?" she whispered as she looked up at him.

"I've been waiting to do this for a long time," he said, his lips the length of a whispered breath above hers, before breathless mouth met breathless mouth. And everything she promised was right there in that first kiss: the heat, the attraction, the sheer bloody bliss of it.

"Oh yes," he murmured into her mouth as her body pulled away from the post at her back and molded to his as if it had been made for it.

They probably looked no different to a lot of other lovers, wending their way down Hannan Street to their accommodation, holding each other close, pausing every now and then to taste each other, with their mouths and with their hands, feeding the simmering tension that bubbled inside, snatching the chance to drink in the feel of a curve or a dip before they pushed apart and moved on a few steps until the next hot clinch.

No wonder it seemed to Scarlett that it had taken forever until they were back in the apartment.

But no sooner were they inside that locked door than she was ripping the clothing from his body. "Oh my god, at last."

He just groaned, and all the things he'd made her feel just yesterday at Bella's, when she'd been dressed up like the hooker she was supposed to be and had been forced to use every weapon in her arsenal to feel nothing in the face of his electric touch and still it was not enough, all those things she welcomed. This was no place to bring out the times tables. This time those feelings felt right. This time she wanted to luxuriate in every single toe curling moment and simply enjoy.

He shredded her clothes from her body as fast as she shredded his, his hot mouth keeping her busy in between the attacks of his hands on her shirt and on her jeans.

"Your boots," he huffed against her ear with hot breath as he wrestled with his own.

"Gone," she said, shrugging them off with her toes. She felt the jeans follow and then his, and then there was nothing between them but air and even that was in short supply where their bodies met.

But who needed air when where their bodies touched

was all kinds of bliss and beyond, flesh against flesh, heat against heat, his every fantasy about to come true. His mouth was busy with the feel and taste of her, his need was her need, or so it seemed as she sighed or gasped with every single stroke of his fingers or tongue.

He was thick and hard between them and her senses and flesh were pulsing with need, the ache between her thighs building so hard that when he took one nipple into her mouth, she almost exploded with it.

"Mitch," she whispered breathlessly, at his next onslaught to the other nipple, "I don't think—I don't—I can't wait."

He growled low in his throat, frustration meshed with need. He'd wanted to take his time, take the slow road, make it as special for her as it felt for him. But with the drumbeat of his blood pounding in his ears, urging him on, he didn't think he was capable. Because right at the forefront of his mind was this desperate need to be inside her. Only that. Hearing her put voice to his need only made him want it more. There was no way he could last now, no way he could wait.

He lunged for the bedside table drawer handle, so far away now, and wished he'd had time to plan, but putting them in his bedside drawer had seemed like wise planning back then and his hopes had only been that. And when he angled sideways, he felt her hand take him, squeeze him, stroke him.

Oh, god. Please god let him last.

And then his fingers found what he was looking for and he ripped the foil with his teeth and pushed her hand out the way to roll it on. He positioned himself between her thighs and rested there a moment. "This is so not the way it should happen," he said, "but you've been driving me crazy a day and a half and I don't think I can last."

"For god's sake, just take me," she said, "and we'll worry about how it should happen later."

He loved a woman with common sense. A woman who could make a decision in a split second. Sure, she might be impulsive, but there was a place for impulsive.

But most of all he loved a woman who was warm and

sexy and who wanted what he wanted. Good times and good sex and no complications. A woman like that had a hell of a lot going for her.

This woman.

He pushed into her, felt her around him, surround him; felt the clench of her muscles and slick heat of her desire, and damn near had to grit his teeth not to come there and then.

"Yes," she whispered, as he pulled back, with her voice like honey and a beckoning sweet body that called him home. "Ahh, like that," when he thrust into her again.

Then there were no more words, only the sighs and sounds of passion, quickening and intense and with only one place to go.

He felt her go, felt her body tense and still and erupt around him like a fireball, consuming his last shred of control as he followed her.

"I just knew you'd be good at that." Sweat-slick and replete, she lay panting by his side, her head against her shoulder, his arm holding her snug against his body.

He kissed the top of her head. "Do I need to tell you how good you were?"

"Yes please."

He chuckled, more like a rumble, and she liked it. "You're amazing. In fact, so unbelievably amazing, that I can honestly say, that you are, without exception, the best Buck I ever had."

"Hey!" she said, sitting up and smacking at him with her hands, "quit it with the Buck jokes."

He laughed and grabbed her wrists. "Make me," he challenged, and she pulled at her hands and wriggled, jiggled and growled and made him laugh all the more until she stilled and said, "I know how to make you shut up anyhow."

"Yeah?"

"Yeah." And she used his arms for supports and dropped herself over his chest and teased his mouth with a nipple.

Oh, yeah, he thought, as he opened wide to accept this unexpected gift, *that'd do it*

Chapter Six

They got away early the next morning on time, a seventy-minute hop to Perth before a short break for the connection to Broome that would have them there around mid-afternoon. Flights were still moving while the tropical storm continued to hover directionless off the north-west coast.

"Damn," she said, as they passed through clouds and the view disappeared. He watched as she flicked through the flight magazine and found the puzzle page and dug out a pen.

"How much have you seen of Australia?"

"Not a lot." she said, as she started jotting down numbers. "A bit of Perth. Kalgoorlie."

"That's it?"

She shrugged. "I'll see Broome. That's a bonus."

"So why Perth? Most people would head to Sydney, especially when they've come from the States."

"Well, I didn't exactly come to be your traditional backpacker-type."

"No?"

"No. So... Perth suited me."

"Okay, are you going to tell me why?"

She screwed up her mouth. "You really want to know?"

"Scarlett, give."

She looked at him, her lips tight. "Only it's not something I'm real proud of or anything."

"Scarlett!"

She pouted. "Okay, seeing you insist 'n' all. It's like this. I came to g—" and whatever else she said was masked under her hand as she turned her head towards the window.

He captured her chin with his hand, and pulled it around. "You came to get what?"

Green eyes sent out an SOS. "You really want to know?"

He was impervious to SOS's sent by green-eyed minxes "Yes. I really want to know."

"Okay. I came out to get married. Well, I thought I was going to get married."

"Seriously? Who to?"

"Just some guy I met."

"What? In Marietta?"

"Well, kind of. I was in Marietta, at any rate."

"Oh Scarlett, tell me you didn't find this guy on the internet?"

"So?"

"You're kidding me. You fell for that?"

"He was nice! And we started out as just friends. We chatted. He told me about Perth, and I told him about Montana. It was fun. He was like a pen pal."

"And so you came out on the strength of that?"

"No! Do you think I'm nuts?" Her fingers flicked at the corners of the magazine, her eyes watching them work. "No, we'd been talking for a while and we were getting to be more than friends. We Skyped every Sunday. He told me I was his soulmate. He told me he loved me. That we belonged together. But it was impossible for him, he said, because he worked such long hours. He couldn't see a way for us to be together just yet. But we would be, just as soon as he could get leave."

Her eyes flicked up to his. Big green eyes that still bore the hurt. It didn't take much to know it hadn't ended well.

"It was his birthday coming up and I wanted to surprise him." A pause, before she continued, her voice flat. "And I did."

"What happened?"

"I texted him once I was in Perth. I said from the airport, '*Surprise, I'm right here in Perth!*' He texted back right away. Said what a surprise and he was thrilled and where was I staying?

"And fool that I was, I couldn't see it even then. I said, with him of course.

"That's when he said he was away on business and to get myself booked in somewhere overnight and he'd fix everything when he came back the next day.

"And I sat in this dingy tiny box of a hotel room, because it was all I could afford after blowing my money on a one way ticket, and there was nothing in it but a fuzzy TV and a Gideon's Bible and a phone book. And because stupid me hadn't ever bothered to find out his address, because stupid me thought he'd be so happy to pick me up from the airport, I wouldn't need his address, I had no idea where he lived. So I looked him up. And I found him."

Her fingers were still troubling the pages of the magazine. Mitch put his hand over hers and she looked up at him, tears swimming in her eyes. "I knocked on the door of this very suburban house in a very suburban street with a car out the front that had kiddie seats in the back and I remember thinking, please god, let me have this wrong.

"He opened the door in the middle of saying something to someone behind him and I remember there was a kid's trike hanging from his hand and toys spread all over the floor. Then a woman appeared from another room asking who it was and she had a belly the size of a basketball and I died on that front porch. I just died.

"And I remember I said, 'Sorry, wrong house,' and he shut the door in my face and went back to his suburban existence and his pregnant wife and his kids and just left me standing there."

Mitch put his arm around her and pulled her close. She shook her head. "I'm not crying because of him. I'm crying because I was so stupid. Everyone warned me and I didn't listen. Because Tara told me I was crazy and that he'd be some sixty-year-old pervert but I knew better, because we'd Skyped and he was so good-looking and I knew she was probably just jealous because she's such a stick-in-the-mud and her Simon is so darn dull. And I just, I just wanted to show everyone that I could do something right."

She hiccupped against his chest, her long braid a heavy snake over his arm. "I'm going to be more like Tara from now on. I'm going to stop being impulsive and I'm going to be sensible and I'm going to think about things."

"Maybe you needed to come here," he offered, his thumb stroking her shoulder. "The big changes in our lives rarely take place with us just wanting them. Usually they come about because of some major defining event."

"You think Travis was my major defining event?"

"Maybe."

"But then I jumped head long into Bella's."

"You were desperate, that's all. Look how long you had to think about my offer, and I thought that was a no brainer. So you see? You are being less impulsive already."

"You think?"

"So long as you remember one thing."

She sniffed and sighed, and he could feel her body relaxing into him, "What's that?"

"Don't try and be someone else, even if it's your own sister. Don't change who you are, Scarlett. I like you, just the way you are."

After a little while, she said sleepily, "You sound a lot like my Aunt Margot."

He kissed her hair. "I knew I liked the sound of her." And as she fell into a doze against his chest he wondered where his words had come from. He'd met her barely two days ago—what did he care about her messy impulsive life that he needed to reassure her, even if it was the truth?

That was the bit that niggled at him the most.

Because he did like her.

A lot.

Broome was hot and humid and her jeans stuck to her legs but after bumping their way down through the clouds, Scarlett was too glad to be safely down on the ground to care. But it was exciting too. Broome was like no place she'd ever been before; even the airport felt tropical and exotic with its palm trees and light spaces and cane furniture. A private car met them and whisked them off to their resort on Cable Beach, the fourteen-mile ribbon of white sand that fringed the turquoise Indian Ocean.

"When do we meet the others?"

"Tonight before dinner. They're all off on some excursion to a pearl farm today."

The wind gusted and tore at the palm trees along the road. "Wind's picking up," he said.

"Bad news for the wedding?"

"From what Robbo was telling me, Kristelle is hoping for her wedding to be blessed with an appearance by the Staircase to the Moon. You can only see it at full moon between March and October and this weekend is the first for the year." He looked up at the cloudy sky. "Don't fancy her chances if this keeps up." They pulled into the gates of a resort. "Looks like we're here."

Her eyes bugged. She climbed out of the car, taking in the long colonial building with its timber veranda decorated with Chinese artefacts and low-slung furniture, the gardens spilling with palms and brightly colored plants. "Oh my god," she said, "I think I've died and gone to heaven."

The driver holding her door smiled. Mitch was smiling too. "Don't mind her," he said, "she doesn't get out much."

The driver laughed and tipped his hat. "A pleasure to meet you both," he said, "enjoy your stay."

"What was that all about?" she asked, as the car pulled away and Mitch took her hand.

"It means they're too used to toffee noses around here."

"Toffee noses?"

"Um, what would Americans say? Let's think: Preppy types. Rich people."

"Oh."

"You're like a breath of fresh air."

She looked up at him quizzically and he added, "He liked you. Then again, maybe he's just met Kristelle."

"Hey." She stopped and he had to stop too. "I know she's your ex 'n' all and you're not sure of her motives, but that doesn't mean she's an awful person. It just means you two didn't get on."

He touched his finger to the tip of her nose and followed it with his lips. "I stand corrected. No more digs about Kristelle."

"Good."

She took a step but he mumbled something under his breath, and she just knew he was going for the last word. "What did you say?"

"Nothing."

She shook her head. "That poor girl didn't deserve you."

"Finally," he said, "something we can agree on."

She pressed her nails into the back of his hand. "She and I are going to get on like you wouldn't believe."

"Right again. Are you going for the trifecta or something?"

She just looked at him. "Unbelievable. It's a wonder she didn't end up in therapy after you."

He smiled and she just looked at him and rolled her eyes. "Like I said: unbelievable."

Check-in was as smooth as silk, and in no time they were in their assigned villa. It was insanely luxurious, a private house more than a mere villa, with a massive king-sized bedroom plus separate lounge and dining rooms and, to top it all off, a private courtyard with plunge pool.

She eyed it with intent and a certain amount of satisfaction. *Take that, Travis.*

"I'm hopping in the shower to freshen up before drinks," Mitch said from inside. "Coming?"

"Sure. Give me a minute, I just need to hang something up." With a bit of luck the closet was so big, he might not even notice it.

"Don't be long."

She smiled. "Not a chance."

A minute later she joined him in the enormous shower. "You know, you were right," he said, reaching for her. "I can't keep my hands off you."

"You're supposed to be saving that for when we're in front of the others," she said, but she wasn't exactly chiding him. Not when her breath hissed through her teeth at his touch. He looked damned fine dry to be sure. But he looked even better dripping wet.

And what he did to her with that bath gel was amazing.

S he was just drying off when she heard him yell, "What the *hell* is that?"

Darn. She had a fair idea where he was and what he'd found and realized that maybe the gown hadn't been quite as well hidden as she'd hoped. After all, there was at least a hundred yards of tulle in the skirt. But there were at least a dozen yards of closet too. Did he have to go opening that particular one?

Anyhow, no point admitting anything just yet. He was a man after all. Maybe he'd just found the ironing board.

"What's what?" she asked innocently, padding barefoot into the room.

"This thing. This—frothy- white—*thing.*"

She peeked over his shoulder. "Oh, so you found it?"

"How the hell was I not supposed to find it? It takes up half the bloody wardrobe. What the hell is it?"

"A mistake. You know how I told you I was impulsive-"

"Hell, Scarlett, I told you I'm not looking for commitment!"

"What? You think I'm planning on marrying you?" She laughed out loud but somehow he didn't share the joke.

"What's so funny about that?"

She laughed even more. "You're funny! First of all you're outraged at the thought I might be secretly planning on marrying you, and then you sound insulted when I tell you I'm not. It's the gown I was going to wear to marry Travis. I brought it all the way from Marietta, Montana to marry that jerkball of a cheating husband in."

If he was relieved, he didn't let it show. "So what's it doing here?"

"It has to hang to get out the creases."

"No." He sighed. "Not *here* in the wardrobe. Here in Broome?"

"Well, I could hardly leave it in Perth."

"Why not? Why take the damned thing anywhere? Why didn't you throw it away? Burn it. Do whatever pissed off brides do when they've been dumped?"

"Because I need the money! It's a two thousand dollar Vera Wang gown, and maybe I bought it on sale for way less than that, but I reckon I should be able to get at least a grand for it."

"So sell it then."

"I am. I'm trying. I've got it listed on eBay. '*New. With Tags. Never worn*'," she quoted, "only that's a bit of a fib because some poor woman before me got stood up almost at the altar in the damn thing, but I could hardly say that."

He shook his head and headed back to the bedroom. He'd never understand women. He hadn't understood a word of what she'd just said.

What he had understood, though, was that she'd thought the concept of marrying him hysterically funny.

Oh yeah, he'd understood that bit perfectly.

And didn't it grate?

"Are you ready? We're due at the bar ten minutes ago."

"You go ahead," she called from the bathroom, "this humidity is turning my hair into seaweed. I'll find you."

Mitch went off smiling, his mind suddenly busy imagining pictures of Scarlett as a mermaid, on a rock, her scarlet hair wending like rivulets over her breasts. Oh yeah, he could see that. That would work. The bar was still only half full and the wedding party no trouble to spot: Robbo and his parents and another couple who must be Kristelle's, plus the bridesmaid he presumed. He scanned the area. No Kristelle. Bonus. He had time to have a word with his mate first.

"Mitch," Robbo called out, as he pulled Mitch into a man hug, clapping him on the back. "It's good you could come."

"Wouldn't miss it for the world."

Robbo peered around his shoulder. "And the friend you were bringing?"

"She's still messing with her hair."

"Oh," he rolled his eyes, "the humidity, tell me about it. Kristelle's been banging on about nothing else but. I told her March would be dodgy up here but she did insist." He laughed, a little uncertainly, and Mitch wondered if all was well in the lovers' nest. "Well, you know what she's like."

He did but still he managed a smile as Robbo started with the introductions. His parents, Virginia and Andrew Farrant, he already knew, and then there were Rolf and Alice Svensson and a sparky brunette, Sharon, who was the bridesmaid. Someone put a beer in his hand and the party got underway before Robbo pulled him aside, an arm around his shoulder. It was a stretch for the shorter man.

"No hard feelings, eh?" he said, squeezing his shoulder. "About me marrying Kristelle? I'd hate for this to come between us."

"I'm here, aren't I?" Mitch said.

"Only I know how hard it must have been when she said no to you."

His head whipped around. "What?"

"When she turned you down. I know you took it rough. I understand it would have been a blow."

Oh good grief, so that was the story she'd spun. "Look Robbo—" He hesitated. His mate was getting married in less than twenty-four hours and he might not get another chance. Besides, he was sure he hadn't imagined the tightness around his friend's features when he talked about the woman he was lining up to marry. "Are you absolutely sure about this?"

"What do you mean?"

"About marrying Kristelle. It is what *you* want, isn't it?"

The hand around his shoulders fell away. "So it's like that is it? You're still sore. Well, let me tell you," Robbo said, poking him in the chest with his finger, "you had your chance, Mitch. You blew it, big time. So suck it up, princess."

Mitch sighed. "Robbo, mate, listen a minute."

"No. Tomorrow Kristelle is marrying me and you are just going to have to learn to live with it."

"All right, I'll live with it," he said, holding up a hand in surrender, when what he would have really liked to do was give his friend a good smack about the head with it and see if that knocked some sense into him.

"Excellent," the smaller man said, flexing his shoulders like he'd just gone ten rounds and come out a champion. "Mates again then?"

"Yeah, mates," he said, and reached for another beer.

He was catching up with Robbo's parents a couple of minutes later when he heard her voice. "Robert, darling, I'm so sorry..."

Mitch stiffened and stood up straight at the bar and he had a sudden insight into why someone had invented the phrase, 'girding your loins', because girding was exactly what his loins were doing right now. "Oh, Mitch," she said, her voice as heavy and sultry as the air, "I didn't know you'd arrived. How lovely to see you."

She did all the moving. She practically glided towards him like a ship on the sea. A warship. *A destroyer.*

She had the capability, that's for sure. She looked amazing, better maybe than he remembered, with her Nordic good looks and blonde hair swept up, her perfectly tweaked and preened body clad in clever layers of silk that shifted as she walked, revealing a glimpse of leg here, a slice of toned belly there.

And a warning inside his head sounded out. *Prepare to repel boarders.*

"How are you, Kristelle?"

She smiled and kept right on coming and reached her hands to his shoulders and pressed herself close. "Is that any way to greet an old friend?" She pushed herself high—blow it if he was going to make it easy for her by bending—and pressed her lips to his mouth, lingering there a moment too long. Mitch cleared his throat and reached along the bar for his beer, feeling Robbo's eyes on him the whole time.

"All ready for the big day?"

She pouted a little as she leaned away, as if she was disappointed with his response, but if he wasn't mistaken, there was a challenge in her eyes too.

"I am. We are. If only this wretched weather would behave." Then she frowned a little, checking who was there. "Robert mentioned you were bringing a friend." She looked delighted when she couldn't find a likely suspect and the challenge in her eyes became an invitation. Nope, he was right not to trust her an inch. "Did you change your mind?"

He took a swig of his beer. "Nope, she'll be along. She's fixing her hair."

"Mean of you to make her arrive by herself. It'd be daunting to have to turn up to a party all on your own."

He thought about Scarlett and grinned. "I doubt it."

In the end Scarlett gave up wrangling with the question of what to do with her hair, and tied it into a simple sideways braid, took a last look in the mirror to check that she looked presentable in the simple little sundress and sandals she'd chosen in deference to the heat and in the hopes of making a good impression for Mitch's sake, and headed for the bar. She was looking forward to meeting everyone, Kristelle especially. She was probably nothing like Mitch had made out. They'd probably end up being best of friends. Ha, wouldn't he just hate that!

The bar was as beautifully decked out as the rest of the resort with white clothed tables topped with crystal glasses, and high-backed cane chairs spilling outside onto a wide deck overlooking the beach. It was glorious. Even with the cloud scudded sky and wind whipping at the palms that lined the shore, Scarlett was seriously loving this place.

She spotted Mitch at the bar, tall and gorgeous and her heart did a little lurch thinking back to that episode in the shower and at the fact that he was all hers for the next two days. He was leaning on the bar, talking with a pair of middle aged couples, the parents she presumed, and there was a younger couple, a man shorter than Mitch with the beginnings of a pot and who looked like he spent a lot of time behind a desk—it had to be Robbo—talking to a younger woman with curly dark hair and a nice smile; if that was Kristelle, she was sure they were going to get along just fine. She was just making their way over to greet them when another woman glided into focus. Tall, svelte and cool as an iceberg in the humid air, she said something to the shorter man before she spotted Mitch, and something about the way his jaw set as he straightened told her she'd been wrong. The brunette must be the bridesmaid. This supermodel-slash-ice queen had to be Kristelle.

She watched as Kristelle seemed to float toward him, her dress like a cloud of liquid silk, watched as she floated right up to Mitch and stretched herself up high like a cat upon his chest to kiss him. And lingered.

Scarlett's blood started to boil.

Nuh-uh, that was so not happening. Not on her watch.

And she looked down at her cotton sundress and simple sandals and headed straight back to the villa. It was time to bring out the heavy artillery.

Mitch checked his watch. They'd be heading for their table soon and there was still no sign of Scarlett. Kristelle was still standing there, talking away, making out like they were best of friends, while the parents had formed their own private collective and Robbo—who had practically warned him off his wife-to-be—was deep in conversation with the bridesmaid. How did that work?

And meanwhile he stuck here getting a blow-by-blow description of the wedding plans, right down to the gazebo and the lily pond and what was on the menu.

Maybe Robbo could hear the conversation and thought there was nothing going on, but it wasn't about the setting or the arrangements at all. It was about Kristelle being oblivious to his signals to give it up and making pretty eyes, come hither smiles and forever moving a hand there, a gesture here, the flick of a bit of invisible lint from his shirt.

He'd just about had a gut-full of it.

"Hey, sugar." The voice was right but the accent was wrong, and he looked around, confused. He was more confused by what he saw. He seemed to remember Scarlett had been wearing something else when he'd left because he sure as hell would have remembered if she'd been wearing this. She was dressed, if you could call it that, in a teensy tiny denim skirt with a teensy tiny white tank with fringing and spangles along the neckline. Not that, he noted, it ventured anywhere remotely near her neck. And if he wasn't mistaken, on her feet were the same pink spangly boots she'd been wearing at Bella's.

Those boots that had been almost enough to make him hard all by themselves.

Those *leave-them-on* boots.

His tongue stuck hard to the roof of his mouth.

Had she been packing those boots all along? Words would be said. But later. Right now he was too busy watching, as she sashayed between the tables, her hips swaying like a pendulum, the fringe at her breasts swaying to the opposite beat. It was provocative. It was mesmerizing. And despite the fans working overtime overhead, the heat in the room went up a dozen degrees.

She stopped just shy of him. "I missed you," she said, and hooked her fingers under his waistband and yanked him close. The other hand snaked around his neck and pulled his head down to her red painted mouth where she damn near sucked out his brain with her hot mouth and clever tongue.

Oh yeah!

When he lifted his head, her eyes twinkled up at him conspiratorially and he made another addition to her impressive skill set. She was the best damned red-headed Rottweiler he'd ever had.

Finally he looked around at the startled group, knowing his lips must be as painted red as hers. "Everyone," he said, "Meet Scarlett."

Chapter Seven

carlett couldn't remember the last time she'd had so much fun. The setting was out of this world and the company was fine too, once they'd recovered from the shock, and even if, she noticed, Robbo's mom did look a bit tense from time to time.

But Scarlett's accent soon brought the topic of travel to the conversation, with plenty of questions about Montana, and it was surreal to conjure up pictures of snow-covered mountains and crystal clear lakes when she was sitting in a tropical beachfront paradise half a world away. Even more surreal to think she'd be back in Montana in a few short days and this would all be just a memory.

Even though she needed to get home—*wanted desperately to get home*—her head wasn't ready to leave this place just yet. Instead she planned to extract every last shred of enjoyment from the experience.

So when the chance came, she let the conversation move on. The long flight to Australia had shown her the world was a far bigger place than just Marietta and Big Sky country. The stories she was hearing now made that world expand even more.

Robbo's parents fought it out with Kristelle's parents for the prize of the best trip ever, to which there was no easy winner, before they headed into the territory of worst travel experience.

There was still no winner until Sharon told the story of

when she'd been waiting for a train at a quiet station deep within the Arctic Circle, and how the train had grown later and later and how she'd grown colder and madder, until finally, shivering her ass off on a lonely seat in a lonely station, she'd figured out that the trains only ran in the summer, and her train wouldn't arrive for another three months. Sharon won the contest hands down. Scarlett liked her stories and her easy laugh.

As for Robbo, he just kept smiling benevolently over at her and Mitch as if her presence had made his day. And when the topic of conversation had moved on and one of the parents asked Sharon what she did, it was Robbo who answered, 'Sharon's an accountant. We only found out when we were having drinks in the bar before. Can you believe Kristelle never mentioned it?'

Kristelle just rolled her eyes. "Maybe because I never knew. It's not like we work together. We're gym friends, aren't we, Sharon?"

Sharon just smiled weakly and reached for her wine.

"Truly," Kristelle continued, "It is fabulous our special friends and family could be here to share this happy event, especially given how suddenly this was all arranged. Darling Robert just couldn't wait a moment longer to tie the knot."

Robbo raised his eyebrows a little at that but agreed with the sentiments. "Hear hear. And we're very grateful our parents could all be here with us and that both Sharon and Mitch could be on hand as our bridesmaid and best man. We're honored to have you all," he said, raising his glass in a toast to them.

They drank and then Mitch proposed a toast to the happy couple and they drank some more and the mood was fine.

Until Kristelle said, with a laugh as she looked squarely at Mitch. "It is funny, though, isn't it, that you're called the best man? When obviously—you're not."

Scarlett, who'd been thinking that maybe she'd just been a bit too hard on Kristelle because everyone was getting along so well, and who'd noticed a definite tic in Robbo's mom's eye every time the bride-to-be spoke, thought again. "Maybe that just depends," she said, with a smile as she wound her arm around Mitch's and laid her head adoringly on his shoulder, "on your point of view. I'm perfectly happy to settle for good ol' Mitch here."

"Hey babe," Mitch said, with a smile, "you're pretty good yourself."

"Hear hear!" said Robbo once more applauding, clearly getting into the swing of things. "Well said!"

"How lovely," said Robbo's mom, looking relieved, "I wonder if there'll be another wedding before too long."

Mitch took Scarlett's hand between his and looked into her adoring eyes, "Well, there's no saying what's in the future for any of us, but if anything does happen between Scarlett and me, you can be sure, as parents of one of my oldest friends, we'd want you there to celebrate with us."

Robbo's parents puffed up. "We'd be honored, son," said Andrew.

"How sweet," Kristelle said with a smile, while her eyes sent a death stare straight to Scarlett.

Scarlett sent a smile back that was so dripping with sugar, it should have come with its own dentist's drill.

There was no time to enjoy the moment because right then, sunset arrived, not with a whimper, but a bang, the way it apparently always did in the tropics. One moment the light was bright and hard, dulled only by the grey clouds, then next the sun had slanted and lit a wick that set fire to the sky. The clouds turned orange and the sea turned gold and the restaurant fell silent as every eye was drawn to the spectacle.

And Scarlett, who back home in Montana had witnessed some of the world's most spectacular sunsets, found one more place where the simple act of the sun setting could rock your world.

"Wow," she said, clutching Mitch's hand as the last of the red light faded into black. And on impulse she turned and pressed her lips to his cheek. "Thank you so much for bringing me here," and he smiled and lifted their joined hands to his mouth and pressed his lips to the back of her hand, and her heart gave a little wobble at what she saw in his eyes.

"The pleasure is all mine."

She wondered at how easily the line had blurred between acting a part to look convincing and honestly expressing her feelings. Or his.

Their appetizers arrived, and Scarlett found she could breathe again, as various amazing offerings of scallops and pearl meat and more found their owners. Mitch and Scarlett laid claim to the shared mezze plate for two, featuring chorizo, harissa prawns, grilled squid, marinated feta, and olives.

"Plain salad, no dressing?" a waiter asked and Kristelle waved her hand. "Here."

"This looks amazing," said Mitch, popping a piece of chorizo into Scarlett's mouth. "Try this."

"Mmmmm." She returned the favor and he took it from her fingers, his tongue licking the slickness clean, and she said "mmmm" all over again and saw the heat flicker in his eyes. *Oh boy.*

Together they demolished the platter, feeding each other morsel after morsel, and nobody could say that they didn't make a convincing couple.

And while a newly discovered voice of sense and reason in the back of mind told Scarlett that she really needed to remember this was a role she was playing, it was all too tempting to blot it out and just enjoy this man's attentions while they lasted. Was it so wrong, she asked herself, to wish that things could be different, that she wasn't a mere day or two away from leaving here and Mitch forever; that there was something more in his heated looks than mere lust?

Then something touched her thigh and she jumped and figured that maybe the answer to question number two was a definite no. Because beside her, Mitch was busy staring the other way while his fingers were attempting to sneak under the hem of her skirt. "'What are you doing?' she whispered.

"Finding out if you're wearing knickers."

She shied away. "You'll just have to wait."

"I can't!"

She smacked his hand away. "Down boy!"

Across the table Robbo laughed. 'Mitch getting a little frisky for you over there, Scarlett?"

She gave an exaggerated sigh. "Honestly, sometimes

he's like a dog with a bone."

The men snorted, the two mothers didn't know whether to be shocked or laugh, Sharon sucked her lips between her teeth to stop herself laughing, and Kristelle just looked glummer and glummer. "I'm worried about the weather," she lamented, looking out at the threatening sky. "What if it gets worse? What if there's no Staircase to the Moon?"

Robbo turned to his fiancée, his hands upturned. "Then there's no Staircase to the Moon, Kristelle, It's not going to be the end of the world. We've still got our wedding to look forward to."

"But it's supposed to be the Staircase to the Moon. It's supposed to be magical."

"It'll be fine, sweetheart," soothed her mother, "your father will fix it."

Rolf spluttered, his eyes nearly popping out of his head. "How, in heaven's name, am I supposed to do that?"

"I don't know, darling," she said, patting his hand. "But you'll find a way, I'm sure."

Scarlett glanced up at Mitch who was way too cowardly to meet her eyes and luckily the entrees arrived and they had more food to concentrate on, the seafood paella for Scarlett, a grilled eye fillet of Kimberley beef for Mitch. Robbo stumped for the lamb shank, and there were a number of fish that gave up their lives in the cause of a very good feed also.

Kristelle, who hadn't ordered an entree, picked valiantly at her salad. She looked accusingly over at Scarlett's paella. "Clearly you're not the one who has to fit into a designer wedding gown tomorrow."

"No, thank god," said Scarlett. "Someone pass the garlic bread."

Mitch was only too happy to comply. "Here you are, sweetlips, we need to keep up your strength."

Kristelle's barely-used silverware crashed to the plate.

Robert looked around. "Are you okay?"

"I'm so sorry," she said with a jagged little laugh. "They must have slipped. Excuse me a moment." And she rose and left.

They all looked at each other. "Should someone go with her?" Scarlett said.

Sharon was already on her feet. "I'll check." She was back inside a minute, her face burning red, her mouth tight. "She said she just wants to be alone a minute or two. She just needed some air."

"Oh, the excitement's getting to her," said her mother. "I remember what it was like before our wedding, Rolf, I was so excited."

Rolf grunted, deep in remembering, his hand firmly wrapped around a tumbler of scotch.

Scarlett looked at Mitch. He took her hand, clearly thinking along the same lines, that it was a different kind of excitement getting to Kristelle than pre-wedding jitters and that she'd probably had enough of being convinced they were a couple for one night.

"We've had a long day. We might call it an early night, if you'll excuse us." He dropped a heap of twenties on the table and saw Scarlett eyeing the stack. "Is that enough?" he said for a joke, and she nodded. "Good tip, too."

Robbo looked disappointed that the party might be breaking up so early. "Mitch," he said, "before you go, can I have a word?"

"Go ahead you two," Scarlett said. "I'll see you back at the villa," and she bade them all a good night.

"I'm sorry, mate," Robbo said, when they were far enough away. "I came on a bit strong before."

"No," Mitch said. "I shouldn't have asked you what I did."

"Well..." Robbo's head bobbed from side to side. "When it comes down to it, I have been having doubts."

"About Kristelle?"

"Yeah, that too. And Kristelle's been so insistent on you being here for the wedding it got me wondering whether she was having second thoughts and I guess you got me at a raw moment. But I can see you're happy with Scarlett and frankly, I can see why. She's a top sheila."

"Yeah. That she is."

"So, no hard feelings. And I really mean it this time."

"Sure, no hard feelings."

He let himself into the villa. "Everything okay?" she asked.

"Yeah," he said, still worried about Robbo. But only until he caught sight of Scarlett in that mini and those boots again.

"Time for bed?" he said, ever hopeful, as he headed for the bathroom to do his teeth.

"I was thinking of a swim in the plunge pool first."

His eyebrows shot up, his toothbrush barely in his hand, as he remembered all those mermaid pictures he'd thought of before. The plunge pool would do nicely in the interim. Very nicely.

"I'll just grab my shorts," he said, about to change his mind and head for the dressing room.

She appeared at the door, wearing only her scarlet hair. "What do you need swim shorts for?"

Good question.

They made love in the pool, slow, slick love until they were too weary of trying to keep their heads above water, and then they moved to the bed, where they made love all over again.

Afterward, as she was lying in the crook of Mitch's arm watching the lazy rotations of the ceiling fan in the shadowed light, she said, "I think I will send a postcard to Travis. And it'll say, '*Having a ball in Broome. Give my love to your wife and kids*'."

"Would you do that?"

"No, tempting though it is. In fact, I actually should thank him. I wouldn't be here with you in Broome without that little disaster." She held out her arms toward the ceiling, "Thank you Travis!" she said to the universe. "You asshat."

Mitch chuckled beside her and she dug him in the ribs. "Hey, you should thank Travis too."

"Me?"

"Sure. You got what you wanted didn't you? A Rottweiler to protect you from the clutches of the evil

Kristelle."

Yeah, he had. But it wasn't Travis he owed thanks to.

Travis might have dropped her in his metaphoric lap, but it was his little sister who'd stopped him from walking away. It was Callie, who'd made him wait long enough to have coffee with Scarlett and make sure she was okay. Callie, who'd given him time to come up with this plan.

Thank you, Callie, he said silently, as he drew Scarlett closer into the crook of his arm.

"You are one hell of a Rottweiler. And there was me thinking you were going to give Kristelle the benefit of the doubt. You came out all guns blazing."

"Yeah," she said, smiling against his shoulder. "So maybe I had a hunch."

He sighed and for a moment she thought he was going to sleep, and then he said. "Now I've got a hunch."

"What about?"

"I'm thinking you should talk to Sharon."

"What about?"

"About her being an accountant."

"Why?"

"Because you're good with numbers. When you're not working out restaurant bills, you're working on those damned puzzles."

She shrugged. "They're just Sudoku."

"Yeah, but they're numbers."

"I thought accountants were supposed to be boring."

"Does Sharon look boring?"

"No, she looks nice. She is nice. I like her." She thought about it for a while. "Mitch, do you think I could be an accountant?"

"I don't know, Scarlett. Like I said, it's just a hunch. Maybe you should talk to her." He squeezed her shoulders. "Now go to sleep."

Scarlett lay there a while, listening to the whisper soft whir of the fan. Accounting. It sounded horrible. But what did she really know about accounting? She'd never met an accountant before. And now she knew two, Robbo and Sharon. But there was a CPA firm in Bozeman near the police department where Tara worked and they had a branch in Marietta. She remembered their signage, *Morison and Daume CPA*.

And she didn't have a clue what they did inside that office of theirs, but if it was something to do with numbers, maybe it wouldn't be so bad. Maybe it was worth thinking about.

Maybe.

The next morning brought good news on the weather front when the weather forecast on the television confirmed what they saw out the windows. The cyclone off shore had blown itself out and winds were easing, the clouds already less threatening, and there was a chance of clearing skies by evening. Mitch flicked off the TV. "Looking good for Staircase to the Moon," he said, and Scarlett would have been excited, except she'd just checked her phone.

With a sigh she put it down on the side table.

"Nothing?"

"Not a nibble." She turned in his arms. Sighed again. "You know, I'm beginning to think it's better if the dress doesn't sell. I mean, some woman in Marietta took it back because she was abandoned at the altar and then the damn thing offered me no joy either. Maybe it's a bad luck dress. Maybe I shouldn't even be trying to sell it because the darned gown is cursed. Why would I want to pass on a dress that's likely to ruin some poor woman's life?"

"It's just a dress, Scarlett. How can it be cursed?"

"I don't know, but it is, and it's a sign that it's not selling. I'm going to take the listing down. I don't want anyone else to buy it."

"Okay, so take the listing down."

"Wouldn't you do the same?"

"If I happened to have a wedding gown that was cursed and that wouldn't sell on eBay, you mean?"

"Now you're just poking fun at me."

"Not at all. It's a fair question. I just need to think about it a while, do a thorough assessment of the pros and cons. You can't be too impulsive about these things."

She sat up and snatched up a pillow. "Mitch Bannister, you are making fun of me!" and she swiped him with it as he lay on the bed.

"Hey!" he said, "don't go hitting a bloke when he's down."

"So get up and fight like a man."

And he did, retaliating with his own pillow, and it was on. They went blow for blow on the already tousled bed until he managed to knock her pillow out of her hands and grab her flailing wrists to drop her bodily to the bed. She was panting and laughing while he pinned her there, her gorgeous breasts rising and falling with her chest, her scarlet hair like a crazy tangled crown around her head, and his lungs squeezed tight in his chest.

"You're beautiful, Scarlett Buck," he growled, in a voice that felt like gravel, as he gazed down upon perfection, from her crazy scarlet crown all the way past her luscious curves to her provocative red tipped toes. "So crazy beautiful." And the green eyes that looked up at him glistened like waterholes that were so goddam deep you could drown in them, and god, he was tempted to jump right on in.

But those toes had given him an idea that might save him from saying anything even crazier before all the blood drained from his brain and headed south.

Though it might not save his sanity.

He reared back on his knees.

"What's wrong?"

"I can't help but feel something's missing," And he disappeared into the dressing room.

"Like what?" she called behind him.

He came out brandishing a grin and her pink sparkly boots. "These."

"Now who's kinky?" she said, reaching for them and pulling them on, before reclining on her side, propping up her head with her hand, the other on her hip. "So, how do I look?"

He looked at her, naked but for those outrageous boots,

and with his mouth watering and his cock standing to attention, knew his sanity was a lost cause.

"Like every cowboy's dream come true."

She smiled, a slow, wide, knowing smile. "Then what are you doing standing all the way up there, cowboy?"

Yet another good question. He loved how this woman's thought processes worked.

He launched himself onto the bed, collecting her in his arms and meshing his mouth with hers and tumbling her across the big wide bed until he stopped with her on top. "Hey cowgirl," he whispered in hot, heavy breaths against her throat, "seeing as you've got your boots on and all..."

"Uh-huh?"

"I thought maybe you'd like to go for a ride?"

Thank god, she thought moments later as he lay sheathed and ready to guide her hips down over that long, hard length of his, some decisions didn't need thinking about.

Some decisions came to you gift-wrapped on a dish.

They made it down to lunch eventually, surprised to find only two of the party at the table. Sharon was laughing and Robbo was grinning and there was no mistaking the way they both sprang back in their chairs at their approach. "Kristelle's at the spa with her mother," Robbo explained as they sat down, "and the others took the chance to grab a helicopter to go sightseeing. They'll be back soon."

"How is Kristelle today?" asked Scarlett, and couldn't help but notice the way Sharon's once warm smile grew tight at the mention of the bride-to-be.

Robbo took a breath, and fiddled with a stray coaster and frowned absently out over the spectacular coastline where the turquoise sea fairly sparkled today. "Nervous. I mean she's happy about the weather improving, and the improved chances for seeing Staircase to the Moon, and now she's aiming for achieving Zen-like calm at the spa."

"Excellent," said Mitch, "maybe we should talk about the plan for the rings."

"The rings! They're in the safe in the villa. How about I give them to you now?"

The men wandered off while Scarlett sat back with a freshly delivered coffee and said to Sharon, "You didn't fancy going to the spa?"

The other woman shook her head. "To be honest, it's nice to have a little space. This is all really weird. I'm still not even sure why I'm here."

"Why? How long have you known Kristelle?"

"See, that's the thing. I started at a new gym a few months ago, and the first time I went, Kristelle asked me for coffee after. I thought it was a nice gesture. So we had coffee and a chat and it just became a regular thing. But y'know? I don't think she actually listens to anything anyone else says, if you get my drift."

"She knew sooo much about your job, right?"

She laughed. "Yeah, exactly. I remember talking about it and then being envious when she said she didn't have to work. She only did it for the—" She rolled her eyes and raised her fingers to make quote marks in the air—"sense of purpose, apparently."

"And then just a couple of weeks ago, she told me she was getting married and asked me to be her bridesmaid, because it's such short notice that nobody else she'd asked could make it. And I thought it was strange that she was asking me, but I had days off owing and it was an all-expenses-paid trip to Broome staying in Cable Beach of all places, and she was in a tough spot and I thought, why not?" She shook her head. "But then I got here and it's like she can hardly remember anything about me. I'm like an accessory after the fact. And I know it's bad, but I started wondering if she even has any other friends." And then she grimaced. "I told you it was weird."

It was weird. But then Kristelle seemed to be one out of the box.

"Maybe she's just stressed."

Sharon nodded. "She's stressed all right."

"Maybe the spa treatment will work."

"Yeah. Maybe." But Sharon didn't look like she believed it and Scarlett had to admit, she had good cause.

"So Sharon," she said, leaning closer, "This might sound strange too, but I'm curious about this accounting thing. Tell me about your job, what do you actually do?"

The men returned a few minutes later and the sightseers returned a little after that, full of all the amazing things they'd seen from the air, and the conversation was lively and lunch was ordered and arrived and was demolished with gusto and the atmosphere was festive.

With two hours to go before the wedding, people were just thinking about making a move to prepare for the ceremony when Alice Svensson bustled nervously up to Robbo's side. "Robert, Kristelle wants to know where you've put the gown."

He shrugged. "I haven't put it anywhere."

Alice blinked and swallowed and tried again. "So where is it?"

This time Robbo twigged. "The dress? You're looking for the wedding dress?"

"Ye-es."

"I thought you had it."

"Oh, god." Alice peeled away from the table and disappeared and everyone around the table blinked, and that was really all there was time for because it was Kristelle who appeared next; Kristelle in a sundress with her skin glowing and hair all pinned up into an intricate and elegant up-do, and how every bride-to-be would want to look, if it wasn't for the rabid eyes and her mother hovering anxiously behind.

"Robert, darling," she said with words that fairly dripped with arsenic, "where is my dress? You know, the one I'm supposed to marry you in. In. Less. Than. Two. Hours. From. Now?"

A sheen of sweat broke out on Robbo's forehead as the coaster in his fingers shredded. "I don't know, darling. Where can it be?"

She laughed, if you could call it a laugh. "You seriously mean to tell me that you don't have it?"

"I thought it was bad luck for me to have anything to do with it before the wedding day. When you weren't carrying it, I assumed Alice had brought it with her."

"Aaaaargh!" She turned on her bridesmaid. "Sharon, you should have done something. Why didn't you think of it?"

Sharon sat bolt upright in her chair. "How? Why?"

"Because you're supposed to be supporting me. You should have known something was wrong. You should have done something about it."

"But you came up the day before me. I didn't know you didn't have the dress."

"You could have asked!"

"And you could have realized then and I could have brought it the next day."

"You're saying this is my fault? You're useless!"

"Hey," said Robbo, "Leave Sharon alone. It's not her fault."

"Then whose fault is it?"

"Oh god," said Rolf across the table, who looked like he'd been visited by the ghost of weddings past, and hailed a passing waiter for a double scotch.

"Calm down," said her mother nervously hovering behind Cyclone Kristelle, "we'll get another dress. We'll go shopping. It'll be fine."

Kristelle's fists clenched at her sides. "We're in a tiny town at the arse-end of the world and I'm supposed to be getting married in less than two hours. Where am I supposed to find a dress?"

"Actually," Mitch piped up, and said, before Scarlett could stop him, "Scarlett's got a dress."

All heads swiveled her way. "What?"

"You wouldn't mind if Kristelle borrowed it, would you, Scarlett?"

She shook her head. "I really don't think..."

"A wedding dress?" all of them said. "You've got a wedding dress? Why?"

"It's kind of a long story."

Kristelle huffed. "This is pointless. Even if *she* had a dress, it would hardly be suitable for me."

"I dunno," said Mitch. "It's white and frothy and takes up half the wardrobe. What did you say it cost? Two thousand dollars? A Vera Wong or something."

"Vera Wang," Scarlett corrected. "But I don't think—"

Alice gasped, her gaze going from her daughter to Scarlett and back again, mentally sizing them up. "You've got a two thousand dollar Vera Wang gown hanging in your closet?"

"Mother, I hardly think—"

"Well think again," her mother snapped. "Because right now there don't appear to be too many other options."

Which was why Kristelle and her mother were standing in their villa two minutes later as Scarlett unzipped the cover on the dress. "Oh my god," Alice said, her eyes popping out at all that tumbled tulle, as if even she hadn't believed this might work. "Kristelle, get your clothes off, right now."

"It gapes," complained the bride-to-be a few minutes later.

"It's bound to," said her mother, who already had the villa's pre threaded needle kit out and ready to go. "You're not as well-endowed as our American friend. But apart from that, it's perfect. Hold still and I'll fix it."

A few tiny stitches under the arm, and it was done. And even Kristelle had to admit, she looked amazing. But still...

"Look, I have to warn you, I don't think it's a very lucky dress."

"Oh, you'd do that, wouldn't you?" Kristelle sniped, "You'd deny me this dress to ruin my wedding day."

Oh good grief, thought Scarlett. "So go ahead. Take the dress."

"It's a dress," Alice said, matter-of-factly as she helped her daughter climb out of it. "It's lucky you had it," she said, securing it back in its protective cover. "I'll see you back at the villa, Kristelle," she said, and left with the gown.

"So long as you understand, Kristelle, this dress has bad luck. Two brides and two disappointments."

"Two?" She blinked, as she climbed back into her own clothes, and then shook the question away. "Well, that's hardly likely to happen to me," she said knowingly, "Robert can't wait to get that ring on my finger. He loves me. Besides, he'd never marry better and he knows it."

"Lucky Robert." Try as she might, Scarlett couldn't keep the snipe from her voice.

Kristelle paused, her hands behind her back at her zipper. "It should have been lucky Mitch, as it happens, but I'll settle. Meanwhile, we all know Mitch can do a whole lot better than you. And he will, because he's not going to marry you, you know. If he wouldn't marry me, he's hardly going to stoop to marrying trailer trash like you."

Wow. Nothing like laying it on the line. Had she just lent this woman a wedding gown? Scarlett found a smile from the nether regions of somewhere. "You know, I really wish there was a way to say this nicely, seeing as it's supposed to be a wedding 'n' all. But I asked Mitch what you were like before we came, and he told me you were beautiful.

"Turns out he was wrong, as it happens, because you're stunning. Super-model gorgeous in fact." Scarlett paused, the look on the other woman's face telling her she was clearly wondering what her problem was.

"What he didn't tell me, because he's too much of a gentleman, is that you're a complete and utter bitch."

Kristelle's face turned as cold and hard as marble. "Trailer trash!" she repeated, as she headed for the door.

"Happy wedding," Scarlett said. *Just don't say I didn't warn you.*

Chapter Eight

Robbo and Mitch were sharing a last pre-wedding tipple at the bar—one of a series of last pre-wedding tipples—when Mitch looked at his watch and stood up.

"C'mon, mate," he said. "Gotta get you to the church on time."

Robbo didn't move, just sat hunched on his stool looking melancholy. "To be honest, I was kind of hoping she'd call it off."

Mitch blinked and sat back down again. He was feeling a bit dazed. The events of the past couple of days were spinning around in his brain and after a few drinks it was hard to pin them all down long enough to make sense of them. "Hang on, mate, what are you saying?"

"I thought it was a solution to everything."

"Don't you want to get married?"

Robbo screwed up his face. "That's a hard one. Ask me something else."

"Do you love her? Do you love Kristelle?"

"Oh, Kristelle. She's beautiful isn't she? Like an ice princess or ice goddess or something. Ice. Cold. Something."

"Mate, do you love her?"

Robbo frowned. "Who?"

"Kristelle!"

"Oh, you still talking about her?" He shook his head. "I dunno. I must. I mean she tells me I do."

"So you don't actually love her?"

"I dunno. How do you know when you love someone? I mean, how do you know you love Scarlett?"

Mitch shook his head. "Mate, it's not like that."

"Of course, it is. Anyone can see you're nuts about her."

"Robbo—"

"And she's nuts about you. The three blind mice could see that. God, it should be you two tying the knot."

"Robbo, listen, this isn't about me. This is about you. You and Kristelle. Because if you don't love her, why are you marrying her?"

Robbo sighed a long loud sigh of frustration. "Because she wanted to get married and I'm scared to bloody death of her! Why do you think? And because when I said I had doubts about getting married so quickly, she said I was nuts if I didn't because I'd never do better." He looked sadly over at his friend. "She was right, wasn't she? I'm too bloody ugly for someone like her."

"Jesus mate, has she got you well and truly stitched up."

Robbo shook his head and drained what was left in his glass. "And then I came here and met Sharon—" he looked at his mate, "Have you met Sharon? She's an accountant, too."

Mitch clapped Robbo on the arm. "Yeah, I know. I've met Sharon."

"Yeah?" Robbo grinned. "Isn't she something else?" He hiccupped and turned his empty glass upside down on the counter. "I need another drink."

"No you don't," said Mitch, signaling to the bartender for two big black mugs of coffee. "What you need right now is a clear head and courage."

"I'd rather have another drink."

"Yeah," Mitch said, "wouldn't we all?"

The elegant gazebo was the perfect site for an intimate wedding. Surrounded by the lush tropical gardens and verdant lawns, the lily pond below lent an aura of tranquility, as silver and golden fish flashed by the surface and lingered a moment before swimming away, and exotic birds made even more exotic calls from the trees around.

It could have been tranquil too, if the groom and best man weren't missing in action.

"I'll go look," offered Scarlett, when the celebrant looked at his watch for about the seventeenth time.

She found them on their way, dressed formally for the wedding, sure, but looking more than a bit frayed around the edges. She caught Mitch's arm and caught a whiff of alcohol with it. "Where the hell have you two been?" Although the answer seemed pretty obvious.

"Pondering the question of life, the universe and everything," Mitch said.

"What?"

"Robbo has to talk to Kristelle. Where is she?"

"She's with her father waiting to walk down the figurative aisle. Where do you think she is?"

Mitch smiled down at Scarlett in the green dress they'd bought together in Kalgoorlie and with her hair tied into an elegant knot. "Geez, you look beautiful, Scarlett." And suddenly, in a bolt from the blue, he had the answer to Robbo's question.

How do you know when you love someone?

You just do.

He blinked as his heart lurched with the enormity of the discovery. He glanced down at his watch. He needed to sit down and work this out a while. "How much time do we have?"

"No time! Are you drunk?"

"Not half as drunk as Robbo." He looked around for his mate. "Robbo?" But his mate was long gone, already wending his unsteady way along the path towards the gazebo. "Shit!"

They chased after him but he had a decent head start and beat them there. "I can't do it," they heard him say to the celebrant and his parents and Kristelle's mother. "The wedding's off. Where's Kristelle? I have to tell her."

"You're not marrying her?" said his mother.

"Nope."

She put her hand to her head. "Oh, thank god for that."

"Virginia!" Andrew chided, gesturing with his eyes in Alice's direction, "Not now."

Virginia put her hand on the other woman's arm. "Nothing personal, Alice, because I like you and Rolf, I really do. But I have been worried about this whole wedding."

"Really?" said Robbo. "I wish you'd told me. I wish someone had told me."

"What *is* going on?" cried Kristelle, marching down the path toward them in her borrowed Vera Wang gown with her father and bridesmaid chasing after her. Quite a sight.

"Wow, that's three hundred and fifty dollars' value right there," muttered Scarlett and earned herself a pinch on the ass from Mitch for her observation.

"Ah!" Robbo turned. "Just the person I wanted to see."

"What is happening, Robert? Why are you so late?" And then she came closer and recoiled. "Oh my god. You reek!"

"I can't marry you, Kristelle."

"What?"

"I can't marry you. I don't love you."

"What are you saying?" She was blinking wide eyes and smiling brightly and really turning it on. "Of course you love me, Robert."

"Nope. I love the idea of you, sure, and I love the idea that someone as beautiful as you might want to marry someone as ordinary as me. But I don't love you. I don't think I even like you."

Kristelle's face turned so hard it looked like it might shatter. "You're drunk."

"And you're an ice... cold...bitch!"

"Oh!" She threw her flowers onto the ground and stomped on them before turning away, about to storm off, before she spotted Scarlett and Mitch on the periphery. "This is all your fault," she said to Scarlett, tugging at the bodice and ripping her mother's clever stitches so that it gaped and sagged and looked as sad as she did. "You knew this gown was bad luck, you knew!" And then to Mitch. "And it's your fault too. You bring this piece of trailer trash to my wedding and look what happens."

There was an audible hiss as everyone sucked air in and held their breath. Mitch looked at the woman before him, the woman he'd once shared a bed with, and didn't that knowledge make him feel sick to the gut. "Be grateful you're a woman," he said, through a jaw so tightly set it was a wonder the words could squeeze through, "because if you were a man, your face would be wearing my fist right now."

There were tears spilling from her eyes, her beautiful face twisted and ugly in her anguish. "Don't you see what she is? Are you blind?"

"Kristelle," said her mother, gently. "Come on, sweetheart. We should go."

She looked around, appealing to them all. "Are you all blind? Mitch should be marrying me! Not her!"

Looks were exchanged. Robbo shook his head. Sharon slipped her hand in his and he leaned into her, and his parents bowed their heads and gave silent thanks. The celebrant just sighed and closed his book and quietly drifted away.

"Come," said Alice and Rolf to their distraught daughter. "Come."

Mitch whisked Scarlett away from Cable Beach where the fallout and recriminations from the doomed wedding were bound to continue, and took her to Town Beach, on the Roebuck Bay side of Broome. Here there was a market set up with stalls selling food and souvenirs, with jugglers and buskers providing the entertainment, as people gathered in preparation for the famous Staircase to the Moon.

He was glad he hadn't said anything foolish to her before the wedding. Now he'd had a chance to think about it, he could see it would have been a mistake. Robbo had simply been so taken in by their acting roles, that he'd actually believed they were in love, and in Mitch's alcohol-assisted brain, he'd almost believed it too.

Lucky he'd sorted that out in time.

Because it would have been the last thing Scarlett would want to hear. She was leaving. Going home to a place half a world away, and possibly as early as tomorrow. And he'd go back to his fly-in, fly-out job and he'd probably forget all about her by the next time he was on leave again.

They wandered around the stalls and ate Indonesian satay and noodles before they found a place on the grass overlooking the bay before things got too crowded. There, as they sat and watched the huge tidal pull suck the bay dry, shrinking it to a tiny rivulet and leaving the muddy flats exposed and glowing under the fading sun, he called his travel agent.

Paying Scarlett in cash was no problem if that was what she wanted, he'd told her, but making a reservation would be quicker and easier on his card, and she'd agreed to that, so long as it didn't cost more than fifteen hundred dollars, or she'd rather take the cash and work it out herself.

And even as he dialed, he was selfishly hoping there was nothing available at short notice, and she'd have to stay a few more hours, even just overnight, until he himself had to catch the shuttle back to the Kimberleys. Was it too much to ask for one more day and one more night? Just twenty-four hours more with a woman who had turned his world inside out and upside down in the space of just a few short days?

But then it had all been an act from the start. And now the failed wedding was behind them, there was no need to act like a couple any longer. There was no need for them to be together any longer. The agent promised to get back to him as soon as he could.

The sun was setting behind them, painting the sky in vivid oranges and lemons. "It's beautiful," Scarlett said, and Mitch agreed, even though he knew the sunset would have looked more spectacular over the sea from Cable Beach.

"Just wait until the moon comes up," he promised her.

She smiled, but only weakly, before she turned her head away to watch the last of the sunset sky.

He was worried about her. She seemed on edge tonight,

as if the failed wedding had knocked the stuffing out of her and even the vibrant market atmosphere couldn't spark her up. Maybe given Kristelle's verbal attack, it was no wonder she was flat. Or maybe she was just feeling like she didn't have to pretend any more. She probably couldn't wait to get home. At least he'd be able to let her know how long she'd have to wait before a flight out.

Scarlett sat there while Mitch went to refresh their drinks. He was making her flight reservation. He wasn't even waiting until tomorrow to give her the money he'd promised. He was making her reservation now. All under the pretext it would be better.

Better for whom?

And although the beach was getting crowded, Scarlett felt utterly alone. She watched the darkening sky erase the last of the color from the sunset, and that was exactly how she felt right now: as if all the color was being sucked from her life. Did he really want to erase her from his life that swiftly?

She'd thought they could have one last night before acknowledging it was over. But Mitch paying so much attention to his phone made it feel like he wanted it over now.

And she did want to go home.

She needed to go home.

Although those two things weren't as closely in sync as they once were.

Because there'd been magic happening here in Broome. Magic in the location, sure, but magic between her and Mitch too.

And while she needed to be home, it didn't stop her wishing that things could be different.

Mitch returned with their drinks and sat next to her and she was so busy thinking of all the reasons she'd miss him, that she all but missed the collective hush that descended over the crowd that had gathered around the edges of the lawn while they'd been waiting. And then the haunting tones of the native Australian didgeridoo music broke the silence as a glow appeared behind the mudflats and kept growing until a silvery burst of light appeared on the horizon and the audience burst into spontaneous applause.

It was amazing to be there, and even more amazing to have Mitch's arm wrapped around her shoulders while it happened, to feel his heat and his heartbeat as this disc of a moon slowly rose from the earth and grew and grew.

And she forgot about leaving, she forgot about everything as she watched the moon grow big and fat and finally slip free of the shackles of the earth and launch itself wholly into the sky.

It was breathtaking, like a giant pearl in the low sky, hanging creamy and white, its glow catching on a strip of the damp mud flats below. And that was when the magic really began, for as the moon climbed higher in the night sky, more of the mud flats were caught in the band of light, illuminating them as the big moon rose, creating the illusion of a staircase rising from the earth to the moon.

Mitch had seen the Staircase to the Moon before but he'd never appreciated the sheer wonder of it until he saw it reflected on Scarlett's face. Her eyes were huge, her lips slightly parted, her breathing faster as if she was moved by the spectacle.

He took her hand and she looked at him, and there were tears swimming in her eyes. "It's so beautiful," she said.

And for all the wonder and beauty of this night, nothing, nothing was more beautiful than she was in that moment. He almost let those words slip again, almost said the words that he'd discounted but that wouldn't go away.

I love you.

"Scarlett," he said, struggling with the discovery. Because she was leaving. Walking away from his world and rejoining hers, half a planet away. The knowledge almost tore him in two. "You're the one who's beautiful," he said instead, and pressed his lips to hers and cursed the cruel fates that had brought them together, only to fling them apart again.

Together they watched as the moon rose, the staircase growing until, as it had once broken free of the horizon, it also broke free of its more tenuous of link to the earth, and the staircase fell away.

Eventually they wandered back through the market

stalls and they found one they hadn't noticed before selling pearls and exquisite pearl jewelry. "You should have a souvenir to take home," he said. "Something from Broome."

She shook her head, even as he saw her eyes fall on one display, of a strand of pearls hung with a single teardrop pearl at its center, with matching teardrop earrings.

"It's too much!" she protested, when he asked if she'd like them, "you've already given me too much," but eventually she agreed to take the earrings.

His phone buzzed as he'd finished the purchase. He looked at the screen and felt his heart sink. "Good news," he lied, "we've got you ticketed right through to Bozeman leaving tomorrow. You'll be home in two days."

"Great," she said, clutching his gift to her chest.

Their lovemaking was tender that night, and sweet. Mitch took his time because that was all he had now and even that was slipping away and he wanted to remember every single thing he could, every freckle, every taste, every tiny detail, about this woman after she'd walked out of his life forever.

He'd never been a forever kind of guy, but right now the thought of never seeing Scarlett again was killing him and if he didn't say something it surely would.

"Stay," he whispered, as their bodies hummed down from the dizzy heights of pleasure. "Even just a little longer. And next leave I can take you to Sydney. Or Uluru. Or Melbourne. There's so much you haven't seen. You don't have to go tomorrow."

"No, I really do have to go."

"Just because some jerkball let you down doesn't mean—"

"No. I never told you why I needed the money so bad, did I?"

"I thought..."

"Yeah, I know what you thought." She pulled his arm tighter around her. "You see my mom's sick. I'd barely arrived in Perth and the doctors finally found out the reason for her falls and her shakes. She's got Early Onset Parkinson's. And Mom's still trying to come to grips with that and Tara's been running her around trying to cover everything and it's not fair that I'm not there to help out, not to mention that I just want to see her." She turned her face to him. "I have to go, Mitch, Mom needs me, but I want you to know I've had the best time with you, really I have."

Home. To Marietta and her Mom and her sister. Scarlett lay on the bed, watching the fan make patterns on the ceiling as the first light of dawn peeked around the curtains. She should be excited. It was what she'd wanted. What she'd set out to do and for once in her mistake-prone life, was going to do.

She should feel proud of herself.

She should feel excited.

Instead she felt empty.

And she knew the reason why.

Because this man had taken her heart and she was leaving here without it.

"Don't come in," she said, when they arrived at the airport and the driver opened her door. "Please, just go."

"Scarlett—"

She held up one hand to him, threw the backpack that the driver had retrieved from the trunk over her shoulder. "No! Really, there's no need. I hate airports and I hate goodbyes and it'll just make my mascara run and I'll look ridiculous and you don't want me to look ridiculous."

He shook his head and smiled. "Do I get to kiss you goodbye?"

She reached up, put her lips to his and breathed in his warm breath for the last time before she drew away. "There. Thanks for everything," she said, and then she had to turn away while she could still see her way into the terminal.

She waited in line feeling utterly miserable, and was never more pleased to get the check-in desk and hand over her documents. All she wanted was to ditch her bag and go hide in a corner somewhere and cry her eyes out.

"You've been standing in the wrong line, Ms. Buck. You're ticketed in business class all the way through to Bozeman, you didn't have to wait in line."

"Business class?"

The attendant smiled as she waited for the boarding passes to print out. "All the way."

"I didn't know."

The attendant handed her the passes. "Then you must have someone special looking out for you."

Mitch. Who'd insisted on buying her tickets for her and who must have planned this the whole time and whom she'd sent away before she could discover his surprise. And she turned towards the windows and mouthed the words she would now never get to say to his face, "I love you, Mitch."

T he cleaners had been through in Mitch's absence and the villa was clean and sparkling again, the big wide bed put to rights. But the place was empty without Scarlett, devoid of life and laughter and even her scent. His gut clenched, he couldn't stay here a moment longer. He only had one more night here but he'd ask for another room. This one held too many memories.

He was on his way out when he noticed them in a corner, and for a moment he thought she'd forgotten them. Until he picked them up and inside one spangly pink boot, he found her note.

To Mitch, with thanks from the best Buck you'll ever have.
All my love,
Scarlett
xx

And he slid down the wall cradling her boots to his chest.

Chapter Nine

Tara came to meet Scarlett, picking her up after one of her shifts. The sisters fell into each other's arms and there were tears and laughter and Scarlett couldn't believe that it had only been a few weeks since she had left, because it felt like so much had happened.

"How's Mom?" she asked, as Tara loaded her bag into her truck and headed for Marietta. "How's she taking it all?"

"You know Mom." Tara shook her head. "Drama queen all the way. But it'll be better now you're back. She's been worried about you, of course, so that'll be one less thing for her to worry about."

"And her illness? Any news?"

"Seems the same. Doctors said she's probably had it a while without knowing and it may not progress too quickly if she's lucky. The drugs should help with that. But she's worried about losing her job of course. It doesn't pay for a nail technician to have tremors."

"Yeah."

"Anyhow, now that you're back, we can all be one big happy family again, right? Unless you've got other crazy plans you haven't told me about? Hmm?"

Well, she would think that. And she'd be justified in thinking it too. "Tara."

The pickup rattled across a railroad track and Tara kept her eyes on the road. "Yeah?"

"I need to apologize. You told me it was a mistake going

to Perth to meet Travis. You warned me it would go bad."

"Hey," she held up a hand. "You already explained what happened. The guy's an asshat."

"Yeah, but I should have listened to you. I should have thought about what I was doing a little more, at least, given myself an escape plan."

Tara pulled her sunglasses down her nose and peeked over them at her sister. "Is this my madcap sister, Scarlett, talking? What happened to you over there, anyhow?"

Scarlett looked out the window at the view. They'd left Bozeman behind and now the thirty or so miles to Marietta were open farmland, dotted with ranches and colored barns and all set off by the snow topped jagged peaks of the mountains behind. A view so unlike the one she'd left behind.

"I don't know. I grew up a bit I think. And I met someone."

"Yeah. Asshat!"

"No. Someone else."

Her sister looked over at her. "Well? Are you going to tell me or do I have to Taser you to get the truth out of you?"

Scarlett laughed. Tara would never change. "Just a guy who helped me work out what I need to do."

"Yeah? Sounds serious. Like what."

She shrugged. "Get a job. Go back to college. Maybe not in that order."

"What doing?"

"I was thinking about asking that CPA firm if they need anyone. You know, the one across the road from you in Bozeman."

"Morison and Daume?"

"Yeah, they've got an office in Marietta too. I thought it worth a try."

"You're going to become a CPA?"

"I thought I'd ask if they had any entry-level positions going, test the water a little."

Her sister hmphed. "Well, good luck with that."

Scarlett smiled. She'd thought it crazy at first too. "Thanks."

"And this guy who helped you work things out. Does he

have a name?"

"Mitch."

"And is he the one who upgraded the fare for those fancy priority baggage tags your bag is wearing?"

Scarlett's mouth fell open.

"Hey, I'm a cop. I'm supposed to notice things. Anyhow, nobody gets off a plane that fast unless they're up the point end. So is he?"

"Yeah, that was Mitch too. I kind of did him a favor and he helped me get home. I didn't expect business class though. That was nice of him."

"Must have been some kind of favor." Her sister looked over at her. "You gonna see him again?"

Scarlett breathed in the sweet Montana air and turned her eyes up to the roof of the car to stop the moisture from trickling down. Even if he had felt half way inclined, the news that her mom had a potentially hereditary illness was sure to put any man off. "I don't see how."

"Yeah," said her sensible sister and slapped her twin on the leg. "Well, maybe that's for the best. You don't exactly have the best track record with men."

Ain't that the truth?

"So how's Simon?" she asked, before Tara could expound on the rest of her character faults.

"Oh, the same."

"You guys still entered in The Great Wedding Giveaway?"

"Yep. Simon's brilliant idea to score a free wedding. Hey, there's a barn dance coming up in April where they announce the semifinalists. You coming to support your big sister? Mom'll be there. You can give her a lift there and back."

"Sure." So nothing had changed here in Montana then. She was back ten minutes and her sister had her organized. But that felt good too. She was back at home and this was the way things had to be, and so she smiled, even though she was over weddings for a while. "Wouldn't miss it for the world."

Chapter Ten

"The name's Mitch Bannister. I'm looking for Tara Buck."

Everyone in range turned at his voice, the police officer behind the counter cocked his head. "You a friend of Officer Buck, sir?"

"A friend of her sister."

"I see." He picked up a phone. "I'll just see if she's available."

Mitch nodded. He sure hoped she was available. He wasn't certain how he'd find Scarlett otherwise, although come hell or high water he swore he would.

The officer behind the counter put down the phone. "She'll be here in a couple of minutes." He gestured to the row of seats along the wall. "Would you like to take a seat?"

"No thanks." He'd been sitting for far too many hours as it was. Instead he turned and watched the people of the good city of Bozeman go about their business through the windows. A busy place, the street filled with shoppers and workers on their lunch break, the parking spaces along the side of the road filled with pickup trucks and SUVs. And somewhere out there in Montana was Scarlett.

So this was Mitch. Tara's eyes narrowed as she checked him out. Not bad from the rear. "Mr. Bannister?"

He turned, his eyes narrowing. "Tara Buck?" And she had to admit the view from the front was pretty good too.

"I hear you're looking for my sister."

"That's right."

"She expecting you?"

"No." He smiled. "I thought I'd surprise her."

"Long way to come to surprise a woman. What if she doesn't want to see you?"

"I'll take my chances. Do you know where I might find her?"

Through the window Tara saw her twin coming back from the deli with the office lunch orders and disappear inside. "Yeah, maybe. You wanna ride?"

"I'd appreciate it."

"Sure, give me a minute."

She grabbed her hat and some car keys and told her co-workers she'd be back in ten.

He'd barely climbed into the black and white alongside her when she pulled out into the traffic. "So what do you do back in Australia?" she asked.

"I'm a mining engineer at an iron ore mine in the northwest."

She took a right. "Yeah? That must pay pretty well?"

"Not bad."

"Not bad? I'll say if you can pay someone to fly home business class, it's not bad."

Mitch smiled. "It's a long trip. I thought Scarlett could at least do it in comfort."

"Very decent of you. So long as you're not expecting anything in return, that is."

"Like what?"

Another right. "You tell me."

"Scarlett is safe with me," he said.

"Yeah," Tara said, with the indicator on again. They waited at the traffic lights before she made another right. "That's what they all say. But Scarlett's come back and she's all settled down and I don't want her shaken up again."

"I appreciate that."

She looked over at him. "So you're not planning on shaking her up again, right?"

"Not if I can help it."

"Good. Then we might even end up friends."

He looked around. The street looked familiar. "I thought you were taking me to Marietta."

Then he saw the police department directly ahead. She pulled up slightly short of it.

"Why would I take you to Marietta?" said Tara, "when Scarlett works right across the street."

He looked out his window, searching for a clue. There was an old timber building, done up and with a sign out the front written in western style lettering.

Morison and Daume CPA

And there inside the glass frontage he saw a flash of color and movement.

Scarlett!

Tara got out of the car and leaned against the fender with her arms crossed. "Now you go see my sister, and I'll wait right here, just in case she's not all that happy with your little surprise."

He smiled and said, "It's been a pleasure meeting you, Officer Buck."

Scarlett picked up the ringing phone, "Morison and Daume CPA, can I help you?" She listened a while and then, "just putting you through." And punched another line before she hung up. Phew. After a week, she had the veritable antique of a switchboard mastered.

The bell above the door rang and she swiveled in her chair ready to give a similar greeting to whoever had just come in. "Welcome to Morison and... Morison and... *Mitch*?"

"Hi Scarlett. Long time no see."

She squealed and jumped up from her chair and flew

into his waiting arms. Mitch spun her around, their lips locked tight in a kiss that said it had been way too long.

"What are you doing here?" she asked, breathless and blushing, her eyes so big and green and alive.

"I missed you."

"I missed you too."

He looked around the office. "What are you doing here?"

"I have a job."

"As an accountant?"

"Yeah. No. Not quite. But I'm learning about the office and I'm going back to college and if I do okay, over the next few months, the firm will let me work part time while I study."

He smiled. "That's great Scarlett. That's really great."

"I know. And I owe it all to you. But hey, how did you even find me?"

"Your sister showed me where you worked. But only after giving me the third degree on the drive here."

She frowned. 'She works right across the street.'

He smiled. "So I discovered."

She laughed and looked out the window and there was her sister, indeed, right across the street, leaning against her patrol car. She waved to her through the window.

And Tara, watching from across the street, waved back and mouthed, "Go Scarlett," and went back to work.

"How long are you here?"

"Not long."

There was a cough behind them, and she turned to see old Mr. Morison sticking his head out of his office. "Everything all right, Ms. Buck?"

"Oh, Mr. Morison, yes sir." And to Mitch she said, "I have to get back to work. Will you wait for me?"

"Sure, I'll take a look around town."

"Oh! And it's the Barn Dance tonight for The Great Wedding Giveaway. Tara and Simon are entered and they're announcing the semi-finalists. I'm going with Mom. Will you come with me? You have to come!"

He smiled. It wasn't quite the way he'd planned the night to go, but he was here and she hadn't recoiled in horror and maybe this wasn't such an insane idea. "Sure, it'd be my pleasure."

The blood in Scarlett's veins fizzed as she slipped on the emerald green dress Mitch had bought for her in Kalgoorlie. It seemed fitting that she'd chosen it to wear tonight. Fitting that he'd arrived today in time to see her wear it again.

Why had he come? Simply because he'd missed her? She'd counted the days off since she'd come home, counted them in blocks of fourteen days on and seven days off. Felt a pang of hope during that seven days that maybe—but nothing. And then fourteen long days on again.

She'd hardly dared hope this time. But he was here.

Her heart was racing. She checked herself in the mirror, knowing she couldn't linger. Right now Mom was entertaining Mitch in the front room and she daren't leave them alone too long. If he thought a grilling from Tara was tough, he hadn't seen nothing yet.

She was half way out the door before she remembered them, the earrings he'd bought her at the Staircase Markets that last night in Broome. Then, with one final glance in the mirror, she was done.

Mitch stood as she entered the room. "You look beautiful, Scarlett."

"You don't look so bad yourself, Mitch."

Her mom flapped and fussed, as if charged by the crackling electricity in the room, fumbling for her purse and a coat. It was Mitch who took the coat from her shaking hands and slipped it over her black sequined top and leopard skin mini.

"Thank you, Mitch. Now we must get going. They'll introduce all the couples and we can't miss Tara and Simon."

Scarlett let Mitch drive, giving him directions to Samuel T. Emerson's big cattle ranch and the magnificent old barn, where the dance would be held, and she was glad she wasn't driving. It meant she could sit back and concentrate on him while her Mom fired question after question.

He looked better than she remembered, and he'd looked damn fine then, and when he looked over at her now, her blood just fizzed some more. He smiled. "What are you looking at?"

"You."

She was so busy watching him that they missed the turn off to the ranch and had to turn around and go back.

Mitch couldn't believe the size of it when he drove up. He'd been expecting something like a shearing shed like they used at home for barn dances. But this was no old tin shearing shed. This was enormous. This was the mother of all barns.

Scarlett's mother was already making a wobbly dash for the entrance when Mitch said, "Tammy—Mrs. Buck—would it be all right if we caught up with you in a moment? I just wanted to have a word with Scarlett."

"I'll see you inside," she said, "I'll save your seats."

And Mitch pulled Scarlett around the side of the barn.

"We don't have long," Scarlett said, but her eyes were bright and hopeful and he was hopeful too.

"This won't take long." He took a breath. "Scarlett, I had to come because I had to tell you something. Something I didn't have the courage to tell you back in Broome and something I thought I'd get over when I got back to work, but I didn't, and I kept looking at that note you left me, and I had to come and find out if you felt the same way."

Her eyes were wide and waiting, her breathing hitched. "Tell me," she whispered.

"I love you, Scarlett. And I need to know if you could love me too."

"Oh Mitch!" She threw her arms around his neck. "Oh yes, I love you! I'm crazy about you. Leaving you was the hardest thing I've ever done. Didn't you know? Couldn't you tell?"

He was spinning her around, laughing and so filled with joy, there were tears in his eyes. "I was too afraid to hope. I was too wrapped up in my own misery." His heart was filled to bursting as they kissed, but there was still room for more.

There was still more he had to ask.

"I know this is sudden," he said, "but I don't have long and I know you've probably had a gutful of weddings for a while, but I need to know." He swallowed. "Scarlett, will you marry me?"

Scarlett stood there, like a deer in the headlights. "You know about my mom, I told you about her sickness. You know there's a chance..."

"Everything in life is ruled by chance, Scarlett. And maybe there's a risk of something happening down the track and maybe there isn't, but I do know that if I don't take this chance on loving you, then I'm the loser, whatever happens."

Her eyes filled with tears, she put a hand over her mouth. "Oh, Mitch. I love you so much. So yes," she said nodding. "Yes, of course I will marry you."

His heart crowed—*buckadoodledoo!*—and the music started up while they were kissing again and Scarlett said, "We have to go inside."

"One more thing," he said. "I don't have a ring for you, but I do have this." He pulled a pouch from his pocket and a string of pearls with one single teardrop pearl in the center. The one that matched her earrings.

And as he fixed it around her neck, he let his lips brush her skin, and felt the heated charge that came with being with this woman, and knew that it was right.

"Where've you been?" whispered Tammy as they took their seats under the crisscrossing fairy lights strung across the barn as the music wound down, "They're about to introduce the couples."

"Mitch asked me to marry him."

"Oh!" Her mother slapped her hands over her mouth. "And what did you say?"

Scarlett smiled. "I said, yes, of course."

"Oh my lord!" Tammy said, and at least a half dozen tables turned their way at the commotion. "First Tara and Simon, now you and Mitch. You have made me the proudest mama."

Scarlett smiled up at Mitch and mouthed, "I love you."

Epilogue

Miss Scarlett Buck became Mrs. Scarlett Bannister a month later under a warm spring sun on the lush lawns of Marietta's Bramble House, an 1890's Queen Anne mansion built on Bramble Lane by one of the founding families of Marietta.

Her aunt Margot gave her away, with Scarlett wearing a gown of organza and tulle with a ruched bodice and long floaty skirt that she'd found at Married in Marietta, though not on the sale rack this time, and not with, Scarlett had made sure, a past. In her hands were the sweetly scented roses that clever Risa Grant from Sweetpea Flowers had formed into a bouquet, and at her throat and on her ears were the pearls that Mitch had given her.

On her finger was the rock he had bought for their official engagement. A one carat Kimberly pink diamond. Nestled right up to the matching wedding band.

Her sister, Tara, looked stunning in her sapphire bridesmaid dress. She and Simon hadn't semi-finalled that night at the barn dance, and while Simon had seemed disappointed, it hadn't fazed Tara at all. She'd just blown off the disappointment and gone back to making their wedding plans the way she'd expected to all along.

Tammy was in her element, her blonde hair back combed to within an inch of its existence, her leopard print silk jacket floating over a gold pantsuit.

Afterwards they had cocktail hour on the white

balustraded balcony and bride and groom mingled with their guests, both far-flung and local. An intimate wedding by wedding standards, but definitely a good one.

Mitch's mum was over from Melbourne, loving every minute of it, and loving Scarlett's mom and Aunt Margot into the deal. This end of town was like her part of Melbourne. She could do leopard print and new age crystals with the best of them.

Robbo had made the trip over too, to be Mitch's best man, and he'd brought a glowing Sharon along with him. "We're getting married ourselves," he admitted after the ceremony, as he pumped Mitch's arm to congratulate him. "Sometime in spring back home, we're hoping. And we'd really like it if you could both be there. Um, especially since we'd like you to be best man, Mitch."

Mitch laughed. "Best man again, huh? Maybe this time I'll get it right."

"You just did, sweetheart," said Scarlett, punching him in the arm, before reaching across to kiss them both, "We're thrilled for you."

And even Robbo's parents had made the trip, just as they'd promised they would.

"A beautiful wedding," sighed Virginia. "I'm hoping our next has a bit less drama than the last."

Andrew wrapped his arm around his wife's shoulders and pulled her close. "You know, we had a lucky escape from the daughter-in-law from hell. We're not sure which of you two we owe the most to, but we just wanted to say thank you."

It was a small wedding, but it was a great wedding. And after all the meet and greets had been done and dusted, and as soon as there was a break in the traffic, Mitch plucked two glasses of champagne from a tray and took his new bride aside.

He wrapped his arm lovingly around his new wife and planted a kiss on her lips before handing her a glass. "How do you feel, Mrs. Bannister?"

"Special. Loved. Like my life is starting over. Like I've been offered a second chance at everything. A second chance at life. A second chance at love."

"A second chance bride?"

And she looked up at him. "Yeah, but this time, I got it right."

"That you did," he said, as he pulled her into his kiss. "That you did."

Almost A Bride

A MONTANA BORN BRIDES NOVEL

SARAH MAYBERRY

Dedication

A huge thanks to the lovely Lilian Darcy and Jane Porter for thinking of me for Tule, and to the rest of the talented ladies who are contributing to the Brides series. Special, super-duper thanks to Trish Morey, for making me laugh and hanging with me in the writing trench. And, as always, I couldn't do what I do without Chris and Max by my side. You boys are my salvation.

Dear Reader

There was so many things I enjoyed about writing this book. I loved writing for Tule Publishing's Montana Born imprint, loved all the amazing women who were working alongside me in this Spring Brides series, loved having Jane Porter cheering me on from the sidelines, and particularly loved having the hilarious and so clever Trish Morey as my wing-woman as we worked together to create a family and history for our twins, Tara and Scarlett Buck.

I can't remember who suggested our heroines be twins, but once the idea took root Trish and I were off and running. The emails flew back and forth as we discussed who our twins were and how they saw the world and how they were different from each other. It was Trish's idea that her heroine be named after Scarlett from *Gone with The Wind*, so of course my heroine had to have a *Wind* reference, too.

I'm not sure if it was the fact that Tara is named after a house, not a person, that gave me the idea that she was the sensible sister. Capable and practical and dependable. Deep down inside, though, Tara is just as scared, impulsive and spontaneous as the next woman - especially if the next woman is her twin. I loved helping Tara understand herself, and I especially loved helping her and her man, Reid, work out what was good and right and amazing for both of them.

If you haven't had a chance to read it yet, don't forget to grab Scarlett's story, *Second Chance Bride*! That Trish Morey is a funny lady, and I'm sure it will leave you smiling. In the meantime, I hope you enjoy Tara and Reid's story.

Happy reading,

Sarah Mayberry

Contents

Chapter One

Reid Dalton pumped gas into his GMC pickup, one ear tuned to the conversation going on between his friends inside the truck. Grant was giving Brett a hard time for missing an easy layup during the basketball game they'd just finished, and Brett was serving it straight back at him with both barrels.

Reid grinned to himself, feeling pleasantly tired after an hour of charging up and down the court, trouncing the Bozeman Fire Department team. The informal competition between the police department and the firefighters had become a regular thing over the past few months. Reid wasn't sure which part of their weekly matchups he enjoyed the most—the rapid-fire pace of the game itself, or the inevitable shit giving and taking that occurred afterward.

"You want to know my opinion?" he asked as the pump clicked off, signaling the tank was full.

"Not particularly," Brett said, which earned him a guffaw from Grant.

"You both need to lift your games. Drink less beer, run a few more miles," Reid said.

Grant made a rude noise, while Brett gave him a one-fingered salute. Reid was still laughing as he headed into the gas station to pay the cashier.

Then he saw the couple exiting the motel next door to the Gas-And-Go Mart and his step faltered.

The girl he didn't recognize, but she was young and

blonde and clinging to her man as though her very life depended on it. Reid watched as Simon Garfield said something before kissing her in a way that left no doubt whatsoever as to the nature of their relationship.

Damn.

Just... damn.

Tara would be devastated.

For a moment he was frozen as he absorbed all the implications of what he'd just witnessed. Tara had been planning the wedding for the past few months and as her patrol partner, there was precious little Reid wasn't privy to. Like the fact that Tara and Simon planned on having the reception at Le Petit Chateau in Bozeman, and that Tara was limiting her attendants to just her twin, Scarlett, and that today she had an appointment at Marietta's one and only bridal salon to pick out her wedding dress...

Belatedly he glanced back at the car, hoping the other guys hadn't seen, but they were both frowning, staring out the windshield at the sordid little drama unfolding in the parking lot next door. There wasn't a doubt in Reid's mind that they recognized Tara's fiancé. They'd all attended the engagement party Tara and Simon held back in February.

Reid mouthed a four-letter word.

What a nightmare.

Simon and the blonde were climbing into separate cars. Reid automatically noted the blonde's license plate before she turned onto the highway, heading toward Marietta.

She was a local, then.

Simon waited until a few cars blew past before following suit.

Reid shook his head in disgust before heading inside to pay for the gas. Both the guys were silent when he returned to the truck. Brett waited until they were heading for Marietta themselves before speaking up.

"What are you going to tell her?"

Reid didn't take his eyes off the road. "The truth."

Because no way was he sitting on this. The last thing he would ever want to do is hurt Tara—the thought literally made his gut ache— but there was no way he was going to look the other way and tell himself it was none of his business.

She'd want to know. Even if the truth was going to tear her world apart.

"When is the wedding?" Grant asked.

"Four months," Reid said.

There was a profound silence in the car as they all processed that particular piece of information.

"You think she has any idea...?" Brett asked.

Reid shot him a hard look. Tara was the most straight-up, no-bull person he knew. She wouldn't live with that kind of deceit. Wouldn't tolerate it for a second.

"Yeah. You're right," Brett said. "Stupid question. Forget I said anything."

Silence reigned for the remainder of the twenty-minute drive into town. Reid dropped both guys off at Brett's place, where Grant had left his car.

"Listen... give me a chance to talk to Tara, okay?" he said after the guys had hauled their gear out of the back of the truck.

Grant looked offended. "Like we're going to be running around telling anyone what we saw. Give us a little credit."

Brett simply nodded. They all knew that Grant told his wife, Sally, everything sooner or later, something that was only underlined by the dull red flush coloring the other man's face. Once Sally knew, it would simply be a matter of time before the story spread like wildfire.

"See you guys tomorrow," Reid said before pulling away from the curb.

His jaw set, he drove straight into the heart of town. The pink and white facade of Married in Marietta came up on his left and he pulled into the nearest empty parking spot. Then he sat and stared out the windshield and tried to work out how he was going to do this. What he was going to say.

Because he needed to do and say something pretty quick—he figured he had a couple of hours max before Grant blabbed to his wife and the phone lines of Marietta began burning up with the news that Simon Garfield was cheating on Tara Buck. Tara needed to know so she could brace herself for the oncoming storm.

First things first, though. Pulling out his phone, he called the station and had a quick chat with Dave on the desk. Sixty seconds later, he had the registration details for the car the blonde had been driving. Paige Donovan. One mystery solved.

It was Saturday afternoon, and there were plenty of people out and about, but Reid didn't register any of them as he stared into the distance. He was too busy remembering the look on Tara's face when she'd told him Simon had asked her to marry him. Her smile had been shy as she'd shown Reid the modest solitaire diamond her fiancé had bought to seal the deal. Reid had said all the right things, asked all the right questions, but there had been a hot feeling in his chest and it had taken him a few minutes to own it for what it was—jealousy. A fruitless and useless emotion, given who Tara was and what they were to each other: partners and friends, nothing more, nothing less. He had no right to be jealous of the man in her life.

And yet he had been, and sitting here now, he couldn't deny that even though he dreaded the upcoming conversation, there was a part of him that was relieved because he wouldn't have to stand in a church in four months' time and watch Tara marry someone else.

Which pretty much made him a selfish bastard of the highest order, he figured.

He shoved the car door open, walking away from his own thoughts.

His heart started to pound as he approached the salon. He wiped his hands down the sides of his shorts. Man, this was going to be hard. How on earth was he going to deliver such a painful blow to someone who deserved only happiness?

Gritting his teeth, he pushed open the door to the salon, entering a plush-carpeted world painted in soft neutrals. Fragile-looking velvet upholstered chairs dotted the space, along with tall vases filled with flowers. The walls were lined with racks bursting with white frothy dresses, a veritable sea of satin and tulle and silk, and a crystal chandelier fractured the light from half a dozen globes overhead.

A couple of women were browsing the racks, and they turned to stare at him in much the same way he imagined they might if he'd wandered into the women's restroom. A slim, middle-aged woman dressed entirely in black bustled out from behind the counter, an alarmed expression on her face.

"Hello. Can I help you?" she asked.

"I'm looking for Tara Buck. She was supposed to be here today, trying on dresses," Reid said.

He was suddenly very aware of his mussed hair, sweat-dampened T-shirt and shorts. Probably he should have taken the time to change into something more appropriate before coming here.

"And you are...?"

It occurred to him belatedly that she was worried he was the groom.

"I'm a friend. We work together."

"I'll just check and see what I can do for you," she said, giving him a dubious head to toe.

"Reid."

He turned toward the familiar voice—and forgot to breathe.

Tara wore a flowing white gown that hugged her body in all the right places—breasts, waist, hips. The way the lustrous fabric wrapped around her mid-section emphasized how slender she was, while a neckline with a little dip in the middle drew his attention to her breasts and the bare expanse of her shoulders. A froth of lace was pinned to her upswept blond hair, completing the bridal ensemble.

She was beautiful, absolutely heart-stoppingly gorgeous, and for a moment he could do nothing but stare.

"What on earth are you doing here?" Tara asked, laughing uncertainly. "I'm pretty sure you're not supposed to see the bride before the wedding. Isn't it supposed to be bad luck or something?"

Scarlett, Tara's non-identical twin, joined them, dressed more conventionally in jeans and a T-shirt, her crazy red hair pulled back in a ponytail.

"That's the groom, doofus," she said. "You are the

worst bride ever. How can you be getting married and know so little about weddings? Lucky Mitch made an honest woman of me in April or you wouldn't have a seasoned pro around to show you the ropes." Her gaze was curious as she glanced at Reid. "Hey, Dalton. What are you doing here?"

"I need to speak to Tara."

Tara's smile faded. "Why do you have that look in your eye?"

"What look?" Scarlett asked, frowning.

"His cop look. Has something happened? Oh, God, don't tell me something's happened to Simon?" Tara's eyes were wide now, and she pressed a hand to her stomach as though bracing herself for bad news.

Reid glanced around, aware that everyone in the salon had stopped to stare at them.

"Simon is fine." For now, anyway. Reid wasn't prepared to guarantee his future good health, however. "Is there somewhere private we can talk?"

"What's going on?" Tara asked, taking a step toward him.

No way was he doing this out here, with all these people watching. He turned to the sales assistant.

"Do you have an office?"

"Yes. It's out the back... "

Reid was already moving, reaching for Tara's elbow as he hustled her toward the rear of the store.

"You're freaking me out, Reid," Tara said.

She came with him willingly enough, though, because she trusted him. Trusted the hours they'd spent in the patrol car together and the confidences they'd shared and the deep knowledge they had of one another.

And he was about to break her heart.

"I'll just wait out here, then," Scarlett called after them, clearly miffed to be excluded from whatever was going on.

Reid spotted an open door, ducking his head in to find a desk, along with a filing cabinet and bookcase. He pulled Tara in after him and kicked the door shut.

They stood there eyeing each other for a long beat. Then he took a deep breath and did what needed to be done.

"I just saw Simon leaving the motel out on 98 with another woman."

For a heartbeat Tara didn't understand what Reid was saying. She was so disconcerted by his sudden appearance during her dress appointment, her brain seemed to be on vacation. He looked so out of place in the salon, with his mussed-up dark hair, broad-shoulders and lean, hard body dressed in work-out gear.

Then she blinked and his words hit home. She opened her mouth to deny him, to insist that he must have gotten it wrong, but Reid was watching her with his coffee-dark eyes and she knew that he wouldn't be here telling her this if it wasn't true. If he wasn't sure.

"Tell me," she said.

"We were heading home from our weekly game—"

"We?"

"Brett and Grant."

She closed her eyes for a long beat. Grant's wife was the biggest motormouth she knew, hands down.

"Did he see them as well?"

She didn't need to refer to Grant by name; she and Reid had been talking in short-hand since their first week on patrol together.

"They both did."

"Okay." She nodded, gesturing for him to resume filling in the blanks. She needed the facts—all of them— before she tried to work out how to respond, how to feel, what to do.

"Maybe you should sit down," Reid said, shoving the wheeled chair her way.

"I'm fine. Tell me the rest."

"There's not much more. We stopped at the Gas-and-Go Mart out on 98, and they came out of the motel next door and drove off in separate cars."

"They were definitely together?" It was a feeble straw,

but she owed it to herself—to the future she'd had planned—to grasp it.

"Yes."

Reid's terse reply and the way he broke eye contact with her said more than any words could. She wondered what he'd seen. Them kissing? Some kind of clinch?

"Who is she?" she asked.

Because she knew without asking that he would have gotten the other woman's plates. She would have done the same for him if she had been in his shoes.

"Paige Donovan. Do you know her?"

Paige Donovan.

She needed the chair then, one hand already reaching for it as her knees suddenly didn't work anymore. She leaned forward in the chair, dizzy with the implications of what he'd just revealed.

Reid crouched down in front of her, trying to see her face. "You're not going to faint, are you?"

No. But there was a good chance she might throw up.

"She's one of his students," she said, somehow getting the words past the tightness in her throat.

She'd heard the girl's name often enough to know. Paige had been a thorn in Simon's side since she'd walked into his class at the beginning of the year. Up until recently, he'd complained about her on a weekly basis.

Reid's expression was stony. "How old is she?"

Something was tickling her face and she realized she was still wearing the stupid veil. Reaching up, she dragged it free, not caring that the pins pulled her hair with them.

"I don't know. She's a senior. Seventeen. Maybe eighteen."

Simon was twenty-eight, two years older than Tara. The age of consent in Montana was sixteen, so even if Paige was only seventeen, he was probably in the clear legally.

Morally... he was toast. On so many levels. He was the girl's teacher—and he was Tara's fiancé. The man she had lived with for two years. The man she'd planned to start a family with, grow old alongside...

Reid took both her hands in his. Hers were icy, his warm and strong.

"Whatever you need, I'm here, okay?"

There was a gravelly note to his voice that made her throat get even tighter. His eyes were full of sympathy, and a worried frown creased his forehead.

"Thanks."

Her gaze dropped to his strong thighs, exposed thanks to his workout shorts. He had a tan, she couldn't help noticing. When on earth did he have time to get a tan, in between pulling shifts at Bozeman PD with her and helping out his parents in their apple orchard?

The absurdity of the thought—the stupid, inappropriate randomness of it—almost made her laugh. She was noticing Reid Dalton's thighs now, of all times?

It's easier than dealing with the truth.

Indeed.

It was tempting to cling to his hands, to use them as an anchor, but this was her mess. Her life. Her fiancé.

She eased back in the seat, slipping her hands free from his, suddenly overwhelmingly aware of the weight of the dress she was wearing. Not so many minutes ago, the heavy satin fabric and the dress's boning had felt comforting, supportive, substantial. Now it felt like a cage. A trap.

She stood. "I need to get out of this dress."

He stood, too, but she was already pushing past him, opening the door. Her sister was hovering near the change rooms, arms crossed over her chest, her expression worried.

"What's going on?" she asked as Tara marched toward her.

"Help me out of this thing. I want it off," Tara said.

She offered her sister her back, every muscle tense as she waited for the hiss of the zipper.

"Can you please tell me what's going on?" Scarlett asked, her voice scared now.

It hit Tara that her sister was probably imagining the worst—death or injury for someone they loved. Nothing as small and seedy as the truth.

"Simon has been having an affair with one of his students," Tara said.

There was a profound silence behind her. Then she felt

the tug of the zipper being undone. Wordlessly she walked into the change room, Scarlett hard on her heels. Her sister didn't say anything, simply shut the door. For the first time Tara was grateful that their mother hadn't been able to attend today's appointment, the symptoms from her recently diagnosed Parkinson's disease having taxed her severely over the last few days. Tammy Buck had never been good in a crisis, and she would be cursing up a storm and weeping and hollering right now if she were here, sucking up all the oxygen in the room and leaving nothing for anyone else.

Instead, there was only Scarlett working silently to help her out of the dress. Only when the satin was piled on the chair in the corner did her sister open her arms, her eyes filled with sadness. Tara's shoulders sagged, and she fell into her twin's embrace.

"I'm so sorry," Scarlett said, her voice raw.

Out of all the people in the world, only Scarlett knew how truly awful this moment was.

Tara had worked all her life to avoid her mother's fate. She had been careful. She had been prudent. She had been wise.

And yet here she was.

Disengaging from her sister's embrace, she reached for her clothes.

"Let's get out of here."

Chapter Two

S omehow Tara managed to hold in her tears until she was safely home, the door shut between her and the world. Scarlett had been adamant about coming home with her, and Reid had hovered while she'd made her excuses to Lisa Renee, the manager of Married in Marietta, but Tara had convinced them both that there was no merit to be had in hashing over everything.

Not that Reid would want to hash over anything. He wasn't the type to talk for talking's sake. He would have sat vigil with her if she'd asked, though. But she wanted to be alone when Simon came home. It was humiliating enough that the whole town would soon know of her fiancé's betrayal; she didn't need witnesses to the ugly little scene that was sure to ensue.

Scarlett had been harder to shake, but Tara's insistence that this was something she needed to do alone had finally sunk in. Her twin couldn't lessen this pain or take it away. This was all Tara's.

Tara glanced around the living room of the town house she and Simon shared, taking in the classic rolled-arm cream-colored couch with its oversized cushions, the recycled Oregon coffee table they'd picked up at a craft fair, the antique oil lamp that had once been her grandmother's.

It all looked so nice and neat and perfect. Like a page out of a Pottery Barn catalogue.

She drew in a shuddering breath. Simon was

supposedly playing golf with a buddy this afternoon. He'd told her he probably wouldn't be home until after three when he kissed her goodbye. Angry tears filled her eyes as she imagined him putting his golf bag in the back of his car—along with whatever it was a person took to a motel room when he planned on cheating on his bride-to-be. Condoms, maybe. Perhaps a bottle of wine, or a small gift for his girlfriend.

Girl being the operative word.

Tears rolled down her face as the reaction she'd fought so hard to hold off washed over her. Her body shook, her teeth chattering with the force of her anger and hurt. How could Simon do this to her? How could he lie in bed next to her, night after night, talking and laughing and, yes, making love with her, while all the while he was bedding one of his students?

It was beyond her. The man she'd lived with for two years simply wasn't capable of this kind of betrayal. He was decent. He was gentle. He was thoughtful and a little stubborn and sometimes overly cautious.

He was also a fantasy, apparently. A figment of her imagination. Because her Simon—the one she'd thought she was going to marry, the man she'd thought she'd spend the rest of her life with—didn't exist. She'd been sharing her life with some other person. A man she didn't know at all. A man who was capable of undressing one of his students—a girl who not so long ago had been wearing a training bra and taking driving lessons and giggling over posters of One Direction and Zac Efron—and lying down with her in a cheap motel in the middle of nowhere.

Bile burned the back of her throat. She wiped away the tears with the backs of her hands, then marched into the bedroom. Bundling the duvet in her arms, she dragged it off the bed and kicked it into the corner. The sheets came next. The pillow cases resisted her efforts to strip them from the pillows and she sobbed with fury as she wrenched first one, then the other free. The duvet cover was liberated, then she took the lot into the laundry room and stuffed it all into the washing machine with vicious, angry jabs. She poured in too much detergent, then slapped the machine on.

Then she slid down the wall until her ass hit the floor. Head bowed, she cried until there were no more tears, and all that was left was a hollow ache in her chest.

Had her mother felt like this the day she came home to find Tara's father gone, leaving her to raise two thirteen-year-old girls alone? Had she felt sick and sad and angry all at the same time? As though the rug had been pulled out from beneath her?

Tara didn't know. She'd never had a conversation with her mother on the subject. In fact, she'd assiduously avoided it, a tough ask given her mother's inability to let go and move on, even after thirteen years.

Tara and Scarlett had grown into womanhood steeped in stories of their father's reckless charm and sense of adventure, every tale ending with the same bitter, wounded observation from their mother—that man had no business getting married.

Despite the fact that she'd had no contact with her father once the divorce was final—her father's choice—Tara had been old enough when he left to have her own memories to draw on. She could remember piggyback rides and impulsive day trips to far-flung parts of the state and being showered with presents for no reason whatsoever, simply because their father felt like it. She could remember his magnetic warmth and infectious laughter, the way people used to gravitate to him. And she could remember his restlessness and dark silences, the way he used to look at her and Scarlett sometimes, as though the walls were pressing in on him.

Most of all she remembered the pain of discovering that he'd lied to her, that his promises had been worth nothing, and that he'd chosen a short redhead with big breasts over her and her sister and their mother.

And yet here she was, staring the same betrayal in the face, despite the fact that she'd done her level best to learn from her mother's mistakes and pick a man she could trust. An earnest man. A man who laughed quietly, who loved history, who had a genuine passion for teaching. A man who was steady and goodhearted.

Safe.

She'd had three serious boyfriends since she started dating in her late teens and a couple of not-so-serious ones, but Simon had been the best of them. Or so she'd believed.

Her tears dried. The hypnotic chug-chug of the washing machine lulled her into a dull-eyed trance as she waited for Simon to return home. She breathed, she tried not to think. She waited.

She had no idea how much time passed before she heard his car in the driveway. Slowly she pushed herself to her feet. The sound of the front door opening and closing echoed through the townhouse.

"Hey, I'm back. How was your shopping trip?" Simon called. "Did you find your princess-for-a-day dress?"

She studied the floor for a second. Then she lifted her chin. He was tossing his car keys onto the hall table when she entered the living room, an easy smile on his face. His chinos were crisp, his dark blond hair perfectly in place.

"Hey—" His smile dropped like a rock when he saw her face. He took a step toward her, one hand extended. "What's wrong, baby?"

She saw the exact moment that it hit him that she knew. His step faltered. His hand wavered in the air before falling to his side.

"You have half an hour to pack whatever you need, then I'm having the locks changed." Her voice sounded distant and foreign even to her own ears.

The color drained from his face. "I can explain."

"You don't need to. Reid saw you and Paige Donovan leaving a motel. That pretty much covers it, don't you think?" Tara took out her phone and opened the timer function, spinning the dial until she had thirty minutes showing. She tapped the screen to start it off.

"Thirty minutes," she said, heading for the front door.

He grabbed her arm as she walked past, his grip urgent.

"Please, Tara. You have to understand. I tried so hard. I didn't want any of this to happen. You have to believe me."

"Take your hands off me."

"It was a mistake. It only happened this one time, I swear. And it will never happen again—"

He knew her history, knew about her father. And still he'd done this to her.

"Take. Your. Hands. Off. Me."

His grip loosened and she pulled free. Eyes straight ahead, she strode to the door.

She could hear him breathing as she pulled it open, panting as though he'd just run a race. Panicking over the fact that his whole world was about to implode around him, no doubt.

She shut the door firmly behind herself, then walked to the nearest flower bed and threw up.

Reid drove straight out to his parents' place after leaving Tara. She didn't want his help, but it didn't feel right to simply walk away. Yet that was what he was doing, because he didn't have any other options.

He passed the dusty sign for Dalton Orchards and turned into the gravel driveway. Apple trees marched either side of the winding road, escorting him all the way to the simple white-washed farmhouse and outbuildings that had been home to Daltons for three generations.

He parked his car beneath the old oak tree and went into the main house. He could hear his mother in the kitchen, banging pots around, a sure sign she was pissed about something. She barely glanced at him as he entered, returning to whatever she was doing in the cupboard next to the oven. He headed straight to the fridge for the pitcher of iced tea his mother always kept there.

"What's he done now?" he asked.

"I caught him up a ladder, checking on the apple scab on those trees down near the western fence." Judy Dalton's voice vibrated with despair and frustration.

Fourteen months ago his father had been involved in a car accident that had broken his right leg and pelvis. He'd been in the hospital for weeks, followed by months of painful rehab. Reid had given up the lucrative private security work he'd been doing in Europe and flown home to help out. It had been a short-term arrangement to get his parents through a tough time before he took off again, but the slowness of his father's recovery had soon changed that plan. After a couple of months of cooling his heels in between helping out around the orchard, Reid had applied for a job at Bozeman Police Department, his old stomping ground, and resigned himself to hanging around for a while in order to take the pressure off his father's recovery.

Running the orchard had always been a part-time occupation for the Daltons, with Reid's grandfather and father both splitting their time between maintaining the trees and running a small law practice in Marietta, but that didn't mean it wasn't demanding work. Depending on the season, the trees needed pruning, spraying, fertilizing. And then there was harvest time...

The four hundred apple trees that made up Dalton Orchards were in the low-maintenance phase of the growing cycle at the moment, however; the fruit was barely budding on the trees. There was no reason for his father to be risking his health by climbing up and down ladders, even if he was worried about the outbreak of apple scab he'd been trying to eradicate for a few months now.

"I'll talk to him," Reid said.

"Fat lot of good that will do. You're both as bad as each other."

Reid eyed his mother. He wasn't sure what he'd done to earn himself a share of her bad mood, but he wisely chose to retreat rather than investigate further. She'd be over her crankiness by dinner time, no doubt.

He tracked his dad down to the barn, where he found him tinkering with the apple press, the contents of his tool box spilling across the dirt floor. At sixty-three, Ross Dalton still had a full head of salt and pepper hair and a face that was worn from too many hours in the sun. He'd lost weight since the accident, and his worn jeans hung from his hips, making him look as though he was wearing borrowed clothing.

"Don't want to hear it," he said as Reid approached.

"How do you know you don't want to hear it when you

don't know what I'm going to say?"

"Did she tell you about the ladder?"

"Yep."

"Then I don't want to hear it."

"You could have waited for me to get home," Reid said mildly.

"I'm fine. You saw my last X-rays. Everything's solid."

"Your reflexes are shot. You know that." Not to mention his father was still trying to rebuild his strength after months of reduced activities. "If you slipped or the ladder fell, there's no way you're fast enough to do anything about it. But I'm not going to lecture you."

"What do you call this, then?" his father asked sourly.

"A conversation."

His father grunted in response, but his mouth curled up at the corners. They'd always got along well, which was a good thing, since Reid was an only child.

"How'd your game go?" his father asked.

"All right."

His father shot him a searching glance, obviously picking up on the heaviness in Reid's tone.

"Something happened on the way home," Reid said. He needed to decompress after breaking the news to Tara, and he knew his words wouldn't go any further. "The guys and I spotted Tara's fiancé leaving the motel up on the freeway."

"I take it he wasn't with Tara?" his father asked.

Reid shook his head.

There was a short silence as his father processed the news. "You told her yet?"

"Yeah."

"How'd she take it?"

Reid remembered the way she'd fumbled for the seat when he'd broken the news about Paige. She hadn't cried, though. Hadn't shed a single tear.

"She's pretty tough," he said.

"Still. She must be upset."

Reid glanced out the door of the barn, remembering the tense set of her shoulders as she left the salon. "Yeah."

"You tell her if she needs any legal advice, it's on the

house, okay?"

His father had been forced to wind up his practice after the accident, but he still took on odd jobs for neighbors and friends.

"Thanks, I will."

Reid knew that Tara and Simon had been together for three years, but he had no idea how complicated their financial arrangements were. He frowned as he thought about all the crap she was going to have to wade through. Moving Simon out of the house, canceling wedding plans, dealing with the inevitable gossip around town and at the station... all of that on top of the hours she already put in helping out her mother.

If he could make it all go away for her, he would. But he couldn't.

"I need a shower," he said, turning away.

He left his father to his tinkering, crossing to the wooden staircase that led to the self-contained apartment over the garage that had been his home for the past year.

Originally built to accommodate visitors from out of state—his mother came from a large family—the space was divided into sleeping, living and cooking zones, with a small bathroom. More than enough to accommodate his needs, and private enough that he didn't feel as though he was living in his parents' pockets.

That didn't mean he wasn't looking forward to having his own place again when he left Marietta. Which reminded him...

Crossing to the laptop he'd left on the coffee table, he called up his email program. There was nothing new, and he pushed the computer away. He'd interviewed for a job with a Chicago-based security company over a month ago now, but they still hadn't gotten back to him.

The Klieg Security Group had offices in most states as well as an international arm, which meant there was plenty of scope for advancement and adventure for a guy who was looking for both. With his overseas security experience and police background, Reid was more than qualified to take on the role, and he was confident he had a good chance of landing it—if they ever got around to shortlisting candidates.

His thoughts shifted back to Tara. When he'd applied for the job, she'd been happily engaged, and the bright lights and challenges of a new role in a new city had held a lot of appeal. With his father coping well, there had been no reason for him to hang around in Marietta...

Don't even think it.

He was only human, however. And he'd been attracted to Tara from the moment he'd walked into the patrol bay at Bozeman PD and been introduced to his new colleagues.

She'd been filling out paperwork at a desk, dressed in her navy blues, her blonde hair neatly braided and pinned at the back of her head. She'd glanced up as he'd walked in with Sergeant Crawford, and he'd looked straight into her clear green eyes and felt the hot pull of instant attraction.

She'd stared back at him, an arrested, uncertain look on her face. Then she'd returned to her paperwork, a small frown creasing her forehead, and he'd known she felt it too.

He was so stupid, he'd been pissed when the Sergeant had put them in the same car. Hadn't wanted to be distracted by his own instincts. But working with Tara— getting to know her—had been the best thing about the past year, hands down.

She was a great cop, conscientious and fair-minded. She was an even better person. Funny and tough, sweet and smart-mouthed. He'd laughed more with her than with any other woman.

And then Simon had proposed, and Reid had realized that it would probably be a good idea to think about moving on. He was overdue anyway, and his dad was getting stronger every day. Hence the job application, and the fact that pretty soon he might be packing his bags and moving on again.

He yanked his T-shirt over his head and tossed it at the laundry hamper. Only an asshole would see any advantage for himself in Tara's situation. She was heartbroken. The future she'd had planned for herself had just come crashing down around her. She wasn't suddenly going to turn to Reid, even if there had been that moment on that first day, and even if there had been other moments over the past year when he'd caught her looking at him or their hands had brushed or one of them had said something and that feeling—that connection—had shimmered in the air between them.

Men and women were attracted to each other all the time and didn't act on it. It didn't mean anything. And even if it did mean something, there were lots of reasons why he and Tara Buck were never going to be an item, not the least of which was the fact that he hadn't had a serious relationship with a woman since he'd broken up with Mary Kent before leaving Marietta six years ago. He moved around too much to do anything other than casual with women. And Tara was not casual. Not by a long shot.

The bottom line was that he was her friend, and that was all she needed him to be right now.

And so that was what he would be.

Chapter Three

Tara knew that Grant had spilled the beans the moment she entered the patrol bay the next morning. One second her fellow patrol officers were lounging around the open-plan workspace, leaning against desks, sucking in coffee and shooting the breeze before the morning briefing, the next they were stiff and self-conscious, their conversations stilted.

Half of them couldn't look her in the eye. The other half watched her with what she could only describe as fascinated pity.

Freaking awesome.

Reid pushed himself to his feet when he saw her, a frown on his face.

"Morning," she said tightly.

A few of the guys returned her greeting. Reid followed her into the briefing room as she made a beeline for the coffee machine.

"I didn't think you'd be in today," he said.

She could feel him watching her as she poured coffee into a mug. She was ridiculously proud of the fact that her hands remained steady.

"Life goes on, right?" she said, shrugging.

"Yeah, but it's not going to grind to a halt if you take a couple of days to get on top of things."

"What's to get on top of? He's gone, I had the locks changed. A few phone calls this afternoon and the wedding will be history."

She shrugged again, even though her shoulders felt stiff and unnatural.

"Tara. Come on. This is me," he said quietly.

She risked eye contact for the briefest of seconds. "Don't be nice to me, today, okay? Don't pussyfoot around or speak in hushed tones or worry I'm going to lose it. I'm fine. Today is just a day, like any other day."

She almost believed her own words. Almost.

She'd had to put eyedrops in this morning to take the redness from her eyes, and her back was sore from sleeping on the couch because even after changing the sheets she hadn't been able to lie down on the bed that had once been theirs.

But she was here, and she was going to do her job, and somehow she was going to get through this.

"Okay. If that's what you want," Reid said.

"It is."

"All right, people, let's get this show started." Sergeant Crawford's voice boomed around the room as he entered, the rest of the crew trailing in after him. The Sergeant's pale blue eyes lingered on Tara for a few seconds longer than strictly necessary and he gave her the smallest of nods.

Great, he knew as well. Was there a single person in the whole of the Bozeman PD who didn't know her private business?

Wrapping her hands around her coffee, she moved to the nearest chair and sat. Reid didn't follow her, but she was aware of him in her peripheral vision anyway, a tall, dark shape that she took great pains not to look at directly. She wouldn't be able to avoid him once they were on patrol, however. Hard to pretend someone wasn't there when they were just a few feet away.

Not for the first time she wished it had been someone else—anyone else, really—who had seen Simon and Paige leaving the motel yesterday. For some reason she couldn't explain, the fact that it was Reid, that he was the one who'd had to break the news to her, added an extra layer of humiliation to the whole situation.

She didn't want to appear pathetic in his eyes.

She forced herself to listen to the Sergeant's rundown of overnight incidents, but there was nothing ongoing for them to worry about and it wasn't long before the briefing was over.

Sergeant Crawford lingered, reading over some paperwork as everyone filed out. Reid waited for her near the door while she dumped her coffee down the sink. Her stomach wasn't particularly food-friendly at the moment; she'd poured the coffee more to have something warm to hang onto than anything else.

"Officer Buck, can I have a word before you head out, please?" Sergeant Crawford said.

Tara's gaze went to Reid, but he was already disappearing through the door with the last of the other guys, giving them privacy.

Bracing herself, she turned to her boss.

"Yes, sir?"

Sergeant Crawford hitched a thumb behind his belt buckle, a sure sign he was uncomfortable. In his late forties, he had thinning grey hair, narrow shoulders and a pronounced paunch.

"You know what this place is like—worse than a high school." He sounded almost apologetic. "We all know too much about each other's private lives."

"Yes, sir."

"If you need some space to sort yourself out, a week, two weeks, you've got time owing, and we can swing it for you. You only need to ask."

Tara shook her head immediately. "I appreciate the offer, but I'm fine. I want to work."

"It's your call."

She summoned up a tight smile. "Like I said, I appreciate the offer."

Reid was waiting for her in the patrol bay when she exited the briefing room, his gaze raking her face.

"All good?" he asked.

"Yep."

They walked out to the yard in silence. It was Reid's turn to drive, so she slid into the passenger seat. Reid started the engine before glancing at her.

"I know you don't want to talk about it, but my dad wants you to know that any legal advice you need is on the house."

She'd been sure she had no more tears left, but she felt the now-familiar hot sting at the back of her eyes at his words. She'd known the Daltons to nod at all her life, harvesting apples at the orchard every October being something of a tradition in her family, but since she'd been partnered with Reid she'd come to know them properly and she liked them a great deal. Every time she trekked out to the orchard to hook up with Reid for one of their cross-country runs, his mother insisted on stuffing her silly with home-baked muffins and breads, while his father was always ready to discuss current events or town politics.

"Thank him for me, but I don't think there will be anything to worry about."

She and Simon rented the townhouse, and while both their names were on the lease, she doubted Simon would be pushing to stay there. They hadn't quite reached the joint back account stage, either, something Tara could only be profoundly grateful for.

Reid looked as though he wanted to say more, but he simply nodded before signaling and pulling out of the yard.

Her phone shrilled to life as he headed south. She pulled it from the slot on her utility belt and checked the screen. Her family and friends knew better than to call her when she was working and Tara's heart gave a panicky squeeze when she saw her sister's name on the screen. Ever since her mother's diagnosis with Parkinson's disease, unexpected phone calls freaked her out. She wasn't sure what she was worried about—Parkinson's was a slow-moving disease, after all—but it didn't stop her heart from speeding up as she took the call.

"What's wrong?" she asked. "Is Mom all right?"

"Mom is fine, mostly because you haven't spoken to her yet, I gather." Scarlett's tone was bone dry.

"I figured there was no rush." Also, Tara hadn't been up to handling her mother's histrionics last night.

And there would be histrionics when she told her mother her news. Tammy Buck did not do calm, never had.

"Why are you at work?" Scarlett asked.

"Because I'm on the duty roster."

"Tara... for God's sake. You're allowed to have a few seconds of weakness, okay? The universe gives you permission to get a little sloppy when the man you were going to marry turns out to be a jerk."

Her sister's voice was loud enough that Reid must also be able to hear what she was saying.

"I'm not made of sugar. Why does everyone think I'm going to fall apart?"

First Reid, then the Sergeant, now her sister.

"Because your heart's just been broken, you idiot."

"We're on patrol, I can't talk now. I'll call you later."

She ended the call. Reid flicked a look at her. She waited for him to say something—anything—but the radio crackled to life, breaking the silence.

"118, 404... "

Tara grabbed her radio. Never had she been so happy to hear her badge number. "118, go ahead."

"118, respond to corner Durston and 19th for a two vehicle non-injury MVA."

"118 copy," Tara said.

Reid was already stepping on the gas and weaving more aggressively through the traffic.

Two hours flew by as they controlled the scene, took witness statements and directed traffic around the cleanup operation. They had a shoplifter to deal with next, then a traffic stop for a car with broken rear tail lights.

Throughout, Tara was aware of Reid's quiet concern. He didn't say anything—he'd said he wouldn't, after all, and Reid always kept his word—but she could feel how careful he was being around her. How sorry he felt for her.

Poor Tara, betrayed by her fiancé. Heartbroken and abandoned and humiliated.

The rational part of her brain reminded her that he was her partner and friend—of course he was concerned for her. He was a nice guy. He was simply looking out for her.

It didn't stop her from grinding her teeth in frustration, and it didn't relieve the burning self-consciousness she felt every time she turned her head and caught him watching her.

She didn't want his sympathy, and she definitely didn't want his pity. What she wanted was to forget. She wanted to give herself over to the job and to simply push all the ugliness that had been bouncing around inside her for the past twenty-four hours into a dark corner and work.

Standing in the open patrol car door, she eyed her partner darkly, watching as he talked to the car owner about the damage to his tail lights. Some of the guys looked goofy in their navy blues, especially the ones who had let themselves get thick around the middle with age, but Reid wasn't carrying an ounce of extra fat anywhere on his tall, broad-shouldered body. He made the uniform look good, and more than one woman gave him a lingering glance as they passed by.

The driver said something, and Reid smiled, his eyes lighting up, making his handsome face even more attractive. Tara looked away, aware of a sudden, terrible urge to march up to him and shove him hard in the chest like a child in the school ground.

No point being angry with Reid. You picked Simon. You agreed to marry the guy.

She did, and she had. Focusing her anger on Reid, resenting his concern for her, was immature and a little crazy. She needed to get a grip.

She turned away so she didn't have to look at him, but the lump of hot anger sitting in her belly didn't go anywhere. Suddenly the need to cry was on her again. Her life was a mess—and the worst thing was, she'd played a part in making it that way.

The radio crackled, saving her from herself, and she leaned in to the car so she could hear it more clearly.

"404 to all units, we have a report of a theft of a motor vehicle in progress with a baby inside near the Post Office on Main."

Tara ducked her head out of the car. "Reid, we're up."

He glanced her way, giving her a sharp nod, and she slid into the passenger seat and reached for her radio.

"404, 118. We are in the area and we are responding."

Dispatch acknowledged her call, relaying the license

plate details of a blue Ford sedan and letting her know that the car was last seen traveling west on Main. Reid slid into the driver's seat, slamming the door shut and starting the engine in one smooth move.

"What have we got?"

"Head west on Main. We're looking for a stolen Ford with a baby inside."

Reid swore quietly. All cops hated incidents like this, especially in summer. No thief set out to steal a car with a baby on board. Most of the time, they realized their mistake almost immediately, leading them to dump the car as quickly as possible. If they dumped it somewhere out of the way, however, the baby could potentially be left in the car for hours before it was found. On a hot June day like today, it didn't take long for a child to become dangerously dehydrated and overheated.

They cruised the area, both her and Reid scanning the passing traffic and side streets, looking for the blue Ford. She checked in with dispatch regularly, and they broadened their search area as other cars reported in.

She was about to report a clean sweep of the area near the Northgate Shopping Center when she spotted a flash of blue out of the corner of her eye. Sure enough, a bright blue Ford was traveling east along a side street. She craned her neck in order to see the license plate.

"Got him," she said, relief flooding her.

Reid's head snapped around, his gaze zeroing in on the car. Tara was already on the radio, calling it in and requesting emergency traffic only over the radio until they could pull off a high risk traffic stop. Dispatch confirmed, informing them that another car was on its way, then the radio began to emit the regular beeps designed to remind officers to use the radio only if absolutely necessary.

They trailed the car as discreetly as possible, not wanting to panic the driver. Once Wadley and Hayes had radioed to let them know they were in position, Reid flicked both lights and siren on.

Tara flashed a glance at him, taking in his intent expression and steady hands on the wheel. Reid was renowned for keeping a cool head in a crisis, one of the many reasons the other officers often deferred to him around the station. That and the fact that he was a natural leader. If he hadn't left the force six years ago and taken off overseas to do private security work, the odds were good he'd be well up the food chain by now.

The Ford sped up, swerving through an intersection and almost taking out an SUV. Reid followed with a smooth surge of power. Up ahead, blue lights flashed as Wadley and Hayes blocked the road with their car. It only took the thief a moment to understand he was trapped. The Ford swerved off the road, tires screeching before the car bottomed out on the curb with a resounding metallic crash. The car plowed into the side of the store on the corner and smashed to a halt. The door popped open almost instantly and a slim, dark-clothed figure slipped out of the car and bolted up the adjacent alleyway. A kid or a woman, Tara guessed, judging by the build and stature.

"404, 118. Car has stopped, suspect has abandoned the car," Tara reported as Reid hit the brakes hard.

She braced one hand on the dash, the other already on the door handle. The moment the car ceased moving, she was out and racing for the Ford. One glance in the side window was enough to assure her that the baby was alive and well, his face red with exertion as he exercised his lungs.

"404, 118. Baby is alive and well. I repeat, the baby is alive and well. 118 in foot pursuit."

She spun away from the Ford, taking off up the alley after the suspect. Reid or the other officers would take care of the baby.

The thief was at the far end of the alley, running like hell. Tara put her head down and gave it her all. Her feet slapped the pavement, her lungs and legs burned, and for the first time all day she felt almost good as she channeled all her hurt, humiliation, and anger into the chase.

Suddenly catching this asshole wasn't just a professional duty but a personal mission.

Digging deep, she lengthened her stride, determined to close the distance.

Chapter Four

T ara took off up the alleyway at a flat sprint, arms
pumping as she gave pursuit. By the time Reid made
it to the head of the alley she was halfway down,
running hard. She'd done track and field at school and he
knew from personal experience that she was fast, but he was
pretty sure he'd never seen her move like this.

"124 in foot pursuit," he told the radio, taking off after
Tara and the suspect.

By the time he got to the end of the alley, he was just
in time to see Tara disappearing down a cross street. Sucking
in air, he pounded after her, not wanting her to come up
against a desperate criminal on her own. She could take care
of herself, he knew, but that didn't mean he liked the idea of
her having to wrangle a freaked-out car thief single-
handedly. The odds were good there were drugs involved,
too, this sort of spontaneous, opportunistic car theft being
typical of strung-out addicts.

He kept Tara in sight as he dodged his way down the
street, sidestepping pedestrians and other obstacles. A part
of him couldn't help but admire her smooth, even gait as she
gained on the thief. She was like a gazelle when she ran—
elegant, born to it, her narrow hips and long legs built for
speed.

Suddenly she veered to the left, disappearing, and
Reid was so distracted he almost went tumbling, smashing
into an A-frame sign a store owner had placed on the

sidewalk.

Shit.

He recovered quickly, once again building speed, streaking around the corner into yet another alleyway. He saw immediately that the far end was blocked by a chain link fence, the top covered with coils of razor-wire. The suspect had just reached it, springing up the chain link like a monkey, hands and feet clawing for traction. Tara was only seconds behind him, and as Reid watched she leaped at the fence, momentum giving her wings as she snatched at the suspect's back. She grabbed the guy's T-shirt, yanking backwards, and the two of them fell to the ground. Tara immediately rolled to her feet, while the suspect stayed low, scrambling toward the fence once again.

Reid was close enough now to see that the suspect was a woman, her face sunken and sallow, hair greasy, eyes bloodshot and wild. Meth user, he guessed, which meant she could be anything from plain old fashioned desperate to out-of-her-mind psychotic.

The woman barely had a grip on the fence before Tara was on her again, wrenching her backward.

"Police! You're under arrest." Tara's words echoed up the alley, strong despite the fact she was breathing hard.

The woman struggled, striking out at Tara. Tara's head jerked backward as a blow connected. Reid's lungs were on fire as he covered the final twenty feet, adrenaline lighting up every cell in his body, the need to get in there and control the situation and protect Tara a primal, undeniable urge.

Tara used her body weight against her assailant, rushing forward and pushing the other woman off balance. For a second the two of them hung suspended. Then they were both on the ground, Tara attempting to control the other woman by throwing her leg across her body. The woman struggled to throw Tara off, but Tara grabbed her right arm, twisting it up her back.

"You have the right to remain silent," Tara panted. "Anything you say can and will be used against you in a court of law. You have the right to consult an attorney... "

Reid slipped his cuffs from his utility belt, dropping to his knees the second he reached the two women. Tara leaned to the side without him having to say a word, allowing him to slip on the first cuff, and within seconds he had the woman's other arm cuffed tightly behind her back. Then and only then did Tara let up, taking her weight off the other woman's body.

"Fucking cop. Fucking broke my arm. I'm going to sue your ass off," the woman screamed, head thrashing from side to side, body bucking.

"You okay?" Reid asked, glancing at Tara.

"Of course."

Her hair had come loose during the struggle, and strands hung around her face. When she turned her head to look at him, he saw a cut and the beginnings of a bruise on her cheekbone.

"That hurt?" he asked, gesturing at her cheek.

Tara lifted a hand, touching her face, looking surprised when it came away with blood on it.

"I want a lawyer. I know my rights. You can't manhandle me like this," the other woman protested.

Tara stood, adjusting her utility belt. "Come on, on your feet."

She reached down and used her grip on the woman's wrists to force her first to her knees, then her feet. Reid called in to dispatch, letting them know they had the suspect in custody before relaying their position. His gaze kept going to the wound on Tara's face. It had been a good takedown, and she was okay, but he hated it that she'd been hurt.

"My arm hurts. I need a doctor, you bitch," the woman said.

"My name is Patrol Officer Buck, and you can request a medical evaluation when we take you in," Tara said.

Her tone was cold and hard, devoid of the professional distance she usually employed. Reid shot her a quick look, registering the stony expression on her face.

"Fuck you, Patrol Officer Bitch," the other woman said. Her expression contemptuous, she spat in Tara's face.

Tara moved so fast, he almost didn't see her, reaching out to grab the woman's T-shirt in her fist, getting right up in her face.

"You want to try that again, you piece of crap?" Reid

didn't recognize Tara's voice, it was so low and hard and dangerous. She shook the other woman, making her head rock on her neck.

"Tara," Reid said.

She didn't seem to hear him, her whole being focused on the thief. He reached out, grabbing her shoulder. He could feel how wound up she was, her body vibrating with suppressed emotion.

"I've got this," he said firmly.

She glanced at him, and for a split second her gaze was utterly blank, as though she didn't recognize him. And then she blinked and he saw awareness rush back in. Her shoulders dropped and she released her grip on the other woman so abruptly the woman staggered, off balance.

Reid concentrated on Tara, aware of the sound of sirens as their colleagues raced to join them.

"Tara?"

She turned her back on him.

"Talk to me, Tara."

Verbal abuse and physical assaults were part and parcel of the job, but he'd never seen Tara react like this before, not in all the months they'd been working together.

She took a deep breath, her shoulders lifting and falling with the force of it. Then she pushed the loose strands of hair back from her forehead and turned to face him.

"I'm sorry."

Her green eyes were clouded, troubled, and she looked close to tears. His gut impulse was to pull her into his arms, but they had a pissed-off meth user to take care of and a patrol car was going to join them any second.

"Go flag the others down," he said.

It was an unnecessary task, but he could see she needed a few seconds to pull herself together. She nodded and started walking to the top of the alley.

"Good riddance, bitch," the other woman yelled after her.

Reid spared her an irritated glance. On another day, he'd probably find some sympathy for the track marks on her arms and the open sores on her face, but not today.

Today, his thoughts were all for the woman walking

away from him, and his inability to take her pain away.

Tara couldn't stop her hands from shaking. She had to clasp them together behind her back to hide the fact while the suspect was read her rights again and helped into the backseat of a patrol car. Tara stood at a distance and kept her head down the whole time, avoiding eye contact with her colleagues. Especially Reid.

If he hadn't stepped in, she had no idea what might have happened. That was the ugly truth of it. She'd been so bound up in the moment, filled with an almost ungovernable anger... she could still feel the purity of it, the way it had burned its way through her body.

Insults often flew thick and fast when people were being called to account for their wrongdoings, but in five years on the job, Tara had never let them get to her. For a few minutes back there, though, she'd been so close to doing something irrevocable. Something that would have changed who she was as a person and a cop.

Shame burned a hole in her gut as she went over and over the scene in her mind. Would she have hit the other woman if Reid hadn't stepped in? A woman who was cuffed and helpless, unable to defend herself? She wanted to believe she wouldn't have—needed to believe it—but she honestly didn't know. In that moment, she'd been so angry, the rage boiling up from some hidden place within her.

"Come on."

Reid's hand landed in the small of her back for the briefest of moments as he encouraged her to walk alongside him. She matched her pace to his, her gaze fixed on the sidewalk.

"Everyone has bad days, Tara," he said after a minute. "Everyone loses it on occasion. You're only human, and if ever it was going to happen, today was probably the day, right?"

Reid's tone was so understanding, so matter of fact

and reasonable. She wanted to believe him, to let herself off the hook, but she'd never gone easy on herself.

"Have you? Lost it like that, I mean?" she asked.

She glanced at him, found him watching her.

"Of course. I'm not a saint. And neither are you."

Some of the tightness left her chest. Not all, but some.

"I always promised myself I was going to be a good cop. Take care of people, do the right thing."

"You are a good cop."

There was no arguing with his statement, he said it so unequivocally.

"I shouldn't have come into work today," she admitted.

He didn't say anything, one of the many reasons she liked him so much.

She could see the patrol car ahead. Someone had put out traffic cones to cordon off the scene. An ambulance crew stood with a woman who was holding the baby, her face still wet from tears. Normally Tara liked this part of the job, the bit where she got to interact with people who'd had good news, a good outcome. She was still feeling shaken and raw, however, and she hung back when Reid stepped forward to check that the mother was okay. She had to force a smile when the woman insisted on coming over so she could thank Tara personally for her efforts.

"I'll never forget this day, and how great you all were," she said, her blue eyes wide with sincerity.

"We're just glad the baby's okay," Tara said.

It was a relief to be in the car, driving back to headquarters. Tara flipped down the visor to check her face, touching the cut on her cheekbone tentatively.

"Should heal okay," she said, flipping it back up.

It was hard to get too worried about a bruise and a superficial cut when there were so many other things wrong with her life.

"You need to learn to duck."

"You need to learn to run faster."

He shot her a dry look and she almost smiled. She was fast, but in a neck-and-neck race they both know he'd beat her.

They pulled into the yard and parked the car. A couple of the guys called out congratulations as they headed inside. Tara was just pleased they had something to think about other than her personal life.

She caught Reid's elbow as they approached the patrol bay, stopping him so they could talk in the relative privacy of the corridor.

"So you know, I'm going to ask Sarge for a week off."

"Good."

He surprised her then by reaching out and brushing his thumb across her cheek, careful not to touch her cut.

"You should get this looked at, too. Just in case."

The contact was fleeting, less than the time it would take a person to blink, but the warmth of his touch stayed with her after he'd turned away. She stared at his retreating back for a long beat.

Then she took a deep breath and went to talk to the Sergeant.

Sergeant Crawford insisted she take two weeks' leave instead of the one she'd requested. She, in turn, insisted she would finish her shift rather than head home immediately. Consequently it was after five by the time she was back in Marietta.

She headed straight for her mother's place. Over the past few months she'd gotten into the habit of dropping in on Tammy every few days so she could take care of any little chores that needed doing—washing, vacuuming, cleaning up the kitchen. Her mother's Parkinson's disease was not yet so advanced that she couldn't still do these things for herself, but she had been struggling with mood changes and depression since her diagnosis, something the doctor was still trying to sort out with medication, and she tended to let things slide if Tara wasn't there to help her out.

And, of course, Tara needed to tell her mother what had happened with Simon.

She took a minute to compose herself when she arrived, listening to the car tick-tick as it cooled, preparing herself for her mother's reaction. Then she drew in a deep breath, let it out, and climbed out of her car.

"There you are. I was beginning to think I wouldn't see you," Tammy said as Tara let herself in the front door.

Her mother was in her favorite chair by the window, a magazine in her lap. Her blonde hair was piled high and sprayed into place, her face perfectly made up, even though she probably hadn't left the house all day. She was wearing a pair of the tight black pants she favored, along with a leopard-skin T-shirt with a bejeweled neckline. The two-inch wedge-heeled mules she usually wore around the house—her idea of a casual shoe—sat beside her chair, at the ready in case someone who wasn't family came to the door.

Tara spared the damned things a dark look. Her mother wasn't supposed to wear high heels any more, her balance having been affected by the Parkinson's, but she insisted that she couldn't stand flat-heeled shoes and that she was too used to wearing heels to stop now.

"I had a few things to sort out at work," Tara said. "How have you been?"

She kissed her mother's cheek, breathing in the smell of hair-spray and Tammy's strong floral perfume.

"Oh, you know. The usual." Her mother shrugged, her mouth pulling down at the corners.

"Do you need me to get any groceries for you?" Tara said. Her stomach was tight. She so didn't want to do this.

"You took care of that last time, remember?" her mother said, giving her a curious look.

"Right." She'd cooked up some meals, too, and frozen them in portions for her mother. "Anything else that needs doing?"

"The bathroom could do with a once-over, if you wouldn't mind."

"Sure. Do you want me to take something out for your dinner?"

"If you like. I haven't been very hungry lately." Her mother attempted a wan smile.

"Well, you need to keep eating. You know that."

"I know."

Tara went into the kitchen and opened the freezer. Half a dozen plastic containers filled the basket, each neatly labeled in her own hand-writing.

"Chicken hotpot or chili con carne?" she called out.

"The chicken sounds good, thank you."

Tara pulled a container from the freezer's depths and left it on the counter. Her gaze went to the cupboard under the sink where the cleaning supplies were stored. It was so tempting to slope off to the bathroom and busy herself with cleaning rather than bite the bullet and do what needed to be done. But delaying wasn't going to make this task any easier.

"Would you like a cup of tea? Margot dropped in with some of that fancy Lady Grey stuff she gets online from France," her mother said from the kitchen doorway.

Without waiting for Tara to answer, she crossed to the counter with the slow, rigid gait that had been one of the first symptoms of her condition. She reached out to flick on the kettle, her hand trembling uncontrollably.

"Mom, there's something I need to tell you."

"Well, go ahead, then. No one's stopping you," her mother said with some of her old sass.

"Simon's been cheating on me. We broke up last night, and the wedding is off."

Her mother's eyes widened. A hand lifted to her chest, pressing flat against her sternum. "Oh. Tara. No. No, no, no." The last words came out on a wail. "This can't be happening. Not again. Tell me it's a mistake. Tell me someone got something wrong. You two are so good together. He's such a sweet man. So reliable and hard working."

"Reid saw him leaving a motel with the girl."

"Girl?"

"She's one of his students."

Her mother's mouth opened, but no sound came out. Tears were rolling down her face now, and the hand pressed to her chest clenched into a fist.

"No. I refuse to accept it. I won't accept it. I simply won't."

"I'm okay, Mom," she said, even though her mother hadn't quite got around to asking.

But her mother was already lost in a world of her own pain.

"Oh, Tara. I can't bear it. This is the one thing I wanted to protect my daughters from. The one thing. People talking and looking sideways at you in the supermarket. Everyone feeling sorry for you. And knowing that they're out there somewhere together, enjoying the happiness they stole from you. Laughing at you. Making up stories for each other to excuse their own weakness."

Her mother was shaking all over now, an emotional reaction and not a Parkinson's symptom.

"This can't be happening. It just can't. I won't let it. Do you hear me, I won't let it?"

The kitchen echoed with the high pitch of her mother's voice, every second word punctuated with a thump of her fist to her sternum.

"Mom, you need to calm down. Simon's not worth this kind of upset."

Her mother moved closer, reaching out to catch both of Tara's hands in hers. Looking into Tammy's faded blue eyes, Tara could see her bone-deep pain, still as fresh today as it had been thirteen years ago. She'd given everything to Jason Buck, and he had left her half a woman when he'd abandoned her. Her mother had never recovered. Worse, Tara suspected she didn't want to, that at a certain point, whether consciously or unconsciously, Tammy had decided that if the hurt her ex-husband had inflicted on her was all she had left, she would cleave to it utterly.

That was how much she'd loved her husband, how devoted she'd been to him.

"You can't hide your hurt from me, Tara. I know how hollow you feel right now. You loved that man, and he's taken all your happiness and trust and left you with nothing. You will never be the same. Never."

No.

The single word came from a place deep inside Tara, an absolute denial of her mother's assessment of the situation. She'd planned a future with Simon, but she hadn't made him her everything. She'd never given a man that kind of power over her life and happiness. She might feel foolish, she might be embarrassed, but she wasn't broken. She wasn't shattered.

She frowned, trying to grasp the realization she sensed hovering just out of reach. Then that moment in the corridor at work today came back to her—Reid's thumb brushing her cheekbone, the heat from the small contact ricocheting through her body long after he'd gone—and something shifted inside her. Blinking stupidly, she suddenly understood something she'd never allowed herself to acknowledge before.

She had never loved Simon the way a woman should love her husband. He had never set her world on fire or consumed her thoughts. He had been good and steady. He had been attentive and kind. A good choice, in other words, for a woman bent on not repeating her mother's mistakes.

"Mom, you'll make yourself sick," Tara said, urging her mother toward the kitchen table so she could take a seat.

Inside, she was reeling as the full repercussions of her epiphany hit home: she'd almost married a man she didn't love.

"I'll take her. Why don't you see if she's got any of her tablets left?" Scarlett said from the doorway.

Tara had been so distracted, she hadn't heard the front door or her sister's footsteps in the hall. Scarlett edged Tara out of the way, giving Tara a sympathetic look before guiding their mother into a chair. Tara seized the reprieve her sister had offered and escaped to the hallway, walking briskly to her mother's bedroom.

She sank onto the end of the bed, feeling a little as though someone had sneaked up behind her and smacked her on the head with a two-by-four. She'd felt foolish yesterday when Reid had told her what he'd seen, but that was nothing compared to the searing sense of her own stupidity she was experiencing right now.

She'd made a deal with the devil, trading off love and passion for security and dependability—and then her stable, safe husband-to-be had cheated on her with a seventeen-year-old.

Her mother's voice floated down the hallway, tinged with hysteria, and Tara pushed herself to her feet. There would be plenty of time for self-recrimination later. Right now, she had her mother to deal with.

Chapter Five

It was past ten that night when Tara opened the door to her sister.

"Well. That was a barrel of laughs," Scarlett said. "Finally got Mom to go to bed. A minor freaking miracle."

At her sister's insistence, Tara had left her sister to finish the Herculean task of calming their mother. Scarlett had argued that with Mitch away, settling his affairs in Australia so he could move permanently to Montana, she had plenty of time on her hands, and Tara had let herself be talked out the door. There was only so much a person could handle, and Tara recognized that she had already pushed the envelope once today.

Now, Scarlett brushed past her as she entered the house, stopping in her tracks when she saw the packing boxes piled all over the living room.

"Don't tell me you're moving out?" Scarlett couldn't look more aghast if she tried. "He's the rat, Tara. He's the one who goes, not you."

"Relax. I'm just packing his stuff." As well as anything that reminded her of him. Which, it turned out, was quite a bit.

"Oh. That's all right, then. Do you need a hand with anything?"

"Sure. Grab a box. Shove some stuff in it. Join the party."

Scarlett gave her a narrow-eyed look. "Have you been

443

drinking?"

"Maybe." She'd needed it after her epiphany.

"Thank God. Hit me with whatever you're having."

Tara led the way into the kitchen, pulling down two glasses and pouring vodka shots for both of them. Scarlet gave her a look.

"You been drinking out of the bottle up until now?"

"Yep."

Tara was well aware that her younger-by-five-minutes sister considered her to be a stick-in-the-mud goody-two-shoes. Scarlett looked as though she couldn't decide whether to be impressed or appalled by the fact that she'd caught her sister drinking hard liquor straight from the bottle.

Tara knocked her shot back, hissing as the alcohol burned its way down. Scarlett followed suit, shaking her head.

"Yow. Okay, that should take the edge off."

Tara walked back into the living room and resumed stacking Simon's books into a box.

"Has he called?" Scarlett asked.

"Five times."

"Did you speak to him?"

"No, ma'am, I did not."

"Good. Have you spoken to the school yet?"

"Why would I do that?" Tara asked, frowning at her sister.

"Because he's screwing one of his students. He needs to lose his job."

Tara smiled grimly. "I think you're forgetting we live in a town with a population of ten thousand people. I guarantee that the school principal knew about Simon's extra-curricular activities about five seconds after I did."

"Good point. So he'll be out of a job first thing tomorrow morning."

"I'm guessing he's already had a phone call telling him not to come in."

Simon's life was in the toilet, no question about it. His career was shot, his reputation ruined. Then there were Paige's parents...

"You know Paige's dad used to be a pro football

player?" Tara said conversationally. The vodka had set up a little heat factory in her belly, sending warmth radiating through her body.

"You're kidding me."

"He played two seasons with the Patriots. Apparently they used to call him The House."

Scarlett pressed her fingers over her lips to try to hide her smile.

"And Paige's mother is the head of the local chapter of the NRA."

Scarlett laughed outright. "No shit."

"No shit."

Scarlett's smile faded as she studied Tara. "You must feel so goddamned betrayed and heartbroken."

Tara glanced down at the box full of Simon's books. "Well, one out of two isn't bad."

"What is that supposed to mean?" Scarlett asked.

Tara eyed her sister, then walked to the couch and dropped into the cushions. She needed to be sitting for this conversation, she was pretty sure.

"I didn't love Simon. At least, I didn't love Simon in the way you should probably love the person you're planning on spending the rest of your life with."

"What are you talking about? You and Simon were great together. You were glowing when he asked you to marry him." Scarlett was looking at her as though she had rocks in her head.

"He was safe." There was a bunch of other stuff she could say, but that was it in a nutshell, really.

Scarlett was frowning, looking confused. "Well, yeah. He's a school teacher. He loves history. Sometimes he wears white socks with jeans. But you loved him, Tara."

"As a friend. As a person that I liked spending time with. But he didn't make me breathless. He didn't make all the little hairs on my arms stand on end sometimes, just because he walked into the room. I didn't dream about him. He was... a good choice. Solid."

Scarlett sat down beside her. "You really mean it."

Tara nodded. It had taken her most of the evening to sift through her own feelings and responses after her moment of clarity at her mother's house. For instance, she now understood that the anger she'd had so much trouble bottling up today had been all for herself, because she had very deliberately played it safe and picked a man who had Good Husband stamped all over him in an attempt to ensure her marriage would go the distance, and life had blown a big fat raspberry at her.

If you stepped back far enough and squinted, the irony of it all was kind of funny—especially if you'd had enough vodka. It was also really, really unfair. She'd been prepared to sacrifice a lot of things in order to secure her future happiness.

She'd been prepared to ignore the way she felt when Reid looked at her or touched her. She'd resigned herself to always wondering, never knowing. She'd accepted warmth and friendship instead of the intensity she'd witnessed between Scarlett and her new husband, Mitch, when he'd flown into town from Australia a few months ago and swept Scarlett off her feet and all the way to the altar.

And for what? Simon had betrayed and humiliated her anyway. She'd sacrificed all the good in an attempt to avoid the bad and gotten the bad anyway, regardless.

"I don't know what to say," Scarlett said, breaking the silence. "No, actually, that's not true. I do know what to say—I'm glad. I'm glad that dirty cradle-robber didn't break your heart, and I'm glad that you aren't going to spend the rest of your life married to someone you don't love."

Tara studied the pale mark on her finger, the only sign she'd ever worn an engagement ring. "I'm not quite at the glad stage yet. But I can almost see it, on the horizon."

"It doesn't mean Simon isn't a complete asshole," Scarlett said.

"Oh, he's definitely an asshole." An asshole with no self-control or ethics, and dubious values.

An asshole who had made it necessary for her to make an appointment for an STD check first thing tomorrow morning.

"Tara... " Scarlett reached out and took her hand. "What happened with Mom and Dad... it sucked. But that doesn't mean we should spend the rest of our lives looking over our shoulders, worried the same thing is going to happen to us."

"You appreciate the irony of saying that when it already has happened to me, right?" Tara said.

"No, it hasn't. Mom adored Dad. He took a part of her with him when he left," Scarlett said quietly.

Tara stared at her sister for a long moment. Then she nodded.

"You're right. It's different." That was the realization she'd had today, after all. The hurt she was feeling was nothing compared to her mother's, because her feelings hadn't been as deeply engaged.

"The truth is, life is a crapshoot," Scarlett said. "You can die choking on a peanut, or you can live to be a hundred." She shrugged. "No one knows. But you know what? I'm not gonna stop eating peanuts. I love Mitch more than I can say, and if something happens to him, or between us, I am going to be a hot mess for a long time. But I'm not going to give him up, either."

Her sister's words had the ring of absolute truth about them. Tara squeezed her sister's hand.

"You're braver than me," she admitted.

"No, I'm not. We're just brave in different ways. I would never have been able to make myself marry Simon, for example. Not for all the security in Fort Knox."

"I would never have taken off for the other side of the world to marry a man I'd met on the internet," Tara said.

Scarlett rolled her eyes. "And look how well that turned out."

"You still did it. There are so many things I have never done because I was too scared or I thought it wouldn't look good or some other stupid, dumb reason."

"Like what?" Scarlett asked.

Tara thought for a moment. "'I've never traveled."

"Easily fixed. Next."

"I always wanted a motorbike."

Scarlett's jaw dropped. "Shut the front door."

Tara nodded. "Not a Harley Hog or anything huge. It looks like fun, you know?"

"What else? No, wait!"

Scarlett scrambled to her feet and rushed into the kitchen. When she came back she was carrying the bottle of vodka and a pad and pen.

"We should make a list, so you don't forget any of this stuff. A bucket list."

"I'm twenty-six."

"Okay, a fuck-it list, then."

They both laughed. For the first time in days, Tara felt okay. Not happy—it was going to be a while before she could forgive herself for the mistakes and decisions she'd made—but okay.

"Item number one: a new haircut," Scarlett said, pretending to write it down.

Tara shoved her sister in the shoulder. "Nice try. Put the motorbike at the top of the list."

Scarlett grinned and did so. "What next?"

Tara gazed off into the distance. There were so many things...

"I want to have a reckless, wild affair with a man I can't say no to," she said, the words popping out of her mouth without her even thinking about them.

"Better than the bike. Way better," Scarlett said, adding it to the list. "I'm putting it at the top."

Tara reached up to scratch her nose, hoping her face wasn't as red as it felt. Thank God her sister wasn't a mind reader, because she didn't want to have to explain why she'd had Reid's image in her head when those words had slipped out of her mouth.

"What next?" Scarlett asked, pen poised.

Tara reached for the vodka bottle. It was going to be a long list.

Five days later, Reid shouldered the ladder and began the walk back to the house. They'd have to start netting soon, the fruit being at a point where birds would soon be interested in trying their luck, but the apple scab his father had been worried about appeared to have finally been vanquished. For now. The battle with Mother Nature was never truly over, and no side ever really won or lost. Growing up on the orchard had taught him that.

"Reid."

He looked up to see his mother making her way toward him, his phone in her hand

"Hey. I was just coming in now," he said.

This was his first day off all week, and he'd spent the bulk of it in the orchard, taking care of all the little jobs his father wasn't quite up to tackling.

"Your phone made a noise. I knew you've been expecting something, so... " His mother passed the phone over.

Reid set down the ladder. "It's probably just one of the guys."

But when he opened the email, the first thing he saw was the Klieg Security Group logo.

"Well?" his mother asked.

"It's from Klieg."

"And?"

He scanned the email. "I've been shortlisted. They want me to go back for another interview."

"I knew it. Congratulations." His mother rested her hand on his shoulder as she leaned in to give him a kiss.

She was smiling, but her eyes were sad as she released him.

"Did they say when they might want you to start?"

"I think all of that's up for grabs," he said. "If I get the job."

"They'd be crazy not to take you."

He slipped the phone into his pocket and hefted the ladder. They both began walking. His mother was uncharacteristically silent, and when he glanced across at her she looked pensive.

"Might as well spit it out, Mom," he said.

Because she clearly wanted to talk about something. His dad, probably. Although why she thought Reid's nagging would have any more affect than hers he didn't know.

"All right, smarty pants." She ran her hand over the

top of her head, smoothing her dark, shoulder-length hair. "Hank Dearborn called me yesterday. He wanted to talk to me about buying out the orchard."

Reid frowned. The Dearborn family had a smaller orchard a little further out of town, and last year they'd started bottling their own cider and marketing it locally.

"I thought Dad rejected an offer from them a few years ago?"

"He did. But things are different now, and I wanted to talk to you before I spoke to your father."

Reid stopped and let the ladder rest on the ground. This wasn't the kind of conversation you had on the run.

"He's going to say the same thing he said last time—no," Reid said.

"He might. Or he might see things the way I do. Neither of us is getting any younger, and since you're not interested in taking on this place, we need to think about the future. If we sell now, we won't have the pressure of it hanging over our heads. Your father can relax a little."

"Dad doesn't want to relax."

"Well, he needs to," his mother said, her tone a little sharp.

"Mom, what's he going to do? Sit around and read the paper all day? He's sixty-three."

"And he's got more metal in his leg and pelvis than that damned ladder you're holding. The fact is, we have to make this decision sometime, Reid, and it's never going to be easy."

Reid glanced up at the Macintosh apple tree spreading its branches over her head. His grandfather had planted it in 1954, along with the Granny Smiths. The Early Golds had come later, and the Cortlands were his father's additions. When he was ten, he'd planted a row of trees, too, and every time he was home he made a point of checking on them.

"We don't expect you to give up your dreams to live ours," his mother said. "But we can't hang onto this place just because it holds sentimental value for you. It's not a pocket watch, it's a dirty, great big orchard."

It was true, his parents had never so much as hinted that they were disappointed he hadn't followed the family tradition and studied law. He'd made it clear from his early teens that he wanted to travel, and they had encouraged him to do so and always been interested in what work he was doing and the places he'd seen. But he didn't believe for a second that they didn't care about the orchard, or that they wouldn't feel it if they had to let it go. Hell, he'd feel it, and he'd always resented the place.

The work he'd had to do before and after school. The fact that there was always something that needed to be done, and that the growth cycle of the orchard dictated so many aspects of their lives.

"I don't know what you want me to say."

"I want to know that you're not going to regret it if we sell," his mother said, her gaze very direct.

"I don't have a simple answer to that question," he said.

Because the truth was, he hadn't hated helping out this past year. In fact, a lot of the time he'd enjoyed it, working in the outdoors alongside his father. As a teenager, life had been elsewhere. As an adult, he appreciated the fresh air and sunshine, the simple straight forwardness of the work.

"I appreciate that, but I told Hank I'd get back to him soon, so we all need to think about this."

"Only because he's made an offer. In real terms, there's no reason why you couldn't hire people in to do some of the work once Dad doesn't feel up to it anymore," Reid said.

"We could, but it would just be putting off the inevitable."

She was right, but it didn't stop him from feeling a twinge of angry resentment that she was forcing him— them—to this decision point now, when it wasn't strictly necessary.

They walked in silence the rest of the way back to the house.

"Are you joining us for dinner?" his Mom asked when they reached the point where he needed to peel off toward the barn.

"Thanks, but I've got something to do," he said.

She caught his arm as he turned away. "I know you

don't want to face this, Reid, but it's not something we can all just ignore. I'm not asking you to make the decision for us, but I am asking you to make it with us."

Reid stared after her as she headed into the main house. One thing about his mom, she had always been great at nailing a person to the wall. She always called a spade a spade, and never bullshitted when the truth would do.

Tara was like that, too. Straight up and honest, even if it was sometimes to her own detriment.

Reid dumped the ladder against the barn wall, aware that his thoughts had once again drifted to Tara. She'd been in and out his head all week, even though he hadn't heard from her since she finished her shift on Sunday. Sergeant Crawford had given her two weeks off, and he'd been doing single-car patrols in her absence.

He'd missed her, though. She always had something to say, and usually it was funny or interesting or both. He missed her light touch, too. No one was better at defusing a tense situation; there was something about Tara's calm common sense that kept people grounded, himself included.

Most of all he missed the sense of having her nearby, and knowing that he had only to turn his head and she'd be there, ready with a pithy comment or a laugh or a smile.

Better get used to that. If you get that Klieg job, you'll see her once or twice a year, if that.

And when he did see her, she'd probably be with some new guy, because it wouldn't take long for some smart bastard to snap her up. She was gorgeous, she was hot, she was funny and smart.

Pretty much the perfect woman.

Jesus. Can you hear yourself? Next thing you know you'll be writing bad poetry and singing beneath her bedroom window.

His dad had left the toolbox near the apple press, and he hefted it back to the workbench where it belonged, dusting his hands on the seat of his jeans when he was done.

It was fruitless to spend too much time brooding over Tara. He'd made that decision long ago. It wasn't just that she'd been in a relationship with Simon the entire time he'd known her—although that was definitely a contributing factor. Tara was a Marietta girl, through and through. She loved the town, the people, the weather. She was content here, saw her future here. More importantly, her family were here, too, and they meant the world to her.

Whereas he'd had itchy feet ever since he'd opened his first atlas and understood how big the world was.

Even if she hadn't been with Simon, that fundamental difference in their outlooks would have stopped him from making a move. He hadn't spent more than eighteen months in one spot since he'd left Marietta when he was twenty-four, and he was on the verge of moving on yet again. He might be powerfully attracted to Tara, but he liked her a hell of a lot, too, and the last thing he'd ever want to do is hurt her. She was a dream. A sweet, hot dream, but a dream nonetheless, and he needed to stop thinking about her.

Determined to put words into action, he headed up to the apartment and changed into his running gear. An hour later, he was sweaty and exhausted and more than a little hungry. He showered, then heated up the leftover spaghetti and meatballs he'd made last night, sitting in front of the TV to eat. The baseball game was on, and he cracked open a beer and settled in for a lazy evening.

The Cardinals were starting their second inning when his phone rang. He didn't recognize the number but took the call anyway.

"Dalton speaking."

"Reid. Thank God. I wasn't sure if this number was current or not. It's Scarlett calling, Tara's sister."

He leaned forward and set his beer on the coffee table. "Scarlett. What's up?"

"Straight to the point, just like Tara." Her laugh was a little nervous.

"I figured that you wouldn't go to the trouble of tracking down my number and calling for nothing."

"True. The thing is, I can't find Tara. I've tried her place, I've tried her phone. I wondered whether maybe she was with you...?"

"No."

She sighed. "Okay. Then I guess my next question is if there is some way you can put an alert out without it being a big deal? In case I'm just being a nervous nelly and freaking out over nothing."

"Her phone battery is probably just dead. Or she could be out with friends, or seeing a movie."

"You think I'm over-reacting, and normally I would totally agree with you. But she only picked up the motorbike the day before yesterday, and even though I know she's probably being super safe and careful, I can't help worrying."

He blinked. "Tara bought a motorbike?"

"On Wednesday. I wanted her to go for the blue one but she had to have red. It's a Suzuki Boulevard something or other. I keep forgetting the model number. "

He was still stuck on the part where Tara handed over cold hard cash for a two-wheeled suicide machine. Between the two of them, they had attended enough road accidents to know how dangerous motorbikes were.

"Why in hell would she buy a bike?" he asked.

"It's a long story."

"Give me the short version."

"She's living a little. Catching up on things she let slide by."

There was a cautious note beneath Scarlett's voice, and Reid guessed he was only getting part of the story.

"So, is there something you can do? Someone you can call in the sheriff's department, maybe, who could just keep an eye out or let you know if there have been any accidents...?" Scarlett asked.

"Let me make a few calls, I'll get back to you."

He swore when he ended the call. What in the hell was Tara thinking? He dialed the sheriff's office, his mind full of horror images from accident sites. He had a quick word with Harrison Pearce, who was happy to inform him that there had been no road accidents involving motorbikes in the area. Then he called Scarlett back, determined to get more information this time.

"No accidents," he said when Scarlett took the call.

"Oh, thank God. Thank you so much for checking."

"When was the last time you spoke to her?"

"Lunchtime. She said she was going to go for a run, then maybe go out on the bike. I was thinking we could get takeout for dinner, but she hasn't answered any of my calls or returned my messages."

Which Reid knew from personal experience was unusual for Tara.

"She didn't say anything else? Mention anything else she might want to do or go?"

There was a pause and he could almost hear Scarlett thinking on the other end of the phone.

"The only other thing I can think of is that she said she wanted to try the mechanical bull at that place near the train line."

Reid was pretty sure he hadn't heard properly. "Did you just say mechanical bull?"

"That's right. What's the name of that bar on the north side of town, the one with the broken neon sign?"

"The Wolves Den."

He stood, unable to stay seated.

"That's the one. They've got a bull there, right?"

"I have no idea."

He hadn't hung out at the Den since he'd first started to drink. Unlike Grey's Saloon and some of the other places in town, the Den was all about getting hammered and it attracted an ugly crowd.

"Maybe I should go over there and check. Just to put my mind at ease," Scarlett said.

Reid had a vision of Scarlett walking through the door at the Den in her usual get-up of tight T-shirt and snug, hip-hugging jeans. There'd be drool on the bar within seconds, and the queue of guys who'd insist on buying her a drink would form to the left.

"Why don't I do a drive by, see what I can see?" he said.

"You don't have to do that."

Yeah, he did. There was no way he was going to be able to concentrate on a freaking baseball game with pictures of Tara fending off drunken idiots or sliding off her brand new motorbike bouncing around in his head.

"I'm heading over that way anyway," he lied. "I can duck my head in."

"Well, okay, then. Although I'm going to feel pretty stupid when it turns out she's gone into Bozeman to shop or something."

He'd much rather Scarlett feel foolish than any of the alternatives his imagination was throwing up. That was the problem with being a cop—he had seen too many bad things over the years.

He pulled on a pair of jeans, put on his boots and shrugged into a T-shirt. Tucking his phone into the back pocket, he took the stairs two at a time. The GMC fired up with a dull roar and seconds later he was shooting up the driveway, gravel spurting beneath his tires. It was only a short drive into town, and he navigated his way from the well-lit center to the less-illuminated industrial sector north of the train line. The Den's neon sign had lost its N years ago, and the neon blue made everything seem gray as Reid turned into the parking lot. There were a handful of motorbikes parked near the stairs to the bar, but none of them were red Suzukis.

He pulled out his phone to call Scarlett, then hesitated when he caught sight of the roof of a black pickup tucked into the corner. Tara had a black pickup.

He cruised up the aisle until he could see the number plate.

Yep, Tara's.

Feeling like he'd slipped down the rabbit-hole, he parked the GMC and headed for the entrance.

Chapter Six

I f anyone had asked Reid, he would have said The Wolves Den was the last place he would ever find Tara Buck.

But apparently he was wrong.

It was a Friday night and the place was crowded, people standing three or four deep at the bar. The mechanical bull was on a raised platform in the rear corner and clearly visible from the front entrance. The rabbit-hole feeling intensified as he spotted a slim, athletic figure astride the bucking beast, her blond hair whipping back and forth in the air as the machine tried to toss her.

He mouthed a four letter word and started pushing his way through the crowd, his gaze glued to Tara's jerking, swaying body. If she came off...

The bull was becoming more and more belligerent, spinning wildly now, throwing her back and forth. Tara had one hand high in the air, the other white-knuckle tight on the strap—and she was laughing and whooping like a good old cowgirl.

A crowd had formed around the safety barrier, cheering her on. Mostly men, Reid noted sourly. And who could blame them? Tara's blue tank top clung to her breasts and torso, while well-worn denim hugged her thighs. She looked wild and a bit dangerous and a lot sexy as she rode the bull like a rodeo champion.

The bull slowed, only throwing out the odd flick here

and there to set Tara swaying. Finally it stopped entirely, and the crowd let up an almighty roar as Tara punched the air.

"Goddamn, you did it, girl," a tall cowboy said, stepping forward and lifting her off the bull.

She was laughing, pushing her hair off her face, her eyes shining. Someone passed her a beer and she chugged half of it down before lifting it high in the air in a triumphant salute. When she lowered it, one of the guys stepped in to top her drink up from a pitcher, filling it to the brim.

Reid muscled his way to the front of the crowd.

"Tara."

Her head swung round. It took her a moment to register him, then her face split into a big, beaming smile.

"Hey! What are you doing here? You just missed my big ride. Four in a row, no falls," she said. "Everyone's telling me it's a new record."

"This girl can ride," the tall cowboy said.

Tara's hair was tangled around her shoulders, her tank top low-cut enough that he could see the shadowy valley between her breasts. She looked Playboy-bunny good—pretty, sexy, fun.

And more than a little drunk, unless he missed his guess.

"Ready to go five for five, sweetheart?" a husky guy behind her asked.

The crowd cheered and Tara laughed.

"Sure. Why the hell not?" She chugged the rest of her beer, banging the empty glass down onto the tabletop.

"Whoa, whoa, whoa," Reid said, stepping forward and catching her upper arm. "Not so fast."

"What's wrong?"

Not wanting to embarrass her, Reid lowered his voice and leaned closer. "How much have you had to drink?"

She blinked, then laughed. "I don't know. Enough to feel good."

"What if you come off?"

"Haven't yet." Her smile was full of cocky confidence.

Reid considered his options—throw her over his shoulder and forcibly drag her out of the bar, or let her have her head.

"Walk a straight line for me," he said.

She frowned, tucking a strand of hair behind her ear. "What?"

"You heard me. Pass a field sobriety test for me and I'll let you climb on board."

"Let me? Good luck trying to stop me, buddy," she said, giving him a look. "You might not have noticed, but women got the right to vote about a hundred years ago."

He didn't say anything, just eyed her steadily.

"I'm not drunk," she said, chin coming up.

"Prove it to me."

Her eyes narrowed. Then she tossed her hair over her shoulder.

"Okay, fine. But if I pass the test, you're next on the bull."

He glanced at the piece of battered machinery over her shoulder. "If that's the way you want to play it."

"It's exactly the way I want to play it, Dalton."

She turned and waved a hand at the opportunists crowding around like starving men at a buffet. "Give me a bit of room, boys, while I prove Officer Dalton wrong."

A few eyebrows went up as his profession was noted and the crowd shuffled backward, clearing a patch roughly three foot by seven.

"Hope you've got a strong grip, because that bull bucks like crazy," Tara said.

"Let's see you stand on one leg first," he said.

Tara lifted one booted foot off the ground and eyeing him smugly.

"Good enough for you?"

No sooner had she spoken than she lost her balance, wavering wildly, arms flailing before catching herself.

Reid crossed his arms over his chest and cocked an eyebrow.

"I didn't fall," Tara said, stabbing a finger at him. "I did not touch my foot to the ground. I want that on the record."

The crowd stirred around them, a couple of people throwing in their two cents' worth.

"Walk and turn. You know the drill," he said, gesturing with his chin.

Tara contemplated the space that had been cleared, then started to walk, each foot placed very deliberately and directly in front of the other.

"Note the straight line," she called over her shoulder.

When she got to the end, she swiveled on her heel, just to show she could, he suspected. For the second time she nearly lost her balance, staggering slightly to the left.

"That wasn't fair," she said immediately. "Let me do that again."

"Too late. You failed, I win. Let's go home," he said.

"I want another test."

"Tough luck." He stepped forward to grasp her elbow.

Tara frowned. "I don't want to go home. I'm having a good time, and I'm doing new things and meeting new people."

Okay, she was definitely three sheets to the wind.

"Why don't we go grab a burger, maybe some coffee?" he suggested.

She pulled her arm free. "I'm riding the bull again, and you can't stop me."

She made a break for the bull, not unlike a child insisting on one last play on the swing set before leaving the park. Reid swore under his breath and went after her.

Plan B it was, then.

Wrapping an arm around her middle, he pulled her back toward him. She squawked out a protest, twisting to face him, and he bent so that his shoulder was tucked against her belly, pulling her off balance at the same time. She toppled onto his shoulder, and he turned and immediately headed for the door, one arm banded across the back of her thighs to lock her in place. It took her a second to comprehend what he'd done, and when she did she started to wriggle and twist around, fists battering his back, doing her best to force him to release her.

He simply tightened his grip, his gaze on the distant exit, and kept walking.

The crowd parted, and seconds later he was outside, bending to set Tara back on her feet.

"I can't believe you just did that," she spluttered, her face red, her green eyes wide.

"Believe it. You want to grab something to eat before I take you home or not?"

She made a face to let him know she thought he was demented.

"No, Dalton, I do not want to grab a burger with you after you just rained on my parade like the biggest wet blanket of all time. What I'd like is for you to stop being the fun police and leave me to my awesome night out." She planted her hands on her hips, her chin tilted aggressively.

So drunk. A part of him wanted to laugh at her, but most of him just wanted to get her out of the seedy end of town.

"Answer me honestly—do you know a single person in that bar?"

"Sure. The tall guy is Jonah. The guy with the white hat is Drew. Or maybe Duncan... something with a D, anyway." She frowned as she tried to remember.

"And how many drinks do you think those good ol' boys have bought you since you've been here?" he asked.

"I'm not stupid, Reid. I can take care of myself."

There was a reckless, almost dangerous light in her eyes. He'd never seen her like this before, and he was pretty sure it wasn't just because she'd had a few too many.

"What's going on, Tara? Why are you hanging out at this dump? Why did I hear from your sister tonight that you bought a motorbike?"

"Because I did. And I love it."

Her chin ratcheted higher. He narrowed his eyes, trying to work out what was going on with her.

"Is this because of what Simon did? Are you trying to prove something to him or—"

"This is about me." She jabbed a thumb at her chest. "About who I am, and how much I've missed out on because I'm such a goody-two-shoes. I'm sick of always doing the right thing, Reid. I'm sick of being the one who always picks up the pieces. And I'm really sick of being so careful all the time."

She was trembling with the vehemence of her words,

her shoulders thrown back as though she was declaring herself or claiming territory for her country. He thought about what he knew of her life—her scatterbrained, irresponsible twin, her melodramatic mom, the way she conducted herself at work, what he'd seen of her relationship with her ex—and he started to get an inkling of where she was coming from.

Because Tara was a good person. She always did the right thing, always stepped up, never said no. She worked hard, pitched in to help her mom out, dug her sister out of rough spots.

"Okay. I get that," he said. "But do you really think breaking your neck on a stupid bull is the right way to fix any of that?"

Tara took a step toward him, her expression fierce. "What do I care about the right way? Don't you get it? I don't want to be afraid any more. I don't want to worry about what people think or what might happen or when people will leave or if they'll stop loving me. I'm over it."

Tears flooded her eyes and her chin wobbled. Her jaw set, she lifted her gaze to the sky and blinked like crazy, trying to suck it all back in.

"It's okay," he said quietly.

He wasn't going to think any less of her for crying.

She shook her head. "No. I've cried enough. I'm done with it."

He wanted to put his arms around her so badly his shoulders ached. But they'd never had that kind of relationship and he figured now was probably a really bad time to start.

"Come on," he said. "Let me take you home."

For a moment he thought she was going to object, but after a short pause she nodded and fell into step beside him as he walked to his pickup. He held the door open for her and she climbed inside. He could feel her watching him as he rounded the front of the truck.

"I'm not taking the bike back," she said as he slid behind the wheel.

He held his hands in the air. "Like you said, I'm not the boss of you."

She sniffed, and he got the sense she was disappointed he hadn't offered her an argument.

"And I could have handled that bull, too. I'm a natural."

He started the truck and put it into gear. "Hip fucking hooray. I'll alert the Nobel Prize Committee."

There was a moment of shocked silence. Then Tara started laughing. The sound was so infectious, he couldn't help smiling as he pulled out of the parking lot and onto the road.

"I knew there was a reason I liked you," she said.

"Only one?"

"I wouldn't push my luck if I were you. I'm still getting over the fact that you just carried me out of a bar like a sack of potatoes."

"You weigh more than a sack of potatoes. For the record."

The corners of her mouth curled into a rueful smile. "You know what the sad thing is? That's the most charming thing you've said to me all night."

"I wasn't aiming for charming."

"You got that right."

The brightly-lit window of the Main Street Diner was coming up on his left. He glanced at her.

"Sure you don't want a coffee?"

"I'm thinking that I probably wouldn't mind a shower," she said, wrinkling her nose. "Is it just me, or do I smell like beer?"

"I wasn't going to say anything. But yeah, you do."

"Your honesty is so refreshing."

"Wish I could say the same for that beer stink."

She huffed out a little laugh. She was still smiling when he turned into the driveway of her townhouse development, driving past the other houses until he reached hers at the end, but her smile faded as he braked to a stop.

"I suppose I should thank you," she said grudgingly.

"You can call me tomorrow if you like, when you'll mean it."

She glanced out at the townhouse but didn't make a move to exit.

"I could have handled that bull."

"You're the expert."

"And you're a smart ass and a wet blanket."

"It was my pleasure."

Her smile was more fleeting this time, and he got it—
she didn't want to go inside.

If he didn't care so much, if he didn't want her so
much, he'd invite himself in for coffee, but he knew that
wasn't a good idea.

"All right. Maybe I'll call you tomorrow and thank you,
maybe I won't," she said, finally moving to open the car door.

The interior light came on, and he saw her face
properly. She looked sad, and more than a little lost.

"What are you doing tomorrow?" he asked.

"Why?"

"Because I asked."

She studied him for a beat. "Nothing, I guess. Except
for collecting my car."

"I'll pick you up at seven. Wear your swimsuit, and
bring a change of clothes."

She blinked. "My swimsuit."

"Seven sharp. Don't keep me waiting."

She thought about it for a second, then she slid from
the car. "I don't suppose there's any point asking what we'll
be doing or where we'll be going?"

"Correct."

She shut the door, shooting him a look through the
window to let him know she didn't think he was funny. He
gave her a mock salute, then put the car into gear and backed
out of the driveway.

When he reached the road and glanced back, the lights
were on in her townhouse, the door safely shut.

He paused for a moment, thinking about what she'd
said to him, what he'd seen. Then he headed for home. He
had an early start tomorrow.

Chapter Seven

The electronic screech of the alarm clock woke Tara at six-thirty, and she batted the damned thing off the bedside table in a futile attempt to silence it. It kept squealing from its new position on the floor near the foot of the bed, and she threw back the covers with a disgusted grunt.

Which was when she registered she was the proud owner of a throbbing headache, and that her right shoulder was inexplicably sore. Then last night came back to her and she realized that her sore shoulder was perfectly explicable, given that the mechanical bull had tried to rip it from its socket several times last night.

The clock was still nagging at her, so she crawled to the end of the bed and switched it off. She flopped back onto the mattress, lying on her belly, her sore arm hanging over the side of the bed, and wondered what Reid would do if she texted him and told him she'd changed her mind about their outing.

He'll just turn up anyway.

He would. He'd knock on the door and honk his horn and bully her until she got dressed and went with him—wherever that might be—so she might as well suck it up and have a shower and try to choke down some breakfast.

The shower was good, the hot water easing some of the stiffness in her shoulder, but food wasn't something she could do, she decided. She'd never been a great drinker, but she'd had two hangovers in the space of a week—one from her vodka night with Scarlett, and today's doozy. Probably time to ease up on her alcohol consumption for the foreseeable future.

She swallowed a couple of painkillers and was just stuffing a towel and underwear into her backpack when she heard the rumble of Reid's truck.

She went to the door but hesitated a moment before opening it. She wasn't sure how she felt about last night, about what he'd done and the things she'd said to him. She definitely felt exposed—that was not up for debate—but she couldn't decide if she was annoyed with him for dragging her out of the bar or grateful or maybe even touched that he cared enough to do what he'd done in the first place.

But her feelings had always been complicated where he was concerned. From the moment he walked in the door at Bozeman PD, she'd been drawn to him. At first she'd told herself it was natural that she'd be curious about him after she'd heard the other guys talk about him so much. He'd only served as a Patrol Officer for four years before heading overseas to work in private security, but enough of the guys who'd trained and worked with him were still around that she'd heard plenty of stories about Reid Dalton.

Then they'd been on foot patrol during their first week of being partnered together, and he'd reached out to catch her when she'd stumbled over a crack in the sidewalk, and she'd been forced to admit that what she felt for him was more than simple curiosity. The echo of his touch had burned through her body, sending heat up into her face and down to places she hadn't wanted to think about, pushing her heart rate sky high, making her jumpy and self-conscious and hyper-aware of him.

She'd been living with Simon for a year by then, and it hadn't taken her long to rationalize the moment into a nice, safe little box. Reid was a good-looking guy, after all. Any woman would get a little hot under the collar if he grabbed her around the waist and saved her from an embarrassing face plant. He also had a dry, sometimes goofy sense of humor, was extremely well-read and well-traveled, and wasn't afraid to let the world know when he cared about something. All in all, a pretty appealing package, and she was only human. It didn't mean anything.

Amazing how long she'd been able to cling to that piece of self-delusion.

She heard Reid's heavy tread mounting the steps to her front door and pulled it open before he could knock. His hair was wet from the shower, making it appear almost black, and a long-sleeved black T-shirt and jeans made the most of his lean, strong body.

Pretty appealing package, my ass.

The man was gorgeous, that was the truth of it, but it was the kindness and intelligence behind his eyes that she'd always found the most appealing. God help her.

"You ready?" he asked.

"Two seconds," she said.

She turned on her heel and went to collect her wallet, house keys and phone. He was standing on the porch when she turned around. Watching her.

She'd gotten pretty good at reading his expressions over the past year. His eyebrows tended to lower a little when he was serious, and his eyes shone with laughter when he was amused. She couldn't read his expression now, though.

"You ready to tell me where we're going yet?" she asked as she shouldered her backpack.

"Thought you might enjoy guessing."

She shooed him down the porch steps so she could lock the front door. "You thought wrong. I hate surprises."

She frowned when she spotted his car. Two big white surfboards were sticking out of the back tray.

She shot him a look. "You're aware that Montana is a land-locked state, right?"

"Shows what you know."

She climbed into the truck.

"I think my geography is pretty solid on this one," she said.

"True. But those aren't surfboards."

She twisted to look through the rear window at the boards. Sure enough, now that she saw them up close, they seemed wider than a normal surfboard, and the middle section was covered with what looked like a layer of rubbery matting.

"You've got me," she admitted. "I am officially bamboozled."

"You ever heard of stand-up paddle-boarding?"

"No."

"Then today is going to be a voyage of discovery." He shot her a grin before reversing out into the street.

"And where is this voyage going to take me?"

"Fairy Lake. Any more questions, Your Honor?"

"I'm good for now. But thanks for asking."

His smile was small but it warmed something inside her to know that they understood—and enjoyed—each other so thoroughly.

He headed north, stopping at a truck stop outside of Livingstone for gas. He returned to the car with a couple of coffees and two grease-marked bags. He tossed one into her lap and Tara was about to explain that she wasn't up to eating when the smell of bacon hit her.

Okay, maybe she could make an exception for bacon.

"Oh, this is good," she said as she swallowed her first mouthful of toasted cheese and bacon sandwich.

"Bacon is nature's cure-all," Reid said.

He pulled back onto the freeway, and she took a moment to unwrap his sandwich for him so he wouldn't have to do it one-handed.

"Thanks."

"Least I can do, since you went to all the trouble of getting me out of bed early," she said.

"Just being a good friend."

He was joking, she knew, but it seemed to her that his words were a timely reminder. They'd gone on dozens of cross country runs together, spent time together at the Bozeman firing range, idled away hours manning speed traps talking about their childhoods, past loves, families, but spending time with Reid felt... different now that she no longer had Simon in her life. For the first time since they'd known each other, they were both single, and the knowledge made her feel distinctly edgy.

Get a grip, Buck. This man is your partner, and you are

an object of pity right now.

Both excellent points, and she made a promise to herself to keep them front and center in her mind for the rest of the day.

The sandwich and coffee went a long way toward curing her hangover, and by the time Reid had turned off Bridger Canyon Drive and onto Fairy Lake Road she was feeling almost human. Which was just as well, because the final stretch of road was unsealed and creased with runnels and potholes, treating them to a bone-jarring ride for fifteen minutes before they rounded a bend and found themselves looking out over Fairy Lake.

The chalky-white cliffs of Sacagawea Peak towered overhead, its slopes dotted with trees. The lake itself was thickly hemmed by tall pines, the still, deep green waters mirroring the surrounds. It was almost painfully beautiful, and they were both silent as Reid turned off the engine.

"Have you done this before? The paddle-boarding thing?"

"Got my own board and everything." He threw her a small smile before exiting the truck.

She followed him, watching as he hauled first one board then the other from the tray.

"So where did you get the other board, then?" she asked.

"A friend."

"I didn't even know this was a thing," she said, frowning as he collected two long-handled paddles and leaned them against the side of the pickup.

"That's because you've lived a sheltered life."

She knew he was only teasing her, but a part of her bristled. She *had* lived a sheltered life, in many ways. That was what last night—and the motorbike—had been all about.

"Says the professional gypsy. Have you heard about that job in Chicago yet?"

"Yesterday, actually. They want me to come in for a second interview."

"What's wrong? Weren't they bowled over by your many charms the first time around?"

"Apparently not. Do you need to change? I can take

these down to the water to give you privacy."

"I've got my swimsuit on already."

"Then keep your shoes on," Reid advised. "The walk down to the water isn't exactly comfortable barefoot."

He reached for the hem of his T-shirt and pulled it over his head. For a heart-stopping moment she thought he was stripping to bare skin, but he was wearing a form-fitting black tank underneath and she was able to breathe again.

A little alarmed by her reaction, she pulled her own sweater off, leaving her T-shirt on over her bikini top. She could see him taking off his jeans out of the corners of her eyes and she popped the stud on hers, too. She'd done a lot of things with Reid, but none of them had included taking off their clothes together. Even though there was nothing remotely salacious or sexual about the situation, she was still acutely aware of the intimacy of the moment as she turned her back and pushed the denim down her legs.

She folded her jeans and sweater neatly and set them on the passenger seat.

"What can I carry?" she asked as she turned to face him.

She almost stumbled over the last word when she saw that he'd stripped to a pair of dark grey swim shorts that left his long, powerful legs exposed.

That explains the tan, then, a little voice noted in the back of her head.

He lifted one of the boards, his shoulder and arm muscles flexing impressively.

"Bring the paddles, I'll come back for the other board," he said before taking off down the slope toward the lake.

She rolled her eyes. Since when hadn't she pulled her own weight? It took her a moment to locate the handhold molded into the center of the board, then she hefted it and started down the slope after him. He glanced over his shoulder when she was halfway, shaking his head when he saw what she was doing.

"Should have known you wouldn't be able to help yourself," he said.

"Then you shouldn't have bothered telling me not to."

He set his board down near the water's edge and

bounded back up the slope at an easy run. She followed him with her eyes until she realized what she was doing, then she snapped her head around and made a big deal out of inspecting the view.

The early morning softness was starting to burn off, and all around her, giant pines reached skyward. She stared at the water, trying to work out what color it was. Emerald green? Azure? A combination of both, perhaps?

She heard the crunch of gravel underfoot as Reid returned.

"It's really beautiful here," she said quietly.

"Yeah. Got to admit, I always feel a little twitchy when I can't see some mountains. One of the side effects of being Montana born and bred."

She gazed up at Sacagawea Peak. She'd never lived anywhere but Marietta; couldn't imagine not waking up to mountains every day.

"So. How does this behemoth work, anyway?" she asked, turning to contemplate her board.

"It floats. You stand on it, you paddle." He shrugged.

"Right. It's that easy," she said dubiously.

"There are a few little tricks to it. When you start out, stay on your knees and get a feel for the board, what your weight does to it and how the paddle feels in the water. Then, when you're ready, you get to your feet..."

He demonstrated, kneeling on his board and then planting a foot before rising smoothly to his feet.

"You might want to stay squatting and get both feet planted before you attempt to stand. Some people find it easier that way. And once you're up, you want to stay in the center of the board with your feet shoulders-width apart, knees slightly bent. The board's incredibly stable, so as long as you don't flail around you won't fall off."

She glanced out at the water. "I bet it's really cold, huh?"

"Refreshing is the word you're looking for."

"Refreshing. I'll remember that when my extremities start dropping off."

Some of the other lakes in Gallatin County had bathtub-warm water in summer due to their shallowness,

471

but Fairy Lake was not one of them. Tara had swum here a couple of times over the years and knew from experience that it was definitely on the icy side.

"The simple solution is to not fall in," Reid said.

"Right. Thanks for that hot tip."

"When you're paddling, remember you need to work either side to go in a straight line." Again, he demonstrated. "You want to turn, just keep paddling on one side and you'll do a big circle. And for sharper turns, work up a bit of forward momentum, stick your oar straight down and hold on tight, and you should spin around. You need to brace yourself when you do that, though, or you'll fall in."

"Okay. What else?"

"That's about it." He flashed a smile at her. "It's not rocket science."

"I guess not."

He pulled off his sneakers and socks. She followed suit, then copied him again as he carried his board out into the water. He went back for the paddles, passing hers over before pushing his board out until the water was knee-deep.

"Here we go. Paddle placed across the board in front of you. One knee on the board... "

He made it look so easy as he slid first one knee, then the other onto the board and picked up his paddle, looking at her expectantly.

She walked her board out, gasping at how cold the water was. Placing her paddle as he had, she slid her right knee onto the board, then quickly clambered on, her arms stretched out for balance as the board started to rock.

"And you're on. When you start paddling, make sure the blade is fully in the water before pushing so you make the most of your strokes."

"Aye, aye, Captain," she said.

"I was wondering how long it would take for insubordination to rear its ugly head."

"Not long. You should know that by now," she said.

She experimented with a couple of strokes, dipping the oar into the water and propelling the board a few feet across the lake. She was aware of Reid keeping pace with her, watching quietly while she got a sense of the dynamics of it all.

"All good?" he asked.

"I think so."

"Good."

She watched as he rose to his feet with cat-like grace.

"Holler if you need me," he said.

Then he took off, paddle digging deep into the water as he propelled himself forward. He made it look so easy, as though he'd been doing this for a million years.

It was tempting to try standing, but she decided to play it smart and paddle around a little more on her knees first. After ten minutes, she took a deep breath and shifted position so that she was squatting on the board, both feet planted like an ungainly frog. Slowly she rose to her feet. As Reid had promised, the board was very stable and steady.

"Way to go, Starbuck," Reid called across the water.

She shook her head. He knew she hated that nickname. Ever since they'd rebooted the old 80's sci-fi television series Battlestar Galactica and recast Starbuck as a woman, she'd been taking guff at the station.

She tried a few strokes of the paddle, keeping her knees slightly bent, and slowly her confidence grew. Soon she was able to stop staring at her feet and the paddle and gaze around herself, absorbing the incredible natural beauty surrounding her.

The sun climbed higher in the sky. A gentle breeze caught at her hair and cooled her cheeks. She watched a bird soar high on a thermal, its wings spread wide, and marveled at how it seemed to hang so effortlessly in the sky. When her legs got tired, she got back on her knees, alternating between the two positions as well as sometimes simply sitting with her legs either side of the board, drifting, letting the lake's currents take her where they would.

And slowly, slowly, the peace of the place, the lap of the water, the warmth of the sun began to seep into her bones and the terrible tension she'd been holding within herself all week started to unwind.

Simon, the incident at work, the painful self-realizations she'd had, her uncertainty about what she wanted for the future... she let it all go, let the wind whisk it away, leaving nothing but a quiet, still calm within her.

She was kneeling on her board, sitting back on her heels as she watched fluffy white clouds scud across the sky when Reid's voice echoed across the water.

"My stomach says it's lunch time. What do you think?" She started and almost fell off the board. It took her a moment to realize Reid was on the shore, one hand shading his eyes as he watched her.

And he'd taken his tank top off.

Even from a distance, his chest and torso looked amazing. She started paddling back toward shore, feeling absurdly nervous about the prospect of standing on dry land with him with so little clothes on.

Partner. Feels sorry for you. Remember?

Reid waded out into the water to hold the board as she jumped off, dragging it up the bank for her. Her mouth went dry at the way his abdominal muscles rippled with the effort.

God, he had an amazing body. Really, really impressive.

She'd always known that, of course—even the utilitarian cut of the Bozeman PD uniform couldn't disguise his great physique—but seeing him like this, almost naked, was a whole other matter.

His pectoral muscles were cleanly defined, his shoulders broad. His belly was ripped, showcasing his zero percentage body fat. Then there were those thighs, and his beautifully sculpted calves...

She dragged her gaze away from him, concentrating instead on the picnic blanket he'd spread on the wild grass covering the slope, a cooler anchoring one corner.

"It's a long way to the nearest McDonalds," he explained.

"Very efficient of you."

She settled on one side of the blanket while he took the other and started unpacking the cooler. She made a point of concentrating on the food he was unloading instead of him, even though a part of her was desperate to ogle him some more.

In some deep, dark, barely acknowledged corner of her psyche, she'd always wondered what his body was like.

And now she knew.

Food. Concentrate on the food.

There were sandwiches, little baby quiches, some of what looked like his mother's lemon cake, apples—naturally—and two amber-colored glass bottles slick with condensation.

That got her attention, successfully distracting her from his body for a few valuable seconds.

"Please tell me that's Dalton cider?" she asked, already reaching for a bottle.

"Courtesy of Dad. He insisted."

"I freaking love his cider," she said.

Reid's family sold most of their apples to the public or to big retailers, but every year his father set aside a certain quantity for his apple cider run. He only ever pressed a few hundred bottles of the stuff, but it was delicious—sweet and full-flavored and fruity—and she was practically drooling as she remembered the last bottle she'd enjoyed at the department barbecue Reid had hosted at the Dalton's place earlier in the year.

"Better enjoy it, then."

There was a dark note to his voice and she risked a look at him. He was gazing out at the lake, a grim set to his mouth.

"Why do you say that?"

He shrugged, and she got the sense that he wished he could take back his words. "It's a limited resource. You know that. Have a sandwich."

He unwrapped his own, taking a big bite.

She mustered all her resolve and managed to stop her gaze from drifting below his chin as she continued to study him.

"Is something going on with the orchard? Is your dad okay?"

Reid frowned, then glanced down at his sandwich. Really wishing he hadn't said anything now if she had a guess.

"You started it, Dalton," she pointed out.

"Thanks for reminding me."

She took a swig from her cider and unwrapped her

sandwich. Chicken, mayo and walnuts. Yum.

"You might as well tell me. I'll get it out of you eventually."

"Going to use your stellar interrogation technique on me, are you?"

"You want to tell me. You wouldn't have said anything otherwise. Might as well just cut to the chase."

He took a long pull from his cider, then tilted the bottle and studied the amber glass for a long beat. She pretended that she didn't want to reach out and wrap her hand around his gorgeously developed biceps and munched away on her sandwich.

"Mom wants to sell the place."

Tara frowned, jerked out of her preoccupation by his words. The Daltons had grown apples for three generations. Selling up would mean giving all that away. Abandoning a legacy.

"Only your mom?"

"She hasn't brought it up with Dad yet. But Mom's pretty persuasive when she's on the warpath. And there's no doubting that the accident shook him up a lot. Who knows? Maybe he'll be relieved to be able to walk away."

"I take it this has come up because you don't want it?"

He frowned, almost as though her words had irritated him. "Something like that."

"Well, either you do, or you don't. I assume your folks wouldn't sell if you were going to step in at some point."

"Maybe we should drop this." He crumpled up the plastic wrap from his sandwich.

Wow, she'd really touched a nerve.

"Do you want the orchard or not, Reid?"

"It's not as black and white as that."

"Why not?"

He sighed, his mouth curling up at the corners as he threw her a rueful look. "You're like a dog with a bone sometimes, you know that?"

She growled deep in her throat before giving him her best dog bark.

"That is... wrong on so many levels," he said.

But he was smiling now.

"Tell me why it isn't as simple as black and white." Having polished off her sandwich, she reached for a baby quiche.

"Because it's not just about me. My grandfather bought that land and cleared it. Planted more than three hundred trees by hand. It doesn't feel like it's mine to give up."

"But you don't want to be tied down by it?"

He ran a hand through his hair. "I used to hate the place, when I was younger. Resented the hell out of it. Took off the moment I could."

"Funny, I thought you'd enjoyed helping your dad out this past year. At least, that was the sense I got." He'd never complained about having to spend his downtime in the orchard. Not once.

"I don't mind the work. Not anymore. In a lot of ways, it's really rewarding."

"But you don't want to be tied down?"

He finished his bottle of cider before responding, setting the bottle carefully back in the basket. His father recycled them, she knew.

"I guess I just never imagined my whole life being played out in Marietta."

"Then I guess that's your answer, then."

She felt sad as she said it. She liked having Reid around. Working with him and getting to know him had been a privilege.

Looking at him wasn't too bad, either.

She distracted herself from her inappropriate and dangerous thoughts by helping herself to a piece of lemon cake. Once she'd demolished that, she brushed the crumbs off her T-shirt and lay back with her ankles crossed, arms behind her head, and closed her eyes.

If her eyes were closed, she wouldn't be tempted to keep staring at him. That was the theory, anyway.

In practice, she was almost preternaturally aware of him moving around, putting food back in the cooler, rearranging things.

"Here," he said, and she opened her eyes to find him leaning over her.

He was so close she could see the individual hairs of his eyelashes and she drew in a nervous breath. Then she realized he'd folded her towel into a pillow for her and was waiting for her to lift her head so he could position it for her.

"Thanks."

She engaged her belly muscles and lifted her head and shoulders, and he slid the folded towel into place. She was powerless to stop herself from breathing in the smell of him as he did so—deodorant and sun-warmed skin and man.

He was back on his side of the blanket in no seconds flat, arranging his own towel in a similar fashion. Her gaze got caught on the dark silk of the hair beneath his arms before darting to the sexy little trail that led beneath the waistband of his shorts. Parts of him she didn't normally see. Parts of him she'd always wondered about.

Traitorous heat unfolded in the pit of her stomach. When she and Scarlett were teenagers, her sister's bedroom walls had been covered with posters of hot guys in various states of undress, but Tara's bedroom walls had been all about the athletes she admired and the movies she loved. She'd never considered herself the type of woman who ogled men or got all squirmy when a well-built guy happened into her orbit.

What a fool.

She concentrated on her breathing, aware that her heart was beating too fast. She needed to calm the hell down and stop thinking like this. If Reid knew what was going on in her head... she didn't even want to contemplate how embarrassing that would be.

Instead, she thought about work, and her mom, and how happy she was that Scarlett had found Mitch—although, strictly speaking, it had been the other way around, since Mitch had come looking for Scarlett, tracking her all the way from the Australian outback to Marietta.

Gradually her hyper-awareness faded and she breathed a sigh of relief.

"So, you ever going to get around to telling me about this motorbike?"

Chapter Eight

Reid's voice was lazy and relaxed, but it didn't stop her eyes from popping open.

"I thought we covered that last night."

"I can think of a million better ways to live a little than buying a motorbike," he said.

She turned her head to find him watching her. If it was anyone else, she'd tell them where to stuff it, but she could see the concern in his espresso-dark eyes.

"Maybe you can. But this is about what I want, and I want that bike."

"You said something last night. About being sick of waiting for people to leave you."

Three cheers for her beer-lubricated mouth.

"Did I?"

"Tell me you don't think you had anything to do with Simon cheating on you? Because that is straight-up bullshit, Tara. It's all on him, all of it."

He sat up, no longer lazy and relaxed. Not wanting to be at a disadvantage, she sat up, too.

"I don't think it's my fault he cheated. But it's my fault for being with him. That's all on me."

He frowned and she could see he didn't understand.

"It's hard to explain," she said, thinking about all the elements that had fed into the unconscious decision she'd made to play it safe with Simon. Her father, her mother, the way things had been after he left...

And then suddenly she was talking, the words pouring out of her, almost as though she'd been waiting for an opportunity to share this part of herself with him.

"When my dad left, my mom fell apart. She loved him so much, and she just... couldn't cope without him, I guess. She was so wounded and hurt and broken, and for a long time all she did was cry and spend days in bed and talk on the phone with Aunt Margot." Tara swallowed past the tightness in her throat. She couldn't think about those hard times without getting emotional. Life had been so precarious, every day had felt as though it balanced on the edge of disaster. "I felt so guilty. So responsible. I did everything I could to help out, but I couldn't bring Dad back and that was what she wanted, more than anything."

"Your dad didn't leave because of you and Scarlett, Tara," Reid said.

"I know. But something happened before he left... " She drew her knees to her chest and looped her arms around them, needing the comfort as she gathered her courage. Then, her gaze fixed on the red and black plaid of the picnic blanket, she told him what she'd never told anyone else. "I came home from school early one day. I had a dentist appointment, and I was supposed to meet Mom at home and she was going to drive me to Dr. Cassidy's. She wasn't home when I got there, though. Dad was. And he was with someone. I could hear them when I let myself in, and I found them in the kitchen, kissing, half-undressed."

She had to stop then, the old memory so powerful she felt physically ill. Reid shifted, turning to face her, reaching out to wrap his hand around her ankle. His touch was so reassuring, so grounding and safe, and she lifted her gaze from the blanket briefly to look at him.

His expression was patiently solemn as he waited for more.

"He told me it was a mistake," she said. "Told me it would never happen again. He cried... I'd never seen him like that. He made me promise that I would never tell anyone. He said he'd make it up to Mom, to me, to all of us. And I believed him."

She saw comprehension dawn in Reid's eyes.

"How long was it until he left?" he asked, his voice gravelly with what she suspected was anger.

And why not? It was an angry-making story. Her father had behaved appallingly. Weakly. Shamefully.

"A month. Just long enough for him to arrange things to suit himself. Take money from the mortgage, sort out a new place to live. Then we came home from school one day and he was gone and Mom was... broken."

And Tammy Buck had never recovered, and Tara has spent the last thirteen years wondering what might have happened if she'd said something about what she'd seen, instead of honoring her promise to her father.

"Your father is an asshole."

Trust Reid to put it so bluntly.

"Yeah, he is. But we all loved him like crazy when he was around. Then he just faded out of our lives, skipping visitation weekends, putting us off until it became clear that he'd rather forget he had us than face up to his own guilt. We haven't heard from him in ten years."

His hand tightened around her ankle. She took a deep breath, determined to get it all out.

"Anyway. Like I said, I did my best to make it up to Mom for not telling her about that day. To make things okay. But I always felt as though there was something I should have done. Warned Mom. Something. That's why I always drop everything when she needs me. Why I can't say no to her or Scarlett."

"Jesus, Tara. It wasn't your fault. You must know that."

"I do. It took a while, but I worked out that I was carrying around my dad's guilt for him, and that it wasn't my burden to bear. I actually thought I was on top of it, which is pretty hilarious in retrospect. It took everything blowing up with Simon for me to realize that I'd been working so hard trying to avoid my mother's fate that I'd almost married a man I didn't love."

Reid's hand tightened around her ankle again, and she forced herself to look up and meet his eyes.

He looked... shaken. And also a little confused. She smiled ruefully. Apparently she'd done such a great job of convincing herself she loved Simon that she'd convinced the world, too.

"You look like Scarlett did when I told her. She actually argued with me. Tried to convince me I was wrong, that I was mad about him," she said.

"I thought you were. When he asked you to marry him... you were happy."

His gaze searched her face as he tried to understand.

"I was happy. He was safe, right? He wasn't going anywhere. He wasn't some outgoing, foot-loose, fancy-free raconteur like my father. He was a history teacher."

She almost laughed at her own naivety and stupidity.

"So you're not...?"

"Heartbroken? No. I'm hurt. He betrayed my trust. I feel stupid, humiliated. But my heart is fine."

There was a profound silence as they looked at one another.

"That's good. I mean, the rest of it isn't, but that part is good." His hand slipped free from her ankle, releasing her.

"Yeah. And that stuff at work last week? My Incredible Hulk impersonation? That was me starting to realize how badly I'd almost messed up my life."

Reid nodded, processing. "I can see that."

"I made myself a promise when I worked all this out the other night. No more playing it safe."

"Right. Which brings us back to the motorbike."

"Yep."

He looked out at the lake, clearly chewing something over. "Promise me you'll be careful on the damned thing, okay?"

"Yes, Mr. Dalton."

He shook his head at her.

"Such a smart ass," he said.

"Thanks. I've been taking lessons from this guy I know."

"Sweetheart, that attitude is all yours, and you know it."

They were both smiling, and something shifted between them. Suddenly she was very aware of how little they were both wearing, and the fact that they were utterly alone. Reid's smile faded and he looked out at the lake again, a frown on his face.

"I might see if I can catch up on a little sleep," she said, settling back onto the blanket. "All that cider and food has made me sleepy."

"Good idea."

She settled back onto her towel pillow, and this time she fell into a true drowse, warmed by the sun and Reid's concern.

He cared about her. He might be leaving soon, but he cared about her.

She had no idea how long she dozed, but gradually she came back to consciousness. When she opened her eyes, Reid was standing beside the blanket, stretching his arms high over his head, his skin burnished by the sun. She blinked as she gazed up at six-foot-two of rock-solid muscle.

It was almost enough to make you believe in the gods of Olympus, it really was.

"You up for another go?" Reid asked when he realized she was awake.

"Sure am."

She stood, and together they walked down to the water's edge. She felt like an old pro as she pushed her board out to knee-deep water. Reid followed suit, and they both paddled out into deeper water before standing.

"Come check out the other side of the lake," Reid said, pointing with his paddle.

His strokes were longer and more powerful than hers, but she did her best to keep up, carefully rationing the number of times she allowed herself to admire his back and butt along the way.

She was only flesh and blood, after all.

When they got to the other side, he pointed out some wildflowers that had sprouted in a fallen log, and they drifted along the edge of the lake, talking and laughing. The sun moved across the sky as they did a slow tour, waving to two hikers and their dog on the far side of the lake, stopping to watch a deer that was grazing in the dappled light beneath the trees.

She was the one who suggested a race, taking

shameless advantage by taking off at a fast clip before Reid could turn his board around. It didn't take long for him to start gaining on her and Tara pushed her oar deep with each stroke, willing her board across the water. She wasn't sure what happened—whether she hit something and the board jostled, or if she'd simply rocked herself off balance putting so much effort into her paddling, but one second she was laughing gleefully over the fact that she was somehow maintaining her lead, and the next the board seemed to slide sideways out from beneath her feet and she was teetering over the water.

She let out a cry of despair.

And then she was in the water, and it was every bit as icy as she knew it would be as she flailed her way to the surface.

The first thing she heard when she came up for air was the sound of Reid's laughter, deep and masculine, echoing off the water.

Kicking her feet, she stretched out a hand for her board before using her free hand to push the hair out of her eyes.

"Nice. Thanks for the empathy, Sir Galahad," she said.

"How's the water?"

"Delightful."

He laughed again. She gave him a disgruntled look before dragging herself across the board and shuffling around until she was lying lengthwise on the damned thing, fully aware that she probably looked about as gracious and graceful as a beached sea cow while doing all of the above.

Finally she was on her feet again, flipping her dripping hair over her shoulder. Her T-shirt clung to her like glue, and she took a moment to make sure her bathing suit was covering everything it should be.

"So, want to make it the best out of three?" Reid asked, his expression deceptively innocent.

"Absolutely."

"And maybe we could both start at the same time this time?" he suggested, eyebrows raised.

"Sorry?" she said.

His smile was knowing as he paddled his board

alongside hers.

"On three," he said. "First to the big boulder. One, two, three."

She waited until he had his blade deep in the water midway through his first stroke before reaching across with her paddle and prodding him firmly in the ass. His head snapped around, an expression of comic outrage on his face, but it was too late, he was already off balance.

She grinned as he hit the water with an almighty splash. Her amusement faded when Reid didn't surface immediately, and she leaned forward to peer into the water. His board was in the way, however, and the water was too murky at this depth.

"Reid?" she called out, panic hitting her. What if he'd hit his head on his board on the way down and she hadn't noticed, or there was a submerged log he'd gotten caught on.. .?

She was about to throw her paddle aside and dive in when her board tilted ever-so-slightly to the rear. She glanced over her shoulder to see Reid gripping the tail, a fiendishly evil grin on his face.

"No."

"I'm afraid so, cupcake."

He pushed down, the board went up, and she went in, arms flailing. He was laughing once again when she resurfaced.

"Okay. I may have deserved that," she conceded.

"You think?"

This time around she didn't have the benefit of sun-warmed skin to keep her warm and she could feel the chill seeping into her limbs.

"Maybe we should call a truce before we both turn into icicles," she said.

"Sounds like a plan." He swam toward her, offering her his hand.

She eyed it mistrustfully.

"What's wrong? You think I'm going to dunk you?" he asked, looking as mischievous as a little boy.

"I know you are, so don't play all innocent with me."

He took her hand anyway, but the smile quickly left

his mouth as he grasped it.

"You're freezing."

"Amazing powers of perception you have there."

"Get back on your board," he ordered, his eyebrows knitting into a frown.

"What a good idea. Why didn't I think of that?"

She reached for her board, once again bellying her way onto it and shuffling around until she was lengthwise rather than across it. Reid, she noted sourly, managed to somehow almost vault out of the water onto his, the big showoff.

She stayed on her knees when she was done, shivering as the wind hit her already cold skin.

"Let's head for shore," Reid said. "We should probably think about going home, anyway."

He wasn't going to get any argument from her. Suddenly the jeans and sweater she'd left in the truck seemed like her idea of heaven.

She stayed on her knees as she paddled back to shore, slipping off in the shallows and dragging the board up onto the bank. Her towel was warm from the sun when she wrapped it around her shoulders and buried her face in it, inhaling the smell of warm terrycloth and detergent.

"Oh, that is so nice."

"You should take that wet T-shirt off," Reid said.

She lifted her face from the warmth of the towel to find him standing there dripping all over the blanket.

"Probably a good idea," she conceded.

She let her towel drop, reaching for the hem of her T-shirt and dragging it up her body. It wasn't until she let it slip to the ground that she glanced down and realized her nipples were hard from the cold, creating two very noticeable points in her aqua blue bikini top. She bent down to collect the towel, carefully tucking it around her torso and securing the end beneath her armpit before looking at Reid.

He was busy toweling himself off, and she told herself he probably hadn't even noticed. Anyway, she was cold. Nipples did the sticking-out thing when people were cold. His were a little puckered, too, she noticed.

Then he glanced across and caught her checking out his nipples and heat rocketed up her chest and into her face.

"I should take the cooler up to the car," she said, turning away to go fetch her sneakers.

She made sure her feet were thoroughly dry before pulling on her socks and shoes, the small task giving her ample opportunity to avoid looking at Reid. Then she grabbed the cooler and lugged it up the slope. Reid passed her on the way back down, one of the boards under his arm.

"Leave the other board for me," he ordered before continuing up the bank.

She considered disobeying him, but she was fully aware that going up the slope was going to be a lot harder than coming down, and the board was big and cumbersome. Instead, she folded the picnic blanket and collected her wet T-shirt and Reid's tank top and headed for the car.

"Good girl," Reid said when he saw she'd listened to him.

"Don't push your luck."

He was smiling as he walked down the hill.

She collected her clothes from the front seat, then glanced around, trying to work out where she could change. There were plenty of pine trees, but not much underbrush, and none of the tree trunks were wide enough to act as a makeshift screen.

Reid appeared, slinging the board into the bed of the truck.

"You take one side, I take the other, and we both pretend we're gentlemen," he said, somehow reading her mind.

"That's going to be a stretch for one of us," she said.

He laughed. "I surely do hope so."

She realized what she'd said then, and couldn't help laughing, too. He moved to the other side of the truck, and she turned her back and pulled her underwear from the backpack. She tried to keep the towel tucked beneath her armpits as she shimmied out of her wet swimsuit, but it kept slipping and in the end she let it drop in the interests of simply getting her underwear on sooner rather than later. The warm cotton felt better than silk against her skin, and soon she was pulling on her jeans and sweater.

"That feels better," she said.

"Does that mean you're decent?"

"No, I'm standing here in my birthday suit, dancing a jig."

"I've never seen you dance."

Reid walked around the front of the truck, his eyes alight with amusement. She couldn't stop her gaze from dropping to his chest. Now that she knew what was beneath his clothes, she would probably never be truly comfortable in his presence again.

A rather alarming thought, given they worked with each other.

Not for long, remember? He's heading to Chicago soon.

He was. And if it wasn't Chicago, it would be somewhere else. So maybe it was okay for her to let herself admire him in his hip- and thigh-hugging jeans that were faded in all the right places.

"Your nose is a little pink," he said.

"That'll happen."

He grabbed her backpack and stowed it in the back of the truck while she liberated a couple of apples from the cooler, tossing one to him when he'd finished. They were both biting into crisp sweetness as he began the bone-jangling trip back to the freeway.

"Can I ask you something?" he said.

"You can."

"That stuff about your dad... have you ever talked to your mom or sister about that?"

"No. And I don't plan to." She frowned at him, not sure what he was thinking. Her mom would hate her if she found out what had happened that afternoon. Tara knew it with every bone in her body. Tammy Buck would work on that single piece of information in her mind until she'd turned it into a missed opportunity, and Tara didn't want to upset her when her mother was already grappling to come to terms with her Parkinson's disease.

"Your decision. It just occurred to me that it might be good to talk it over with your sister. Scare a few ghosts out of the closet."

"That ghost is an old one. I'm happy to leave it where

it is, thanks."

"Like I said, your call."

She made an effort to shift the conversation then, asking him about his second job interview in Chicago and ragging on him about wearing a suit.

"I can't imagine you all gussied up," she said.

"Like a bear in a tuxedo, you think?"

"Yeah. Exactly like that."

"I have it on good authority that I scrub up okay."

"Pretty sure your mom doesn't count, Reid."

That earned her a smile.

"I have other people willing to vouch for me."

"I bet."

They stopped for dinner in Livingstone on the way through, both of them having worked up an appetite, and they rolled into Marietta just as dusk began to blur the world and the street lights were flickering on.

Tara felt an odd sense of disappointment as Reid turned into her driveway and cruised toward her townhouse. It had been such a great day, she'd felt so good, enjoyed Reid so much...

She didn't want it to end.

The knowledge burned in her belly as he came to a halt in front of her single-car garage, slipping the car into neutral.

"Fair warning, you might have sore legs and feet tomorrow from all the work counterbalancing on the board," he said.

"Noted. I'll be sure to remember you fondly as I hobble around."

"You do that."

She twisted to face him, her gaze going over his mussed hair and his beard-shadowed cheeks. He'd given her a much-needed circuit break today, taking her away from all the crap she'd been marinating in and blowing fresh air into her head. He'd also listened and let her vent without judging or trying to solve anything.

"Thank you," she said. "I think you might have just saved my ass today."

"Only your ass? I'll have to lift my game." His smile

was small and slightly self-conscious.

Typical Reid, bold in everything except accepting heartfelt appreciation.

"You've been a good friend to me, Reid Dalton. I'm going to miss you like hell when you abandon us and head to Chicago."

"Might not get the job yet. Don't go counting your chickens."

"They'd be crazy not to take you."

She scooted across her seat a little and leaned in to kiss his cheek. They didn't normally kiss and hug or do any of that touch-feely stuff, but it felt right for today. It felt necessary.

Her hand landed on his shoulder, and she inhaled the good, fresh scent of him as she pressed her lips to his cheek. She must have surprised him, because he shifted a little and his stubble rasped across her lips, the lightest of abrasions.

She pulled away, instinctively licking her lips to soothe them. Reid's gaze followed the movement, and she was close enough to see his pupils dilate and his nostrils flare.

She went very still. And then she did something she'd been wanting to do for a very long time: she leaned close and kissed him, properly this time.

His mouth was warm, and she could taste the sweetness of the lemon meringue pie he'd had for dessert. She waited for him to respond, to do something, but he seemed to be waiting for something else. Something more.

Well, might as well go for it. Feeling bolder than bold, she ran her tongue along the closed seam of his lips, asking for entry. There was the smallest of pauses, then some of the tension went out of him as he opened to her, his tongue stroking hers, his mouth starting to move at last. His hands found her waist, his fingers gripping her warmly as his kiss became more demanding, more urgent.

God, yes. Urgent was how she felt, and she'd never been greedier, more ready, more eager in her life. Her heart was already racing, her body flooding with heat, the need for more, more, more a drumbeat in the back of her head.

She made a small encouraging sound as his hand left her hip and smoothed its way up her torso. If he touched her breasts, she was pretty sure she could almost come on the spot.

Suddenly he stilled, pulling back slightly so he could look her in the eye.

"Tara... this is a bad idea."

"No, it isn't." It was the best idea she'd had in a long time. "You'll be going soon. I know that. But I want to know before you go, Reid. I need to know."

A whole year they'd been sitting side by side in that damned patrol car, denying the pull of desire between them.

She was sick of denying it. She was sick of playing it safe.

His gaze searched her face, and whatever it was he saw seemed to satisfy him, because the next thing she knew he was kissing her as though his life depended on it.

Fierce and demanding, taking no prisoners. She gripped his shoulders as his hand slid onto her breast, the friction of his thumb gliding over her nipple making her shudder with need.

It felt so good, he tasted so good. Operating on blind instinct, she threw a leg over the center console and slid into his lap.

"Jesus, Tara," he said, his hands gripping her ass as she straddled him.

They kissed again, bodies grinding together. He pushed a hand beneath her sweater, tugging her bra out of the way to reach her breast.

She couldn't get enough. The taste of him. The feel of his hands on her body. She was on fire, her sex hot and wet for him. All she could think about was having him inside her, filling her. She slid a hand between their bodies, feeling the hard, long length of him through his jeans.

This. She wanted this. She wanted it now.

She fumbled at the stud on her jeans, breaking their kiss so she could maneuver more easily.

"What are you doing?" Reid asked, his eyes glinting in the darkness.

"What does it look like I'm doing?"

She rolled to the side, already pushing her jeans down her legs, taking her panties with them.

"Don't worry, I'm on the pill," she said.

Reid's hand found her bare ass as she kicked off her jeans, his fingers curling into her flesh possessively.

"Just as long as you know we're in the driveway in front of your townhouse," he said, and she could hear both the amusement and the desire in his voice.

"I can't wait."

She couldn't, and it was dark enough and they were private enough down here at the end, away from her neighbors.

Reid took care of his belt buckle and button fly, and together they pulled his jeans down. His erection sprang free, thick and long and hard, and she wrapped her hand around it, reveling in how hot he was.

Need driving her, she straddled him once again and guided him into place. The exquisite pressure of him filling her, stretching her, made her clutch at his shoulders as she took him all. His hand slid to the back of her neck, squeezing lightly.

"Give me a second," he said, his voice very low, his hand holding her still.

She understood. She'd expected it to be good, but she hadn't expected it to be profound.

This felt right. Right and so good and absolutely essential.

Reid pressed his mouth to her neck. "I've wanted this for a long time."

"Me, too."

Even though she'd been too scared, too stupid, too blind to acknowledge it.

His hands found her hips as he thrust up into her, and together they started to move, quickly finding a rhythm that was all their own. Reid's hands slid from her hips and up her torso, pushing her sweater out of the way. She leaned forward, offering him her breasts and he took her left nipple into his mouth and tongued it avidly.

She was so wet, so aroused, she could already feel her climax bearing down on her. She drove her fingers into his hair, holding him to her as she rode him. He switched to her other breast, biting her nipple gently before drawing it into his mouth.

"Reid," she breathed.

And then she came apart, sensation rippling through her in delicious waves, her sex throbbing around him, her knees locked to his sides.

One of his hands found her ass, pulling her more tightly to him, and he thrust himself deep, his whole body shuddering as he found his own pleasure.

She was breathing hard, her body damp with sweat, her breasts and face tender from his stubble. And yet she'd never felt better, more alive, more herself than ever before in her life.

Bowing her head, she rested it on Reid's shoulder, pressing a kiss to his skin.

She would never regret this. Ever.

.

Chapter Nine

Reid woke to the smell of apple blossom. Stirring lazily, he smiled as memories from last night rushed over him. Then he pushed Tara's hair out of his face, sliding a hand around her body and tucking himself more snuggly behind her.

They'd slept well together, he and Tara—when they'd finally slept. She'd asked if they could go back to his place rather than do the obvious and go to hers. He had been more than happy to eschew the ghosts of her former relationship, driving out to the orchard and kissing her every step of the way up the stairs to his apartment.

They'd barely made it to the bed the second time, tearing each other's clothes off, the room echoing with their roughly-voiced words of encouragement and appreciation. Making love to Tara had been... extraordinary, in the truest sense of the word.

He'd never had such intense, fun, gratifying sex in his life, and just lying here thinking about it was making him hard all over again.

He nudged his hips a little closer, enjoying the pressure of her ass against his erection. She stirred, her behind pressing back into him more firmly, and he realized she was awake.

"Morning," he murmured, pressing a kiss to her shoulder.

"Morning."

She was smiling. He couldn't see her face, but he knew it. Could feel it.

He spread his hand over her belly. Her skin was soft and warm, and she smelled so good, like sunshine and soap.

"I have a question for you," he said.

"Mmmm?" She wiggled her backside against him, teasing him shamelessly.

"Are you a morning person?" he asked, gliding his hand down her belly and into the silk of her pubic hair. She was wet and swollen with wanting and he got even harder as he stroked the seam of her sex.

"What do you think?" she asked.

He shifted, rolling on top of her, and she welcomed him with widespread thighs and arms. This would be their fourth time making love, and he still had to stop himself from simply plunging inside her, his need for her was so powerful.

Instead, he kept a tight rein on himself, using his erection to tease her, sliding back and forth, loving the way her head dropped back and her mouth opened, her teeth just showing as she started to pant.

"Want me?" he asked.

"Yes. Stop being a tease."

Her hands gripped his ass, encouraging him to push inside her, and he gave into her urging, beginning the slow slide to ecstasy. She lifted her legs, locking them behind his hips, and he slid his hands under her ass and used his grip to tilt her hips as he stroked into her.

She was flushed and tousle-haired, her green eyes cloudy with desire, her nipples budded into taut peaks. He drew one into his mouth, savoring the taste of her, relishing all the little sounds she made: the catch of her breath, the low moan in the back of her throat when he stroked her deeply, the little rushed exhale as he stepped up the pace.

He stoked her desire, holding his own in check, until finally he couldn't wait a second longer. She panted out her encouragement as he pounded into her, then he felt her tighten around him, and she was gone, her gaze dazed and shaken and lost as she came.

Her pleasure fed his, and he pressed his face into her

neck and inhaled the essence of her as he gave himself up, his body shuddering into hers.

Her arms held him tightly afterward, denying him when he would have rolled away to relieve her of his weight. He was only too happy to stay. In fact, if he had his way, the world would stop turning altogether so they could remain like this forever.

"What's your best guess?" she asked, her voice husky and low.

"About what?"

"Whether I'm a morning person or not?"

He was still inside her, and he felt her muscles tighten around him. He smiled against her neck.

"I'm thinking yes."

"I'm thinking I might be an afternoon and evening person, too, when it comes to you."

He lifted his head so he could see her face, supporting himself on his elbows. She had a strand of hair across her forehead and he brushed it gently away. She watched him a little warily, although her lips were smiling.

"Tara—"

"No, don't. Let's not say all the things that need to be said. Let's just enjoy this while it lasts. Be a little reckless."

He brushed a thumb along her cheekbone. She was so freaking gorgeous. It made his chest tight, being this close to her and seeing the many different shades of green in her eyes.

"Okay. If that's the way you want it."

"It is."

"There's still the small matter of work."

"But not for much longer."

"As much as I enjoy your faith in me, I haven't got the job yet."

"You will."

Her confidence in him was simple and unequivocal, and he brushed his thumb along her cheekbone again.

"We'll see."

A knock echoed through the apartment, and they both glanced over his shoulder toward the door.

"That's locked, right?" Tara asked a little nervously.

"It should be."

"Reid?" His mother's voice sounded clearly through the door. "I'm making waffles. Should I save some for you?"

"Yes, please," he called.

Tara started to giggle quietly.

"Tara would like some, too," he added.

Her eyes went wide then, and she slapped his shoulder, doing her best to push him off her.

There was a telling silence. Then:

"I'll open up another bottle of syrup. Morning, Tara."

"Morning, Mrs. Dalton."

"Judy is fine, dear."

They heard the sound of his mother retreating down the staircase and Tara gave a mighty heave, successfully wriggling out from under him.

"That was a dirty stunt, Dalton."

"I thought you liked waffles?"

"You are lucky you are so good in bed. That's all I'll say for now."

She slid to the edge of the bed, evading him again as she stood and headed for the bathroom.

"I need a shower."

The thought of Tara naked beneath streaming water was enough to have him bounding out of bed to go after her. Her smile was small but knowing as he joined her beneath the spray.

"What took you so long?"

They ran the tank dry washing each other, and when they emerged the bathroom was cloaked in steamy fog. He flicked on the exhaust fan and dried himself off, watching while Tara did the same. She was so freaking sexy, with her long, athletic legs and slim hips. As for her breasts... he'd lost sleep fantasizing about her breasts, and they more than lived up to his imagination, her nipples a pale browny-pink, the shape round and full.

"I thought you wanted waffles?" she said, giving his crotch a significant look.

He was hard again, his erection straining against his belly.

"You're the one standing there all naked and

gorgeous," he said, hooking an arm around her waist and kissing her.

She let him have his way for a few minutes before pulling back.

"I don't suppose your parents will believe I slept on the couch."

He smiled slowly. "Why, Ms. Buck, don't tell me you're shy?"

"No." She frowned slightly. "It's just they know about Simon and that we work together and it might be weird."

"My mother is probably in the kitchen doing a victory dance," he said. "She loves you. They both do."

She looked pensive for a second, then she shrugged. "All right. I'm sure I'll survive the walk of shame." She turned to head into the bedroom.

He frowned, reaching for her and pulling her back into his arms. "There wasn't an ounce of shame in what we did last night."

She looked a little surprised by his vehemence. "I know. Sorry, that was a bad choice of words."

He studied her face, needing to be sure that she meant what she said.

"It's okay, Reid. I want to be here. I don't regret anything. I couldn't." She pressed a kiss to his mouth before exiting to the bedroom.

They dressed in silence, then Tara brushed her wet hair and pulled it into a ponytail and announced herself ready to face the music and the waffles.

He led the way downstairs and across to the main house, slipping his hand into hers as they entered the foyer.

"In the kitchen," his father called as the door clicked shut behind them.

Tara stood a little taller, and he kissed her quickly. "Don't be an idiot."

"Good morning," his mother said brightly as they arrived in the kitchen.

Four places were set around the old oak table, and a pitcher of freshly squeezed orange juice sat in the middle, along with a jug of maple syrup.

"Hope you're hungry," his mother said, her gaze

bouncing from him to Tara and back again.

"Come sit next to me, Tara," his father said, pushing the seat out for her with his foot.

Tara smiled at them both. "Thanks. And I am hungry, thank you."

His father started talking about the weather, and his mother dished up the first round of waffles. Sitting across the table from Tara, he watched as she slowly relaxed.

As he'd said, his parents loved her. Far from disapproving of the idea of the two of them together, they were far more likely to push him to make it permanent, his parents never having been shy about their desire to see him happily settled.

A concept that had always sent shivers up his spine— until recently.

The whole notion of being "settled" had always conjured up visions of making-do and conceding in his mind. But that wasn't how he felt when he looked across the table at Tara. She wasn't a concession, she was the grand prize. She was a lifetime of laughter and generosity and challenge.

When he looked at her, he didn't feel trapped. He didn't want to check the specials board at the local travel agents. He didn't want to loosen his collar and check where the exits were.

She made him want to stop and stay.

"Reid? Are you with us or not?"

He glanced up to find his mother standing beside him, a plate full of waffles in hand.

"Sorry, did you say something?"

"I asked how many do you want?"

"As many as you're prepared to give me."

His mother was frowning slightly as she loaded up his plate and he wondered how long she'd been standing there.

The waffles were great, and Tara's bright smile and sparky comebacks to his dad reassured him that she'd let go of any misgivings she had about going public with his parents regarding their... situation.

Because it was too early to call it a relationship, even though everything in him wanted to. There were too many question marks hanging over everything for him to let himself go there. Tara might be whole-hearted after her break up, but there was no getting away from the fact that she was still recovering from the wreckage of her engagement. And then there was the Chicago job to consider.

Tara insisted on helping clean up after breakfast before suggesting it was time she went home. She still had to collect her pickup from The Wolves Den across town, and she had "things to do."

"We can head into town now," he said as they both hung up their kitchen towels to dry.

"Thanks. And thanks, Judy, for a great breakfast. Best waffles I've had for a long time."

"Vanilla essence in the batter," his mom said with a wink. "Works every time."

Reid stared at her. His mother was notoriously cagey about her recipes, yet here she was, handing out one of her most closely guarded secrets without being held at gunpoint.

"I'll have to remember that," Tara said.

"Reid, I need help in the laundry room, if I can borrow you for a moment," his mother said. "It will only take a second."

The look she gave him was loaded with meaning.

"I'll wait outside," Tara said diplomatically.

His mother disappeared into the laundry room and Reid took a deep breath and followed her. The moment they were alone, his mother pushed the door closed.

"What are you doing, Reid Dalton?" she hissed the moment it thudded shut. "That poor girl has just had her whole life turned upside down, and all you can think to do is snake-charm her into your bed?"

He flinched away from the vehemence of her words, a little taken aback by the depth of her feeling.

"Whoa. You want to calm down there a minute?"

"I know you've always had a thing for her, but she is not one of your easy-come, easy-go women, Reid. I'm really disappointed that you've allowed your libido to put you in a situation where you're going to hurt a person who deserves a lot better."

He was starting to get irritated by all the assumptions his mom was making. Sure, he hadn't dated anyone steadily since he came home to Montana, but he wasn't an alley cat.

"I didn't realize you had such a high opinion of my morals," he said sharply.

His mother set her hands on her hips and eyed him critically.

"I love you, but I'm not so one-eyed I can't see your faults. You're charming and handsome, and women have always come too easily to you. Which is fine, except when they want things that you aren't prepared to give."

"You have no idea what I'm prepared to give Tara," he said.

"A home? Your heart? A ring? Because those are the things that Tara wants and needs."

"You know what? I'm not having this conversation with you. What's going on between Tara and me is our business, and I don't have to justify myself or explain myself to you."

"No, you do not. But I just hope you can look yourself in the eye when you go sailing off to this new job in Chicago and leave her behind."

"For Pete's sake, will everyone stop going on about the Chicago job as though I've got it already? It's a second interview. Nothing is set in stone."

"If it's not this job, it will be another one, Reid. Be honest with yourself, at least. You always leave. The grass is always greener, life is always elsewhere. And that's okay, it really is, as long as you don't set up expectations that you aren't going to fulfill."

"You must think I'm a real asshole," he said, thoroughly pissed off now.

He yanked the door open and exited angrily to the kitchen before heading for the front door. Tara was waiting by his truck, her head downturned, when he emerged from the house.

She scanned his face as he approached. "You okay?"

"Yep."

He held her door open for her, and she considered him for a beat before climbing into the truck.

She waited until they were pulling out of the driveway and onto the road into town before speaking.

"I hope you and your mom didn't fight over me."

"She thinks I'm going to love you and leave you," he said shortly.

"Did you tell her that I was on board with that?"

"No. It's none of her business."

He scowled at the road, his mother's voice still echoing in his head. He wasn't going to apologize for having a broader horizon than her. And he definitely wasn't going to apologize or justify his private life. He always made sure that he was as honest as he could be with anyone he was involved with, and he'd had his fair share of wounded feelings and broken hearts over the years, too.

"It's very sweet of her to be so protective of me. Maybe I should have a word with her," Tara said. "Explain to her that we both know this is only temporary."

"It's none of her business," he said.

Her hand landed on his knee, warm and welcome. "It's still nice that she cares."

His shoulders dropped a notch as he let go of some of his irritation. "That's because you're a better person than I am."

"I've just had more experience dealing with a high-maintenance mom. Yours is a piece of cake compared to mine."

"True."

She squeezed his thigh. "Count your blessings."

She'd managed to tease a smile out of him by the time they turned into her street. Then Tara's own smile faded as she caught sight of the bright blue bomb parked in front of her townhouse.

Scarlett.

"Shit."

"What's wrong?" he asked.

"I forgot that Scarlett was coming over today to be here when Simon turns up to collect his stuff."

"You think she's been waiting long?"

"It's not that." Tara tugged on her ponytail nervously.

"What is it, then?"

"She'll see you."

Right. And that was a bad thing, apparently.

"Not that that's a bad thing," Tara said quickly, clearly picking up on his reaction. "It's just I was kind of hoping we could keep this just between you and me."

"And my parents."

"And your parents."

Scarlett had already exited her car and was standing watching them, arms crossed over her chest, her expression unreadable.

"Can I see you tonight?" he asked.

Truth be told, he didn't give a fat rat's caboose who knew about him and Tara, and that included the crew down at the station. She was the only thing that was important, nothing else.

"Um. Okay, if you want to."

"I want to." He leaned across the hand brake, palming the nape of her neck as he lowered his mouth to hers.

She tasted sweet, and she opened to him, her own hand coming up to tangle in his hair.

"What time should I come?" he asked when they finally parted.

"What time would you like to come over?"

"Early."

She smiled, the slightly-dazed look fading from her eyes. "Okay. I'll see you early, then."

She pressed a last kiss to his lips before grabbing her backpack and sliding from the truck.

He watched her walk over to greet her sister, aware of a deep reluctance within himself to let her go. It wasn't just because she'd be facing her ex today.

It felt as though he'd been waiting a life time for Tara already.

Unsettled by his own thoughts, he headed for home.

"Wow. You are powering your way through the Fuck-it list, aren't you?" Scarlett said as Tara approached.

Tara couldn't quite interpret the expression on her sister's face. "Excuse me?"

"Have a fling with a hot guy. Remember that one?"

"Right." Tara had honestly forgotten that stupid list. After her day at the lake and her night with Reid, it didn't seem very important.

A day beneath the big Montana sky had put things back into perspective for her. The truth was, she liked most of her life, was comfortable with most of the choices she'd made.

And those she wasn't so happy with would be in the past once Simon had collected his things today.

Scarlett followed her as she let herself into the townhouse and dumped her backpack on the kitchen table.

"You know, I always wondered about you and Reid," Scarlett said.

"Did you?" It was news to Tara.

"Yeah, of course. He's hot, you guys are stuck in a car together all day. If it was me, I would have jumped him a long time ago."

"I was engaged, remember?"

Scarlett dismissed Simon with a flick of her fingers. Tara couldn't help thinking that it would be nice to be able to do the same. She really wasn't looking forward to seeing him today. If she and Scarlett were identical twins, this would totally be a situation where she would be prepared for her sister to pretend to be her.

"So, has this been one of those simmering-beneath-the-surface things for the whole year you've worked together? Or did he just pounce on you out of nowhere? Or did you pounce on him...?"

Scarlett's eyes were bright with interest and Tara knew her well enough to understand where she was going with this.

"Don't get too excited. Reid is leaving Marietta soon, so this isn't a star-crossed lovers scenario."

She pulled her wet swimsuit and towel out of the

backpack and went through to the laundry room to dump them in the washing machine.

When she turned around, Scarlett was standing in the doorway, and some of the sparkle had gone out of her eyes.

"Why is he leaving?"

"There's a job in Chicago. Also, he's a gypsy." She shrugged, offering her sister a wry smile.

"But you jumped into bed with him anyway?"

"I'm living on the wild side, remember?"

Her sister pursed her lips.

"What's wrong?" Tara asked.

"Are you sure you know what you're doing?"

"Of course. I'm going in with my eyes wide open. I'm going to have a good time with a great guy, and it's going to be okay when he heads off into the wild blue yonder."

Scarlett looked unconvinced.

"You don't believe me?" Tara asked.

"It's all great in theory, sweetie. But you didn't see your face when you got out of his truck just now."

"What about my face?"

"You looked happy. As though the lights were on, and someone was definitely home, and there was a party going on."

"I like him. So sue me. But I also know him, and I'm not stupid."

"Okay."

For some reason it was suddenly very important that she convince Scarlett that she meant every word that she said.

"He's got a second interview for a job on Tuesday, and when they offer him the job, they'll probably want him to start as soon as possible. So we're talking a couple of weeks, a month, before he's on his way. I can handle that."

Scarlett held up her hands. "Hey, I believe you. You've convinced me."

Tara narrowed her eyes, but she knew that if she kept pushing, she'd be getting into "doth protest too much" territory.

"You want me to start stacking the boxes near the door?" Scarlett said.

"No. He can lug them around. He's lucky that I packed his stuff up in the first place."

The house had been dotted with boxes and garbage bags full of stuff all week, and it would be good to have it gone.

"I heard that he's lost his job, as predicted."

"Good."

"I also heard something else, but I'm not sure if I should tell you or not." Scarlett tucked her fingers into the front pockets of her jeans as she waited for Tara's response.

"Tell me." Whatever it was, Tara could handle it.

"There's a rumor going around that Simon and Paige are engaged."

Tara set a hand on the cool metal of the washing machine. Simon was marrying her. That was...unexpected.

"Is she pregnant?"

"Who knows?" Scarlett moved closer, reaching out to rub her arm. "Sorry. But I thought you might hear it someplace else, or he might say something today, and I wanted you to be prepared."

"No, it's okay. I'm okay. It doesn't make any difference to me."

It really didn't. She'd made her peace with the mistake she'd almost made. Simon's betrayal wasn't any more or less palatable because he might end up married to a girl who was ten years his junior.

"Good," Scarlett said.

She told her sister about her day paddle boarding then, and Scarlett told her that Mitch was due to land the day after tomorrow, having escorted his mother home and sorted out his affairs in Australia so he could join Scarlett in Montana permanently.

"Any leads on a place for the two of you yet?" Tara asked.

Scarlett had been living with their mother since she returned from Australia, not an ideal situation when you were a newly-wed woman.

"I found a place yesterday, actually. Where's your laptop?"

They were scrolling through the photographs on the local

real estate website when a knock sounded. They both looked at the door, then each other.

"It must be douchebag o'clock," Scarlett said.

Tara smiled, reaching out to squeeze her sister's hand. It was good to have her here for this. Not something she would have necessarily said about her sister not so long ago. But Scarlett had changed—and maybe Tara had, too.

Taking a deep breath, she went to answer the door. Simon was standing on the other side, hands shoved into the pockets of his chinos, shoulders tense.

"We'll wait out on the deck while you clear your stuff," Tara said, not bothering with greetings.

She might be relieved that she wasn't going to marry this man, but that didn't excuse his bad behavior.

"I was hoping we could talk."

Tara crossed her arms over her chest. "About?"

"I wanted to explain. About Paige."

"I'm really not that interested, to be honest."

"I love her. We're going to move to Vegas, get married. Start over away from all of this."

Tara sent a silent thanks to her sister for forewarning her.

"I'm sure it will be a lovely ceremony. Don't forget the stuff in the garage."

She turned way and Simon stepped forward, reaching out to try to stop her. She shot him a look and his hand fell to his side. Nice to know he'd learned from last time.

"I'm sorry, Tara. I never meant for any of this to happen. For the record, I loved you. I loved you a lot. But the moment Paige walked into my class room at the start of the year I knew I was in trouble. I can't explain it better than that, I'm sorry."

He looked so tortured, guilty and stressed that for a second she felt a little sorry for him. But only a second.

"You're not the man I thought you were," she said. "You lied. You abused the trust of a student. You betrayed me. I don't know what you want me to say to you, but I'm not going to give you a free pass, Simon."

"I don't want that. I know what I did was shitty and wrong."

"Good. Then we're on the same page. Like I said, we'll be on the deck if you need anything."

Scarlett gave Simon a scathing head to toe before turning and leading the way to the deck. Tara actually had a smile on her face by the time they were outside in the early morning sunshine.

"You have to teach me how to do that sometime. I swear, I could hear his balls shriveling," Tara said.

Scarlett looked at little startled by her laughter. Then she smiled, too.

"That's my Medusa look. I use it on grabby employers. It's all in the lip. You have to get a little curl in it, and look down your nose."

By the time Simon had cleared the house of his things and rapped on the back door to let them know he was done, Tara had mastered the Medusa look. She was tempted to try it out on Simon, but her heart wasn't in it.

She was better off without him, in so many ways.

"Well. I guess this is it," Simon said on the front porch.

"Yep. I'll send you your share of the security deposit sometime next week," Tara said.

"Keep it. It's the least I owe you."

"I'll send it ," she said firmly.

He nodded, then glanced at the ground. His throat bobbed a couple of times, and when he looked back up at her his eyes were glassy with tears. "I'm sorry. I'm going to miss you."

She stared at him for a long moment. He really was an idiot. A messed up, foolish idiot who had made a lot of really dumb moves.

"I hope it works out for you," she said. Otherwise all of this, all the ugliness and hurt and embarrassment would be for nothing.

He nodded, then turned and headed down the stairs.

Tara shut the door and leaned against it, waiting for him to go. She was aware of her sister watching her. Together they waited until the sound of Simon's car had faded.

"Well, that's that, I guess," Tara said, pushing away from the door.

Scarlett came and put her arms around her. "You're my hero. If ever this happens to me, if I can be one tenth as classy as you, I will be so proud of myself."

Tara blinked away sudden tears. Not because she was sad about Simon, but because she knew she was lucky. She had good people around her. People who loved and cared about her.

They held each other tightly for a long beat, then eased apart.

"Now, how do you feel about driving me over to The Wolves Den so I can collect my pickup?" Tara asked.

Reid spent the day working with his father in the orchard. His thoughts were on Tara almost the whole time, mulling over the things she'd said to him and the time they'd spent together last night.

At four he went up to the apartment and pulled out his suit, checking to make sure he didn't need to get it dry-cleaned before his interview on Tuesday. It was fine, and he hung it with a fresh shirt, ready to be ironed the night before his departure—he'd already booked flights, and he planned to leave early Tuesday and get back late the same night.

He was aware of a heaviness within himself as he contemplated the whole process. The flight, the interview, all the jumping through flaming hoops that would be required of him. Then he reminded himself that it was a great job, and an excellent opportunity. Three times the money he could make at Bozeman PD, and he'd be living in the vibrant, cosmopolitan city of Chicago.

He walked to the window and stood staring out at the orchard. Trees stretched into the distance in orderly lines, branches swaying in the wind. He knew from his time out there today that the fruit was coming along nicely. Soon it would be harvest time and they'd be opening the orchard to the public.

His mother hadn't raised the prospect of selling to the

Dearborns again, and he had no idea if she'd spoken to his father about it.

It's not just going to go away because you want it to.

He turned away from the view and headed for the bathroom, stripping his sweaty work clothes and stepping beneath the shower. He took the time to shave carefully, splashing on aftershave before pulling on his good jeans and a linen shirt he'd bought in Rome.

He admitted to himself that he was nervous as he drove to Tara's place. He wasn't sure why. He wanted to see her very badly. Wanted to hold her again. Touch her. Look into her eyes. He was also aware of the clock ticking. All modesty aside, he knew he had a good shot at the Chicago job. Which meant his time with Tara would be limited.

The moment he acknowledged the thought, he started coming up with out clauses for himself. There was no reason, for example, why he couldn't fly home a couple of times a month to see her and help his folks out. She might be willing to fly out to Chicago, too. She'd talked about wanting to travel more as they floated around Fairy Lake. Maybe they could manage a long distance thing for a while.

And then what? a voice asked in the back of his head.

Long distance was only worth enduring if there was the prospect of an end in sight. And it was pretty well established that Tara was not about to uproot herself from Marietta.

She opened the door when she heard his car in the driveway, watching as he exited the truck. Her hair was up, and she'd put on a little makeup, making her eyes smoky and sexy and her mouth pink.

She looked good enough to eat.

"Hi," she said. "How was your—"

He stole the rest of her words with a kiss, his arms wrapping around her, hands gravitating to her perky little ass. She gave a murmur of approval as he backed her toward the doorway.

He had her top off by the time they'd reached the couch, and seconds later her bra was off, too. Filling his hands with creamy smooth flesh, he tongued her nipples and relished the way she trembled in response. She started fumbling at his belt buckle, pushing her hands into his jeans. He broke from her briefly to push them all the way down, helping her do the same, then he set her on the arm of the couch and slid inside her. She wrapped her legs around him, kissing him avidly as he began to move.

"You feel so good," he whispered in her ear. "I want to do this forever."

"Yes."

He reached between them to find the place she needed him the most, stroking her inside and out until she tightened around him, her knees gripping his hips. Only then did he let himself go, pleasure swamping him.

She pressed a kiss to his chest afterward, and he wondered if she could hear his still-pounding heart.

"I guess it's lucky my sister went home earlier, huh?" she said.

She tilted her head to look up at him, her face full of laughter, and his chest got tight the way it had that morning when he'd looked into her eyes.

If he got the job, he was going to be walking away from this woman.

Good luck with that one.

Chapter Ten

T he next three weeks were the most bittersweet of Tara's life. She spent the remaining week of her leave helping out with her mother, reorganizing the townhouse and spending time with Reid. He took her paddle-boarding again, this time to Ennis Lake, and they made love on the shore beneath the warm sun. By mutual consent they didn't talk about his job interview much, apart from general details. Reid didn't seem eager to hash it over, and she wasn't sure she could maintain the pretense that she would be happy for him if he got it.

The night before she was due back on the job, they had a discussion about the potential weirdness of their work situation. They both agreed that there was nothing they could do but wing it and trust each other, as they always had.

Tara turned up the following morning feeling crazy nervous and very exposed, albeit in a very different way from the day after she'd found out about Simon. Her colleagues were pleased to see her, however, and there was nothing in Reid's greeting or demeanor to let on that she was anything more to him than his patrol partner.

She did her best to hold up her end of the deal, even though it was hard when she was so vitally aware of everything about him. The sheen of his hair, the warmth in his eyes, the texture of his skin. His smell, the way he walked, the timbre of his voice.

After twenty minutes in the patrol car, however,

ingrained habit and instinct kicked in. They were on the job, and anything else between them fell back a step as they went about their duties. It helped that she'd always respected him—looked up to him, really—as a cop, and that they were kept busy with the usual rash of complaints. Break-ins, domestic disputes, MVAs. It was different, working together now they were lovers, but it wasn't difficult or impossible. Best of all, she was confident that none of their colleagues or superiors had a clue what was going on between them, which was just the way she liked it. She'd had enough of being the source of department scuttlebutt. She was more than happy to cede the floor to someone else's life dramas.

She helped out on the orchard whenever there was work to be done, enjoying spending time with Reid without having to monitor her behavior. His parents were so welcoming, she caught herself on the verge of explaining the finite nature of her relationship with Reid half a dozen times, but each time she reminded herself that they knew about the Chicago job. They knew Reid would be leaving soon.

Reid surprised her by offering to help out at her mom's place, too, taking it upon himself to mow her lawns and do a few odd jobs around the place that neither she nor Scarlett had felt up to. Mitch was good to pitch in, too, and the Buck women found themselves in the novel position of having two healthy, strong men at their bidding. Watching Reid and Mitch joke around with each other and her mom was but one of many moments that made Tara acutely aware of the hole Reid was going to leave in her life when he finally packed up and went.

But she'd known that, going in. She was prepared for it.

At least, she thought she was.

Then she woke on a Sunday morning almost three weeks exactly after Reid had taken her to Fairy Lake, and slipped from the bed to make use of the facilities. On her way back, she diverted to the kitchen to turn the coffee maker on. She was about to pad back to bed, her head full of all the delicious ways she could wake her lover, when her gaze fell on the thick envelope sitting on the kitchen counter. The Klieg Security Group logo filled the top left corner, and she found herself taking a step closer.

Don't, a voice in her head said, but she was already lifting it. It was empty, its contents sitting beneath it on the counter. She stared at the bold words across the top of the page. Confidential Employment Contract.

So.

Her gaze went to the postage mark on the envelope. It was dated earlier in the week, which meant Reid had been sitting on this news for at least a couple of days.

You knew this was coming.

She did. She'd prepared herself for it a dozen times. But nothing she'd imagined came even close to the way she felt right now—as though the bottom had fallen out of her world.

Which was stupid. So stupid.

She pressed a hand to her stomach, blinking rapidly to dispel the tears that were burning at the back of her eyes.

She was going to lose him.

The pain of the realization was visceral, like a blow to the solar plexus.

Which, again, was so dumb. This wasn't an ambush. She'd bought into their fling knowing it would end, and soon. Now it was time to pay the piper.

She set the envelope back on top of the contract and turned to the sink, running herself a glass of water. Her hand shook as she lifted it to her mouth.

I didn't think he'd go.

She closed her eyes as she admitted the truth to herself. Even though she knew Reid, even though he'd regaled her with tales of his travels, his eyes bright as he described a bazaar in Turkey or a weekend market in Paris, she'd sold herself a secret fantasy where Reid decided that he'd had enough of seeing the world, that being with her was more important than any of that. And she'd bought it, hook, line, and sinker, because she was wildly, crazily, passionately in love with him and didn't want to let him go.

You fool.

She set the half-full glass on the drainer, unable to swallow past the lump of emotion in her throat.

For a moment she was so overwhelmed by the loss she

was about to endure that the urge to sink to the floor and curl into a ball was almost irresistible.

Her mother had been like that after her father left, she remembered. She'd sobbed until her eyes were so red and puffy they were almost raw, she'd refused food, she'd spent hours in bed, not talking to anyone. Standing in Reid's kitchen, for the first time in her life Tara truly understood her mother's helplessness in the face of her grief.

It would be very easy to let the pain take over, as her mother had, to succumb to it and let it swamp her. Right now, it felt like a tsunami crashing down on her, unavoidable, sweeping everything in its path.

But Tara was not her mother. She'd worked diligently all her life to be different. She'd trained herself to be disciplined, to be capable. To be resilient. She was resilient.

She would be okay when Reid left. It would hurt. It would hurt like hell. But she would be okay. There would be no sleeping for days on end for her. She wouldn't abandon herself to pain. She couldn't.

Her knuckles were aching, and when she looked down she realized she was gripping the edge of the sink so tightly her fingers were white. She forced herself to let go. Suddenly the need to be outside, away from Reid, was so strong that she didn't dare disobey it.

She'd brought her running gear with her last night in anticipation of a cross-country outing with Reid today. She would put it on and slip out and run until this feeling in her chest—this tight, suffocating, painful heaviness—was gone. And when she came back, she would wait until he told her his good news and she would be happy for him.

She would.

She walked quietly into the bedroom to collect the bag with her running gear. Reid was sprawled across the mattress, the sheet tangled around his hips. She stood looking at him for a long moment, aware of the urge to climb into bed beside him and cling to him. Maybe if she asked, he would stay. Maybe if she begged him.

She retreated to the kitchen before she could allow the thought to take root. She pulled on underwear, fastening her sports bra with cold, fumbling hands. Then she pulled on her running leggings and a tank top, and finally her shoes and socks. She tied her hair back into a ponytail, then took a moment to leave a quick note on the pad of paper near the phone.

Felt the urge to run. See you soon, sleepyhead. T.

She left the note propped against the coffee can and made her way to the door.

"Where are you going?"

She glanced over her shoulder to find Reid standing there in all his naked glory, one arm raised to scratch his head. It said a lot that even now, when she was on the verge of falling apart, she still felt the burn of attraction as she looked at his beautiful body.

She forced a smile. "I'm just ducking out for a quick run," she said. "Just felt the urge."

"Give me five and I'll come with you."

"That's okay. You go back to bed. We can still go out together later."

She loved their runs together, and she wasn't about to give one up when it might very well be their last.

"Don't be silly. I'll be two minutes, tops." He closed the distance between them, wrapping her in his arms and his smell and his warmth.

She kissed him, swallowing the burn of tears. She couldn't object without crying. Without losing it. And she didn't want to lose it.

Not with him, anyway.

"Okay."

She hovered by the door as he pulled on running shorts and a tank top, sitting on the couch to tug on socks and his shoes. He ducked into the bathroom to stick his head under the tap and gulp down a glass of water, then he was back with her, his eyes alert now as he studied her.

"Is everything all right?" he asked, and she knew that he could sense her tension and upset.

He'd always been tuned into her. Always.

"Yep. Just feel like blowing the cobwebs away."

She led the way down the steps, going through the motions of doing some warmup stretches even though she really just wanted to run.

And then they were heading up the driveway, the gravel hard underfoot, and the terrible pressing-down feeling seemed to recede as she picked up the pace.

Very deliberately she cleared her mind, concentrating on her stride and her breathing, feeling the stretch in her hips with each step, visualizing her mid-foot hitting the ground and pushing off again.

Her muscles became liquid and warm as she slipped into the groove. The wind rushing past her felt good, the burn in her legs and lungs felt good, the perfect distraction from the hollowness inside her. She increased the pace, barely looking at Reid as she pushed harder and harder.

Then, somehow, she was sprinting, arms and legs pumping, her whole body on fire as she ran as fast, as hard as she could. Her feet slapped the ground, her eyes streamed, every muscle and sinew screamed for relief.

Still she kept running, relishing the burn, embracing the pain because it was so much easier than dealing with the hurt inside herself.

I love him, I love him, I love him. Don't leave me, don't leave me, don't leave me.

And suddenly she couldn't breathe, and she couldn't see, and she had to stop as tears flooded her eyes and her throat. She staggered to a halt, gasping for air, her chest heaving with sobs, tears pouring down her face.

"Tara." Reid was panting, too, his face twisted with concern as he reached for her.

She shook her head, unable to accept his comfort when she wanted—needed—it so badly. His hands fell to his sides as he frowned, his gaze never leaving her face.

"What's going on?"

She turned her back on him, walking a few paces away, trying to get a grip. But the words she wanted to say were rising up inside her, and she couldn't stop them, even though pride and history and experience told her they were pointless.

"Would it make a difference if I asked you to stay?" she said, her back still to him.

"Tara."

His arms came around her from behind, his big body

enveloping hers. His arms were like steel bands, and she felt the rasp of his morning beard against her cheek as he pressed his face alongside hers.

"You don't need to ask. I'm not going anywhere, doofus."

She frowned, not understanding. "I saw the contract, Reid."

She struggled free from his grip, turning to face him. Needing to see him.

"I called them on Thursday and told them I didn't want it."

Reid's dark eyes were steady on her as he waited for her response.

"But you don't want to live in Marietta. You can't imagine your life playing out here."

"That was before us. Before I understood that what I've been looking for all my life is right here. Tara, I love you. I've been crazy about you since the moment I met you. Wherever you are is where I want to be. It's that simple."

She shook her head. It wasn't that simple. Her father had been like Reid, a born gypsy. Restless. Always wanting more. He'd handled being domesticated for thirteen years before his nature had gotten the better of him.

"I'm not going to make the same mistake my mother made," she said. "You want to be out there. You love exploring new places. What is there for you in Marietta, besides me?"

"My parents. The orchard. Mountains. Lakes. A life with you by my side. The children we will have together. Believe me, that trumps Rome or Egypt or Mumbai every time, Tara."

She shook her head again. She wanted to believe him. He was offering her everything, her heart's desire. But she couldn't believe him. She couldn't.

He reached out and caught her hand, pulling her close, his other hand reaching up to tilt her chin so he could look into her eyes.

"Let me tell you the way I see this working. My parents move into town, and we take over the house. Anything you want to change, you change, with my blessing. I've got some savings, and we sink a bit of money into modernizing some of the machinery to make things easier. We both take our detective's exam, and when the time comes when we want to have kids, we work it out between us. Maybe I take some time out, then you take some time out. Whatever. And at least once a year, we turn our backs on all of this, and we go somewhere just for us. Somewhere new, somewhere we can discover together."

"Stop it," she said, desperately trying to hang onto her hard-earned sense of self-preservation.

"You don't like any of that? Fine. The only part that's not negotiable for me is you. I've gotten a lot of things ass-backwards in my life, Tara, but this is right. I love you, and I will always love you. You are my future. Only you."

He was holding her face in both his hands now, his thumbs brushing her tears away.

"I want to believe you so much," she whispered.

"Then believe, baby. I promise that if you fall, I will catch you. And I know you'll do the same for me."

Tara felt dizzy, as though some fundamental anchor within herself had just snapped free. If she did this and it didn't work out—if they tried and failed—the pain she'd just stared in the eye would be nothing.

If Reid left her, it would destroy her. She would become her mother.

Reid leaned forward and kissed her lips, and she tasted the salt of his sweat and her tears, and she felt the gentleness in his hands, and when he pulled back she saw the fierce love in his eyes.

"I love you," she said.

"I know, sweetheart. I love you like crazy. I love you so much I'm going to pretend I don't mind about that damned motorbike, and I cannot wait to start my life with you."

He kissed her again, deeply this time, his tongue stroking hers, one hand palming the nape of her neck, the other sliding down her back to urge her closer. She felt his arousal against her belly, and the flare of her own desire, and knew that even though she was terrified, even though life had taught her that this was the most dangerous thing she would ever do, she couldn't not do it.

To do so would make a lie of everything she had ever tried to be, and mean she would be turning her back on a man who filled her with love and pride and heat and need.

"Yes," she said. "Yes. Let's do it. All of it. The house, the exams, the babies, all of it. All of it."

"Good answer," he said, and then he kissed her to seal their deal.

Epilogue

One Year Later

"I'm going to bed now, but you are not to touch anything, Tara, do you hear me?" Tammy Buck said as she pushed herself upright from her seat. Bottles of nail polish, emery boards and polish scattered the kitchen table in front of her, along with a number of soiled cotton balls. "The last thing we want to be doing is fixing your nails tomorrow when you'll have a million better things to do."

"Like getting married," Scarlett chimed in.

Tara waggled her fingers in the air. "I'll be good, I promise."

"You did a good job, Scarlett. There's a career there if you want it," her mother said approvingly. Between them, she and Scarlett had transformed Tara's nails from workaday practical to wedding glamorous, shaping them and buffing them and finally painting them with a pale pink varnish that was pearlescent in the overhead light.

"I would be high as a kite on all those fumes, Mom. And all I did was follow your expert instructions," Scarlett said.

"Don't blow smoke up my skirt, I know how good I am. At least, how good I used to be."

Tara resisted the urge to offer to escort her mother to bed. In recent months, her mother had reached a sort of peace with her illness, and a new independence had grown out of her acceptance. These days, she liked to do as much for herself as she could, claiming that there would be plenty of opportunities for them to fuss over her in the future.

Scarlett waited until they heard the bedroom door click shut before standing.

"You want some of the good stuff now?"

"Yes, please."

Their mother preferred sweet spumante, always had, but Scarlett had bought a bottle of French champagne to celebrate Tara's last night as a single woman.

The pop of the champagne cork echoed in the kitchen, and Tara accepted a brimming, frothing glass from her sister.

"To sunny skies tomorrow and for the rest of your lives," Scarlett said, raising her glass in toast.

They clinked glasses, both making appreciative noises as they swallowed a mouthful of yeasty, dry goodness.

"So good," Tara said.

"You nervous?" Scarlett asked.

Tara shook her head instantly. "No. Excited, but not nervous."

Tomorrow, she was going to become Mrs. Reid Dalton, and the next stage of their life together would begin. While the thought of all the theater of tomorrow's wedding made her feel a little twitchy, she didn't have a single doubt about the man she would be marrying.

He was her rock, her heart, her everything. She adored him. She admired him. She lusted after him. She couldn't wait to walk down the aisle and make her vows.

"You love him," Scarlett said in a childish, sing-song teasing voice.

"Yep," Tara said, grinning unashamedly.

"Good thing Mr. Douchebag had a thing for cheerleaders, then, huh?"Tara shuddered as she thought about the terrible mistake she'd almost made.

"Don't remind me. I was such an idiot."

"You had your reasons," Scarlett said, her green eyes warm with understanding and acceptance.

Tara felt a rush of love for her twin. For so many years, they had pulled against one another, each attempting to carve her own place in the world. Somehow, though, their mother's illness and the changes in their personal lives had led to a new accord between them. Scarlett had let go of the need to always be the rebel and the entertainer, and Tara had resigned from her role as family protector. For the first time since they were little, they were friends, and it felt good.

"You want some chocolate, too?" Scarlett asked.

She was already on her feet, heading for the pantry. Tara smiled at her sister's fluffy-bunny slippers, paired with a pair of rather sexy shorty pajamas.

"You wear that outfit at home?" she couldn't help asking.

"Hell no. Mitch won't let me wear anything to bed. He's an impatient man."

Tara laughed.

Scarlett returned with a big box of chocolates bearing the Copper Mountain Chocolates logo, sliding the lid off as she placed it in front of Tara.

"Wow," Tara said, surveying the decadent array in front of her. Sage Carrigan's chocolates were legendary in Marietta, and there were enough here to make her teeth ache.

Scarlett passed her the little booklet which told her which chocolate was which. "Save me a coffee cream, but the Turkish Delights are all yours."

"I thought you loved Turkish Delights," Tara said, looking up from studying the booklet. She could remember having to strategize like crazy to get her share as a kid.

"Nope. Dad was the one who loved them, remember?"

She said it so matter-of-factly, but the mention of their father stole the smile from Tara's lips. Even though it had been a long time since he'd been a part of her life, she'd been haunted by thoughts of him lately. Only natural, perhaps, in the lead-up to the wedding, but a little disconcerting, too.

She picked a caramel from the box and passed the guide to her sister.

"Did you miss him at your wedding?" she asked quietly.

Scarlett took a second to answer. "I thought about him. I didn't miss him. He's been gone so long, I can't really remember what it was like to have him in my life."

"Yeah." Tara pushed the tray of chocolates away.

"Hey. You okay?" Scarlett's forehead was wrinkled with concern.

"I need to tell you something. But I'm scared you'll hate me," Tara confessed.

"I will never hate you. Ever.".

Tara glanced down into her lap at her perfect pearly nails.

"A month before Dad left, I came home from school and caught him and Wendy in the kitchen."

Scarlett blinked a couple of times, processing. Then she mouthed a four letter word. "What did he say?"

"He cried. Told me it was a one-off." Tara reached for her champagne glass and took a big gulp to ease her dry throat. "He told me it would never happen again, and made me promise not to tell Mom."

"What an asshole."

It was so not what Tara had been expecting she almost laughed. It came out as a sort of hiccup, and she had to blink away tears again. Scarlett was watching her closely, her head tilted to one side.

"Wait a minute. You were worried I'd hate you because of this?" Scarlett asked, her tone incredulous.

"When we came home that day and he was gone and Mom was crying with Aunt Margot... It took me ages to accept that Dad wasn't coming back. That he'd lied to me. And Mom kept on saying that she'd had no warning, no idea that it had all come out of the blue, and all I could think was that if I'd told her what I'd seen, maybe they could have fixed things... " She broke off to wipe away the single tear that had found its way down her cheek.

"God. And you've been carrying that around all these years. If I knew where he was, I'd hunt him down and kick him somewhere it hurts," Scarlett said fiercely. "Tara, you were a kid, and he was a liar and a cheat and too charming for his own good. Everything that happened was his fault. All of it."

"I know that. I do. I just...There will always be that question inside me, you know?" Tara said.

Scarlett scooted her chair closer and wrapped her

arms around Tara.

"Let it go, Tara Banana. Let it go."

Scarlett hadn't used the childish nickname for years, and Tara had to blink away more tears as her sister embraced her.

"You have been an amazing sister, the backbone of this family," Scarlett said. "When I think of all the shit Mom and I have put you through over the years... please don't blame yourself for his selfishness. Please don't think that that was anything to do with you."

Her sister's words were a balm, the forgiveness and acceptance that Tara had needed for fourteen years. Resting her chin on her sister's shoulder, Tara let herself cry, clinging to her twin.

"I love you so much," she said brokenly.

"Back at you, baby. So back at you," Scarlett said.

They were both red-eyed and wet-cheeked when they drew apart. Scarlett sniffed and used the back of her hand to wipe her face.

"Boy do we know how to party," she said dryly.

Tara smiled, and the next thing she knew she was laughing. Scarlett watched her with a bemused smile.

"You okay there?"

"Yes. I think so. How about you?"

"I'm good."

They smiled at each other, then Scarlett nudged the box of chocolates toward her. "You get another pick now because you're so tragic," she said.

Tara shot her a mock-outraged look. "I'm going to take it, too."

She made a big deal out of searching for the coffee creams, making lots of yum noises when she bit into one. Scarlett commandeered the box then, stockpiling the remaining coffee creams in a pile in front of her.

"Can I ask you something?" Tara asked as she watched her sister be a pig. "Do you think I should tell Mom?"

Scarlett was silent for a moment as she considered the question. Then she shook her head. "I don't see the point. It will only upset her, and it won't change anything."

The last of the weight Tara had been carrying lifted

from her shoulders.

"Reid told me I should talk to you about it," she admitted.

"He's a smart guy. Great taste in women, looks hot in jeans. You should totally marry him as soon as you can."

Tara smiled. "That's a good idea. Why didn't I think of it?"

"Because I'm the ideas twin."

"Right, that must be it."

They talked till midnight, then Tara went to bed in her old bedroom and stared at the ceiling, chocolate, champagne and emotion buzzing through her body. Finally she drifted off to sleep, waking early the next morning. The nerves she'd denied last night made a late appearance, and she went for a quick run to burn off some adrenaline before jumping into the shower. She and Scarlett did each other's makeup, then their mothers, then Mitch arrived looking outrageously good in a dark suit.

"Good God am I glad you married me," Scarlett said, kissing him hello.

Mitch gave her an appreciative head to toe. "Am I allowed to touch any of this or is it for display only?"

He didn't wait for an answer, dropping a kiss onto her lips.

Tara cleared her throat. "If you don't mind, I'd like to hit the road. I believe there's a certain someone counting on me turning up."

Mitch let out a whistle when he saw her. "Looking good, Mrs. Dalton. Someone's going to be very happy to see you."

Tara blushed, pleased. She was excited for Reid to see her in her figure hugging, lacy gown, complete with a modest train. She felt beautiful, and she hoped he would think she was, too.

Mitch ushered them out to the car, helping their Mom into the front seat while Scarlett helped Tara wrangle her gown into the back. Tara's belly danced with butterflies during the short drive to the orchard. The front gate was decorated with white balloons that danced on their strings as they drove past. Tara could see the snowy white peaks of the tent that had been erected for their reception as they stopped in front of the house. Scarlett helped her out, and Tara took a moment to catch her breath and arrange her veil before her sister passed her her flowers.

"Okay, let's do this," Tara said.

Walking slowly in deference to their mother's compromised gait and Tara's long gown, they rounded the house and emerged on the lawn where chairs had been set up in front of a garden archway covered with flowering apricot roses. The celebrant stood beneath it, a tall, dark-haired, broad shouldered man by his side, his back to the gathered guests.

The violinist they'd hired for the ceremony started playing when he caught Tara's eye, and the dark-haired man turned.

Tara looked down the aisle at the man she was about to marry and couldn't stop her mouth from curling into a smile. An answering smile curved Reid's mouth, and warmth expanded in her chest. This man made her so happy. So happy. Thank God she'd been brave enough to trust his love.

Her heart keeping time with the music, a warm breeze tugging at her veil, she took her first step toward her future.

About the Authors

New York Times bestselling author **Jane Porter** has been a finalist for the prestigious RITA award five times and has over 12 million copies in print. Jane's novel, *Flirting With Forty*, picked by Redbook as its Red Hot Summer Read, went back for seven printings in six weeks before being made into a Lifetime movie starring Heather Locklear. A mother of three sons, Jane holds an MA in Writing from the University of San Francisco and makes her home in sunny San Clemente, CA with her surfer husband.

Visit Jane at JanePorter.com

Accidentally educated in the sciences, **Kelly Hunter** didn't think to start writing romances until she was surrounded by the jungles of Malaysia for a year and didn't have anything to read. Kelly now lives in Australia, surrounded by lush farmland and family. Kelly is a USA Today bestselling author, a three-time RITA finalist and loves writing to the short contemporary romance form.

For more from Kelly, visit KellyHunter.co.

USA Today Bestselling Author **Trish Morey** has written thirty romances for the internationally bestselling Harlequin Presents line and her stories have been published in more than 25 languages in 40 countries worldwide, including being published in Manga comic book form in Japan, and as Trish Moreyova in the Czech Republic. Trish was awarded Romance Writers of Australia's Romantic Book of the Year Award (the Ruby) for short, sexy romance In 2006 and again in 2009, as well as being a finalist in the Romance Writers of America's prestigious RITA Awards in 2012. A qualified Chartered Accountant by trade, Trish was employed as financial manager at a major business school prior to her first sale.

Trish lives with her husband, 4 daughters and assorted menagerie in the beautiful Adelaide Hills.

For more from Trish, visit TrishMorey.com.

Sarah Mayberry is the award-winning, New York Times bestselling author of more than thirty novels. She was born in Melbourne, Australia, and is the middle of three children. Sarah picked up a love of romance novels from both her grandmothers and has always wanted to be a writer. In line with this ambition, she completed a Bachelor of Arts degree in Professional Writing and Literature. It took her ten years and multiple attempts before her first book was accepted. During that time, Sarah worked in magazine publishing and the television industry, contributing to the internationally known Australian serial drama "Neighbours" and co-creating teen drama series "Karaoke High". Sarah currently splits her time between writing for television and writing novels.

She lives in Melbourne by the bay with her husband and a small, furry Cavoodle called Max. When she isn't writing, she loves reading, cooking, going to the movies and buying shoes.

For more from Sarah, visit SarahMayberry.com.

Thank you for reading

Love Me Tender

Be sure to look for the next two anthologies in the Great
Wedding Giveaway series:

Love Me True

&

Love Me Always

For more information about our authors and stories visit us
at MontanaBornBooks.com!

TULE
PUBLISHING

Printed in Great Britain
by Amazon

17385248R00308